DECK THE HALLS . . . WITH BLOOD

What could be jollier than a glass of eggnog and a corpse for Christmas? It's holiday horror fit for a scrooge when the ghost of Christmas Past has a score to settle and putting together your kid's bike can, literally, be murder. And who is that hanging next to the stockings . . . ?

'Tis the season of Santa and slay bells and Ann Crowleigh, Connie Feddersen, Louise Hendricksen, Toni L. P. Kelner, J. Dayne Lamb, and Pat Warren have gift-wrapped all the clues. So gather round the tree and enjoy six intriguing tales of murder, mayhem, and mistletoe. But you'd better watch out . . . you never know what's going to come down the chimney.

BOOK YOUR PLACE ON OUR WEBSITE AND MAKE THE READING CONNECTION!

We've created a customized website just for our very special readers, where you can get the inside scoop on everything that's going on with Zebra, Pinnacle and Kensington books.

When you come online, you'll have the exciting opportunity to:

- View covers of upcoming books
- Read sample chapters
- Learn about our future publishing schedule (listed by publication month *and author*)
- Find out when your favorite authors will be visiting a city near you
- Search for and order backlist books from our online catalog
- Check out author bios and background information
- Send e-mail to your favorite authors
- Meet the Kensington staff online
- Join us in weekly chats with authors, readers and other guests
- Get writing guidelines
- AND MUCH MORE!

Visit our website at
http://www.zebrabooks.com

MURDER UNDER THE TREE

ANN CROWLEIGH • CONNIE FEDDERSEN
LOUISE HENDRICKSEN • TONI L. P. KELNER
J. DAYNE LAMB • PAT WARREN

Zebra Books
Kensington Publishing Corp.

http://www.zebrabooks.com

ZEBRA BOOKS are published by

Kensington Publishing Corp.
850 Third Avenue
New York, NY 10022

First Printing: November, 1993
10 9 8 7 6 5 4 3 2

Printed in the United States of America

CONTENTS

The Ghost of Christmas Past

by

Ann Crowleigh

If *It* was in the next exposure, she would scream the house down! Or strangle the nearest statue.

"There, Clare . . . if you will but straighten Grace's shawl a trifle . . . and fluff up the red ribbons on the boxwood and holly garlands," Mirinda Clively directed her twin.

This photography session—which had started with tea and biscuits at ten this morning—had now extended until well past noon. And still the family grouping was not quite right. Good grief! The Michael Bedfords wanted only this holiday season's *cartes de poste,* a family portrait *en costume de Noël.* What they were getting, instead, were stiff backs, glazed eyes, and a child whose fidgeting accelerated by the second.

Still, the tot's mother, Grace, the American-born wife of the M.P. for Redding, managed to be true to her name by holding a smile and cooing to her two-year-old son.

"We will be but a moment longer, John. Here, lean back against Momma's skirts and rest your eyes until Lady Mirinda is ready for us to pose again."

Lady Mirinda had been ready for two hours. As had Michael, Grace's husband. But every damned plate Mirinda had exposed had, so far, been ruined. She jammed in another precious colloidal glass plate and slammed shut the covering. One more try. Then she would admit defeat.

No! Never! No Clively had been defeated in all the family's history—now, in 1875, they had survived more than six

9

hundred Christmases. But she wasn't sure she and Clare would survive this one.

A fiasco, it was turning out. A fandangoed fiasco.

Here was she, Mayfair's—nay, London's—preferred social photographer, and today she could not get a perfect exposure. It should have been a simple task. She had done everything correctly. The lighting. The drapery. The subject's positions. All looked like Art. And was.

Grace was lovely in her pale blue tea dress with its miles of subtlely shaded satin skirt. When the photograph was finished, that color would be shimmering pale mauves with deep purple-gray shadows. Entrancing. And to be topped with that shawl! My God, some Spanish lace maker must have spent a year producing that intricate pattern. Grace had instinctively known what a contrast the black *pointelle* would make against the stark simplicity of her skirt. Then there was her blond hair. With its one soft blue ostrich feather, it was—and this was *not* trite—her crowning glory. And a face such as hers was exactly right for the young mother she was . . . an American beauty. Delicate of brow, with fine bones; pointed, little nose; full lips; and the saddest blue eyes Mirinda had ever seen. She was perfection. Except for that sadness. There was a tale there. And Mirinda hoped to capture a speck of it in her lens.

The father, Michael, was her opposite. Tall where Grace was petite. Strong where Grace was delicate. A dark angel, his deep-set hazel eyes contrasted with his swarthy complexion and midnight hair. Mirinda had been hard-pressed to find a background to complement both mother and father.

She hadn't tried with the son. She didn't have to. John Michael Bedford had the light brown hair and blue eyes of a cherub. The disposition, too, judging from his compliance with the past two hours of drudgery. But she could only assume that John was used to compliance. His physical nature demanded it. He had a club foot and his built-up shoes were so heavy, his mother had hinted they inhibited his walking.

10

Well, they didn't inhibit his twinkling eyes or the mischievous grin that threatened to ruin yet another plate.

But this delightful child was not to blame for all that morning's disasters. *That* Mirinda attributed to sloppiness in preparing her equipment. Even Clare was getting peeved with Mirinda's inefficiency. And if tolerant Clare saw fit to frown at her twin, then Mirinda knew it was long past time to reexamine exactly what she was doing. She might even have to reschedule this sitting. After all, they would soon lose the noon sun and sun, alone, could expose the photographic plates. The brighter the sun, the less the subjects had to sit still. She could not bear to jam their heads into iron stanchions to hold them immobile. That child had agonies enough with his foot. And the mother would lose the grace with which God blessed her.

Quickly, in a routine which Mirinda could now do in her sleep, she polished the glass, coated it with a solution of nitrocellulose in alcohol and ether, with a touch of potassium iodide. She positioned her quarter plate camera, adjusted the black drape over her head, and slipped one corner of the plate into the exposure box in the back. One exposure for each corner, turning over the plate and reversing it for the bottom two—that was how she made the *cartes de poste* and *cartes de visite.*

"This must work," she muttered under her breath. There were only three weeks to Christmas and the Bedfords surely wanted to mail their postal cards a fortnight in advance. If she rescheduled, she would spend hours in her darkroom to produce the three hundred *cartes de poste* they had ordered.

She tinkled her bell—her signal that the family look into the lens. "Do not smile," she warned. A smile could not be held the five to ten minutes needed to expose the plates. "Merely relax and remain still as stone." She put her hand on the light-proof cloth so she could quickly duck under, and fixed a steely gaze at John. "Now!" she said, slipped under the cloth, and pulled aside the aperture covering. One exposure finished. She juggled the plate and slipped in the oppo-

11

site corner. And all the while, Mirinda judged the amount of light coming in the room. She calculated what it would take to get a sharp photograph.

During the ordeal, even Clare held her breath.

One minute. Two. Three. And . . . thank God . . . the family held their places. Though John's tiny fingers looked white with fatigue where he grasped his little tin flute.

"Only three more minutes," she called out. "Think of Father Christmas coming soon." The little boy's eyes glistened at the idea. Outside the drapery, Mirinda kept time like a metronome with her finger so John might find these last few seconds bearable. "Sugarplums and Banbury tarts. Christmas pudding and . . ." She shoved in the aperture covering, whipped the drapery off, and sighed.

". . . an' Papa Kithmith . . . my friend."

"Yes," Mirinda agreed as—with her hands still underneath the dark cloth—she dropped the colloidal plate into the solution in the developing box. "Father Christmas is my friend, too. He brings me my heart's desire."

Well, almost. He couldn't bring her Gus all wrapped in a big red bow. But now that Gus had been posted to London as Bismarck's special envoy, Father Christmas would place her in Gus's presence for a few precious moments. It would have to do. Less had done for the last twenty-five years. This year, when she received the Christmas blessing from Uncle George, she would give great thanks for all He had already given her. Gus.

Clare leaned over Mirinda's shoulder and watched her sister's busy hands as she slipped them into rubber gloves, removed the plate from the developing box, and dipped it into several bowls of chemical solutions. As soon as the ritual was complete Clare asked, "Well?"

Mirinda pulled off her gloves, poured water into a basin and soaped her hands to remove all traces of the chemicals clinging to them. "Two more minutes. Why don't you serve them some of that cold tea?"

Michael snickered. "Brandy might be better this time of day. Revive the spirit and all . . ."

John piped up, "Thpirt . . . Papa Kithmith . . . Thpirt!"

Grace patted her son on his glistening curly locks. "Yes, dear, we know. Father Christmas is going to be very good to such a good little boy as you."

Michael stretched his limbs, pulled his mistletoe boutonniere out of his lapel, and straightened his cravat. "Well, I tell you, Lady Mirinda, if this last plate hasn't done it, Father Christmas may have to bring me a new spine." He went to the sideboard in Bedford Hall's tastefully furnished drawing room and poured brandy into four delicate cut-crystal snifters. He handed one to each of the ladies and quaffed his own with obvious relish.

Mirinda sipped hers. "We shall give it time to dry and then . . ." She shrugged, wiped her hands on a towel she had tucked into her voluminous white apron, and sipped once more. All the while she kept one eye fixed on the plate as the solution dried unevenly. When it was ready, she picked it up and groaned.

It was there again! In all four exposures . . . on all four corners.

God, and what could it be?

There was nothing on the curtains. The light was different in each exposure. Of course. The day had waned. And she had prepared these plates carefully. She was known for her attention to detail. Besides, how could each and every plate be defective in exactly the same way on four different corners of a perfectly good photographic plate?

It was impossible! Yet, she had twenty-seven ruined plates, four ruined exposures each, to prove it happened.

"I'm sorry," she said, and plopped into the nearest Louis Quinze chair. Her elbows sought the comfort of the armrests. Her back, too, was stiff from exertion and exhaustion. Her feet blazed with fatigue. And her hands, which had been drowned in developing solution for two hours, were wrinkled and puffed like bloated raisins.

"I can't understand it! I simply cannot! I don't know how to apologize to you for such failure."

"Now, dear," Grace said, as she rose regally from her perch, "you've done the very best you can for us. I know it. And Michael does, too, don't you, dear?"

Michael smiled wanly. "But of course. We will merely reschedule, as you suggested, Lady Mirinda. I will have to look at my appointment book." He rang the bellpull and directed Budge, his butler, to bring it to him. Then he, too, sought out some comfort, this time in an overstuffed chair. He stretched his arms and his very long legs and relaxed the muscles in his neck.

Mirinda understood his appeal to the lovely American heiress. He had little money since he was only the third son of a minor branch of the great Russell family. The Dukes of Bedford had proliferated since one famous John had thrown in his lot with Henry the Eighth. This was the Redding branch of that noble family. Impoverished but proud. Handsome but in some cases vain.

Michael, however, was far from vain. And he had much for which to be proud. Not only was he handsome with those changeling eyes and that thick brown hair and handlebar moustache, but he was also a hard-working member of Parliament, a staunch Conservative—but Mirinda wouldn't hold that against him.

She drained her glass of brandy and almost asked for another when her attention drifted to the table on which she had placed those damned twenty-seven ruined plates.

John, restless and curious as every two-year-old, stood on his tiptoes to peer at her ruined day's work. He pointed to one plate. "Papa Kithmeth." He pointed to another. "Papa Kithmeth." Another. And another. And chatted away, talking in his baby babble which was part English and part wishful thinking.

"Papa . . . toyth . . . thore . . ." The boy nodded as he looked at the plate. "Want thore, too."

"Yes, son," Michael said. "We are all sore. It has been a long day."

John looked quizzically at his father. Then he clomped in his heavy shoes over to a huge portrait which dominated the west wall. It was of an eighteenth-century courtier in all his Court regalia, including a great shiny saber with a scabbard thick with rubies and the Bedford crest. "Papa Kithmeth. Thore." He pointed upward. "Want thore, too."

Michael bit his lower lip. "Yes, that does look a little like Father Christmas. The white wig and the regal red garb . . . but," he bent to his son's level, then scooped him into his arms, "that is your Great-great-great-uncle Thaddeus, not Father Christmas."

"Friend," John said. *"My* friend."

Grace's laugh was like a tinkling bell. "This must be his newest imaginary friend." She, too, surveyed the portrait. "Well, he could do worse. Thaddeus was one handsome devil." She glanced at her husband. "Just like the rest of you."

Michael sat again, his son in his lap. "Yes, but good old Thad, I'm afraid, was not like the rest of us. 'Tis his grave on the high ground near the formal gardens. Unchurched. Unsanctified." He sighed. "A long story."

And one Mirinda and Clare had heard often from their Aunt Prudence. Too often. It was not something Mirinda cared to have repeated.

The Judas, they called Thaddeus Bedford, the first son of the first Viscount Redding. Traitor to his King, George the Third. Betrothed to Rachel Symons, daughter of his father's best friend. Whispers of debauchery. Proof of treachery and treason. A Christmas Eve suicide from the third-floor gallery, throwing himself at the feet of the woman he had loved, and who had spurned him. Her melancholy, leading to madness.

Too horrible for words. With almost a century of enmity between two proud families as bitter legacy. No, Mirinda did not want to hear it.

Instead, she busied herself corking her chemicals into bottles and placing them carefully into the special box with a

15

very good lock. She had to leave them there. And she wanted no tragic accidents . . . especially the kind that happened when a house housed an inquisitive boy. The plates went into another box; but she left a few on the table because John was so fascinated by them. Later, she would clean all of them thoroughly and recoat them for the next session with the Bedfords. And this time they would *not* have those four damned spots!

Out, damned spots! But this time, thank goodness, it was not blood to be washed away.

While her sister did those things mysterious which made her the artist and businesswoman she was, Clare Clively-Murdoch could not take her eyes from the child who, by laying on of hands, sought something from those plates.

She glided up behind him and the urge to run her fingers through his tight locks overcame her. So like Ian's, her stepson's, at a young age. So, too, was John's demeanor like Ian's. Bright. Inquisitive. Adamant that *this* was Father Christmas.

This spot. And this spot. And this spot.

She stretched her aching back, looked again at those spots which intrigued the little boy, pulled over a stool and sat at John's eye level. "John," she put her finger on the grayish spot, *"this* is Father Christmas?"

He beamed at her in reply and nodded. "My friend."

She looked more closely at the few plates which Mirinda had left for John to view—the ruined plates her sister so carelessly cast aside without examining them in detail. In every corner, Mirinda had seen a whitish gray spot behind and above Grace's right shoulder and been furious as one by one the plates revealed the same blight. But could it be possible that Mirinda—that paragon of organization and efficiency, not to mention perfection—could have missed what Clare saw? That these were not ordinary bubbles or swipes of finger soil which had ruined her sister's work?

No, not these. They were marred in four different places,

16

but exactly the same in each. They were too much of one shape. Too *shaped*. For they did possess a shape. A real shape. A human . . .

She took another look. It couldn't be.

Why not? *There were more things in heaven and earth than are dreamt of, Clare.* The older she became, the more she knew it of a certainty.

She rounded her eyes at John. "Does your friend come to play with you often?"

The little boy nodded. He pointed upward. "Thairs."

"On the stairs?" Another nod. "First floor?" A shake of the head. "Second?" Another shake. "The third?" A nod with a bright smile. "On the *stairs*," she emphasized.

John frowned. He thought a minute, as young children do when they want to be precise, and she waited patiently. Ian had been the same. So accommodating. So explicit.

John made a motion with two hands as if he created a bird. Clare's eyebrows shot to her forehead. "You mean to say your friend flies?" He agreed eagerly. "From place to place?" John hoisted his left arm and sent his right hand flying over it and down. "Your friend flies over the . . . the . . . over the rail upstairs in the gallery?"

"Yeth!" John clapped. And pointed to the spotted plates. "Flieth."

Clare rose, took one of the plates, sat back on the stool, and gathered John close to her. "He looks a fine friend, John. I wonder who he could be?"

John threw a glance over his shoulder. "Thore."

Clare's head swiveled. "Thaddeus? Your friend is Thaddeus?"

"Thad. Yeth. Flieth." That settled, John clumsily skipped off to retrieve the last three biscuits on the tea tray.

Well . . . what did she do with this information? Tell Mirinda the spots she saw before her eyes were really the manifestation of a century-old family ghost? Oh, yes. And be Bedlam bound, for certain.

The only question that remained was . . . why had Thad-

17

deus Bedford manifested himself? Had he been here all along? Why choose John? And whom should she ask without sounding like a dithering old fool?

Ghosts! Most people would not credit them, nor anything else they could not touch, see, hear, smell.

But the instinctive part of herself which her family termed her *Clare-voyants*—a mysterious realm which told her things no one else could ken—that part of her understood anything was possible. Ghosts and all phenomena unexplainable. Ghosts and the hereafter. Ghosts and the invisible. She could sense the phenomena, sometimes see them.

Why had John seen this one? Why had she not?

Why had it been necessary to have it manifested four times, times twenty-seven, on photographic plates to bring it to her attention?

Perhaps because it was not meant for her?

Did this ghost know of Mirinda's new bent—oh, all right, hers, too—for investigating crimes laid at their doorstep? The baby in the chimney. The emasculated Chinese bannerman.

Now they were investigating crimes *not* on their doorstep, but on someone else's marble foyer.

Crime?

She looked at the portrait of the bewigged Georgian gentleman. Crime? How so? Had he not committed suicide?

Had he *not?*

Had his body laid in that unsanctified hilltop for no reason . . . or for the best of reasons?

It was coming to her . . . the reason . . . the *voyant.*

But a cold hand on her shoulder came, instead. She reached up and patted . . .

Naught.

Yet the hand was still there, still squeezing her shoulder blade. She did not move. She knew he did not expect her to. She thought, *I am on the right track, am I not?* A friendly pat made her smile.

"It will be all right. Mirinda and I will make it all right. You will see."

The hand left.

"To whom are you talking?" Miranda asked. "Over here all by yourself, Clare! Are you well, sister, dear?"

Clare bounced up onto her feet and handed Miranda the plate. "I'm perfectly fine!"

They were hardly seated in their new-old coach (their cousin Robin's castoff) when Miranda whipped back the oiled curtain separating the interior from the coachman's seat.

"Hurry it up, Connery," she called up to their footman cum coachman. Miranda consulted the watch pinned to her lapel. "I've a portrait sitting in twenty minutes!"

"Oh, Indy, we have no time to breathe. And if it takes you as long this afternoon as this morning's sitting, you will be late for tea."

"Posh! I am most efficient. I shall attend in the conservatory, as usual." She leaned back and shut her eyes. "I cannot understand what I did wrong."

"Perhaps you did naught wrong," Clare suggested. While she might feel the ghost was real, she—and Miranda—were of this world. She needed a dram of proof that her *voyant* was accurate, her conclusions irrefutable. Miranda would need buckets. "It might be the plates, you know."

"Those plates are fairly new. There should be nothing wrong with them. I have used them previous and found no imperfections within the image. This time, when I prepared them, I must have done something to mar them."

"All of them? In the exact spot on all four corners?"

"I know. It hardly seems likely. Yet I have no other explanation."

"I might. But I need to confirm it first."

Miranda opened one eye and glared. "Confirm away. Now!"

"You know me better than that, Indy. When I have evidence, we will talk."

"And, pray, when might that be?"

19

"Don't be so acerbic! If you do as I bid, we shall have the proof."

"Your servant, madam. I am too tired to argue."

"Well, then . . . for this appointment you have, I wish you to use at least one of these damaged plates. Do not scrape them. That is what you do, is it not?"

"No. But I understand. No clean sweep, correct?"

"Correct. Just the minimal resurfacing. Unless, of course, you have any unused ones from this batch left . . . ?"

"Fine. We shall use two of each. Two cleaned and resurfaced now. Two prepared from yesterday. I should be able to get good *cartes de poste* for Catherine Symons."

"I do not believe it! You scheduled one sitting in the morning for the Bedfords and another in the afternoon for their mortal enemy? Are you daft or merely dangerous?"

Mirinda chuckled. "I love to stir up the stewpot."

Clare groaned. "You and Aunt Pru."

"As a matter of fact, it was Aunt Pru who referred Catherine to me. She's taken an interest in the young lady who spends all her time reading to her blind father."

"The social register no longer considers twenty-five-year-old women *young.*"

Indy fixed Clare a baleful eye. "You and I are still young at fifty. Or do you dispute it?"

Mirinda smiled when Clare picked at her newest frock, which was more youthful and gay than that which most debutantes wore . . . and looked better on her indubitably.

"Certainly not," Clare affirmed. "And our social calendars agree. We have the Royal affair at Cousin Julia's next week, an at-home at the Brennans' new town house on December twenty-second, Uncle George's annual Christmas Eve concert and luncheon, the Bedfords' Christmas Eve wassail celebration, and the dinner and ball at Jenny Churchill's tonight, mind. And I intend to wear my newest Worth creations. Tonight the turquoise silk organza with those wonderful shirred sleeves, wide black satin curaisse, and inset jet and pearls."

Mirinda rolled her eyes. "My green velvet from two seasons ago will serve me well."

"You shall have Grandmother's emeralds and diamonds. They will outshine those of the American beauties'. Although I hear those Frost sisters have diamonds as big as your elbow."

"If that's true, Clare, they must all have hunched backs."

"Oh, Indy."

When they arrived at Scarborough House, Clare was pleased to see that the staff had already draped the mirrors in her center hall with boxwood and big red bows. And a delightful spray of holly and pine cones decked the staircase rail. A tussy mussy filled with aromatic cinnamon and cloves made the house begin to smell like the holidays.

She inhaled as they divested themselves of their pelisses and hats. Then Hopkins announced that Miss Catherine Symons awaited Mirinda in her studio.

"And Lady Prudence is ensconced in the conservatory, mum," he informed Clare. "Pence is serving her a late luncheon."

His demeanor indicated he considered this completely unwarranted since High Tea was only two hours hence.

"Thank you, Hopkins," Clare said. "I will attend my aunt." She swished down the hall, then turned. "You won't forget, Indy. Two plates from the ruined batch, mind."

"Thank you, Clare. I would have forgotten since we only talked about it five minutes ago."

Mirinda hurried through the door which connected Clare's half of Scarborough House with hers. The servants had been busy on her side of their combined house, she noted. But where Clare went in for traditional Christmas ornamentation, Mirinda had insisted on something more avant-garde. Her collection of Ming vases topped an occasional table in her hall. And in them the staff had placed long dowels, atop each of which was a perfect, round orange studded with cloves and cinnamon. No red bows. Only greenery on the lintels of her doors. And smack in the middle, another orange to match those in the vases. It smelled the same. But the effect was totally different.

As it should be for twins of differing bents.

Scarborough House reflected that difference. The renovation of the venerable Howard estate had resulted in the grand old mansion becoming two separate town houses. Hers was only slightly smaller than Clare's; but when Clare's newest scheme was finished, Mirinda's would be larger. Ian, Clare's stepson and a new recruit for the Yard, would have half the first floor and the majority of the second for his own apartments.

How Grandmother Howard would love to see her favorite residence once more bursting with Family! Though she might not appreciate the photography studio in her front parlor. *The smells, you know,* she would have said.

But the old dear *would* have loved that Mirinda and Clare were no longer dependent on the whims of fortune or the men in the Clively family. She would have appreciated Mirinda's and Clare's "useful" solution—turning Scarborough Downs into Clively Close, the newest and foremost address in Mayfair. Twelve new town houses now lined the curving drive which wound around the central park, where the statue of Gen. Clarence Clively held center stage. Twelve town houses, six on each side, and half rented. The income was most welcome.

So were Mirinda's clients. She swept open the door into the front-room studio and smiled warmly at the younger woman who sat intently reading. By the binding, the book in her hand had to be one of Mirinda's favorites: Browning's *Dramatis Personae.*

"Thank you for waiting, Miss Symons."

The young lady rose quickly. Her height took Mirinda by surprise. She stood taller than most men. With that mass of platinum curls carelessly piled on her head, she could have been six feet. The dress she wore was becoming to one with her translucent skin and purple-tinged eyes. The plum satin tea dress emphasized her every asset—and it would photograph beautifully against the stark Elgin Marbles drop which Mirinda had recently installed.

And that widow's peak! Combined with Catherine's dainty brows and the mole on the corner of her left cheek, which drew the onlooker's gaze to her smile . . . Well! Mirinda could tell Catherine had earned those tiny lines in the corner of her mouth.

Generous cheekbones. Rounded jaw. Long neck. Straight back. Squared shoulders. Small breasts. Small waist. Generous hips.

Yes, I can do something with that!

"Will you follow me, Miss Symons. I do apologize for my tardiness. The session previous ran overlong. The Bedfords—" The stricken look on Catherine's face made Mirinda realize what she had said. Enemies. This was one of the Bedfords'. "Oh, dear, I am sorry."

"No, no! It is quite all right." Catherine waved a hand for Mirinda to precede her. "I am quite used to people mentioning the Bedfords and then biting their tongues. But I tell you, it is such an old family story, I find it all rather moot. I am afraid I am the only one, however."

Above all else, Mirinda noticed anger and a tinge of sorrow. What had occasioned that?

"Old family rivalries do moulder one's perspective."

The young woman hooted. "If they would only moulder in the grave, our present lives would be much happier."

Mirinda's interest soared. As she pulled out the wedge-shaped corner chair which would afford Catherine some comfort, she arched her brow at the young woman and grinned. "And whom would you like to moulder in his grave?"

"Her grave, Lady Mirinda."

Mirinda frowned. "I thought you were the only female remaining in your family."

"I did not say my family, my lady." She took a seat and arranged her skirts so the folds swept gently to the floor. "Rivalries extend beyond one's personal sphere."

23

"The only rivals of the Symons were, I always thought, the Bedfords."

Catherine merely smiled, looked up, and said, "Is this what you wanted or should I pose another way?"

Mirinda knew avoidance when she heard it. Her interest had been politely spurned. Catherine had been reared to know when rectitude was important. Obviously this was one of those times.

"That will be fine. The afternoon sun will give good, strong shadows for your face. It will arrest the interest."

Connery arrived carrying that morning's collection of plates and deposited the box inside the studio door. Mirinda hurried to rescue the five which had not been used. As she had promised Clare, she selected two. But she did what she usually would not do. She quickly washed off that morning's residue and recoated the plates. She did not polish them before she added the colloidal solution. That would have been cheating. And it would not show the defects once again. Merely recoating them would.

Then, from the pile on the long deal table against the far wall, she selected two which were not prepared. Quickly she repeated the routine which had frustrated her so at the Bedfords'. She finished quickly, a startling contrast to that morning's eternity of failure.

Clare slipped into the room. "Aunt Prudence insists that Miss Symons stay to tea. And we would be delighted if you could. Would that suit?"

Catherine beamed. "Most assuredly. But I must send word to my father."

"Use the desk in my waiting room to pen him a note. I will have our footman Burton deliver it," Mirinda ordered.

Her mind registered when Catherine left the room, but her attention was on the four completed negatives which she had lined up on the deal table.

It—the four times four *its*—were not there.

The plates, all four, were pristine clear. No spot where spots had been. No shadow where shadows once loomed.

"Blast and tarnation!" She looked up to Clare. "You knew."

"I suspected. Now I *know.*" She smiled with secret self-satisfaction and Mirinda scowled. "Never fear, dear doubting sister, I am revealing it. You have a ghost in your plate. That is, *four* ghostly figures made by the same one man. Long dead. Who now befriends young John. And has come, I believe, to *us,* Mirinda."

"I'm sending for a doctor for *you.*"

Clare caught Mirinda's sleeve. "I'm quite serious."

"I'm quite appalled. I don't want to have to shut away my sister."

Clare chuckled. "Oh, Indy, bear with me. We shall discover more. With Aunt Pru's help, I do believe."

"Oh, lovely! Excite the seventy-nine-year-old dear. It is truly good for her heart. Not to mention my indigestion!" Mirinda flounced to the hallway, heading straight for the conservatory and leaving Clare to do the honours with Catherine.

"Thaddeus!" Prudence nodded and thunked her cane into the terrazzo tile. Her lace day cap bobbed on her carefully coiffed white curls. And her aquamarine eyes twinkled like the Severn on a sunny day. "Oooh," she rubbed her hands together, "I do like a good ghost story. Perhaps I can use it in my next novella. *He Walks in Westminster.* Or *The Ghastly Ghost of Gravesend.* Oh, I am wonderfully creative this afternoon."

Mirinda ground her teeth together. *"Creative* and *ghost.* I never thought to hear them uttered in the same sentence. Especially by you, Aunt."

"Folderol." Aunt Prudence replaced her teacup in her saucer and eyed their guest. "But, of course, we all know why he walks again, don't we?" She smiled at Catherine.

Catherine blushed and refused to look anyone in the eye. "I do not know to what you refer."

"But of course you do, my dear. Your good father was remarking on it just last week."

"Father?" Catherine blanched. "He . . . he *knows?*"

Clare inched to the edge of her chair. "Knows? What, pray? Would it help explain this phenomenon?"

"I cannot see how," Catherine huffed. " 'Tis my affair. No one in the . . . the *Bedford* household would have wind of it. So I do not see how any ghost could." Her purple eyes blackened. "And I do not believe in ghosts! I do not."

"But one believes in you, dear," Prudence said. "Else, how explain it?" She patted Catherine's hand. "Now, naught is amiss in your . . . um . . . relationship . . . with Artie is there?"

Catherine sucked in her breath. "Absolutely not! There is no relationship." Suddenly her bottom lip quivered. "His mother . . . oh, dear!"

Prudence nodded. "Yes, as I thought! Maud is so over-proud of that viscountess title she queers every attempt to become the dowager. Which would happen if Arthur married."

Mirinda was afraid her mouth would never close. She forced herself to swallow. "A Symons and a Bedford? Marrying? Good God!"

Clare folded her hands, pleased with herself. "The ghost walks for very good reason. The pattern repeats itself. He must wish a different resolution this time."

Catherine was up out of her chair. "Oh, my! Oh, never say that! Artie is too sweet, too full of the joy of life to ever consider suicide!"

"Was not Thaddeus also sweet and full of the joy of life?" Clare asked quietly.

"So the legend goes," Catherine said. "But he was also a traitor and when found out . . . you know the result."

"Death before dishonor?" Clare asked.

"Yes."

"But there *was* dishonor. It was already broadcast in the land, according to what Aunt Prudence has always told us."

She looked to Pru for confirmation and received a calculating and proud nod. "Why, then, Catherine, Mirinda, did Thaddeus entertain the necessity of suicide?"

For the first time, Mirinda began to understand to what Clare alluded. "Do you suggest there was no suicide?"

Catherine dropped with a plop and whoosh of her skirts to the settee. "No suicide? That's impossible."

"No," Clare affirmed. "It is *not* impossible. I consider it highly probable. Whose word do we have that Thaddeus was a traitor? What proof? Do you have any, Catherine? Does Arthur? Did any of your ancestors? Or was it mere gossip? Conjecture? Perhaps intrigue? This occurred, after all, during the American uprising. And Thaddeus spent five years in the Colonies as an emissary for George the Third. Five years of absence—time enough for someone to spread rumors, time enough for some of those rumors to be believed and for poor Thaddeus to be branded traitor with no means to defend himself."

"But his family . . . *they* believed it true. They must have had some proof, else why would they lay him in unconsecrated ground?"

"I don't know," Clare said. "But I do believe old Thaddeus wants us to find out."

Prudence rose and gathered her reticule and lace shawl. "What you are proposing is an investigation, Clare?"

"Yes, Aunt."

"Of a century-old mystery."

"Murder, Aunt."

"Ah, yes. Of course. That would follow, would it not?" She swept dramatically along the terrazzo path among the ferns, orchids, and miniature roses. Before she left the conservatory, she turned to survey the younger women. "Yes. If it were not suicide, then Thaddeus must have been pushed over that balustrade. Pushed to his death. It is our duty . . . *your* duty, Mirinda, Catherine, and Clare . . . to discover who, what, and why, and to allow that soul to rest in peace."

Mirinda stared after her. "Well, I'll be hornswoggled!

While Clare could set aside the investigation to ready herself for Jenny Churchill's ball, Mirinda fussed and fumed over Pru's hegemony. Ordered to delve into a century-old mystery and to solve it! The women—both Pru and Clare—were mad. Present-day murders were hard enough. But where in the world were they to find the evidence they needed to rectify old injustices? And how to help Thaddeus . . .

Oh, posh!

Here she was, thinking the ghost real. She should think about Gus. Conversing with him. Dining. Dancing.

Well, she was lucky. Because if what they had learned this afternoon were true, Catherine would not be able to dine or dance with her beloved. Not openly. Not ever.

And Mirinda knew that pain. She did not wish such suffering on another. So . . . she would help her daffy sister and her imperious aunt. But not for the reason they would assume she did. Because Mirinda wished true love to run an easy course. A natural course. And murder or suicide was never natural.

Nor was that barge of a viscountess natural, Mirinda decided as she glared across Jenny Churchill's enormous ballroom. Greenery and Christmas baubles everywhere but all Mirinda saw was Maud Lavinia Bedford, age sixty, at the very least, hanging onto Gus's arm as if she were a debutante.

Maud Lavinia Bedford. Big breasted. Big boned. Big hipped. Ruffled and laced to make her a gingerbread battleship. She might once have been lovely, lithe, and lively. Now she was dried, desiccated, and deadly.

And only Mirinda could see in Gus's copen blue eyes the agony he suffered having to smile courteously, courageously, and continuously.

Mirinda put her fan to her face to cover her snicker. She could imagine what Gus would say if they could be alone to discuss it. *"Ach, du liebe! What I do for the Kaiser!"* She giggled. But her giggle sputtered short when she saw Maud pull her eldest son, Arthur, away from a black-haired American beauty named Felicity Whitney. One American beauty in the Bedford family was one too many, it seemed, because Maud hurriedly shepherded both Gus and Arthur to a bevy of that season's British debutantes. Blond. Bland. Boring.

Mirinda wanted to laugh; but the image of Catherine's tortured face intruded. And one look at Arthur's bemused reaction told Mirinda volumes.

We are not amused.

Ambitious mothers! A pox on them!

Mirinda had one choice, one devilish desire. And she took it.

Following her Grandmother Howard's dictum: *Shoulders back, chin high, Howards do not hesitate,* she sailed across the crowded ballroom floor and interrupted Maud's chatter.

"My dear," she said to Arthur, tucking her arm into his and drawing him—and his mother and Gus—away from the young girls, "have you heard of the disaster at your brother's photographic sitting this morning? Too, too dreadful!"

Though she wanted to eat Gus with or without a spoon, she focused on Arthur. His hazel eyes twinkled in merry gratitude, and his flashing, toothy smile confirmed his joy.

Maud huffed. "I heard you were completely incompetent. Or was my daughter-in-law in her usual dither?"

Arthur stilled.

Even Gus, with his usual grace and aplomb, blinked.

Mirinda summoned The Haughty Howard Look; and Maud, true to most human's reaction to that Look, quelled.

"No, Lady Redding, your daughter-in-law was in her usual delightful phase—she is so serene. I could only wish to sample some of that myself one day."

"Mother, truly, Michael is blessed with his wife and that lovely child. I could wish for much less."

"You had best do much more, Arthur. Thirty-six and unmarried! Why, that . . . that *child* will be viscount if you do not do your duty, accept your responsibility to sire an heir. A British heir. From the best stock. Yes. That's what we need."

Venting his anger for the first time, Arthur all but spat, "Enough, Mother. You forget where you are."

Through it all, Gus stared blankly at Mirinda, but his eyes shone with an emotion only she could read. It mirrored her own. Outrage. For Arthur. For themselves. For what was lacking in far too many lives—love and affection.

Poor Thaddeus had lacked it and evidently had died for or because of it.

Or had he?

Here she was, dithering away her time with this beastly woman, when she should be putting her investigative skills to best use. And the best place to start was with the beleaguered viscount.

"Your Highness," she addressed Gus, Prince Hesse-Bogen, "perhaps Lady Redding would enjoy a turn about the floor?"

She bit her lip when Gus stared daggers at her. But she regretted her offer when Monstrous Maud tilted her head . . . giggled! . . . and tucked her arm inside Gus's, making damned sure his elbow felt the *softig* bounty of her bosom. Grrr! People should be able to bare their teeth and growl.

Smiling, Gus grasped Maud's hand and led her out in a waltz, where it was all too evident to the agile prince and all else that his partner had feet of concrete.

Viscount Redding choked on his guffaw, took Mirinda's hand, and kissed the back of her kid glove. "Most grateful, Lady Mirinda. I love her dearly, but she does wear on one."

"Come, Arthur, let us get punch and have a chat. I am a mite tired and I would dearly love to have a handsome man's company while I rest."

"Delighted."

Mirinda waited patiently while Arthur retrieved two glasses of champagne punch from one of the five buffet tables. They settled in a corner which Jenny had probably reserved for lovers, but did nicely for Mirinda's purposes.

"So . . ." she said, cocking her head, "I shall be blunt, dear boy."

30

"I expected no less, Lady Mirinda. Your reputation would be ruined, else."

She laughed. "Then you will not blanch when I ask. You and Catherine . . . Ah! 'Tis true, then."

"How the deuce did you know?"

"I had the pleasure of doing her portrait today. What few of my clients see is how well *I* see beneath the surface they affect. But I had some help discerning the truth. Aunt Pru, it seems, is in Catherine's father's confidence."

"Oh, no! We thought we had been discreet."

"You were, dear boy. You were. But parents, it seems, have sensibilities and those who suffer the loss of one sense compensate in many ways. Stephen Symons intuits, if you will, his daughter's admiration for you. Probably from acute auditory facilities. It is in Catherine's voice, you know . . . her admiration . . . her frustration . . . her bereavement for what cannot be. I heard it myself today. And we must do something about it, dear boy. Aunt Prudence orders it."

Arthur gulped and fought back moisture in his eyes. "My gratitude knows no bounds, Lady Mirinda. For you and for your aunt. Catherine has always admired Lady Prudence. I do believe she takes the place of the mother Catherine lost at an early age. But I doubt you or anyone can change what history has decreed."

Mirinda could not picture Prudence as a mother at all— natural or not. "We shall see. We Howards and Clivelys persist where others quake. So, to begin: how will you explain this affection to Maud?"

"I cannot. The history of the families . . ."

"Yes. Decidedly unpleasant."

He sighed heavily. "Unpleasant is the kindest term. Mother calls it dastardly when over the years the Symons have found every means to ruin the Bedfords. In the Regent's time, they manipulated one stock market offering and took over our import-export trading company. A decade later—in 1827 to be precise—they almost killed our shipbuilding firm in Portsmouth. By the time Victoria took the throne, the Symons

31

managed to get control of most of the Bedford estate loans. And until my father's death, Catherine's uncle always called our loans in early. Only the Bedford loans. In fact, if it weren't for my sister-in-law Grace and the van Allyn dowry, all the Bedfords would be on the street. Yet that was a bitter pill for Mother to swallow. American money to shore up British poverty. Over the years Mother has come so close to it because of the Symons that now she vibrates at the mere thought of a Symons on her doorstep. Could you imagine her reaction if she were to discover that her eldest son—the viscount—wishes to take a Symons to wife."

"Still, you choose Catherine."

"Absolutely." He spoke almost to himself, and Mirinda smiled at the intensity of his emotion. "I met her quite by accident but I loved her on the spot. Try to deny it though I might, I cannot. She has done the same. We are caught in the hideous tangle of betrayal. It haunts us mightily."

"You don't know how true that is." She rearranged her skirts and laced her fingers around her crystal goblet. "Tell me, Arthur, have you ever seen the family ghost?"

He chortled. "Yours?"

"That is answer enough." She patted his hand. "No, dear boy. This ghost is yours."

Arthur reached out and gently tugged at her glass. "Lady Mirinda, you will have no more champagne punch."

She slapped his hand away. "Such impertinence! I *am* your elder, young man. And I am not tipsy, nor mad. Though for one moment I thought my sister was when she brought me this tale." She was getting more adept at describing the phenomena. This time it took but a couple of minutes before another's mouth opened in utter disbelief. "Yes, I know. My reaction, just. But the proof is in the pudding. Or in this case my photographic plates. I cannot argue with the results I saw on them. It could not be otherwise. No, it could not!" She allowed Arthur time to chew over the implications, then asked, "Clare and I would like to peruse your family histories. You do have them, do you not?"

"Oh, yes. The second-floor library is filled to the rafters with diaries and journals and day books. And the butler's sitting room contains household accounts. Would they be useful?"

His tone implied indulgence. It was no matter. She had accomplished what she needed. "I will not know until I inspect them. Thank you, dear boy. And I do wish you well with your Catherine. But if you wish us well and all goes well, your Christmas wish may come true."

"Then by all means, Lady Mirinda, I wish you Godspeed."

The second photographic session with Grace, Michael, and John went swimmingly. Clare was in a jovial mood—until the butler closed the door of the Bedford library. She groaned. Books and journals, boxes and bags of detritus rose twelve feet on every paneled wall in dizzying disarray. "Grace's money was desperately needed, but not one penny was spent on this room."

"Nor on staff. Mrs. Minnow and the maid ascending the stair look to be Aunt Pru's generation. And Budge, the butler, has outlived the Visigoths!" Mirinda looked around her in distaste. She dug in her reticule and found two old pairs of rubber gloves. "Thank goodness I always carry these. Your new white kid would be ruined from all this . . ." She waved her arm, dislodging dust whose residence had been fixed in the air for decades. Sighing, she handed Clare a pair of gloves, then donned her own. "We must to it, dear. Tallyho and all that rot!"

Two hours later Clare scratched her head and stretched to relieve tension in her neck. "I say, even we Clivelys do not rave on about ourselves as much as these Bedfords."

"Shh. You will wake the dead," Mirinda grinned. "Have you found anything of any import?"

"Menus of dinner for three hundred. Receptions for the King. Thirteen letters from some merchant named Brennan complaining of underhanded tactics in New Amsterdam and bringing his business close to ruin. He actually says that 'ye undercut others' prices, bring goods in without ye proper tax stamps, and use pirate vessels to subvert ye King's Admiralty and Revenue Courts.' Now, Mirinda, is that not merely another way of calling Thaddeus a traitor? Gad. With all that folderol, what *am* I expected to pursue?!"

Mirinda rolled her eyes. "My dear, you are usually the one to tell *me* that bit of news. Where are your powers today?"

"I did not bring them. It is this atmosphere. So dreary. Musty. Sorrowful. A good dusting and rug-beating would do this library proud. Please, Indy, sometimes you are as perceptive as I. Point me in the right direction and I might be able to draw up my *voyants*. But as it is. . . ."

Mirinda closed yet another diary, and a cloud of dust wafted from the pages. "We are looking for the time the ghost walked on this earth as a man. Seventeen-seventy-five through the end of the uprising should be enough."

Clare grumbled as she opened another butler's tome, "And too much." She squinted at the crabbed hand and slammed the book shut. "No. I refuse. *Voyants* are easier. Give me something less dry and ordinary, Mirinda."

Mirinda stood and waved her hand over an expanse larger than their conservatory. "I give you the Bedford Library! Take what you will, my dear."

Clare mashed her teeth together. Then, she rose to stalk the confines of the gloom. Shelf after shelf of diatribes. Lectures. Sermons. Papers of credit. Wills. And not a novel among them.

Gad. Had no one bought a book in seventy years?

She trailed her hand along one wide window ledge crusted with grime. She fingered the velvet drapes and they disintegrated before her eyes. *Maud will have your head. Well, bother Maud.* She squared her shoulders and knelt on the window shelf to open the casements. Seventy years? One hundred seemed more like it. She pushed with all her might and was rewarded finally by hinges creaking with fatigue of historic proportions. One more shove and the window flew open, causing her to lose her balance.

"Indy!" She sprawled—half in and half out of the library—and stared into an abyss which seemed endless. Suddenly she knew *this* was what Thaddeus had felt that fateful night. She clutched madly behind her and the drapes ripped from their supports. "Oh, Indy!"

Strong hands supported her, pulling her away from that inexorable void. A warmth flooded her. Tears came so easily. "Oh, Thaddeus, how awful it must have been," she whispered, her heart understanding at last what only her head knew previous. "I am sorry. So very sorry."

Mirinda's head whipped up at Clare's cry. She was out of her chair in a heartbeat.

And then stood stark in her tracks.

The light from the casement blinded, yet did not blind. A gray mist swirled around Clare. A Clare with her arms raised as if someone embraced her. Clare rose and stood against the window ledge. And smiled into the gray mist.

Good God! The mist moved.

Dust coalesced, swirling round *It*. Mirinda blinked hard. Her eyes must be overtaxed from the day's duties. First the photography, now the gloomy tomes . . .

And then gray became puce. Puce, pink. Pink, scarlet.

And she saw him.

Thaddeus, of a certainty. Thaddeus, as he must have looked on that last night. Thaddeus, in his most splendid regalia. Scarlet cutaway jacket trimmed in miles of gold passementerie with a royal crest attached prominently to the left. Blue dress trousers. Black shiny boots. Wide black belt with gold buckle. Jewel-encrusted scabbard, empty of the sword shown in his portrait.

He stood tall and proud, smiled invitingly, and held his hand out to Mirinda.

Automatically she moved closer.

And Thaddeus moved away.

He stood beside Clare, his hand on her shoulder. He beckoned Mirinda forward . . .

And laid his other hand against the framework of the window ledge.

His finger curled as if pulling something. Curled and tugged. Curled and tugged.

But there were some things even a handsome, virile ghost could not do.

The frustration and sadness on his face ripped away all Mirinda's hesitation or disbelief.

"Yes, Thaddeus. I understand. We shall prevail. Clare, you, and I."

"Oh, Indy. You see him, too."

"How could I not? If ghosts wish to be seen, they *are* seen. Now, he wants us to search here."

Attuned now to the needs of Thaddeus, the Viscount Redding, dead these one hundred years, she ran her fingers along the window casement where Thad's ghost had grasped at something. A blast of cold air left her gasping.

"The fresh air is appreciated, Clare. But 'tis freezing out there!"

"And the ground is three floors away."

"You nearly plunged to your death."

"Thaddeus would not have permitted it." As Mirinda probed the window casement, Clare surveyed the damage her enthusiasm had occasioned and giggled. "How *do* we do it, Indy?"

"Luck, my dear."

And then Mirinda felt it. One gloved fingernail caught in a chest-high depression and a warm flush crept up her throat. She stole a glance at Clare whose reddened cheeks had more to do with excitement and interest than the cold air coming from the window.

"Yes, Indy. I see it. So does Thaddeus. Now do as he wishes."

"I will. I will. 'Tis only that this seems so . . . so . . . Dickensian, does it not?"

"Indy, if you will not complete Thaddeus's bidding, then I will."

"You should. He manifested himself to you first."

Magnanimously Mirinda stepped back and allowed Clare to feel the depression for herself. And at the same moment, Thaddeus laid his hand on Mirinda's shoulder, cocked a smile and a salute at Clare. And slowly vanished. Scarlet to pink. Pink to puce. Puce to gray. Then nothing.

"It is all up to us now, Indy."

"Yes. Do hurry, dear."

Clare swept her gloved finger around the circumference of the depression. "A flash of brass. A ring."

"A ring?"

"No. And yes. Larger than anything which goes on a finger. But small enough for two fingers to fit inside. Now if I can but pry it up . . ."

With it came a section of the side of the window shelf!

"Oh, Indy." Clare peered into the recess. "Two shapes. Square. Dark."

"Boxes?"

"I do believe so, yes."

"Another cache? Delightful," Mirinda enthused.

Clare sniffed. "Delighted if you like mouse droppings and four hundred kinds of spiders! I do not. Here. You take the boxes out."

"Oh, Clare. Your fastidiousness sometimes ruffles my feathers." Gingerly she extracted two small, iron-bound cedar boxes. "They appear to be old seafaring chests." She sniffed. "They smell like it, too!"

"Simply put them on the reading table. These are my finds, Indy."

Mirinda bobbed in a curtsy as Colette, Clare's maid, would do. "Yes, my lady. And should I prepare tea?"

"No, but you could ring for it."

Mirinda plunked the two boxes down and gave the sturdy bellpull a yank. Within moments, the Bedfords' venerable butler shuffled into the room.

He squinted through thick lenses and bowed. "Miladies?"

"Tea, please, Budge."

Nothing on the butler's body did budge except his eyebrows, which went for the rafters when he spied what destruction Clare had wrought. And they disappeared into his rim of fuzz when he saw what she riffled. "Miladies!" he croaked. "Where did you find those?"

She could not tell him a ghost had directed this discovery. Budge would believe her mad. And he'd tell the entire household. Maud would know. And once Maud knew, all London would be atitter. So Mirinda simply pointed to the opening in the window ledge.

"Perhaps if the drapes had been taken down and shaken at least once this century, you might have had benefit of these memoirs before we discovered them, Budge."

"But, miladies, your discovery is one the family sought for decades. My father told me of the treasures to be found in two old ditty boxes, long lost to us . . . to the Bedfords."

Clare's head jerked up. "Treasures?" She pawed through the contents and at the very bottom discovered what the Budges considered treasures. She laid them out on the table one by one, all in a row. She smiled.

"A brooch in the shape of a crest. I do believe I have seen one like this. Quite recently, too. A pair of aquamarine earbobs. A small bloodstone and pearl cockade. A pearl-encrusted thimble. An illustrated quarto of Shakespeare. Numerous pieces of delicate scrimshaw. Hand-forged golden scissors. A very heavy gold seal ring. And the *pièce de résistance,* a tiny woven reed sewing kit." Her eyes met Indy's. "A delight. For whom, I wonder?"

"For his lady," Budge confirmed, his hands calm as a minister's over his Bible.

"Whose lady?" Mirinda and Clare asked at once.

" 'Tis written, my father said, on the lid."

Clare swallowed her distaste and did what had to be done. With her delicate lace-edged handkerchief, she wiped the grime from the cover of both boxes. Burned into one of the surfaces were the words, *Thaddeus. Bedford.* And on the other, *Rachel. Symons.*

Shock etched Budge's already coruscated face. "We never speak of this gentleman," he croaked. "The scandal seems fresh as this morning's bread."

"Of course it does," Mirinda said. "This is a house of mourning. And the Lady Redding keeps it so."

As if her words evoked the devils in the dust, the very lady sailed through the open door. Abruptly she bid them all good afternoon and came to stand beside Clare. She peered at the assemblage on the table.

"Jewelry. Are you selling or giving it away?"

"Neither," Mirinda said. "It is not ours to give. It is, I believe, Rachel Symons's."

Maud's fingers grasped at the high neck of her day dress. "Never use that name in this household! The calumny! The treachery! The agony it invokes!"

The melodrama made Mirinda's jaw ache. "It seems my sister has recovered lost memorabilia. Quite priceless, too."

A calculating look came into Maud's eyes. "Yes. Of course." Her fingers left her throat and lightly caressed each jeweled piece. "Of course, these came from *him*. Look here, the family crest."

Laurel wreath surrounding an emblazoned charge from the Bedford coat of arms: A perfect rose, topped by a viscount's coronet.

"The arms are a field of gold with a bend sinister in blue. The rose is white, laid into the sinister base . . ."

A bastard in the family somewhere. Mirinda smiled. The old battle-axe wouldn't admit it, of course. She was too family proud.

". . . while the viscount's red coronet sits in the dexter chief. Of course it is all laid upon a cloth of gold to represent the first Redding's service to Henry Tudor."

Maud picked up the brooch. "Pearls," she cooed. "All perfectly matched. And the enameling . . . I shall wear this to the Brennans' on Thursday." She rang for Budge. "Take these

39

two pieces to your pantry and clean them. After, take the other things to Lord Redding's study. He will wish to catalog them. Then perhaps I can persuade him to allow me the pleasure of this lovely seal ring as well."

Clare gnashed her teeth. The audacity of this woman to appropriate not only the family crest, which was rightfully Arthur's, but also to covet the viscount's seal. Maud could curdle fresh cream with one touch of her greedy fingers.

If I never felt it before, I vow now to ensure that Artie has the prerogative to bestow these two treasures on his Catherine.

Clare rose from her seat, doing what she must to obtain Maud's cooperation. "Very well. Take those. But I would like you to know that Arthur has given us permission to examine everything at our leisure at Scarborough House. If you wish it, we will sign a release . . ."

But Maud was too engrossed in her newfound wealth. She waved an imperious hand at the sisters. "Take what you like. But return them in the condition they were found."

Clare's hands balled into fists. For the first time in her life she wanted to strike at someone. Not even her close brush with a murderer had occasioned that response. Imagine, returning memoirs *with* all the dust intact.

The sisters spent the next several days stretched between their usual occupations, preparation for the holidays, and their unstinting devotion to the Bedfords' vexing history.

"How are we expected to make something of this?" Clare asked Mirinda five days later. "Thaddeus asks much of us."

"And much we will give, sister."

"At least Thaddeus's love letters break up the monotony. He must have truly loved Rachel."

Mirinda snorted. "He loved what he thought the girl was. Listen to this:"

" 'I see you more beautiful than Boticelli's Venus, more steadfast than Penelope, more regal than Juno.'

"Does that sound as if he were writing to a real woman? Would you have believed Robert had he written such to you?"

Clare mashed her mouth together. "Robert's loving phrases were firmly grounded in reality. He never even compared me to a summer's day."

"I should hope not. A husband and a lover should see you as you are, and love you for or in spite of it. But this . . ." Mirinda tossed Thaddeus's missive into the center of the pile that had accumulated on her dining-room table. "Even one hundred years ago this was drivel."

"Don't tell Thaddeus."

"My dear, I do believe he already knows. After all, the steadfast Rachel spurned him more rapidly than aspic hardens."

"Poor Thaddeus. He did not fare well . . . in any aspect of this sorry incident. No wonder he walks. I'd run."

Mirinda chuckled. "He does sound a bounder. These letters from his American mistress—what was her name?" Mirinda pulled over a small note and squinted at the tiny signature. "Abigail Gray. Good heavens! It looks like no feminine hand! Not a misspelling in the whole thing. And I thought Americans had little education—especially among the class who would consent to become a mistress to one already affianced. And then have the audacity to confirm it on paper! Would any woman do such?"

"Hardly, Indy. Not when they know the letters might be opened and read."

"Yes, that was one of the quirks of the American post, I do believe. Dumping letters on an inn trestle! Or on a cracker barrel at the general store where anyone could open them and read the contents! Abominable!"

"Yet Abigail writes glowingly of the nights she and Thaddeus spent together. And in most graphic prose, Indy. *Not* one of our kind at all."

"Not one of our kind? No, decidedly." *Perhaps in more ways than Clare now understood.* "But there is another ques-

41

tion of far more import. How did these letters get from Thaddeus to Rachel? We found them in her box, remember."

Stunned, Clare had to move to coalesce her thoughts. She rose and paced from sideboard to table, from table to window seat, and back again. "Why, it never occurred to me. Did Abigail send them? No. That could never be. She would have sent them to Thaddeus. Did she, then, make copies of the ones she sent and then mail them to Rachel? No, that could never be. How would she know where to send them unless Thaddeus told her. And I cannot credit that our wonderfully handsome rogue ghost had mush for brains. So how did they get into Rachel's possession?"

"That was my question five minutes ago."

"There is no explanation."

"There is one. Someone else sent them to her."

"Oh, Indy, who would do such a thing?"

Mirinda riffled through the letters. "A friend who was no friend. And many of these correspondents fit that description. One writes that Thaddeus was 'a man of too much sympathy for the Rebellion. A man given to clandestine midnight meetings with imprudent acquaintances of revolutionary bent, especially his hosts, the van Allyns.' " She dropped the letter to her lap. "The van Allyns? Is not that Grace's family name?"

Clare smiled. "And from the city and state of New York. When do you think New Amsterdam became New York?"

"Both names are used in these letters. They were probably interchangeable prior to the uprising."

"Those were busy days, Indy. Even house parties had a hint of intrigue in the air."

"When have they not?"

"But then a simple liaison could have monumental consequences. This house party at the Roger Morrises', for example . . ." She pulled over a letter that had arrested the interest of both of them. "Plots and counterplots. Spies and counterspies." She shivered. "Not just gossip, then, Indy. Life-threatening, these intrigues were."

"Thaddeus's life." Mirinda frowned. "Three bitter accusations that Thaddeus had actually helped plan the New Amsterdam tea party—and in the process had made the King's ministers and officers look the fools! The men who signed the accusations—British loyalists to the core—were duly rewarded by King George following the war. But if I remember my history, they grumbled that George's offerings were not enough. Roger Morris—George Washington's friend and fellow surveyor—expected at least a viscount title and British lands. He received lands but no title."

"Horst van Zett and Wendell Brennan also. Only Warren Standish was knighted. But not for what he discovered at Roger Morris's Christmas Eve house party. Rather for his privateering, which added revenue to George the Third."

"That must have grated after what they had done."

"Oh, Indy. Such things on which men build hope . . . What they unearthed was so minor. Discovering a plot to dump tea in the Hudson and alerting the British Army was admirable. But when they failed to catch any rebels, think of the humiliation."

Mirinda nodded. "Yes. Which was why they looked for a reason for their failure."

"And found it in Thaddeus."

"Well, all evidence pointed to him. He boarded at Allwynd in the Hudson Valley, a home known, Roger Morris says, to be 'rife with rebel sympathizers.' Thaddeus's hosts were known revolutionists. And he was at Roger Morris's when the plot was discovered. The four believed he warned the van Allyns of the impending British action and the van Allyns had warned the rebels, who postponed their activity for a night when British patrols were unprepared. The New York Junta tea party succeeded just as the Boston one did."

"Unfortunately for Thaddeus."

"Most decidedly. Because when it did, those four men singled Thaddeus out as the one man with the capability and opportunity to turn traitor. What I don't understand from all these missives is why, when they accused him, Thaddeus would not refute it but allowed them to hound him—in print, in person, by letter—until he was recalled to England to face a charge by the Privy Council. A charge of treason."

"Thus Thaddeus's suicide seemed to confirm their suspicions."

Clare's excitement grew as the pieces started to fit together. "But if it were not suicide—and of course it wasn't—then the accusations were quite false."

"Yes, dear. Quite false. Why then the tone of the letters and articles? Why the Privy Council's quick acceptance of the charges?"

Clare's eyebrow raised in that clearly Howard hauteur. "I have a ghost of an idea, Indy. But I will need to make a quick trip back to the Bedford library to be certain. We did not bring the missive I need to confirm my suspicions."

"Tell me now."

"No, Indy. You know I like to be quite certain."

Mirinda's only reply was to grind her teeth and stalk out of the room. She, too, had her own suspicions. And if Clare would not divulge hers, then Mirinda saw no reason to reveal her own until she, too, was certain.

Suspicions frayed the nerves. And the Brennans' Holiday At Home bore the brunt. Clare snapped at Colette, her maid, who starched Clare's bonnet ribbons too severely. Mirinda sent her own maids, elderly Ida and Lettie Smart, scurrying to sponge out spots only she could see.

The carriage ride to Kensington, just south of the palace, took them mere minutes. It was not too soon for Mirinda, who hated the silence in the carriage and longed to walk Brennan House unfettered. For once, she could not expect to see Gus there, and that was all the better. She had other things on her mind this afternoon.

Murder. Not romance.

The Brennans—all twelve—lined up for the reception. Couturier houses had been picked clean for this afternoon's

44

fete. Mirinda saw enough organza and ostrich plumes to last a lifetime; and she was glad when she could politely excuse herself and prowl the drawing rooms and studies.

A fine example of Georgian architecture, Brennan House. Lovely marble columns graced each doorway. Ceilings soared to trompe l'oeil clouds. Angels adorned mantel pieces. And the terrazzo floors sparkled in bare brilliance. She could see herself in their reflection.

What she saw most were, of course, the Brennans.

This generation eschewed mauve and plum velvet gaucherie. They ignored the current penchant for mirrors, black-and-white prints, and tabletops aswim in gewgaws and photos, photos, photos. She liked this simplicity, this classic order. She also appreciated the family heirlooms. The Wedgewood. Holbeins. Two Romneys. And one portrait of a loose-lipped, bewigged Georgian gentleman whom the nameplate declared was none other than Wendell Brennan, 1742-1792. The articles the portraitist had grouped around this Wendell showed him to be a merchant. They did that in those days—defined a man by his accoutrements.

Mirinda turned and walked across the room to the opposite wall rich with armaments—silver-chased and pearl-handled pistols, two old blunderbusses, three kinds of maces, a collection of daggers and swords. She stared at the eighteenth-century memorabilia, obviously Wendell Brennan's, obviously from his prominence in the room, the scion of this family, the one who had made their fortune, made their name.

Her head jerked up and she looked over her shoulder. Wendell Brennan. *Thaddeus's* Wendell Brennan?

The dates certainly fit.

She took three steps to bring into closer perspective Wendell's portrait. Yes! There, in portrait proclamation . . . a map of the New World, of New York harbor.

Wendell Brennan, merchant adventurer. For, after all, was establishing a merchandising business in the New World not an adventure? A risk? Most assuredly,

So . . . this Wendell had been one of Thaddeus's accusers.

She spun on her heel, intent on finding Clare to reveal her knowledge, when the sun flashed off an item that stopped her in her tracks. Chills swept her body. She drew her shawl high against her neck and craned her head to get a better view of . . .

Dear God!

It was there on one of the Brennan artifacts. An embossed *B*. A circlet of gold laurel leaves. A coronet studded with pearls. And one perfect, simple rose.

The sight had her reeling. The shock sent her blindly back out into the hall in search of Clare.

With one hand rubbing her pounding temples, she could not see where her feet took her until she collided with one solid figure.

She looked up; but the gentleman into whom she had tottered was too preoccupied with someone across the Brennans' drawing room to know what had occasioned.

Arthur Bedford's eyes brooded over the elegant figure of Catherine Symons as she bent over her father's chair.

Arthur's inertia gutted Mirinda. She had felt what he was feeling. She had probably looked the way he looked.

For years. For decades. Much too long.

How long must it take for lovers to acknowledge what cannot be denied? Why should two people who so obviously loved each other remain apart? What did they gain from it but pain and heartache? And who was Maud to stand in her son's way? More to the point, why did he allow it? Could he not see what it did to him . . . to Catherine?

"Arthur," she said, winding her arm in his so he could not escape her, "enough is too much! You eye that woman across the room as if she were your very breath."

"She is," Arthur mourned.

"Then, by God, do something about it! You bear the viscount coronet. You have the power."

"Our families . . . the history . . ."

"History is made by men and women who dare to risk all for a cause. I can think of no cause greater than love."

46

"You speak as if you know tragedy."

Mirinda nodded. "Much like yours, my love must be ignored, denied. But unlike yours, I have no way to mend our broken hearts. Law prevents our union. This is not so in your case. Only habit—a nasty reason for anything—stays your hand. Yet you have suzerainty over your family. Every one of them. Use your coronet, Arthur. Claim the woman you love."

"What? Here?"

"Why not?" Mirinda smiled. "It would make the Brennans' at-home an afternoon to remember."

She pushed him through the archway, and after one faltering step he strode purposely forward, bowed before Catherine, and held out his hand.

The at-home at the Brennans' became the talk of London. *The Tatler. The Illustrated London News.* Both embroidered the intricate rumors of an hysterical Maud, a shattered Stephen Symons, an embarrassed coterie of Brennans. An ecstatic Catherine and a glowing Arthur. Dancing. Laughing. Ignoring the whispers, the parents, the history.

Their engagement announcement was anticipated through seven days of gossip columns. When Christmas Eve approached—and so did the Bedfords' wassail celebration—Mirinda and Clare climbed into their coach with glee and trepidation.

"You do think that Maud has come round by now, do you not, Mirinda?"

"I have brought my smelling salts—along with the other things we have—for anyone whose stays are much too tight or whose emotions run much too high."

Clare's kid-gloved fingers ran lightly over the long oak case which straddled both their laps. She straightened the red bow which camouflaged its significance. She had decided to make it appear only another of the small tokens they had brought for exchange of gifts—an innovation Grace had imported from America.

As their brougham made the wide turn into Bedford Hall, it pulled up directly behind Aunt Prudence's new Chariot d'Orsay. The lady alighted, securing her gloves and carved walking stick.

She grinned at her nieces. "Prepared for the unveiling, are we?"

The imperial *we,* as if she had done the legwork! Mirinda smiled with gritted teeth. "Aunt, are not Howards prepared for anything?"

"Precisely, child. That is why I knew you could solve this riddle."

She linked her arm with Mirinda and allowed Clare to help her up the wide brick stairway. Behind came footmen bearing both the sisters' gifts and Aunt Prudence's. Mirinda eyed them suspiciously. They were all of a size.

"No! You did not!"

"What, dear?" Prudence asked guilelessly.

"You did not wrap copies of your latest dreadful!"

"But of course. What better token of my affection than a piece of myself?"

Clare groaned. "Oh, Aunt. Why not candied fruits?"

"I do *not* make candied fruits. I make books." She patted Clare's hand. "They will be appreciated, you know. They always are."

"People are too cowed by you to tell you different, Aunt Prudence. You do manage to quell anyone's objection."

Prudence snorted. "The prerogative of age, my dear. You will discover it soon enough."

"Probably within the next hour," Mirinda muttered.

"Chin up, as Mother would have said. We are Clivelys. They will listen for that reason alone."

Clare rolled her eyes at Mirinda. They had enough trepidations between them to sink the Royal Navy. Knowing they were Clivelys was not enough to still her trembles or slow down her triphammer heart.

And the expression on Budge's face as he opened the door did nothing to calm her fears.

They divested themselves of their outerwear, and the footmen deposited the smallest of the Clivelys' offerings among an already teetering pile on a long Tudor table. The long gift, which Mirinda had carefully cradled in the carriage, the footmen placed on the floor.

"How are we this evening," Clare whispered to the venerable butler.

"Terrible, my lady." His eyes slid to the drawing room and back, and he bent closer to Clare's ear. "Such rantings and ravings you have never heard. *I* have never heard."

"And Lord Redding?" Mirinda pursued.

"I have never seen my lord smile so broadly, yet persist in his desires so forcefully." He rocked back on his heels. "I am quite proud of him."

Clare nodded. "So you should be, Budge. We all are."

Mirinda interjected, "And after this evening many people shall stand taller, straighter, happier with their lot in life."

The tableaux which greeted the sisters and Aunt Pru were telling in their divisiveness. Maud, surrounded by elderly matrons who threw steely glances across the room at dear Catherine. Stephen Symons, Catherine's father, at the other end, straining to hear since he could not see. Arthur, rising from Catherine's side and joining Grace and Michael to do the honours and welcome their newest guests into this icy fold.

"Good evening, dear Clare and Mirinda." Grace threw a fearful glance over her shoulder at Maud, then bowed her head. "Lady Prudence. We are delighted you could join us."

"Some of you are."

Grace sighed. "We are carrying on."

Pru took the young woman's hands in hers and squeezed. "Rather well, too, my dear. You do your family proud. You will fit in here, I promise you. Bear with us as we finally accept you Americans as equal."

Grace grinned. "I anxiously await the day, Lady Prudence.

It has been a hundred years since we declared ourselves equal."

"We British are slow learners. Some of our doddering old fools don't learn until the lids on their boxes close out the last vestiges of the British sun."

When Arthur would have taken Pru's arm and led them farther into the room, a shuddering crash startled them.

"What in the world . . . ?" Arthur exclaimed.

Stephen Symons rose to his feet and pounded on a nearby table. "What is happening? Catherine! What is happening?"

Catherine put her hand on his shoulder. "I will see, Father. Please, don't disturb yourself."

"Don't leave me alone with these—"

"I won't." She tucked his arm in hers. "Come. Artie and the Clivelys are investigating. We shall follow."

Mirinda and Clare surveyed the wreckage of the foyer and smiled at each other as the small figure of John Bedford played with the item which they had brought.

"My thore," he said with pride as his fingers brushed across the jeweled hilt. His eyes traveled up to the gallery. Mirinda's and Clare's gaze followed.

They were not surprised by what they saw.

But all the others gasped.

There, at the gallery rail, in all his scarlet and blue splendor, shimmered the ghost of a Christmas Eve long past.

"Papa Kithmith," John breathed. "My thore. Thee?" He turned for his mother. "Thee, Mummy? My thore. He gived it to me."

Grace barely knew where to look, what to say, so torn was she by the sights below in the foyer and above, on the gallery walk. She leaned against her husband, bent to snatch the sword from John before he could cut himself, and held it gingerly on two outstretched hands.

"How did this get here?"

"We brought it, dear," Mirinda said.

Maud shouldered her way to the front of the gathering.

Her eyes calculated the worth of the artifact, then lit strangely at the sight of the hilt. "The Bedford Crest!"

"Yes, Maud. The *Bedford* Crest."

"Where . . . how . . ."

Mirinda cast one glance at the unmoving figure which still manifested itself above them. " 'Tis a long story. One hundred years in the telling."

Clare popped in, "And weeks in the discovery."

"Perhaps they should sit for this," Prudence said.

"No, Aunt," Mirinda said. "I wish to demonstrate, and we should be here . . . where it happened . . ."

"You see," Clare began, "it started with a ghostly image on Mirinda's photographic plates." She told them quickly about what they had surmised and why they had begun the investigation. ". . . which led us to the Bedford library and the family history kept there."

"And then Thaddeus appeared . . . as he is now," Mirinda said, raising her arm to the figure above. "The ghost most of you refuse to acknowledge. But he is real. And he has been wronged. We found evidence of it in this very library. We did not know its significance at the time. Not until the Brennans' wassail celebration. Then, one turn about their trophy room gave me enough evidence to connect the dots."

"And after we told them what we suspected, the Brennans were gracious enough to return Thaddeus's sword to you," Clare said to Arthur.

"I wondered why they sent around regrets after having initially accepted," Grace said. "I thought perhaps they were so mortified by the uproar created by Mau—" Grace bit off her words, but all knew she meant the screaming fit Maud had pitched when Arthur had claimed his Catherine.

Maud herself knew it. But she had other concerns. She stepped forward, one hand out. "Thaddeus's sword? This is Thaddeus Bedford's sword?"

"Indubitably," Mirinda said.

"You said the Brennans had it?"

"Yes, Lady Redding."

"How did they get it?"

"Wendell Brennan took it away with him after he murdered Thaddeus Bedford. He hid it in his stores; but at his death it was found and someone mounted it on the wall, assuming the *B* was for Brennan. As soon as I saw the crest, however, I knew whose it must be."

Clare beamed at the shocked faces around them. "And then she knew that Thaddeus had never committed suicide, that the Symons were not to blame, that the one hundred year enmity was all the result of jealousy and hatred. Rachel Symons, you see, was manipulated by Wendell Brennan to believe Thaddeus did not love her, was, in fact, unfaithful. Wendell Brennan and his cronies convinced the Privy Council that Thaddeus was a traitor. And the King did naught to disprove it, even though he knew Thaddeus was one of his own spies. But to acknowledge it would expose Thaddeus to dangers. When Thaddeus returned to England—the King—I am speculating here, but I do believe I am correct—would have quelled the false rumors. He did not have the opportunity. And even he must have believed Thaddeus committed suicide, else he would have spoken up to dispel any lingering doubts."

Maud's lips mashed together, then her eyes flicked upward . . . and just as quickly down. "You must be mistaken. The history is quite explicit. Thaddeus was completely discredited. He tried to effect a reconciliation with his betrothed, Rachel Symons, and she spurned him. In grief and anger, he threw himself over the railing to die at her feet." Maud pointed down. "Here. Right here." Her chin lifted and she inhaled. "That is why Rachel lost her senses and retired to a cloister. She spurned Thaddeus. She spurned a Bedford!"

Prudence harumphed. "Something no sane person should ever do. Correct, Maud?"

"Precisely so."

Mirinda took the sword from Grace. "I am sorry to crack your illusions, Maud. But you are very wrong. I shall demonstrate."

She had to carry the ponderous thing all the way up to the third-floor gallery. When she got there, Thaddeus hovered about her. "Shall we show them, my lord?"

In answer, he shimmered brightly about her and then darted to a darkened corner, where the Bedfords kept a tall chiffonnier. His transparent hand gestured to a space between it and a suit of armour. Mirinda cocked her eye at him and he seemed to grin. She looked down at the eager assembly below her. "There is a hiding place, just here." She wiggled into the space which took up more than a body's width. "Wendell Bedford must have lain in wait for Thaddeus." A vigorous head shaking from the ghost told her she had not taken the right tack. "Then, what, Thaddeus?"

He flitted towards a large door at the end of the hall.

"Just one moment," she called down. She followed Thaddeus and opened the door. "His study!" Once more she looked over the rail. "Thaddeus's study, Maud?"

"Yes," the viscountess admitted.

"Then Thaddeus and Wendell must have been in there. Arguing, obviously." Mirinda paced back to the center of the gallery. "Arguing about Wendell's shrinking business and how he blamed Thaddeus for it. Arguing about the letters Wendell had forged and sent to Rachel. We know they were forged because they did not have the van Allyn imprint on them, as all his other American letters did."

Maud's head swiveled to Grace. "Van Allyn?!"

"Yes, Maud," Clare said. "Grace's ancestors housed Thaddeus in New York. He made their house his headquarters. They were his friends."

"That's what all the questions were about when Mirinda came to see me the other day?" Grace asked.

Clare nodded. "We had to be certain you were the direct descendant of Thaddeus's van Allyns. We believe it is your presence here, as well as the parallel relationship between Arthur and Catherine, which drew Thaddeus out. In you he saw an ally. And in John he saw hope for the future, since none had been found in the past."

"Then John's Father Christmas is . . ." Grace looked upward and smiled at the ghostly, hovering spirit. ". . . him," she breathed. "And not imaginary at all."

"Oh, dear, no. Not imaginary. Though there will be few who will credit what we are seeing."

Maud's supporters murmured agreement.

"But it matters naught what others believe," Prudence said. "It matters that we put things to right."

"Yes," Clare agreed. "Mirinda," she called up.

"Yes, dear. I will proceed now."

Mirinda and Thaddeus now moved as one. He, a few steps before her; she, stalking behind him. As they approached the center of the gallery rail, she raised the sword and poked Thaddeus in the back. The sword went right through the ethereal figure. "But if he were human flesh," she called down, "he would be at a great disadvantage. Wendell must have been frantic . . . perhaps crazed at this point. He had called Thaddeus traitor; and now Thaddeus was in England and could prove the charges false. Wendell had sent Rachel forged love letters written to another woman. The wax seal bore a circled *B* but the letters were so perfect, so *unlike* Thaddeus, that we saw in an instant they were forgeries. But Rachel would have torn right into them and not noticed the difference in the wax seal or in the way the letters were written. The shock, you see . . . So Wendell was about to be exposed. Thaddeus would not let him merely fade away. Charges would have been brought. Wendell would have been ruined, probably served a severe criminal penalty. Most assuredly he would have lost his business, his fortune, his reputation. So to say he was crazed is probably not an exaggeration.

"Thus, he had to take action. He was unarmed, naturally, since this took place at a Christmas Eve celebration. But Thaddeus wore his dress uniform as a member of the king's guards and he would have donned his dress sword. So, Wendell took what was to hand, Thaddeus's own sword, to push him, force him, to the rail.

"Then one quick, unexpected thrust . . . like so!"

The guests gasped when the sword went through Thaddeus and he began to topple over the rail, just as it must have been one hundred years previous. But Thaddeus's ghost righted himself and Mirinda heard a collective sigh of relief. *At least they would not be witness to the horror Rachel must have seen.*

"So," she continued, "Thaddeus misjudged his step, doubling backward over the rail to his death. And while everyone below was mesmerized by the death—as you just were when the ghost of Thaddeus nearly repeated history—Wendell hid himself in the gloom between the chiffonnier and the suit of armour. He must have slipped away later, taking Thaddeus's sword with him."

"But why did he have to do that?" Arthur asked.

Clare answered, "What else could he do? He could not throw it down. Someone would have noticed and remarked on it. With it gone, it could be assumed that it was lost in the tumult created by the incident."

"Thus," Mirinda said, "Wendell had to keep it with him, hidden in his house, the only witness to and evidence of his foul deed. We can but wonder what it did to him, knowing that Thaddeus was innocent of all wrongdoing, that Wendell had killed for nothing more than money. Not honor. Not family pride. Not to save his country. Not even for love—for I cannot credit that a man who loved a woman would send her forged letters. No, he did it only for money."

Clare turned to confront Maud. "And Wendell Brennan left in his wake an enmity between the Symons and the Bedfords that had no foundation." Maud had the grace to blush and sputter.

With that, Mirinda glanced at the dancing spirit. "Did we do well?"

For answer, he floated above the gallery rail and hung there for one breathless moment. Then his scarlet jacket changed to puce. Puce to pink. Pink to gray. Gray to . . .

Naught.

John wailed. "Papa Kithmith!"

Grace hugged her son to her. "He will return, John. Tonight he will fill your stocking and leave your gifts under the tree. And next year you will see him again. And every year forever after that."

"And in the meantime," Arthur said, taking his nephew into his arms and chucking him under the chin, "you shall have his sword to hang in your room. You cannot play with it, of course, because it is too sharp. But it shall be yours forever."

"Arthur, do you truly mean to give a Bedford heirloom to that . . . that . . . child?" Maud demanded.

"Who better?" Arthur said. "He it was who first saw Thaddeus. To him, Thaddeus came. Not to you. Not to me. To John Michael Bedford, an innocent child who would not spurn him as adults once had. John accepted and loved him."

Grace hugged her son to her, tears mingling with her bright, loving smile.

Michael knelt to the young boy. "John, you do not totally understand what has happened. But we all owe you a great debt."

"The debt is paid," Prudence said. "Each of you had a hand in it. Now let us retire to the drawing room and welcome in this blessed season, a season which unites two wonderful young people and two warring families. A season which, thank God and Thaddeus, gives them, us, and Thaddeus our hearts' desire. Peace. And love."

About the Author

ANN CROWLEIGH is the pseudonym for the brilliant and prolific writing team of Barbara Cummings and Jo-Ann Power. Both are residents of Maryland and members of Sisters in Crime. The characters of Mirinda and Clare Clively are taken straight from CLIVELY CLOSE, their popular mystery series set in Victorian England and published by Zebra Books. Titles available in the series include DEAD AS DEAD CAN BE, WAIT FOR THE DARK, and coming in May 1994: SILENCE, COLD AS DEATH. In addition to CLIVELY CLOSE, Barbara and Jo-Ann collaborate on contemporary women's fiction, written under their own names. RISKS, published by Pinnacle Books, is their most current title available.

The Santa Claus Caper

by

Connie Feddersen

It was the Christmas season in Vamoose, Oklahoma. The volunteer fire department had wrapped red and white tinsel around the light poles that lined Main Street. The small farming community, with its laid-back atmosphere and welcoming sign posted at the city limits that read "If you like it country-style, then Vamoose" had become a land of gigantic candy canes. The windows of Last Chance Café had been painted with snowflakes that swirled around a colorful Christmas tree. Thatcher's Gas and Oil boasted a life-size mechanical Santa Claus that waved to passersby. Velma's Beauty Boutique was decorated with winking green lights that encircled the eaves and surrounded the front lawn.

Amanda Hazard's Accounting Agency had one measly night-light candle burning in the window.

Even that was a concession on Amanda's part. She had suffered the Scrooge Syndrome for years. The season was entirely too commercialized to suit Amanda's tastes. She still believed in those simple, basic traditions that made the season what it was originally meant to be. True, the small town of Vamoose came closer to projecting the quaint, down-home atmosphere of Christmas than life in the fast lane of Oklahoma City, where Amanda had worked in recent years. But she was still searching for that warm, comforting feeling that Christmas was supposed to be all about.

And how was Amanda ever going to get into the Yuletide

spirit when confronted with the disturbing news she'd heard earlier this morning?

Amanda had become highly suspicious after stopping by Last Chance Café for her customary morning cup of coffee—the one she doctored with enough cream and sugar to make it taste like hot chocolate without the marshmallows—and discovering that one of her clients had been plagued by a series of accidents.

Pulling her coat tightly around her to ward off the biting wind, Amanda locked her office door and headed for her Toyota. Immediately upon hearing about Oliver Klusmeyer's calamities, Amanda made arrangements to consult with the most dependable gossiper in town. Velma Hertzog, the community's one and only beautician, had her pudgy finger on the pulse of Vamoose.

Under the pretense of getting a holiday haircut, Amanda was confident she could determine if Oliver Klusmeyer was the target of attack or simply a victim of a string of bad luck. As far as Amanda knew, crime didn't take a holiday, and her suspicions refused to allow her to ignore Oliver's mishaps. Being the conscientious accountant she was, Amanda not only kept her clients' tax records straight, but she was also fiercely protective of her clients themselves. Amanda was the assertive kind of individual who believed in heading off trouble before it struck—if humanly possible.

The minute Amanda sailed into Velma's Beauty Boutique, a fog of hair spray swirled around her. The Amazon beautician stood in all her splendor, decked out in her tent-style blouse and stirrup pants that clung to her tree-stump legs like sap. Every strand of Velma's dyed red hair was glued in place. The fake eyelashes Velma swore she didn't wear set like black fans above her chunky cheeks. Meaty hands, adorned with crimson-colored acrylic nails, were clamped around a bottle of aerosol spray and a comb. The queen of gossip was chomping on her chewing gum and chattering like a magpie.

"Hi, hon." Chomp, crack. "I'll be with you in two shakes." Snap, pop. "Just have a seat."

Amanda parked herself beside Millicent Patch—another pruner and nurturer of the Vamoose grapevine. Sixty-year-old Millicent was thumbing through a magazine while her steel-wool hair was stuck under a humming dryer. Since Amanda was on her lunch break, she didn't have time to dawdle. She needed to scare up a few facts, trim her shoulder-length blond hair, and hightail it back to her accounting office.

"I heard Oliver Klusmeyer is limping around on a cast," Amanda baited. That's all it took to activate Velma's tongue.

"Can you believe that man!" Snap, crackle, pop. "I never knew Ollie to be so accident-prone." Velma teased Lorraine Gilbert's salt-and-pepper hair until it stood straight up on her head.

Amanda stifled a smile while she stared at Lorraine's teased hair. The woman had always reminded Amanda of a female version of Abraham Lincoln. Lorraine looked eight feet tall with her hair standing at attention.

After coating every strand of Lorraine's hair with spray, Velma teased it again for good measure. "Three weeks ago Ollie was trying to burn the weeds out of the bar ditch in front of his farmhouse and almost caught himself on fire when the hose to his propane torch sprang a leak."

Millicent Patch, who had ears like a fox, leaned out from under the dryer to tug her green polyester skirt over her bony knees. "Two weeks ago Ollie was mowing around the corrals on his open-air tractor and the seat broke. He was nearly chewed to pieces by the Brush Hog he was pulling behind him. If not for his hired man, Oliver would've been fish bait. He was dragged to safety in the nick of time."

Amanda knew farming and ranching were high-risk occupations, but this was ridiculous! If Amanda could rescue Oliver Klusmeyer from another dangerous mishap and determine who might be out to get him, she would have done her good deed for the holiday season.

"Sometimes people are most susceptible to accidents when they've been under stress. Has Oliver been upset about anything lately?" Amanda inquired. Or more to the point, was anybody *upset* with *Oliver?*

"Yes, come to think of it, he has." Smack, chomp. Velma spun The Chair sideways to attack a recalcitrant strand of hair that refused to succumb to her demands. "Ollie is unbelievably competitive when it comes to his Duroc hogs. He and Adley Willis raise the top show hogs in the area. Oliver and Adley usually finish first and second in the county and state fairs."

"Oliver and Adley have developed a fierce rivalry over the years," Millicent contributed. "They're always sneaking around to see what the other one is doing to upgrade livestock facilities and check on what type of rations are being used to improve weight gain."

"I heard Adley and Oliver got into a shouting match last month at the Tulsa fair." This from Lorraine who could hold her own in the gossip department. Lorraine shifted in The Chair and crossed her long, skinny legs at the ankles. "My son was there and he said Adley accused Oliver of padding the judges' pockets to win blue ribbons and the grand champion trophy in the barrow and gilt divisions. Push came to shove and the bystanders had to pull the two men apart in the parking lot before they came to blows."

"All because of a couple of blue ribbons and a trophy at a stock show?" Amanda questioned skeptically. It sounded as if those two grown men were squabbling like children over toys. Jealousy and spitefulness must've had a fierce and mighty hold on both Adley and Oliver, she concluded.

"We're talking big business here." Pop, crackle. Velma smoothed her baseball-glove-sized hands over the haystack of hair that capped Lorraine's head. "Ag teachers and their students come from all parts of the country to buy those high-powered hogs. When you bring home grand champion trophies from the fairs, you receive top dollar for your livestock. Adley and Oliver both want to be the biggest name in the hog industry. You know, hon, it's just one of those male-ego things."

Amanda was beginning to wonder if revenge and greed may have been the motive that provoked Adley Willis to sabotage his competitor. If Oliver *accidentally* met with disaster, it would certainly eliminate threatening competition, now wouldn't it?

"It's a wonder Ollie didn't break his neck instead of his leg last week." Crack, snap. "He had no business propping a ladder in the truck bed and climbing up a tree in that high wind."

"Why was he doing that?" Amanda inhaled a deep breath when Velma set off another polluting fog of hair spray that was guaranteed to cut gashes in the ozone layer.

"It was my fault actually." Velma stepped back to examine her latest creation—a stiff beehive that the fiercest gale Mother Nature could blow at Oklahoma wouldn't touch. "Every year Ollie sends his older sister in Washington a box of mistletoe and she mails him a package of holly. I asked Ollie to bring me several clumps of mistletoe for the decorations at our annual Christmas pageant. I'm the chairperson this year." Snap, crack. "Ollie's farm is loaded with trees that are thick with mistletoe."

"Do you think Ollie will give into his wife and finally move to town after this rash of farming accidents?" Lorraine asked as she levered herself and her beehive hairdo out of The Chair.

"Oliver move?" Velma snorted. "Not a chance. His ancestors staked a claim on that homestead during the Land Run of 1889. He's sunk all his cash into machinery and improvements. Doris Klusmeyer couldn't drag Ollie off that place with a tow truck."

When Velma crooked a fake fingernail at Amanda, she approached The Chair with her customary reluctance. One of Velma's flamboyant, outdated cuts was the price Amanda always had to pay when she wanted information about her clients' relationships with other citizens of the rural community. Turning the scissor-happy Velma loose was dangerous business. Amanda could find herself scalped when Velma started whacking at the same accelerated speed she talked. But then, a woman had to do what a woman had to do to gather facts and protect her clients from impending disaster, Amanda reminded herself.

"I don't know how Doris puts up with Oliver," Millicent piped up. "Have you seen that house Doris has to live in?"

"The shabby one that sits beside the monstrous barn that's bumper to bumper with all Ollie's high-priced tractors and machinery? Who hasn't?" Chomp, crackle. "And Doris Klusmeyer resents the fact that all their profit from cattle, hogs, and alfalfa revert back to farm improvements and machinery, I can tell you for sure!"

Another set of alarm sirens clamored through Amanda's head. It sounded as if the only way Doris would ever get off the farm was if Oliver was buried out there with his pioneer ancestors. Since Amanda handled Oliver's accounts, she knew—to the penny—how much money was invested in that homestead. Amanda had also discovered that Oliver's greatest loves were his hogs and cattle. Wasn't it just like a man to take his wife for granted? Oliver ought to be shot . . .

Good Lord, what was she saying!

"And what about that farrowing barn Oliver and his hired man constructed for those prize pigs!" Millicent sniffed in disgust as she uncoiled a roller to test the dryness of her hair. "Why, those critters live higher on the hog than poor Doris does."

Poor Doris may have taken drastic measures to remedy the situation, Amanda decided. From the sound of things, Oliver Klusmeyer might find himself nailed inside a pine box and stuffed under the Christmas tree if he didn't watch out!

"Did you know Ollie spent five thousand dollars on that state-of-the-art heating system to keep his sows and baby pigs warm in his farrowing barn?" Velma spun Amanda toward the mirror and took scissors in hand. "Poor Doris has nothing but a wood stove to keep her warm in winter."

Amanda flinched when the whack of the scissors sent shafts of blond hair drifting through the aerosol vapors. Although Amanda put more stock in her abilities as an efficient accountant than in her physical attributes, she preferred to look presentable. If she didn't put a clamp on Velma, Amanda would walk out of Beauty Boutique looking like the accountant from hell!

"Just a trim, please, Velma." Amanda grabbed the Amazon beautician's wrist as the blades swooped toward her scalp.

"Sure, hon." Snap, crackle, pop. Her eyes twinkled with anticipation. "I saw a hairstyle in one of my magazines that would suit you to a T. With your oval face and fine figure, it would look terrific on you. I've been dying to try it out."

Amanda inwardly groaned. She was about to become Velma's guinea pig, all because Amanda wanted information about Oliver's suspicious misadventures. "Whatever you think, Velma. You're the expert."

"And your new do will attract plenty of attention," Velma guaranteed with a grin that put creases in her full jowls. "Nick Thorn will sit up and take note when he sees you."

Amanda very nearly came out of The Chair when Velma popped her gum. It sounded as if a pistol had exploded beside Amanda's ear.

"It's a puzzle to me why you and Nick haven't gotten together." Chomp, snip, whack. "The two of you would make a striking couple. He's tall, dark, and handsome and you're a pretty, blue-eyed blonde."

Millicent leaned out from under the dryer to add her two cents' worth. "You'd be perfect together."

Amanda smiled to herself. Her relationship with Vamoose's chief of police was the best-kept secret in town. Even Velma didn't have a clue that Amanda and Thorn had become exceptionally well-acquainted while she conducted her first amateur investigation of an "accident" that turned out to be a cleverly arranged murder. Using what Amanda had learned from watching reruns of "Magnum PI," she had cracked a difficult case that Nick Thorn had been reluctant to classify as murder. But in the end, Nick Thorn had come around to Amanda's way of thinking, and the two of them had . . .

"You really should give Nick a call." Crackle, snip. "Invite him over for dinner sometime, hon."

The matchmaking beautician was relentless, but Amanda had become an expert at keeping her, ah, relationship with Thorn off Velma's wagging tongue. Being a veteran of the divorce wars seven years past, Amanda had become cynical when it came to men. Her ex had had an extramarital affair, and Amanda had been the last to know. She'd made a pact with herself to proceed with extreme caution henceforth and forevermore. Nick Thorn—gorgeous hunk though he was—was no exception. Amanda was determined not to become the victim of another broken heart or the subject of juicy gossip. What she and Thorn did with their private time was nobody's business but their own.

"That reminds me . . ." Snap, crackle, snip. "Nick Thorn agreed to play Santa Claus for our Christmas pageant. You'd make a great Mrs. Claus, hon."

It was on the tip of Amanda's tongue to decline—until her eyes locked with Velma's in the mirror. The Amazon beautician loomed behind Amanda. One stubby hand was wrapped around a clump of hair and the scissors hovered two inches above the scalp. If Amanda didn't provide the answer Velma wanted to hear, the repercussions could be disastrous. Amanda would have to wear a hat for months. Years maybe.

"Well, what do you say, hon? It would give you and Saint *Nick* the chance to know each other better. You'd also be doing me a great favor." Chomp, pop.

Amanda gulped when the scissors inched closer to the patch of hair on the crown of her head. "I'd be happy to," she chirped like a partridge in a pear tree.

Velma loosened her grasp on Amanda's hair and smiled triumphantly, causing her double chin to wrinkle like an accordion. "Thanks, hon. I knew I could count on you. I have your costume in my storeroom. Rehearsal for the program will be Wednesday night after choir practice. All the churches in Vamoose have banded together for this celebration. It'll be a humdinger holiday pageant."

Amanda clamped her hands around the arms of The Chair when Velma attacked in full force. Blond hair flew in all directions. Edward Scissorhands had nothing on Velma Hertzog. She could clip hair and chew gum faster than anyone alive.

Ten minutes later, Amanda stared at her reflection in the mirror and stifled a scream. Her hair had been swept up and anchored in place with at least fifty bobby pins and two cans of spray. The worst blizzard ever to hit Vamoose couldn't dislocate a strand of hair on Amanda's head. Good God, it looked as if she were wearing an igloo!

"There, hon. All done. How do you like it?" Crack, chomp.

Amanda wouldn't want to be caught dead in this do, much less alive! "It's—"

"It's really you, isn't it?" Velma interrupted, beaming proudly. "Now let me get your Christmas costume before you leave. You can drop Nick's outfit by his house for me, too."

Laden down with a box of red suits, padding, and wigs, Amanda stepped out to face the howling December wind. Just as predicted, her new do didn't budge a millimeter.

Amanda crammed the heaping box in the back seat and plopped behind the steering wheel. Lord, the sacrifices she made to scare up information about her clients! Well, if Oliver Klusmeyer's life *was* in danger, this new do was a small price to pay, Amanda consoled herself. And Velma Hertzog was happy. She had filled the position of Mrs. Claus for the pageant which was held on the lawn of City Hall, and she had thrown Amanda and Thorn together to satisfy her matchmaking tendencies.

Amanda had only driven two blocks before she noticed the approaching police car in her rearview mirror. When the squad car lit up like a Christmas tree, Amanda pulled off on a side street, waiting for Officer Nick Thorn to swagger toward her. She rolled down the window to greet Tom Selleck's clone—minus the moustache. Although Thorn annoyed the hell out of her when he went into his Andy of

Mayberry routine, the man oozed sex appeal from his pores. He could also inspire erotic fantasies when he cut loose with one of his devastating grins that made his eyes sparkle like black diamonds.

She gave herself a mental slap for letting her thoughts detour down sultry avenues and said, "Geez, Thorn, surely you aren't giving me a ticket for failure to come to a complete stop. Getting a little picky, aren't we?"

A wry smile dangled on the corner of Nick's mouth—a very full, sensual, and expressive mouth, Amanda noticed as she wiped the drool off her chin.

"No, Hazard, I'm citing you for failure to *yield*. Do you know how long it's been since you and I have had any time alone?"

Amanda knew exactly how many weeks she'd been deprived of Thorn's amorous attention, thank you very much. But it was hardly her fault that this part-time country cop and farmer-stockman had been busy with his obligations and she'd been up to her eyeballs in paperwork and new clients.

Thorn had been meeting himself coming and going— planting wheat, doctoring calves, and patrolling the streets. After cracking her first murder case, Amanda had gained so much notoriety that a steady stream of Vamoosians had poured through her door with sacks and boxes of bills, receipts, and canceled checks. Everybody in Vamoose and the nearby community of Pronto wanted Amanda as their accountant—all except Thorn. He refused to let Amanda get her hands on his tax returns. However, that was the only restriction he'd placed on where she could put her hands since this, er, relationship blossomed.

Amanda reached over to turn down the blower on the heater. Recalling the few times she and Thorn had snuggled up like two polar bears in hibernation was enough to put her internal thermostat on too-hot-for-comfort.

Nick braced his arms on the side of the compact car and leaned down to confront Hazard face-to-face. His expression registered shock and then wary consternation when he noticed her igloo-do. "Okay, Hazard, what's up? The only time you pay visits to the Beauty Boutique is when you're on one of your self-appointed investigations. To my knowledge, nobody around Vamoose has bit the dust in weeks."

Her teeth clenched. As compatible as she and Thorn were in the boudoir, he refused to give her credit for her reliable detective instincts. That rankled.

"Nobody's dead—yet. I plan to keep it that way, Thorn."

"Now, Hazard, we've been through this before. I'm the head honcho of Vamoose PD and you're an accountant. Cops don't appreciate armchair detectives poking their noses in places they don't belong."

"When one of my clients falls victim to a series of calamities, am I supposed to sit back and wait for fatal disaster to strike?" There. Let him argue with the one-ounce-of-prevention-is-worth-a-pound-of-cure theory!

"Come on, Hazard. It's Christmas," Nick grumbled. "All I want is a little relief from this drought of affection and for you to get into the spirit of *giving*, not *investigating*. Cut me a little slack here, will you?"

Amanda's chin and her igloo-do tilted to that characteristically determined angle Thorn had learned to recognize at a glance. "You know perfectly well that Christmas isn't my favorite season."

"Yeah, right. Too much materialistic commercialism and all that."

"Exactly. I prefer to concern myself with Oliver Klusmeyer's recent accidents and determine their true cause."

Nick groaned in frustration. Knowing how Bloodhound Hazard delighted in sniffing out clues, Nick predicted he was about to be dragged on a goose chase—Hazard-style. True, this blond bombshell had unraveled a difficult case a few months back, but that didn't mean every accident was potential murder!

"And what ill-founded conclusion have you jumped to this time, Hazard?"

71

"I don't leap to conclusions, Thorn. I'm analytical and methodical," she said defensively.

"Fine. Who do you think is trying to bump Oliver off and why?" he patronized as only a man could.

Amanda wanted to slap him. Nobly she restrained herself. "That's what you're going to help me figure out. While we're gathering mistletoe on Klusmeyer Farm for the Christmas pageant, we can examine the scenes of these supposed accidents. And by the way, Saint *Nick,* I was shanghaied into playing your Mrs. Claus."

A deep chuckle reverberated through his broad chest. "What did Velma do? Hold a pair of scissors over your head to get you to agree?"

"Yes, damn it. It was either a scalping or this igloo hairdo," Amanda muttered. "As usual, Velma was determined to pair us up."

"I don't see why our affair has to be classified as top secret—"

Amanda flinched at the A word. "We have a . . . relationship," she corrected and then scowled when Thorn rolled his thick-lashed eyes at her. "We have reputations to uphold, after all. I don't want to be the latest gossip posted on the bulletin board at Last Chance Café or the hottest news buzzing around Beauty Boutique."

Nick tossed up his hands in resignation. Sure, he knew Ms. Propriety and Extreme Caution was adamant about keeping her high-profile image untarnished and that she had been soured by her divorce. Trusting men didn't come easy for her, but Nick was *not* her ex and he didn't appreciate being judged by good ol' Jason's low standards, either.

Fact was, Nick liked this sexy accountant who considered her Nevada showgirl figure the curse of her life. She had gumption, class, and style, and she could send his testosterone count right through the roof when she let her hair down.

"Okay, Hazard, we'll keep the affair under wraps if that makes you happy, but the point is that my glands are about to explode. It's been a helluva long time since you and I—"

"I realize that, Thorn. Enough said. If you can get Deputy Sykes to cover for you tomorrow afternoon, we can gather the mistletoe for the pageant, examine the scenes of Oliver's accidents, and spend some time alone together at my place."

Nick felt ten times better already. He could tolerate Hazard's fetish for investigation if it meant they could steam up a few bedroom windows when the sun went down.

"I'll pick you up at three o'clock tomorrow afternoon and we'll gather mistletoe."

"Thanks, Thorn. I have the inescapable feeling that one of my clients is on a collision course with catastrophe."

Amanda stepped out of her Toyota and poked her head into the back seat to retrieve the Santa Claus costume. Meanwhile, Nick enjoyed the view of a well-rounded derriere and hose-clad legs. Although Hazard preferred to be admired for her brains rather than her curvy bod, Nick had no complaints whatsoever about the shape of things. Hazard had a fabulous fanny that drew masculine eyes and wolfish whistles whether she was wearing a business suit or trim-fitting jeans. The rest of her was nothing to scoff at either . . .

His thoughts evaporated when Hazard dumped the fuzzy red costume and wig in eager arms that preferred to be holding *her*. Nick was still hugging his Santa Claus suit when Hazard sped off. He watched her whiz into the parking lot of Last Chance Café before returning to her office.

The café and Velma's beauty shop were the hubs of gossip in this one-horse town that sat two hops and a skip from the thriving Oklahoma City metropolis. Nick knew Hazard made it a policy to frequent both establishments when wheedling information to support her theories. Odds were, the born crusader/amateur detective had stopped at the restaurant on the off chance that another piece of evidence concerning Oliver Klusmeyer's recent mishaps might unveil itself.

If there was one thing to be said about Amanda Hazard CPA, it was that she was relentlessly persistent when her suspicions were aroused. She had the unswerving determination and directness of a guided missile.

Nick shook his dark head and climbed into the squad car. This was probably another of Hazard's crazed escapades, but it would give him the chance to enjoy her company, et cetera, et cetera. . . . Their affair, he was sorry to report, was progressing at a snail's pace. Things, however, were looking up. Tomorrow night he could tie a red ribbon around himself and "ho-ho-ho" his way into Hazard's cautious heart.

Hot damn! It would be a fun time in ol' Vamoose tomorrow night!

The jingling phone broke Amanda's concentration. For a half-hour she'd been immersed in analytic thought. Her pit stop at Last Chance Café had been productive. Not only had she picked up a high-cholesterol-content hamburger and greasy French fries to tide her over until supper, but she had acquired evidence to support her suspicions.

According to coffee-shop talk, Doris Klusmeyer had threatened to divorce Oliver the previous summer. Rumor was that Doris had her fill of hogs, cattle, alfalfa, *and* Oliver. She wanted to replace the broken-down household appliances and furniture—or else.

The waitress at Last Chance Café was Doris's sister. Faye Bernard had confided that Doris had packed up to leave before Oliver took her demands seriously. Oliver had also been persuaded to give his wife the consideration she deserved by Doris's two-hundred-twenty-pound brother Milton who had backed up the demands with a pair of meaty fists. Milton was a rodeo steer wrestler who could rope and throw a calf in ten seconds flat. He set a new record on his bullheaded brother-in-law.

The incident served to prove you couldn't swing a dead cat in Vamoose without hitting or offending somebody's kinfolk. The community was a conglomeration of fiercely devoted friends and relatives. There were tribes of double cousins, aunts, uncles, siblings, in-laws, and kissing

74

cousins—some of whom should've been a lot more careful about whose cousin they were seen kissing!

Thanks to Milton's strong-arm tactics and ultimatums, Doris had acquired a long-awaited dishwasher and a new La-Z-Boy recliner. The marriage had survived another six months.

Amanda wasn't sure Oliver would last that long . . .

The phone blared again and Amanda reflexively plucked up the receiver. "Hazard Accounting Agency."

"Mandy? It's Billie Jane Baxter."

Amanda despised being called Mandy. It was the nickname her ex had given her. "Hello, Billie, what can I do for you?"

"I need a favor, Mandy," Billie crooned.

In Amanda's opinion, what Billie Jane needed was a new voice. It still amazed Amanda that Billie Jane had made it big in country music. The former Vamoosian had moved to Nashville to cut records. Surprisingly the human gong had made a fortune. There was no accounting for some people's tastes. Billie Jane sang like a howling tomcat.

"As you know, I've agreed to sing for the Christmas pageant while I'm home for the holidays."

That was news to Amanda. She could hardly wait to hear the human gong's rendition of "Silent Night." All the baying hounds in Vamoose would be harmonizing with her, no doubt.

"You know what a terrible time I'm having with the house under construction on the land I bought from Cousin Preston," Billie Jane yakked. "With my hectic concert schedule, I just can't keep up with details and finances. I don't have a head for business."

That was the understatement of the decade! Billie Jane had jingle-jangled into the accounting office in skintight denim. Her silicone-injected figure had been draped with gaudy silver and turquoise jewelry and she had been toting a boot box of canceled checks and wadded receipts. It had taken Amanda days to sort through the mess and put Billie's fluctuating account at Vamoose Bank in proper order. The human gong was a walking financial disaster.

"I'm flying in from Nashville next weekend and I wondered if you could balance my bank account so I can pay the contractors for their work. I swear, I'll never build another house. It's a nightmare!"

"I'll do what I can for your checkbook," Amanda agreed without enthusiasm.

"Thanks, Mandy. You're a peach."

Amanda dropped the receiver in its cradle and glared at the phone. Hazard was nobody's peach. She shouldn't have taken Billie Jane on as a client. The woman was an airhead who gave the fairer sex a bad name.

Glancing at her watch, Amanda strode off. She had just enough time to reach the bank before it closed. If she stayed up half the night, she could unscramble Billie Jane's account. Tomorrow she would devote full time to Oliver Klusmeyer's "accidents," she promised herself. And tomorrow night she'd give the sexy country cop all the consideration and attention he deserved, without the gossipmongers of Vamoose getting wind of it. Amanda had every intention of being discreet— but thorough—when it came to Thorn . . .

Amanda didn't bother buttoning her coat on her way out to face the Polar Express that had swooped across the Great Plains from Canada. Thoughts of Thorn's exceptional prowess generated enough heat to melt an iceberg.

Dressed in Justin Roper boots, Wrangler jeans, and a Mo'Betta shirt, Amanda met Thorn at the front door of her rented farm home that sat three miles from Vamoose. Her gaze traveled over his tall, muscular frame in feminine appreciation. Damn, this country cop was too easy on the eye and exceptionally hard on her hormones. He was dressed in a brown Western shirt and matching Levi jeans that fit his six-foot-two-inch frame like a glove. With his wavy raven hair, olive complexion that denoted Indian ancestry, and that ex-marine physique, Thorn reminded Amanda of a life-size Hershey Kiss. She felt a fierce and sudden craving for chocolate. Amanda popped a breath mint in her mouth to curb her appetite.

Those black eyes, rimmed with long black lashes that Velma the beautician would kill for, completed the picture of a striking, heartthrob of a man. Around Vamoose, getting arrested was more of a turn-on than an inconvenience. Who wouldn't want to be frisked by *that?*

"Ready to go find some mistletoe to stand under, Hazard?" Nick drawled and waggled his eyebrows suggestively.

Amanda jerked her thoughts out of the gutter and whizzed out the door. "We're conducting an investigation, Thorn," she reminded him *and herself.*

"Ah yes, how can I forget that somebody is trying to do Oliver in?" He ambled toward his truck, watching the hypnotic sway of Hazard's hips and thinking things that had more to do with investigating all those feminine curves than digging up information about Oliver's accidents. "Any suspects in this case you dreamed up?"

Amanda ignored the goading question and piled into the black four-wheel-drive truck with its hydraulic-cylinder-operated hayfork protruding from the bed. The sturdy farm vehicle reminded Amanda of a bumblebee with a stinger. The truck was Thorn's pride and joy and an invaluable piece of equipment in his farming operation. The man could lift thousand-pound round hay bales with the touch of a button. What would experts invent next to eliminate backbreaking farm work? she wondered.

When Thorn shifted into drive, Amanda fastened her seat belt. It was an automatic reflex. Mother had harped at Amanda since she was a teenager and still harped to this day. Of course, Mother harped on every subject. Mother was a card-carrying nag who believed her thirty-two-year-old daughter's infantile brain had frozen at age thirteen.

Amanda muttered as the pickup bounced over the washboarded roads. The country byways around Vamoose were notorious for flinging vehicles out of frozen ruts and landing passengers in ditches. Commissioner Brown and his road-grading crews had turned their backs on this section of the county, much to Amanda's outrage. She cursed Brown weekly for his negligence.

"What do you know about Doris Klusmeyer?" Amanda quizzed Thorn as he sped across Whatsit River bridge and bumped over another gravelly road.

So much for small talk, thought Nick. Hazard was in her detective mode again. "Don't tell me Doris is your prime suspect," he smirked.

"Until I'm convinced Oliver has become accident-prone, everyone who has any connection with him is suspect, his wife included."

Nick resigned himself to responding to Hazard's third degree. "Doris was a Bernard before she married Oliver. She has a brother and a sister—"

"I already know that, Thorn. Get to the good stuff."

"Doris has never cheated on Oliver as far as I know," Nick continued. "And Oliver has been faithful to Doris—"

"Except that his precious hogs and cattle are his first two loves," Amanda inserted. "Oliver equips his barns far better than his own home."

"The man does worship his Duroc pigs," Nick conceded. "But I hardly think Doris is the vindictive type who's attempting to murder Oliver because he spends more time catering to livestock than he does to her."

"You might be surprised, Thorn. Being stuck in a run-down house and ignored can do strange things to the mind."

"Get real, Hazard, Doris wouldn't hurt a fly."

"Maybe not a fly, but she may have it in for Oliver— Ouch!" Amanda yelped when the truck dropped into a rut, flinging her head against the side window. "I'm going to shoot Commissioner Brown first chance I get! Doesn't he ever grade these country roads? The terrain in the Rockies is smoother than this!"

"Give the guy a break, Hazard. It's Christmas. Where's your charitable spirit?"

"It's stuck in these fricking ruts that never get graded!" she erupted like Mount Saint Helens.

"You know what your problem is, Hazard? Your bah-humbug attitude is getting you down. If you'd start spreading a little holiday cheer, you'd feel better."

"I'll feel better when you start taking my suspicions seriously, Thorn," Amanda grumbled. "And I certainly wouldn't want to rain on your Christmas parade, but I think Oliver is in trouble. You choose to ignore his accidents because you think it's the season to be jolly!"

"Look, Hazard, take it from a man who's been involved in farming and ranching most of his life, accidents happen all the time. I've had more than my fair share, but that doesn't mean someone's out to get me. Any time you're working with heavy equipment with moving parts or contrary livestock, there are certain risks involved."

"Those risks multiply when somebody wants you out of the way," Amanda contended.

"Sheesh! I may as well argue with a wall," Nick snorted. "Once you've chiseled a suspicious thought in that rock you call your skull, there's no talking you out of it."

"Ah, here we are at the Klusmeyers' run-down, shamelessly neglected home," Amanda noted. "If I were Doris I'd certainly have something to say about the deteriorating conditions, believe you me!"

"So what else is new, Hazard? You have an opinion on everything."

Nick didn't know why he was so irritable. . . . Hell yes, he did. Sitting within three feet of this voluptuous blonde always caused his male juices to percolate. Sexual deprivation spoiled his good disposition. Hazard, on the other hand, had a mind like a steel trap when hounded by suspicion.

For all of Hazard's foibles and hang-ups, Nick reluctantly admitted that she couldn't be faulted for her unfaltering loyalty to her clients. She possessed a tough, strong-willed exterior, but she had a soft, caring heart. If there was a remote chance that

Hazard could rescue Vamoosians from disaster, she was ever ready to pursue her missions for truth and justice.

Since Hazard had resigned her full-time position with Nelson, Blake, and Cosmos Accounting Firm and only traveled to the City once a week to confer with her associates, she had devoted her time and energy to catering to elderly rural clients and fellow Vamoosians. The only one around here who didn't receive the benefit of her care and concern was Nick. Hazard had come to the conclusion that the ex-marine, ex-detective from OKCPD and part-time rancher could take care of himself. Nick didn't know whether to be flattered or insulted. He chose to be insulted since he hadn't been getting the affectionate attention he thought he deserved in this turtle-paced affair that was kept under the covers—literally!

"Amanda? What are you doing here?" Doris Klusmeyer's attractive features registered stunned amazement. "Did Oliver call you? He didn't say anything to me about your making a house call while he's laid up."

Amanda assessed the forty-year-old brunette who had aged gracefully, despite the lack of luxuries Oliver offered. Doris had maintained her girlish figure and her complexion hinted at only a few wrinkles. She was an attractive woman who could still catch men's eyes. Too bad Oliver's tastes ran more toward hogs. The blind fool.

"Actually, Officer Thorn and I are here to do a favor for Velma—"

"Who is it, Doris?" Oliver's tenor voice rang above the drone of the television.

"It's Amanda Hazard and Nick Thorn," Doris called.

"Well, don't leave them standing out in the cold. Invite them in!"

Doris stepped aside and glanced self-consciously at the interior of the house. Amanda inspected the threadbare carpet and faded furniture and silently scolded Oliver for his neglect.

80

It was outrageous to have high-dollar barns sitting beside this dilapidated house. This was where Doris and Oliver lived, for crying out loud!

"Have a seat," Oliver insisted from his throne of the new La-Z-Boy recliner. His elevated leg boasted a cast. A set of crutches was propped against the only new stick of household furniture—which he had designated as his chair, of course. "I've been going stir-crazy since I fell off that dad-blamed ladder trying to gather mistletoe. Now Leo Snittiger has to do all my chores.

"I'm trying to get ready for the hog show at the City and that sneaky Adley Willis keeps snooping around to figure out what grain ratios I'm using in my rations to put weight on my livestock. I caught Adley slinking around last week and I warned him that I'd have him arrested if I caught him near my hog barns again!"

While Oliver was muttering and scowling about his rival, Amanda sank cautiously into a rickety chair. Its broken leg wobbled precariously beneath her and a loose spring stabbed her in the posterior. She scrutinized the dark-haired Oliver who was showing signs of turning gray around the temples. No doubt, a few more near brushes with disaster and he would have a head full of white hair. His nose resembled a broken branch. Some of Milton Bernard's handiwork, Amanda speculated. In comparison to Doris, who had aged with dignity, Oliver appeared older than his forty-three years. His leathery face looked like a few miles of Commissioner Brown's bad roads.

"I was sorry to hear about your injury," she commiserated. "Thorn and I were sent out to collect mistletoe for the pageant."

"I hope you brought a sturdy ladder," Oliver grunted as he resituated his bulky body in his tufted throne and adjusted his green John Deere suspenders. "My ladder broke all to smithereens."

Amanda glanced discreetly at Doris whose carefully blank expression revealed none of her emotions. Doris didn't ap-

81

pear overset by her husband's condition. If anything, Doris probably considered it fitting that Oliver was stranded in this shabby excuse for a home with its drafty windows and peeling wallpaper.

"I heard you had a run of bad luck," Nick put in.

"Damn right. I nearly burned myself to a crisp with the propane torch. It was fortunate I turned off the fuel valve before the truck burst into flames."

"He did singe his eyebrows and hair," Doris inserted without glancing at her husband. "Those torches are much too dangerous."

"Then I nearly got run over by the Brush Hog attachment behind my tractor when the seat broke," Oliver added as he gestured for Doris to fetch his drink which sat all of one foot out of his reach.

That rascal, Amanda fumed. Oliver had Doris fetching and heeling like his devoted puppy. The man had no respect or consideration for his wife! Doris was probably ready to club the big oaf over the head . . .

The thought activated Amanda's suspicious mind. She couldn't wait to snoop around outside. Instinct told her that Oliver hadn't seen the last of his accidents. "We won't take any more of your time. We'd better collect the mistletoe before dark."

"Take all you want," Oliver generously offered. "We've got enough around here to choke a hog."

The minute Doris closed the front door, Amanda rounded on Thorn. "Well? What do you think?"

"I think Oliver has a broken leg," he diagnosed with a mock innocent grin.

Amanda glared him down before marching toward the shed to inspect the propane torch. The instant she spied the sooty hose attached to the propane tank, she was certain foul play had been involved.

"Am I right or am I right, Thorn?" she demanded, indicating the punctured hose.

Nick gnashed his teeth until he wore the enamel thin. He

always hated it when she said that. And it did look as if Hazard might be onto something, though he'd rather shoot himself in the foot than admit it. The hose did look to be in good condition, except for the puncture that allowed flammable leaks. However, there could be any number of reasons for the hole in the hose . . .

"And don't give me that baloney about there being a number of logical reasons for the puncture, Thorn."

Damn, the woman could read his mind! "There are, you know."

"But there's a legitimate margin for doubt."

Nick scowled. "You've been watching too many episodes of Perry Mason."

"I'm trying to make a point," she said, her chin tilting to that characteristically stubborn angle—again.

"Point taken."

Nick rose to full stature and strode toward the small John Deere 2040 tractor with its broken seat. Amanda was one step behind him for a change. Usually the crusading accountant was one step ahead of him. He hated that more than her wisecracks about being correct in her assumptions.

"I'd like to take a look at the broken bolt that held this seat in place," Amanda mused aloud. "Ten to one, somebody tampered with it."

"If you want to get down on your hands and knees and dig around in the manure in the corral to locate it, be my guest. But I've broken a few seat bolts myself in the past, so don't go thinking the incident is an earth-shaking rarity!"

The man was being unnecessarily obstinate, Amanda decided. That innocent-until-proven-guilty-routine of Thorn's was fine and dandy for murders already committed. In Amanda's estimation, the theory was worthless when investigating possible impending disasters.

"Hi, Nick, Ms. Hazard. What are you doing here?"

Leo Snittiger—or Snittie as he was called by friends and relatives—ambled into the shed with a pipe wrench in one hand and a plastic plumbing fitting in the other. At forty-five,

Snittie, the hired man, was in excellent physical condition, having spent most of his life outdoors as a jack of all trades. He was tall, tan, green-eyed, and had an engaging smile.

"We came to gather mistletoe, but we got sidetracked after hearing about Ollie's accidents," Nick explained before Hazard took command of the situation as she had an annoying habit of doing. He couldn't call her overbearing exactly, only intense. That intensity in the boudoir was one of the things he adored most about Hazard. So who was he to complain about her dominant traits?

"Of all the rotten luck for a man to have," Snittie said with a shake of his brown head. "I've never seen the like. Ollie probably didn't even mention running over his foot while trying to short across the cellinoid with a screwdriver when this temperamental tractor wouldn't start."

"No, he left that accident off the list," Amanda put in.

"Ollie didn't realize the tractor was in gear. He was standing between the front and back tires when the tractor lurched forward," Snittie reported, leaning a brawny arm against the tractor hood. "Then there was the Mad Hog Incident week before last. One of the sows rolled over on her piglets and Ollie tried to rescue them before they were crushed. That sow went after him with teeth bared. Six hundred pounds of angry pork can tear you to pieces. My mother's cousin was killed by a sow whose maternal instincts caused it to go hog-wild."

"I see, so it's all right for a sow to accidentally smash her babies, but don't let a human hand touch one of them," Amanda paraphrased.

"That's exactly right, Ms. Hazard." Snittie grinned. "Ollie overlooked that important rule. And speaking of overlooking rules, I forgot to pay attention myself two days ago. Ollie's bad luck must be rubbing off on me. I nearly electrocuted myself while I was welding. I didn't notice the insulation was peeling off the wiring attached to the plug. I got a buzz like you wouldn't believe!"

Amanda frowned warily, wondering if Snittie's accident

84

was meant for Oliver. Snittie could very well become a victim of circumstance!

When Snittie walked off to repair the malfunctioning hog waterer in the farrowing barn, Nick grabbed Hazard's arm and steered her toward his truck. "Let's take a look at the scene of the most recent accident before we leap to a few more wild conjectures, shall we, Hazard?"

"Fine, Thorn. Drag your feet like you usually do when I'm right and you don't want to admit it. What is it with you men? Do you feel your manhood threatened when a woman conjures up an idea that hasn't first been conceived by the male of the species?"

"Lay off, Hazard," Nick grumped. "We both know you're suspicious by nature and by habit. I believe in examining evidence, motive, and gathering facts rather than assumptions before I slap on the cuffs and haul suspects to the slammer."

"And in the meantime, Oliver could wind up a stiff, stuffed in his Christmas stocking." Amanda fastened her seat belt and stared straight ahead. "That's the trouble with our judicial system, Thorn. Victims get no respect or consideration, and criminals get all the breaks. Heaven forbid that we offend murderers, rapists, and thieves!" Her voice amplified every word until she was very nearly shouting her opinion.

"Get a grip, Hazard. I agreed to investigate and I am. I doubt Oliver is in danger now that he's cooped up in the house, nursing a bum leg. His only risk is falling on his way to the bathroom—"

"That dilapidated house could crash down around him," Amanda cut in. "I'm not even married to the man and I could strangle him for letting that place fall to ruin. Client or no, Oliver needs an attitude adjustment. Doris is embarrassed to have guests in her home. Who knows? Our visit could send her right over the edge."

"So you're saying Doris has just cause to murder her inconsiderate husband?" He sounded incredulous. He *was* incredulous!

"I'm saying Doris has cause to complain," Amanda

amended. "She may use drastic methods to convert Oliver to her way of thinking. Or—" She frowned ponderously. "Brother Milton may have decided to drop by to see if Doris was being treated fairly and became annoyed at the state of things. Or Adley Willis could be out to dispose of his competitive rival in the prize stock pig industry."

"Damn it, Hazard. The next thing I know you'll have Santa Claus on your list of possible hit men!"

In stilted silence they followed the sandy path through the pasture to a grove of pecan trees beside Whatsit River. The broken ladder was lying on the ground with a clump of wilted mistletoe beside it.

Amanda bounded out of the truck to examine the wooden ladder. Although splintered wood protruded from one side of the ladder, the other side looked suspiciously smooth.

"It's my opinion that someone partially sawed the rung so it would crack under Oliver's weight," Amanda said with great conviction.

Nick scoffed. "You, of course, are an expert on the subject. Just how did you acquire such a vast and sundry knowledge of tools and machinery while being raised in the City, Hazard? Was your father a carpenter?"

"No, but—"

"You took shop classes in high school, then?"

"Well, no, but—"

"Your ex must have been a whiz at woodwork, right?"

"Confound it, Thorn, stop ridiculing me! You'll be sorry as hell if Oliver winds up dead and I'm saying 'I told you so' every other minute."

Nick let out his breath and cursed his surly disposition. "Okay, Hazard, so maybe someone did tamper with the ladder, causing Oliver to fall."

When Amanda opened her mouth, Nick flung up a hand to forestall her. "I said *maybe* and that's all I'm saying. I'm not going to arrest Doris because you think she's trying to bump off her husband who puts his precious hogs and cattle before her wants and needs. Neither am I going to march

Milton and Adley in for questioning because you think they might have sabotaged Oliver out of family loyalty or vengeful greed."

"But you're willing to agree the accidents might be suspicious?"

"Yes," he said reluctantly. "I will agree to that."

Amanda flung her arms around Thorn's broad shoulders and kissed him right smack-dab under the mistletoe. He reacted instantaneously, savoring every succulent drop of long-awaited physical contact.

Nick had never been able to get enough of this gorgeous, crusading accountant. When she showed the slightest interest in hugging him, he wrapped his arms around her, prepared to kiss those lush lips right off of her. His hormones went wild and his hands blueprinted her well-designed architecture. Holding Hazard was like charging the voltage in his male battery and revving his turbo engine. One touch and she could open the throttle of his choke and send his synchromesh transmission into high gear.

It was several minutes before Amanda found the will to retreat a respectable distance. Damn. It had been a long time, she realized as she sucked air in great gulps. She could feel the biological and chemical combustion generating inner heat which spread through her body like a nuclear meltdown. Thorn always had a potent and profound effect on her. He could cause her brain to short-circuit and set nerves to tingling in nothing flat.

Yikes! She could become a full-fledged wanton around Thorn if she didn't watch herself. Lord, the gossip she'd endure if she fell head over heels for this Magnum PI and Andy of Mayberry all rolled into one tempting package of atomically charged charm and radioactive sex appeal.

Amanda cleared her throat and cursed the fact that she had emulated Mother's annoying mannerism. "Now, about the mistletoe, Thorn."

Although Amanda tried to hide her volatile reaction, it showed. Nick noticed and smiled to himself. Ms. Propriety and Extreme Caution still had the hots for him. The feeling was mutual. Hazard, of course, was intent on concealing her passionate nature from the rest of Vamoose, but she wasn't fooling Nick one bit. They set sparks in each other—always had, always would. This affair could've proceeded at a rapid and satisfying pace if Hazard wasn't so leery of commitments. But just wait until tonight . . .

Nick felt himself grow harder with masculine anticipation. In his state of arousal, he wasn't looking forward to climbing up the ladder and inching across the tree limbs like a caterpillar.

"Being an independent, liberated woman, I imagine you'll want to gather the mistletoe yourself. I'll get you a ladder," Nick volunteered.

Amanda stared at the green vegetation high atop the tree. Being a woman who prided herself on keeping her feet solidly planted on the ground, she had a slight aversion to heights. "Can't we just shoot the mistletoe down, Dead-eye Nick?"

"We could." Nick propped the ladder against the tree. "But we'd most likely blow it to bits. Cutting it loose in clumps is best. Go ahead, Hazard. Have right at it."

"And wound your manly pride and your overactive machismo? Certainly not!"

It wasn't his pride he feared bruising. Nick didn't want to risk injuring any part of his anatomy and spoiling his plans for the night.

"Go on, Thorn. Impress me with your fearlessness," Amanda challenged him. "I just love seeing a big, strong hulk of man like you in action. It sets me all atingle." She tried to look properly helpless and batted her eyelashes for effect.

"Knock it off, Hazard. I'm not falling for that swooning female routine."

Amanda smiled impishly and stared at the part of his anatomy that had yet to recover from their steamy kiss. "If you hurt yourself, Thorn, I promise to give you a massage."

Nick was up the ladder, marveling at his instinctive need

to impress Hazard every chance he got. Although he was a mature thirty-five-year-old, he was behaving like a teenager in heat. Hell, he was in heat—period. Hazard had caused his male hormones to riot the first time he had laid eyes on her; they were still rioting.

Amanda surveyed Thorn's jean-clad backside and powerful shoulders as he made his way into the tree. *Admit it, Hazard. The man's a veritable hunk. Why are you so all-fired determined not to let him know you're absolutely crazy about him?*

Because I don't want to get hurt again, Amanda responded to the needling voice inside her. Jason's betrayal had hit her hard and damaged her self-confidence when it came to men. She was a woman who never repeated her mistakes. She wasn't going to stumble blindly into a, uh, relationship only to be humiliated again. *And thank you, Jason—you big jerk— wherever you are!*

"What was that, Hazard?" came the voice from above.

It wasn't God; it was Thorn.

Amanda winced, unaware she had muttered aloud. "Nothing, Thorn."

She watched Thorn cut several clumps of mistletoe loose with his pocketknife, place the vegetation in a trash bag, and scoot across the limb to retrieve more.

"Be careful—!" Amanda choked on her breath when Thorn lost his balance and struggled to steady the dangling trash bag, and himself, on the swaying branch.

Thorn's teeth gleamed in the afternoon sunlight as he stared down at Amanda's alarmed expression. Mother adored sparkling teeth, and Thorn had the kind of pearly whites that deserved to be displayed in toothpaste commercials.

"So you do care, Hazard. That's nice to know."

"Of course, I care, you big ape. I don't want to scrape you off the ground, haul your mangled body to the emergency room, and miss supper."

"Thanks, Hazard. I like you, too."

Thirty minutes later, Nick climbed down with his bulging

sack of mistletoe. Amanda grabbed the ladder and laid it in the truck bed.

"Velma will be forever in your debt, Thorn. Nothing would do but for her to have scads of mistletoe dangling all around City Hall for the holiday celebration."

"I didn't risk busting my butt for Velma," Nick said as he slid onto the seat. "I went out on a limb for you, Hazard. The pageant will be my only chance to kiss you in public without your flipping out."

Up went the chin. "I never flip out, Thorn. I'm emotionally stable, sturdy as an oak, solid as a rock, and all that."

"Oh, yeah?" One thick black brow elevated in contradiction. "Then why are you behaving as if publicizing our affair ranks right up there with threatening national security? Don't you think a country bumpkin cop is good enough for a high-class city slicker like you?"

"Of all the idiotic things to say, Thorn, that really takes the cake. I'm not a snob!" she said, highly affronted.

"Then what the hell are you?"

"Discreet, practical, and sensible!" she flung back at him. Amanda could have gone on, but if she continued to toot her own horn, Thorn would probably arrest her for disturbing the peace. Not that the peace hadn't been disturbed already, thanks to thick-head Thorn's dumb deductions!

Thorn glowered at Hazard. Not to be upstaged she glowered back.

"I think I've finally hit on the crux of the problem," Nick declared. "You think you're intellectually superior. I graduated from the marine's academy of hard knocks and OKCPD's eye-opening homicide and narcotics squads while you gathered college degrees galore."

"That has nothing to do with anything, you moron!" she spluttered.

"Now I'm a moron." His thick brows formed a single line over his stormy black eyes. "That's just what I thought you thought."

Her chin went airborne. "Take me home, Thorn. You're in

90

one of your irascible moods. Talk about arguing with stone walls!"

Nick floorboarded the accelerator, giving Amanda whiplash. She swore he hit every rut and bump on purpose, just to annoy her; it worked. To further infuriate her, Nick detoured to his farm to feed a round hay bale to his cattle herd. Lowering the hydraulic hay fork, he slammed the pickup into reverse and rammed the bale like a knight of old goring a challenger with a lance. Amanda's neck popped when the collision konked her head against the back window. She glared meat cleavers at Nick. He made a spectacular display of ignoring her.

Still fuming, Amanda clung to the door handle while Nick surged over the ridge of the terrace, leaving the truck bouncing on its suspension springs. The only sounds inside the cab were the whine of the hydraulic cylinder lowering the bale and the bellow of hungry cattle.

Nick mashed on the emergency brake, hopped out, and slammed the door behind him. Amanda silently cursed while Nick cut the nylon strings off the bale and hurled them into the pickup bed. When he slid beneath the steering wheel, he didn't glance in her direction, nor she in his. The cold December wind had nothing on the frigid temperature in the pickup cab.

After a wild ride through the pasture and a launch off the terrace ridge, Nick stopped at the barn to feed his flock of sheep. "Get out, Hazard," he ordered in his gruffest tone. "I catered to your suspicions. Now you can help me with the chores.

Amanda had already had one run-in—literally—with Attila the ram. The cantankerous creature had made Amanda's derriere the target of attack when he trotted around the corner of the barn to find her doubled over the feed trough. Amanda suspected Thorn planned to let Attila do the dirty work. Thorn didn't believe in physically abusing females who aggravated him; he was going to let the ram rough her up a bit.

Reluctantly Amanda climbed out of the truck and followed

in Thorn's wake, determined to protect her blind side and pump Thorn full of pertinent questions, despite his reluctance to take her suspicions seriously.

"Speaking of Oliver's accidents—" she began, only to be cut off by Thorn's disgruntled snort.

"Damn it, Hazard."

There were times when Amanda swore Thorn thought Damn It were her first and middle names.

"What do you know about Adley Willis?" she persisted.

Nick dropped a sack of sheep rations into Hazard's arms and gestured his head toward the feeder. "Adley has his fingers in every facet of the hog industry. He supplies feed lots in Iowa with pigs to be fattened for slaughter, and he raises show pigs to sell at top dollar to FFA members and their instructors all over the country. He judges hog shows in the Western districts and at the national farm show in Kansas City."

"And Adley has no love for Oliver Klusmeyer," Amanda added as she dumped the feed into the long trough at the back of the barn.

"No, he doesn't," Nick concurred before he grabbed a square alfalfa bale. "Adley and Oliver have been rivals since high school. They competed in stock shows for state and national honors and they both dated Doris—"

Nick slammed his mouth shut and glanced over his shoulder at Hazard. He could see the cogs in her brain cranking, assimilating facts.

"The eternal triangle," she said consideringly. "Adley covets Oliver's wife and his registered Duroc hogs."

Nick let loose with a whistle that nearly blew out Amanda's eardrums. Judging by the disgruntled expression on Thorn's bronzed features, she suspected he was leaving it to Attila to knock that suspicious notion out of her head—via her posterior. Attila bounded around the corner to wolf down his feed and to attempt to bowl Amanda over.

Amanda artfully dodged the ram and plastered herself against the side of the barn as the flock of sheep, looking like mobile cotton balls, stampeded inside. Attila's black eyes zeroed in on Amanda. The ram reminded her of Thorn in his cantankerous moods. They could both be butt-heads when they felt like it.

"Nice boy," Amanda cooed while she and Attila stared at each other like duelists at twenty paces.

She wished she'd kept her mouth shut. Attila lowered his hard head and charged. Amanda scrambled up the side of the metal feeder and hung on the steel rafter like a slab of meat.

"Get that crazed maniac away from me!"

Smiling in ornery satisfaction, Nick left Hazard hanging on tenterhooks. "Geez, Hazard, what a big chicken you're turning out to be. Attila won't hurt you."

"Oh, yeah?" Amanda peered down at the giant ball of smelly wool-on-the-hoof. "You better tell Attila that. I don't think he knows it—Yikes!"

Amanda coiled her body upward like an acrobat when Attila bounded forward. His head slammed into the wall, leaving a dent in the tin. Only when Thorn waved a block of alfalfa hay under Attila's nose did the ram trot toward the far corner. Amanda dropped to her feet when the Great Pyrenees—Napoleon, protector of the flock—moseyed inside.

While using Napoleon as a shield of defense against the ram, Amanda turned her thoughts back to her interrogation. "Why do you think Milton Bernard is so protective of his sister Doris? According to reliable gossip, he's threatened Oliver a time or two."

Nick filled Napoleon's bowl with dog food and heaved a sigh of resignation. This amateur sleuth wasn't giving up—come hell, high water, or ram attack. "The Bernards had a rough childhood," he explained as he grabbed another alfalfa hay bale. "When the kids were just toddlers, their father abandoned them and ran off with a woman from Pronto. Anna Bernard died in a car crash when the kids were in high school. Milton was the oldest child and he assumed the responsibility of raising Doris and Faye. Milton never did care much for the older generation of Klusmeyers or Oliver's fanatic approach to building a name for himself in the national hog-raisers' circles. Milton wants Doris to have all the finer things in life that his struggling family couldn't provide."

"So the reigning pooh bah of the Bernard clan takes offense when his kid sisters don't get a fair shake. Milton, of course, is big enough and tough enough to throw his weight around," Amanda speculated.

"And Sissy Klusmeyer turned down Milton's proposal and married the banker's son," Nick confided before he realized he had handed Hazard another weapon to add to her arsenal of suspicions. "Oh hell, Hazard. You know how small towns are. There are generations of families linked together by birth and marriage, with feuds and resentments festering on the perimeters. Just because Milton fell for Sissy and was jilted, and Oliver doesn't give Doris the proper respect, doesn't mean Milton wants to dispose of his brother-in-law."

Amanda quickened her step when Thorn strode out of the barn. "No? Men always exhibit their Neanderthal characteristics of surliness, resentment, and spitefulness when their sex lives are in turmoil. Milton never married because he's still carrying a torch for Sissy. He holds a grudge against the Klusmeyers, who probably didn't think the down-on-his-luck cowboy was good enough for their daughter. And I doubt the Klusmeyers think Doris is good enough for their darling son Oliver, either. They probably believe Oliver is giving Doris as much as she deserves. Am I right?"

Nick muttered under his breath and climbed into the pickup. "Not being good enough seems to be a problem all the way around, doesn't it, Hazard? Sissy married for money and social position and she's miserable. Milton travels the rodeo circuit in the spring and fall, hoping distance will cool his banked fires. Adley Willis is frustrated because he couldn't land the catch he wanted—the one his worst rival ended up marrying, much to the Klusmeyers' disappointment. Adley's first marriage ended in divorce because he settled for second best and was never satisfied."

Nick glared at Hazard as he rammed the standard shift into

second gear. "And I'm frustrated because I only qualify as your occasional bed partner. I'm just a cop in a podunk town and you're holding out because you think you can do better. You don't want to be tied down in case your Mr. Right comes along."

"Curse it, Thorn! For a man who's been lecturing me about tidings of comfort and joy and good will to all, you've suddenly turned into a holiday grouch!"

"It must be the company I'm keeping that's curdling the milk of my human kindness. That, and the fact that our affair—"

"Relationship!" she corrected in a voice that resembled a supersonic boom.

"Affair, Hazard," he insisted just as loudly. "Affairs are clandestine activities kept hush-hush. You can't even say the word, and you're ashamed to let Vamoosians know we have something going. You're driving me nuts and I'm getting no respect or satisfaction. Maybe I should take my Yuletide cheer and spread it around places where it's welcome and appreciated. You and your scrooge attitude can deal with the ghosts of Christmas Past, for all I care. Go deck your halls with boughs of cactus. You certainly don't appear to enjoy being *stuck* with a no-account, farm-grown cop like me!"

"Of all the stupid—" Amanda's seat belt clamped around her like an octopus and her breath came out in a whoosh when Thorn popped the clutch and slammed the stick shift into third gear.

"Oh fine, now I'm a *stupid* moron." Nick scowled and put the pedal to the metal.

"You're speeding, Thorn," Amanda wheezed as they soared over hills and craters that compared to the landscape of the moon. "I ought to have you arrested."

"I may as well be behind bars. You've already got me tied in knots."

Amanda gave Thorn her most scathing glare; he returned it with equal intensity. The silence was so thick that a blade of straw could have drifted to the floorboard and it would have sounded like a meteor crashing to earth.

There seemed to be no way to make Thorn understand how difficult it was to let go of cautious habits and long-harbored hang-ups. True, Thorn had suffered a devastating blow himself. The woman he claimed to love had died at the hands of a vengeful drug dealer whom Thorn had clamped down on while working the narcotics division at OKCPD. But Thorn hadn't been humiliated or had his self-esteem ripped to shreds the way Amanda had.

Amanda had lived in the war zone of divorce and she was still carrying around a lot of emotional baggage. Confessing her deepest feelings didn't come easy. Thorn simply didn't realize Amanda needed to test the waters before leaping in over her head again. Thorn thought she was ashamed to be seen in public with him. He had it all wrong, but he wasn't in a receptive mood, and Amanda had difficulty baring emotions that had been locked in cold storage for so long. Put simply, Thorn didn't know where she was coming from because he hadn't been there.

After a high-speed race down gravelly paths that Commissioner Brown's road graders hadn't touched in months, Amanda found herself in her driveway. She felt as if she had just touched down after orbiting the earth at the speed of light.

"Don't forget to keep the mistletoe cool so it doesn't wilt," Nick instructed, staring everywhere except at Hazard.

"And where am I supposed to put it, Thorn?"

He turned his raven head toward her. A sardonic smile thinned his lips. "Why don't you stuff it—"

Amanda's blue eyes narrowed menacingly, daring him to say it.

"—in your refrigerator," Nick continued cattily. "There's nothing in there anyway. Your gourmet meals include canned meat and crackers. If your microwave broke down, you'd be helpless in the kitchen. And by the way, don't bother carving the Christmas tuna on my account. I'm not staying for supper . . . or dessert."

"Fat chance the invitation would still be open after all your insulting quips!" she sniffed as she climbed out of the truck. "Bad tidings and good riddance, Thorn. I hope Santa Claus poisons your eggnog and crams rocks in your stocking!" she punctuated her holiday curse by slamming the door and stalking off.

The pickup slung gravel as it blazed off. Amanda stormed into the house to be greeted by her two-foot tall, undecorated, metal Christmas tree. *Some holiday season this turned out to be,* she thought as she peeled off her coat and automatically hung it in its proper place on the left side of the hall closet. Amanda stormed toward her alphabetically arranged kitchen cabinets to grab canned tuna and crackers. Her hand stalled in midair, recalling the snide crack Thorn had made about her culinary talents. She opened the refrigerator, discovering he was right. There was plenty of room for the mistletoe on her empty shelves. Damn it, she really hated it when that mulish man was right . . .

The blaring phone sliced through Amanda's black mood. She snatched up the receiver to grumble an unsociable "hello."

"Hi, doll. It's Mother."

Great. Just what Amanda needed after her exasperating tiff with Thorn.

"I just called to make sure you sent out your Christmas cards. You *did* get them out on time, didn't you, doll?"

"Yes, Mother."

Mother cleared her throat the way she always did when she wanted to draw attention to herself or switch topics of conversation. "Did you get all the gifts on the list I sent to you?"

Mother's Christmas tradition was to jot down the items, prices, and stores where each gift could be purchased, as if Amanda didn't have the good taste or ability to make her own choices for the family. And Thorn wondered why

Amanda suffered the Scrooge Syndrome? He hadn't met Mother.

"I've done all my shopping, thank you, Mother."

"Good, doll." She cleared her throat; Amanda gnashed her teeth. "Your brother and that scatterbrained wife of his are behind schedule—as usual. I still haven't figured out what to get those two juvenile delinquents your sister-in-law is raising. Your brother needs to take charge of those yahoos before they wind up in a detention center."

Mother considered herself an expert at parenting. She doled out free advice every chance she got.

While Mother continued her Yuletide yammering, mentioning every gift she had purchased and the price she paid, Amanda applied the Dewey decimal system to the stack of books and magazines on her coffee table.

"So . . . how's that new man friend of yours, doll? When are you going to bring him over to the City so Daddy and I can see if he's good enough—" Mother cleared her throat for the millionth time. "That is to say, when do we get to meet that country cop and part-time farmboy, hmm?"

"Thorn won't be joining us for Christmas dinner," Amanda replied in the most civil tone she could muster. "We had a spat."

"It's just as well, doll. You have to watch yourself, you know. Some men are after your money . . . and other things, if you catch my meaning."

Amanda smiled in spite of her glum mood. If Mother tried to utter the word *sex,* it would probably strangle her.

"Now then, doll, did you make your dental appointment? You know how important it is to keep your teeth in good condition. Your Uncle Dean was neglectful and now he's sporting dentures and biting his tongue."

Ah, that Mother would bite *hers* occasionally!

While Mother rattled about the benefits of regular brushing and dental flossing, Amanda laid down the receiver to fetch a couple of crackers to counteract the gnawing in her stomach before she suffered heartburn because of her unsettling confrontation with Thorn. When she returned, Mother was just winding down.

"Now try to be on time for Christmas dinner, doll. Your daddy misses you. We never see you much these days, what with your accounting agency taking all your time."

Amanda felt herself being boarded on the Guilt-Trip Express. "I'll be there Christmas Eve, Mother."

"Of course you will, doll." Queen Mother sent her royal summons over the line. "Where else would you be?"

In the sack with Santa would've been nice, Amanda thought. Unfortunately Saint Nick had driven off in a fury in his four-wheel-drive sleigh. She didn't expect to see him until the pageant rehearsal. And wasn't that going to be loads of fun, Santa was in a snit. Amanda was all atwitter with anticipation of *that* encounter.

"Well, I've got to go, doll. Now don't forget to buckle up. You know how holiday traffic can be. All the crazies are on the roads."

Not all of them, Amanda silently amended. *Mother* was on the *phone.*

When the line went dead, Amanda tossed the receiver in its cradle and trudged off to dine on tuna and crackers. What next? A visit from the ghosts of Christmas Past and Future, just as Thorn had wished on her?

Amanda took two Tylenol—Aspirin upset her stomach as much as her row with Thorn did—and went to bed.

Sure enough, the Christmas hauntings began around midnight.

Christmas pageant rehearsal was a fiasco. Velma Hertzog, chomping on her gum, shoved the participants into their places and marched them through their scenes to practice their lines. Thorn made a noticeable display of giving Amanda the silent treatment, much to matchmaking Velma's dismay. Amanda got the idea that Thorn preferred she pack

99

up and vamoose from Vamoose, leaving the role of Mrs. Claus to someone else.

Amanda's suspicions were again aroused when she saw Doris Klusmeyer standing in City Hall parking lot, chitchatting—or was she plotting murder?—with brother Milton and Adley Willis.

Milton Bernard reminded Amanda of a bull with his sturdy, compact shoulders and stout build. A tuft of dark hair tumbled down his broad forehead, and his weather-beaten features were set in a stern expression that suggested he wasn't accustomed to smiling.

Adley Willis was no shrimp himself. Towering at six foot, one inch, Adley was decked out in his Western finery to impress Doris. He was a muscularly built man in his mid-forties with blond hair and reasonably good looks.

Amanda wondered if Doris regretted her choice of husbands. From the look of things, Doris could be making a few New Year's resolutions.

When Amanda tried to stroll nonchalantly past the threesome to eavesdrop, they scattered like quail. Amanda had no proof that they had called a fiendish pow-pow, but she wasn't one to turn her back when she sensed trouble. Amanda was also certain she had missed her calling as a private detective, and she promised to keep her eyes and ears open in case something new developed in this perplexing case.

The rest of the week proved to be drudgery deluxe. Amanda moped through the paces at the accounting office with the enthusiasm of a slug. She paid one visit to Oliver Klusmeyer, whose only accident was spilling coffee down the front of his shirt while he sat enthroned in front of the television in his crumbling castle. Amanda was beginning to wonder if Thorn was right—God forbid! Maybe she *had* dashed off a cliff and leaped to ill-founded conclusions. Perhaps her woman's intuition had malfunctioned—just this *one* time.

After several days of lonely existence, Amanda stuffed herself into her Mrs. Claus suit and crammed in the padding until she looked as if she'd gained an instant fifty pounds. With a waddle in her walk and her mouth turned down at the corners, Amanda flounced into her Toyota—or at least she tried to. She could barely squeeze beneath the steering wheel.

She sang a few fast-tempoed carols to put her in the holiday mood as she drove to City Hall, admiring the winking lights that adorned the homes of Vamoose. Nothing helped. The Christmas Grouch had taken a bite out of her good disposition.

When she arrived at the pageant, Velma was in a tizzy. Her fake eyelashes were batting ninety miles a minute and she was chewing her gum to beat the band.

"Hon, you've got to help me out." Chomp, crack. "The angels are squabbling with the shepherds and one of the wise men just konked Joseph over the head with a gold-painted brick."

"Not to worry, Velma," Amanda reassured the frazzled beautician. "You line up the community choir, and I'll handle the hoodlums."

"Thanks, hon. I'm ready to pull out my hair!" Crackle, pop.

When Velma lumbered off, Amanda veered around the props and backdrop of scenery to find the pint-size shepherds batting angel wings with their staffs while the wise men tossed the frankincense and myrrh around like baseballs. Amanda jerked up an angel and shepherd by the napes of their costumes and glowered at them through her wire-rimmed spectacles.

"Santa is going to be none too happy when he sees you pounding on each other. This is supposed to be the season of peace and good will."

"There isn't a Santa Claus and you aren't his wife," a nearby wise man, who had delegated himself spokesman of the mob, scoffed. "And we're only here because our moms made us come. You think we like walking around in these long, funny dresses?"

Amanda rounded on the unwise little man in his crimson robe and turban. "You don't believe in Santa Claus?" she questioned with just the right amount of shock and indignation.

"Certainly not, lady. I'm eleven years old."

Amanda loomed over him in her padded red dress, bending lower to poke her face in his freckled features. "Would you and hell's angels like to live to be twelve, kid?"

The wise man turned pea green and swallowed his Adam's apple.

Just then, the giant star that hung over City Hall flared brightly against the dark of night. The jingle of bells broke the sudden silence. Measured footsteps clanked against the stage.

"Having trouble, Mrs. Claus?" came the booming baritone voice.

She wrapped her arm a little too tightly around the little wise man with the big mouth and pivoted to see Santa's tanned face framed by flowing white hair and long whiskers. Black eyes glittered as they swept over the suddenly angelic-looking host of cherubs, shepherds, and wise men.

"We have a few nonbelievers in our midst, Santa dear."

"Is that so?" Santa clomped around the huddled group with his gloved hands clasped behind his back, pausing at irregular intervals to study the young faces. "It seems you have misinterpreted the spirit of giving, my little friends. Handing out punches isn't what Christmas is all about. Christmas is love, kindness, and sharing. Your younger brothers and sisters are sitting in the audience, waiting to see the nativity recreated. We are here to remind them of the real meaning of Christmas. *For* them, you will become the Christmas magic. And *to* them, Mrs. Claus and I are the anticipation of dreams coming true once a year."

When the choir burst into "It Came Upon a Midnight Clear," Santa spread his chunky arms in an encompassing gesture. "Let's make this the best Christmas program Vamoose has ever seen."

It must have been the way the gigantic star sparkled on Santa's hair and beard and the long shadow cast by his six-foot-two-inch frame. . . . Or maybe it was Christmas magic itself that turned the mob into a host of seraphs moving quietly into position. Whatever it was, Amanda felt a warm tingle of anticipation filtering through her as the choir harmonized in the still of the night beneath the beaming starlight. She looked up into the twinkling black diamond eyes of Santa Claus and felt the jolt all the way down to the soles of her shiny patent-leather boots.

Santa spoke not a word, but there was a hint of a smile on his lips as he laid his forefinger beside his nose and faded into the shadows formed by the props and scenery that had been painted and donated by Cecil and Cleatus Watts, owners of Vamoose's Auto Repair and Body Shop.

Amanda shook herself out of the trance brought on by the glowing star and voices lifted in song. She circled the stage, keeping to the shadows to watch angels in harnesses hover above the manger. The tug on her heartstrings put moisture in her eyes. Although Amanda prided herself on being a tough, savvy modern woman, she decided she was a gummy marshmallow on the inside.

Now this was what Christmas was about, she thought as she mopped away the tears that clung to the edge of her spectacles. Vamoosians had turned out in full force, sitting shoulder to shoulder, smiling and whispering to each other as the shepherds knelt and wise men approached.

Even Billie Jane Baxter had acquired the magical gift of a new voice when she swanned onto the stage, decked out in turquoise and silver jewelry, to sing her solos. Gone was the human gong's nasal twang.

Amanda was really getting into the festive spirit until she glanced sideways to see Doris Klusmeyer making her discreet appearance. Oliver was nowhere to be seen. Yikes! The man could be in serious trouble! With warning sirens resounding in her brain, she wheeled around and dashed off to locate Santa. Intuition told her that this was the perfect night for Oliver to meet with disaster—if he hadn't already!

"Come on, Santa, you may have to work a little of your magic at Klusmeyer Farm."

Santa pushed away from the tree against which he'd been leaning, enjoying the musical performance. He glanced down to see Mrs. Claus's hand wrapped around his elbow.

"Gimme a break. I'm having fun for the first time in days," Santa grumbled.

"Oliver won't be enjoying himself if these niggling suspicions that are hounding me prove correct," Mrs. Claus insisted, giving Santa a fierce and insistent tug. "The stage is set for another accident. Practically the whole population of Vamoose is in attendance and Doris just arrived without Oliver. I have the unshakable feeling Oliver is in perilous danger."

"We have to be on stage in thirty minutes in case you've forgotten," Santa muttered.

"I haven't forgotten, and you are wasting precious time dragging your size-eleven boots. Move it, Claus!"

"If you're wrong and we miss our performance, I'll hold it over your head for the rest of your life."

"Fine, be that way." Mrs. Claus bustled Santa away from the crowd. "Just put your sleigh in overdrive and get us to Oliver's house PDQ!"

Although Santa didn't have a red-nosed reindeer to guide his four-wheel-drive pickup, he made tracks through town. When he spotted Deputy Sykes in the squad car, Santa flashed his headlights, poked his head out the window, and requested a backup.

"Follow me to Klusmeyer Farm," Santa demanded.

"Klusmeyer Farm, right," Benny Sykes repeated.

In a cloud of dust and a hearty "Hi-ho Santa," the pickup and squad car reached speeds matching a flying sleigh. Mrs.

104

Claus held on for dear life as the truck soared over Commissioner Brown's rough roads and veered through the entrance gate on two wheels.

The instant the truck skidded to a halt, Mrs. Claus bounded out and charged toward the house. With a sense of urgency and impending doom hounding her, she burst through the door to hear the television blaring, but to see the La-Z-Boy recliner vacant.

"Oliver! Where the hell are you!"

"Watch your tongue. It's Christmas," Santa snapped behind her.

Mrs. Claus lurched around and headed for the only place she could think Oliver might have gone—provided he was still alive to go anywhere.

"Is she all right?" Deputy Sykes questioned as he watched Mrs. Claus take off like a speeding bullet, leaping the porch steps in a single bound.

"No, she's a fruitcake in a red suit," Santa muttered before he gave chase.

The sound of snorting hogs caught Mrs. Claus's attention as she raced toward the farrowing barn. And what to her disbelieving eyes did appear but none other than Leo Snittiger shoving Oliver Klusmeyer backward on his gimpy leg. A howl burst from Oliver's lips when his hip slammed against the four-foot tall hog panel. He cartwheeled into the pen, landing squarely on the six-hundred-pound sow that took quick offense to having her territory invaded and her ten squealing piglets attacked. The sow's mouth clamped onto Oliver's cast. It was all that saved him from a vicious bite.

While Mrs. Claus was jackknifed over the metal panel, frantically trying to upright Oliver and remove him from harm's way, Santa and Deputy Sykes arrived upon the scene to lend a hand. White-faced, Oliver was dragged to safety while the irate sow charged the panel, grunting and snorting in threat.

"Snittie, what in the hell did you think you were doing?" Mrs. Claus raged at the hired man.

"I said watch your mouth, Mrs. Claus," Santa scolded as he set Oliver on his wobbly legs and handed him the crutches.

"I was doing Doris a favor," Snittie growled, glaring laser beams at Oliver.

"Doris asked you to dispose of Oliver?" Mrs. Claus interrogated.

"Hell, no, she's too good a woman for that. Too good for the likes of him! I'd treat Doris like a queen and give her all the things she deserves." Snittie flashed Oliver—who had half-collapsed against the wall in shocked disbelief—another mutinous glower.

"You're in love with my wife, too? You and Adley both?" Oliver croaked.

"Someone around here ought to love her, and it doesn't appear to be you!" Snittie snapped. "These hogs get preferential treatment while you ignore Doris. You never take her anywhere except to hog auctions and the stockyards."

"You took it upon yourself to get rid of Oliver so Doris could have all the things you think she deserved," Mrs. Claus summarized.

"Either get rid of him or keep him laid up in that dilapidated house until he wisens up," Snittie said with a scowl. "I hadn't decided which yet."

"Oliver, do you want to press criminal charges?" Santa questioned, checking his watch. Time was running short. He and Mrs. Claus were due to make an appearance at the pageant in ten minutes.

"No." Oliver rearranged the shirt the sow had twisted around his neck. "Snittie is right and so is Milton. I've been an inconsiderate fool, and Doris has suffered because of my obsession with breeding the best Duroc hogs in the county."

"Damn right, she's suffered. And you don't have to bother firing me because I quit!" Snittie blared. "Buddy Hampton offered me a job on his horse ranch and I'm taking it. If you don't treat that angel right, I'll come back and feed you to your precious hogs. And unless you want to lose your wife to another man, you better change your ways, Klusmeyer!"

"I intend to. Doris will be rewarded for standing by me all these years." Oliver propped himself on his crutches and stared gratefully at the chunky Mrs. Claus. "You saved my life. How can I ever repay you?"

"By giving your wife the attention and affection she craves and deserves," said Mrs. Claus. "We all like to know we're needed and wanted." Her gaze darted momentarily—and meaningfully—to Santa. "It's never too late to make amends and share a little of that magical Christmas spirit with those who are near and dear to us."

She heaved a satisfied sigh, adjusted her sagging padding, and smiled at Oliver. "And now, if you'll excuse us, Santa and I have to perform at the pageant. I'm sure Deputy Sykes will be happy to escort you back to the house so you can decide where and how to begin remodeling."

"I'd be happy to help, right," Deputy Sykes repeated in his characteristically enthusiastic manner.

Santa and Mrs. Claus jogged to the truck. The dashboard lit up like holiday decorations when Santa switched on the headlights. They surged off in another cloud of dust, arriving at City Hall with only a minute to spare.

Billie Jane Baxter was hitting high notes while three members of the volunteer fire department were setting off fireworks in the open lot across the street. Children's laughter and delighted giggles filled the air when Santa and Mrs. Claus appeared on stage in a blaze of sweeping spotlights. Billie Jane Baxter burst into a chorus of "Santa Claus is Coming to Town," and children flocked to the stage to greet Saint Nick. Several other members of the fire department distributed sacks of fruit and candy, all of which had been donated by the businesses in Vamoose—Hazard Accounting Agency included.

Velma Hertzog grabbed the microphone from Billie Jane to point out the clumps of mistletoe that hung overhead, insisting that tradition should be followed. With a mischievous twinkle in her eyes, the Amazon elf, garbed in garnet green from the top of her dyed-red hair to the curled toes of her felt slippers, suggested that Santa and Mrs. Claus demonstrate the proper Christmas kiss to all of Vamoose.

A wry smile pursed Santa's lips as all eyes turned toward the spotlighted stage. "Are you game, Mrs. Claus? I know how you cringe at public displays."

"Reject Santa Claus two days before Christmas? Gee whiz, how big a fool do you think I am—?"

Santa's kiss packed quite a wallop. It was difficult to tell which way was up when Santa bent her over backward and plastered her against his heavily padded contours. For a minute there, Mrs. Claus feared the stage beneath her had tilted sideways when her self-reserve came tumbling down.

Applause filled the air and cheers rippled through the crowd like tidal waves. Husbands started kissing wives and cousins hugged cousins. There was nothing like a down-home, country-style Christmas celebration to uplift spirits.

Toting her sack of treats, Mrs. Claus wedged her rotund body into her compact car and drove home. The phone was ringing when she waddled through the door.

"Hi, doll. It's Mother."

Not even Mother could spoil the gaiety of the evening. A life had been spared tonight, and Vamoosians were celebrating the success of their pageant. All was right with the world.

"Hello, Mother," she said cheerfully.

"Why don't you come over to Uncle Dean's tonight? We're having a little get-together. Nothing fancy. Casual dress will be fine. Some of your cousins will be there."

The creak of the front door caused Mrs. Claus to swivel her bewigged head around while Mother yammered about which cousins would be in attendance and how high everyone's cholesterol count would be after sampling Aunt Lydia's Christmas candy.

"May I come in?" came the raspy, masculine drawl from the front door.

"Since when does Santa need an invitation? Why didn't

you come down the chimney? It would've been more dramatic, Claus."

"What was that, doll?" This from Mother.

"Nothing, Mother. I can't come to Uncle Dean's. I have company this evening."

"Who?" Mother snoopily demanded.

"Santa Claus is here."

"Who did you say?" Mother persisted.

"You know, Mother, the man in the red suit that hangs out with reindeer."

"Doll, sarcasm doesn't become you . . . or have you been drinking? There isn't a Santa Claus and you know it. I told you that when you were seven years old."

"You lied to me, Mother."

"Lied to you!" Mother yowled. "What a thing to say to the woman who spent half her life sacrificing, caring, raising you, and seeing to it that you had orthodontic braces to ensure straight teeth! I knew I should have insisted that you come live at home after your divorce, instead of letting you move to that rinky-dink little town—"

Mother was still squawking like a plucked Christmas goose when the receiver *accidentally* dropped from Mrs. Claus's fingertips and rattled in its cradle.

Santa pulled off his moustache and beard and tossed them toward the sofa. "I came to apologize."

"For what?" Mrs. Claus questioned as she removed her frizzy white wig and spectacles.

"For behaving like an ass."

"Watch your mouth, mister. It's Christmas," she teasingly scolded him.

"You were right and—" The padding swelled on his muscular chest as he inhaled a fortifying breath and blurted out, "I was wrong. You saved Oliver's life and I'm sorry I didn't believe those accidents were the prelude to disaster."

"And tonight you coaxed several hoodlum angels, shepherds, and wise men into giving an impressive performance. I suppose we both did our good deeds for the day."

Nick stared into those lively blue eyes that could melt him down like burning candle wax. "We've already kissed," he murmured huskily. "Now can we make up?"

"Make up what, Thorn?" she asked elfishly, while doffing her costume.

Nick swallowed his tongue and the words on the tip of it. Hazard was wearing nothing but a smile and skimpy red silk lingerie. Certain parts of his male anatomy rose in salute to her excellent taste in feminine apparel.

Amanda cocked a perfectly shaped eyebrow. "One of us is inappropriately dressed for making merry during the holiday season. I'll be in the bedroom while you decide which one of us it is."

With a drumroll walk that would've done Cleopatra proud, Amanda sashayed down the hall, tormenting Thorn with visual temptation.

Nick plugged his eyes back in their sockets and battled his way out of his padded suit with all the haste befitting a man who had been deprived for weeks on end. Boots, socks, and polyester stuffing formed a path from the living room to the bedroom door.

Amanda gave Thorn the once-over twice while he stood there, filling the doorway to overflowing and staring at her like a starved man drooling over a feast. "My, my, what big . . . eyes you have, Santa," she teased.

"That line was meant for the big bad wolf," Nick growled as he approached the bed.

"So which one are you?"

"Lately I've been the Thorn in your side," he admitted as he sank down beside her. "Hazard, we need to get something straight between us—"

She giggled and surveyed his muscular torso. "I think we already have, Thorn."

Nick broke into a wide grin, displaying gleaming white teeth. "I plan to spend the entire night wishing you a Merry Christmas, Hazard, because, as crazy as you are sometimes, I'm still nuts about you . . ."

When Nick leaned down to take up where he'd left off with that sizzling kiss that began under the mistletoe at the pageant, the witty comment Amanda intended to dazzle him with flew out the window. If there was one thing to be said for Thorn, it was that he was masterfully thorough in spreading Christmas cheer. But then, Amanda had always known there was something special about Nick Thorn. Woman's intuition had told her that months ago.

Woman's intuition proved her right again tonight . . .

A Note to Readers

Happy Holidays. I hope you enjoyed "The Santa Claus Caper" and that you had the chance to read *Dead In the Water,* an October Zebra Mystery. *Dead In the Cellar* will be released in May 1994.

Amanda Hazard will be back with Thorn at her side, faithfully serving her clients in Vamoose and Pronto. Velma, the gum-chewing beautician, Deputy Sykes, and other good citizens of the community will appear from time to time. You will also meet a cast of other lively characters—or dead ones, as the case might be.

Until we meet again in Vamoose,
Connie Feddersen

About the Author

Connie Feddersen has written more than thirty best-selling historical romances under the pen names of Carol Finch and Gina Robins. Her "Dead In" mystery series features the characters you met in "The Santa Claus Caper."

Seasons greetings to one and all, and welcome to the goings-on in small-town America . . .

No Cookies for Santa

by

Louise Hendricksen

A crimson-edged footprint stained the angel's white satin skirt.

"Damn," Dr. Amy Prescott muttered, eyeing the fallen tree-top angel . . . and a man's body stuffed under the tinsel-draped Christmas tree. "I knew I shouldn't have let myself get talked into coming along."

"But Amy." Her father hoisted the load he carried onto the porch. "This is the first time we've had a chance to work together." Slab wood boards creaked as he mounted the steps and eased into the doorway. He regarded her with a hurt expression. "I thought you might want to see how we do as a team."

Amy shoved her fingers through short rain-soaked brown hair. "Sorry, Dad, I'm kind of edgy." She shucked off her raincoat and laid it on a crudely made bench. "The roads were sheet ice from Seattle to Anacortes. And the ferry to Lomitas acted like a roller coaster."

Dr. B.J. Prescott flung his coat on top of hers and drew graying brows together. "Darn it, kitten, you should have told me you were beat."

A child's keening cry erupted in another room and spiraled upward. Amy's gaze met her father's. "Do they have a child?"

B.J. peered around the shack's murky interior. "God, I hope not." He pushed back his leather fisherman's cap and wiped his sodden mustache and Van Dyke beard on the sleeve of his jacket. "Don't know much about them. They're new on

117

the island." He grabbed the evidence vacuum and his forensic satchel and carried them inside.

Amy closed the front door, trapping an admix of mold, gunpowder, and death. She set down her satchel and propped the stand of her father's work light against kitchen shelves curtained with faded blue gingham. As she wiped her glasses dry, she gazed around the room. "Where's the deputy?"

"Can't be far." B.J. plunked his equipment onto linoleum worn to a color that matched the sand dunes visible through a cracked window facing Bridger's Cove.

Both she and B.J. pulled on paper shoe covers, a routine that had been his long before it became hers. The year she turned thirteen, he'd been appointed Lomitas Island's medical examiner. She'd been hearing his dictum ever since: Don't contaminate the crime scene. She drew on a pair of plastic gloves. After she'd started working at the Western Washington Crime Laboratory in Seattle, she'd found the strict rules he'd drilled into her an immense help.

A clatter sounded inside the closed room on their right. A man emerged and pushed the door shut.

Amy felt an almost forgotten twinge at sight of him. Same wide shoulders. Same lean, square-jawed face.

So that's why her father had insisted she come along. He was on another of his matchmaking missions. She clamped her teeth together so hard her scalp ached, sidled through a narrow doorway, and found herself in a windowless lavatory. The room reeked of pine cleaner, but the stench of urine-saturated flooring won out.

Feeling embarrassed and foolish, Amy pulled the door toward her until she could see out, but the two men couldn't see in.

"Hiya Doc." Making a wide circle of the crime scene, Deputy Scott Margeson grasped B.J.'s proffered hand. "Sure glad you got here fast. This one's going to be a real bummer."

B.J. ripped open a paper packet and fitted white plastic gloves over his stubby fingers. "How'd you find out about this?"

"His wife flagged down a fisherman."

B.J. jerked his head toward the room from which Scott had emerged. "Who's in there?"

"Elsa Gardner and her two kids."

Amy squeezed her fist against her midriff where gastric juices seethed like an erupting volcano. The people left behind—they daunted her most. To her, facing them had proved to be the only drawback to forensic medicine.

"Shouldn't someone be with them?"

"I've searched Mrs. Gardner and the room. She's not going anywhere. The owner nailed the window shut and installed metal bars across it to keep out vandals."

Amy shifted her position so she could rest her gloved hand on the wall and her foot struck a container sitting under the leaky sink. Metal clanked against metal. Great! She might have known her stupid ruse wouldn't work.

Scott whipped out his .38, braced his arms, and sighted along the barrel. "Step out where I can see you."

Muscles at the back of her neck tensed. Now he'd know she was the same screwup she'd always been. She moved into the dim, gray illumination provided by a single window.

"Amy? . . . Amy Prescott is that you?" Scott holstered his weapon and squinted at her from under the rim of his peaked deputy hat.

She hunched her shoulders and ducked her head—a stance she'd often assumed during her gangly, zit-plagued adolescence. Angered at herself, she swore under her breath. It had taken years to break herself of that habit. "Yes, I'm afraid it is." She located a light switch and flipped it on.

He flashed the lopsided grin that had ensnared the hearts of half the girls in the twelfth grade. "Been a long time."

She straightened her spine and met his scrutiny square on. "Twelve years."

He shoved back his hat, causing his thatch of wiry sandy hair to spring up in its wake. "You're looking good."

She searched his face for traces of sarcasm. "Oh? . . ."

The tips of his ears turned pink. "Real good."

Bushwah! No way would she believe a compliment coming from him. She lifted her chin. "You too, Scott." Her voice quavered slightly and a flush heated her cheeks. Blast him, he could still turn her to Jell-O.

She plunged her hand into her over-sized shoulder bag and yanked out a notebook. "What have you got here?"

His smile vanished and cool professionalism took its place. He pulled a pad of paper from the pocket of his police-blue cruiser jacket. "The dead man's name is Lukas Gardner. Does odd jobs around the harbor and marina."

B.J. scrutinized clotted crimson rivulets snaking out from under the toppled Christmas tree. "How'd he die?"

"Can't say for sure. You said not to touch anything." Scott pointed to a .22 caliber handgun on the floor. "It's been fired." A crocheted blue afghan covered a child's bed near the bedroom door. Red stains dotted the afghan's white yarn border. Six feet away, scattered around the splintered base of the Christmas tree, lay three brass shell casings.

"The gun belong to him?"

Scott shrugged and blew out his cheeks. "His wife told me his name and where he worked. That's all." He slapped his pad against his blue-twill-clad thigh. "The woman's got blood all over her."

Amy jotted down the information. "How old are the children?"

"The girl's three. The boy's five."

"Did you question them?"

"I only got a few words out of the girl before she started—" he grimaced and flung out his arm, "—that godawful wailing."

A soft humming accompanying the child's lament turned to crooning words. "Hush little baby, don't you cry. Mama's gonna . . . Mama's gonna—" The singing stopped.

Scott let out a long breath. "The boy won't talk. Just sits there, rocking himself back and forth."

Amy knew the answer but she had to ask, "You going to arrest the mother?"

120

Scott lifted his shoulders and spread his hands. "I've got no choice."

Amy took preliminary photographs while Scott kept the evidence log and made a sketch of the room on the graph paper she'd given him. Exact measurements would have to wait until her father finished using the evidence vacuum.

"Include these in your log and your sketch, Scott." B.J. pointed to a dime, two pennies, and a lipstick case near the shack's door.

"This is terrific, Doc." Scott finished writing and clamped his pencil on a clipboard. "I don't get much chance to do any hands-on stuff. When Tom's around, he takes over."

"You shouldn't let him!" Amy triggered the camera's flash. "What Sheriff Calder knows about processing a crime scene you could write on a matchbook cover."

Scott folded his arms. "He does a passable job."

In a pig's eye! Her father had been doing a good share of the sheriff's investigations ever since the town council had hired the man five years ago. "Wouldn't hurt him to get some training."

B.J. shut off the vacuum. His sour expression indicated he neither understood, nor approved of the barbs she kept throwing at the deputy. He took several brown paper sacks from his satchel and held them out to Scott. "Why don't you bag the clothes Mrs. Gardner's wearing."

Scott's cheeks reddened and he backed away. "I can't do that, Doc. We're supposed to watch the prisoner undress."

B.J. turned to Amy. "Would you mind doing it?"

She regarded Scott coldly. If high-school rumors had any basis, he didn't use to be so bashful about seeing girls get undressed. He recoiled from her sharp scrutiny as if he'd read her mind.

Score one for her side. She set the camera on a cigarette scarred counter she'd already dusted for prints, took the bags, and entered a room that had space for a double bed and little else.

Two blond-haired children sprawled asleep on a blue hand-tied quilt. The boy clutched a teddy bear that had lost one leg and half of its stuffing.

At the window, a woman who couldn't have been more than five-foot-one, stood staring out. A long drawn-out sigh floated up from her and lingered like smoke in the stagnant air. Amy fought an urge to tell her everything would be all right. It wouldn't, she knew all too well, and if the woman didn't realize it yet, she soon would.

"Mrs. Gardner . . ."

The woman peered over her shoulder.

Amy caught her breath. She'd sat across the aisle from her on the ferry not more than three hours ago.

Amy hadn't noticed her until the ferry blasted its horn at a fishing boat and the woman gave a small yelp. Then Amy'd studied her fellow passenger over the edge of the book she was reading on the use of disguise by criminals. The woman, perhaps without even realizing it, had found her own method. Long, pale hair, an equally pale face, washed-out dress and jacket caused her to blend into the surroundings.

The poor creature sat with her legs splayed to accommodate a pregnant abdomen that appeared much to large for one so frail to carry. Tears coursed down her face, yet she neither made a sound, nor lifted a hand to wipe them away.

After a few minutes, Amy went over to her and asked, "Can I do anything to help?"

The woman gripped her purse to her chest and stared up at her with fearful eyes. "No, no," she'd said, shaking her head. "I'm fine, just fine."

Amy stared at Mrs. Gardner. Why hadn't she sat down beside her, gotten her to talk. Everything about the woman had set off alarm bells, warning Amy that she needed counseling.

Amy bit her lip. Some fine doctor, she was. If she hadn't

been so wrapped up in her own problems, she might have taken the time to get involved.

She glanced at the sleeping children. Where had they been while she was on the ferry?

She forced a smile and took a step forward. "Could we—"

Elsa Gardner, her eyes darting right and left, backed along the narrow space between bed and wall until she reached the corner.

"Don't be frightened." Amy rested her hand on the rusty metal panel at the foot of the bed. "I'm Dr. Amy Prescott," she said, making her tone as quiet as possible. "I'm here with my father, Dr. B.J. Prescott." She moved closer. "You may have heard of him, he's the Island's medical examiner."

Elsa's blue eyes flared wide. Shivering, she clutched her arms across her chest.

A fine trembling began in Amy's innards as she searched for the proper words. "We're only here to find out who did this to your husband."

Elsa mashed her fingers against her face. "What you want in here?"

"Please, Mrs. Gardner," Amy stretched out her hand, but the woman shrank away from her, "try to understand. We need the clothes you're wearing."

Elsa's teeth began to chatter. "Why?"

Several answers raced through Amy's mind. She chose the simplest one. "For lab tests."

Elsa's red-knuckled fingers gripped and ungripped the long sleeves of her beige turtleneck . "All . . . my clothes?"

"Yes, please."

"But there's nowhere—" The woman turned in a circle as if seeing the room for the first time. "I can't . . . not with you." She lifted her arms and dropped them to her sides in a helpless gesture.

Amy leaned toward her. "I understand. Really I do, but the deputy says I have to be here."

Elsa flung her a narrow-eyed look, dragged a cardboard box from under the bed, and tossed out a shirt and tent-shaped jumper almost identical to the ones she wore. Turning her back on Amy, she grasped the hem of her dress and tried to pull it over her head. It hung up on her stomach.

Amy hurried forward. "Here, let me help you with that." She eased the knitted fabric upward until it came free and she could drop the garment into the open sack. As she set the sack aside and opened another, she noticed blood oozing down the woman's neck. "Are you injured?"

"Huh-uh." Elsa worked her arms out of the turtleneck.

"But you are. Do you mind if I see?" Before Elsa could object, Amy parted strands of blood-matted hair. "How'd you get this gash in your scalp?"

Elsa shrugged and pulled her shirt over her head. "Fell down, I guess." She tossed the shirt into the bag. "I fall down a lot these days."

"Oh, G——" Amy clamped her lips closed to hold back the rest. Elsa, who now wore only a bra and underpants, had bruises on her neck, her arms, and her breasts. On the woman's swollen abdomen, an ecchymotic blotch overspread one side and purple streaks of extravasation extended halfway down her thigh.

Elsa, noting Amy's shocked expression, snatched up the clean jumper and held it in front of her. "I ta—took a tumble off the front steps th—this morning."

Amy knotted her fists until her nails bit into her flesh and tried to calm her breathing. "Have you——" she tried to swallow and found she didn't have any spit—"have you seen a doctor about . . . about your pregnancy?"

"Sure, a couple of times." Elsa put on her turtleneck and followed with the knit jumper, yanking at her clothes when they didn't go on smoothly.

"When?"

Elsa set her hands on her hips and stared back at Amy, her gaze as frigid as the waves battering the rock-rimmed cove. "Before we moved to this godforsaken island. That's when."

* * *

124

Scott, under B.J.'s low-key direction, measured distances, made triangulations, and recorded them on his crime-scene sketch. "How'd you make out?" he asked, without taking his attention from the task at hand.

"So-so." Amy whisked aside gray fingerprint powder on the green Formica-topped table and placed the labeled sacks next to the bagged Christmas-tree angel. Nearby, her father had arranged a stack of Tamper-Guard-sealed polyethylene pouches, each containing a single filter disk speckled with debris gleaned from a designated section of the room.

With camera in hand, she returned to the business of recording the crime scene on film. As she worked, she mulled over how to approach Scott. Under ordinary circumstances, she might not have worried about denting his self-confidence. After all, he'd once totally shattered hers. Nevertheless, she couldn't let old wounds disrupt her father's investigation.

She cleared her throat. "You might consider taking Mrs. Gardner to Dr. Ryan's office before you cart her off to jail." She grimaced at her poor choice of words.

Scott's lips came together in a hard line. Bending closer to his sketch, he erased a line and drew in another. After several minutes, he squatted back on his heels. "What for?"

"She has a bad scalp wound."

He clenched his pencil with whitened knuckles and a muscle bulged in his neck. "I didn't see a wound."

Had he been hesitant about searching a woman in Mrs. Gardner's advanced state of pregnancy? "Easy to miss, her hair's badly matted."

"Oh?" He studied her, his features revealing nothing.

"Uh-huh, scalp wounds bleed like crazy." She adjusted the camera lens while she decided how to reveal the rest. If she came off sounding arrogant, he could get miffed and refuse to let her assist her father. "Might be wise to get an OB exam, too." She snapped close-ups of a few blood spatters on the wall behind the children's bed.

"She's pregnant?" B.J. groaned, pushed himself to his feet, and massaged his lower back.

"Very." Amy stepped over a wooden box that held several sticks of wood and leaned across the stone-cold wood heater to inspect a weathered plywood wall.

"That could present a few problems." B.J. took an evidence bag from his jacket pocket, knelt, and held the bag open while Scott deposited the gun inside. "She been seeing a doctor?"

"Not since she came to Lomitas."

Scott straightened. "When's she expecting?"

Amy tried for a clear camera shot of the wall behind the Christmas tree but gave it up. "Won't be long. Either she's close to term, or she's expecting twins."

She hunkered down beside her father who had squatted beside the body. "She's got some severe contusions." She avoided Scott's questioning gaze. "Worst one's on her abdomen."

"Damn, that's bad." B.J. passed her some small cotton-lined packets. With a pair of tongs he'd padded to fit his needs, he picked up the brass shells one at a time, inscribed them with an I.D. mark, and placed each in a separate pack. "Are her contusions recent?"

Amy could feel Scott hovering in the background, so she took her time sealing and labeling each item. Finally she rose to her feet. "The one on her abdomen is. The rest are older."

Scott scowled and slapped his notepad against his thigh. "She mention how she got them?"

Amy blew out a breath that ruffled her bangs. "She says she fell off the porch."

Scott's intent hazel-eyed gaze pinned hers. "She'd tell another woman if her husband had been knocking her around . . . wouldn't she?"

Warmth flooded Amy's body. Perspiration gathered under her arms and dampened her sweater. Mitch had done it to her and she hadn't told anyone—not even the judge who'd granted her divorce. She tore her gaze from Scott's. "Women seldom do."

"Ain't that the truth." B.J. gestured toward the Christmas tree. "You can move it now, Scott."

As Scott lifted the fir tree, Amy noticed the trunk's gnawed appearance. "Good Lord, Mrs. Gardner must have cut it herself."

Scott raised his eyebrows. "Nothing to brag about. Never saw a scrawnier-looking excuse for a Christmas tree."

Amy frowned at him. "Picture her down on her knees with a hatchet."

Scott gazed at the ceiling and exhaled heavily. "Wouldn't have been easy for her, I guess." He leaned the tree against the far wall.

"Proves she's stronger than she may appear," B.J. said, making a chalk outline of the corpse. The braced Christmas tree had held Gardner's body in an odd position. It crouched on knees and elbows as if about to crawl into a hole.

"So?" Amy recorded the film number and camera angle in her log book and took several pictures of the body.

B.J. glanced up at her. "She could have been so enraged, she shot him and jammed him under the tree."

"Why? It doesn't make sense."

"Yeah, it does." Scott stared at the toes of his black engineer boots. "Maybe she thought she was giving herself and the kids a Christmas present."

Amy tasted gall as she remembered the woman's silent tears on the ferry, her expression as she clutched her purse. Despite her wan appearance, Elsa Gardner's features had held a determined set.

Amy drew her lips taut. "I hate cases like this."

"Come on now, kitten, you been in this business long enough not to let yourself get emotionally involved."

"You're a great one to talk."

"We-ell, then, do as I say, not as I do." B.J. lifted Lukas's eyelid. "His eyeball's beginning to flatten." He loosened the man's clothing and took a rectal temp. "All things considered, I'd say he's been dead approximately two hours."

B.J. turned the man onto his back. Black curls tumbled over even features that managed to be handsome even in death. B.J. attempted, not too successfully, to straighten the man's legs.

Amy cocked her head. "Pretty early for rigor to be setting in."

"Some sort of exertion before he died could have brought it on faster." B.J. leaned forward to inspect three closely spaced bullet holes in Lukas's blood-soaked cashmere sweater. "Hmm, should be more gunpowder particles if the killer stood where the gun was."

Amy studied the body. "Pretty hard to tell with all that blood, Dad. His skin may tell you more." She jotted down a cursory physical assessment: Height, five foot eight, approximately 142 pounds. Black hair, blue eyes, athletic build.

A small gold hoop dangled from his right earlobe. A heavy gold chain gleamed above the dead man's boat-necked sweater, a Seiko watch encircled his wrist. Black Italian-cut trousers shrieked Giorgio Armani, and he wore handsewn calfskin loafers so new only a few scuffs marred the soles.

Amy remembered what Elsa had worn on the ferry—her limp faded dress, the thin cotton jacket that hadn't even buttoned over her stomach. "What a dirty rotten bastard."

"That goes double." Anger darkened Scott's features. "Gardner's odd jobs must pay a helluva lot better than law enforcement."

Amy and Scott's search for the two lead slugs that had exited Lukas Gardner's back turned up nothing. Amy scanned the room. "What about the children's bed, Scott? We haven't looked there."

"But there's nothing to indicate—"

"I know, but that smooth coverlet has been bothering me ever since I walked in here. In this narrow room, I can't believe it's possible. A struggle took place, a tree was knocked over, a man got shot, and the bed still remained unruffled." She shook her head. "It's not logical."

Scott pulled the knitted afghan from the bed. The striped

128

blue mattress beneath didn't have a blemish. "Well, there goes your theory. He couldn't have been shot here."

She leaned against the wall. "Damn, now what?"

Scott continued to study the mattress. "Surely the kids had blankets. They aren't in the bedroom. So where are they?" Suddenly he grabbed the bottom edge of the mattress, heaved it up against the wall, and stared at the bloody underside. "Jesus, Amy, this is crazy. Why would anyone go to all the trouble of turning the mattress?"

"Good question." While she and her father probed the cotton batting for slugs, she pictured Elsa shooting Lukas as he lay asleep on the couch. With an abusive man, that might be the only opportunity she'd get. But why had she dragged his body off the bed and turned the mattress before running out to the road and flagging down a passerby?

Amy shoved satchels and equipment into a special compartment in the back of her father's canopy-covered truck.

"Coming through," B.J. sang out, and she stepped out of the way. He and Scott lifted the body bag and placed it inside.

The icy wind-driven rain slashed her face. Ducking her head to shield her glasses, she pushed through leathery-leafed Rose Bay bushes to a stand of Sitka spruce that bordered both sides of the long narrow lane leading to the shack.

Scott and B.J. trudged over to her. "Well, that's that," Scott said, letting out a long sigh. "Now I guess I better go get Mrs. Gardner."

Amy regarded him. "What do you plan to do with the children?"

A horrified expression spread over his face. "Jesus! I never even—" His glance darted to B.J. and back to her. "My God, I've never faced anything like this before."

B.J. rested a hand on his arm. "Whoa now, don't panic." He thought for a moment. "I got it," he said, snapping his fingers. "I saw Sedonia Tombe in the store the other day. Her family isn't coming home for the holidays. Maybe she'll—"

"Geez, Doc, Sedonia must be pushing sixty by now."

B.J. recoiled as if Scott had hit him.

Amy smiled to herself. The fair-haired eligible male had just shot himself in the foot. Her father's fifty-sixth birthday loomed on the horizon and he'd grown touchy on the subject of age.

"Sedonia could teach you young folks a thing or two," B.J. snapped.

Scott looked stricken by his sharp tone. "Like what?"

"Unconditional love for your fellow man."

Scott's expression turned to puzzlement. "Oh . . ." He hunched his shoulders and stared down at his feet.

"Well, do you want me to call her or not?"

"Sure . . . I . . ." Scott turned to Amy as if asking for help. "But where . . ."

"They can stay at my house. I'll ask Sedonia to stay several days as well." B.J. jammed his hands in pockets of his raincoat.

Amy tried not to show her concern. Sometimes his quick temper backed him into a corner. "Dad, are you sure that's what you want?"

He jutted his chin and his blue eyes blazed as if she'd attacked his sore point, too. "Of course, I'm sure. There's room for a family of twelve in that big old house."

"What about the noise, the clutter?"

"I might enjoy a little noise for a change. Did you ever think of that? I'm not a doddering old man, you know." He stomped down the lane to the shack to get the rest of his gear.

Scott wiped a hand over his face. "Boy, I really stuck my foot in it, didn't I?"

Amy giggled, enjoying his fall from grace.

"It's not funny."

Her smile broadened. "Oh, yes, it is. He practically dragged me out here, and I suspect it's all because of you."

"Me? But what—" His eyes widened. "Oh . . ." He regarded her from under cinnamon brown lashes. "Was that such a bad idea?"

"Yes." She took out her notebook to put an end to the subject. "Did you see any fresh tire tracks in the lane?"

"None. I inspected the entire road."

"Mrs. Gardner arrived on the twelve o'clock ferry from Anacortes."

"How do you know that?"

"I sat across the aisle from her."

Scott planted his hands on his hips. "How come you didn't bring this up until now?"

"That's not important."

Scott caught hold of her shoulder. "Okay, so you've hated my guts since the twelfth grade. That doesn't give you the right to—"

"How would you know? You weren't even aware I attended high school."

He leaned forward. "Which goes to show you weren't as all-fired smart as the teachers thought you were."

She backed up a step. *Which goes to show . . .* She tried to translate his convoluted sentence and failed.

He shook his finger in her face. "You've been whittling on me from the minute you walked in on my investigation. You got that, Amy, *my investigation.* Now either you get off my back, or—or you can—" He stared down at her and his Adam's apple bobbed, "you can . . . dammit, Amy, I don't need this right now." He wheeled and headed for the shack.

She stared after him, trying to make sense out of his peculiar actions. After a moment she pushed the enigma to the back of her mind and dashed after him. The investigation came first—personality conflicts could be worked out later.

"Scott, Scott." She slipped on a patch of wet leaves and fell onto all fours.

He came back, helped her to her feet, and scraped sodden leaf mold from her slacks. "Sorry I blew up."

"I deserved it. I was angry at you, Dad, and the world."

"Amy . . ."

His fingers brushed her face as he picked a twig from her hair, and she felt a soft rush of warmth.

131

His hand came to rest on her shoulder. "Will you go to Dr. Ryan's with me?"

She looked up into topaz eyes flickering with green lights and her heart jolted as if she'd been zapped by an electric paddle. She wet her lips. This situation was taking a turn she didn't care to take. "Why, Scott? My Aunt Helen will be there and you've known her for years."

"But what if the kids start crying? I've never been around little kids."

"We-ell, I—I . . ." He squeezed her shoulder and her pulse began to race.

"Thanks, you're a lifesaver."

B.J. came out onto the porch. "I'll tell Joe Ryan you'll be by in awhile. Amy, you coming?"

"She's going with me, Doc."

The corners of B.J.'s mouth curved upward, and he beamed at them. "Good idea. I'll have Sedonia wait in your office."

Scott returned his smile. "That'll be great."

Amy eyed her father with suspicion. She'd been divorced for a year and he was bent on getting her paired up with a "decent" man. She gave an inward sigh. For the moment she might as well let him think he'd succeeded. "Dad, I'd like to go over Gardner's clothes later on."

"That'll work out fine. Thought I'd do the autopsy as soon as I get to the morgue. We can process the evidence later in my lab at home."

Amy carried Marne, the little girl, down the steps. Behind her, Kyle, who had refused to let Scott near him, held his teddy bear with one hand and gripped a fold of his mother's dress with the other. Scott, with a cardboard box of children's clothes, brought up the rear.

"How'd you get home?" Amy asked, turning to Elsa.

"Walked, like I always do."

"Were the children with you?"

"Yes, I picked them up at Mrs. Tombe's house."

"You and the children walked a mile and a half in this weather?"

"I pulled them in the wagon." She pointed to a rusty child's wagon that held two rain-soaked paper bags, and her shoulders drooped. "I forgot to take in the groceries. Lukas will—" Her face twisted, and a tear ran down her cheek. "Guess it doesn't matter now."

Amy set Marne down, took the groceries inside, and hurried back. "Does your husband have a vehicle of any kind?"

Elsa glanced around the yard. "An old Ford truck." She frowned and scanned the clearing again. "Wonder where it is?"

"We'll find it, Mrs. Gardner." Scott shooed the bedraggled group ahead of him. "The patrol car is parked out on the main road."

When they drove into the empty parking lot of the medical clinic that had once been her father's, Amy exchanged a look of relief with Scott. Mrs. Gardner wouldn't have to face other people's prying eyes.

The bell over the front door tinkled as they entered a birch-paneled waiting room. Through a bank of windows, Amy saw the ferry dock lights go on. Farther out, on Rosario Straits, glided a freighter, a black silhouette on an ebony sea scalloped with white lace.

"Amy!" A tall, erect woman rushed out of the inner office and enfolded Amy in her embrace. "Glad you're home, honey." A second-generation Scot, she still rolled her r's.

Amy returned her aunt's exuberant hug. At last she felt as if she'd truly come home. Helen had been her surrogate mother, long before her biological mother deserted her and her father.

Helen held Amy at arm's length. "You're not eating enough."

Amy sized up the other woman's ample bosom, the extra

pounds that had gathered on her angular body, and her eyes twinkled. "You are."

Helen Prescott patted graying reddish blond hair. "An older woman's privilege." She planted a kiss on Scott's cheek. "And that's another."

Helen then took Marne's hand and attempted to take Kyle's, but he stuck it behind his back. She ignored the rebuff and directed them to the children's corner. Kyle, still clutching his one-legged teddy bear, seated himself on a couch and sat stiff as a statue. Marne found a soft doll, climbed up beside him, and began to sing in a soft sweet voice.

Aunt Helen escorted Mrs. Gardner to an examination room, leaving Amy and Scott alone. Amy wandered around the familiar room, peering at fish darting through fantasy castles in the aquarium, examining an earth-tone wall hanging woven by her aunt. Finally she picked up a magazine and settled herself in a chair.

Scott, who'd been following in her wake, selected a National Geographic and sat down near her. "I knew things would go smoother if you came along."

Amy glanced up from an article she'd been staring at without seeing the words. "Wasn't me, Scott. Aunty Helen works her magic on everyone." She turned a few pages. "I suppose the sheriff will be at the courthouse when we arrive."

Scott shook his head. "He had to go to the mainland. His mother had a heart attack."

"I don't wish his mother any bad luck, but I hope Calder stays away for a week or two."

Scott lay his book aside. "What kind of a grudge have you got against old Tom, Amy?"

"He takes everything at face value." She leaned toward Scott and lowered her voice. "He'd have been convinced of Mrs. Gardner guilt the minute he walked into that shack."

"There weren't any signs of forced entry. No actual evidence that anyone else had been there." He puckered heavy brows. "What other conclusion is there?"

Amy rammed her spine against the chair's upholstered

134

back. What she had to say wouldn't win her any points. "The first rule they taught me in forensic science was never assume anything. I've seen trace evidence turn a whole case around."

Scott's scowl turned fierce. "Great! Just what I needed to make this a merry Christmas." He slumped down in his chair and pulled his hat over his face.

An hour later, Aunty Helen ushered her patient back into the waiting room. Elsa hurried across the room and pulled her children into her arms.

Scott rose to his feet. "How is she?"

"All right, considering what she's been through."

Scott ran his hand over his face. "Did you take some polaroids."

"Naturally. She's not the first battered woman we've seen, Scott."

"You mean guys here on the island . . . ?"

She gazed up at him. "That's right. Rich and poor, old and young . . . it happens."

Scott squirmed uncomfortably. "Well, we'd better get going. I appreciate you and Dr. Ryan staying late."

Helen touched his arm. "If she starts having pains, let the doctor know right away. Her labor only lasted two hours with the last one."

Scott groaned. "Thanks a lot, Helen, you've made my day."

While on the way to the courthouse, Amy learned Sedonia Tombe had also cared for the Gardner children while Elsa went to Anacortes a week ago as well as today. The time frame sparked a new worry—legitimate handgun dealers required a five-day wait.

When they arrived at the sheriff's office, they found Sedonia hunkered down in an overstuffed chair upholstered in leather a shade darker than her sepia-toned skin. Her spare, pint-sized body came nowhere near filling Sheriff Calder's recliner.

She bounced out of the chair a big smile wreathing her face. "Amy, girl. Come here, child, and give old Doanie a hug."

135

Although Amy was only five feet seven, she towered over the woman. A lump clogged Amy's throat as she remembered they'd once been the same size. Where had the years gone?

The children eyed them with puzzled expressions as they embraced. Amy smiled at them. "When I was a little girl, Doanie was my sitter, too."

Sedonia winked at the children. "Worst tomboy I ever did see. Always climbing trees or jumping off of something she wasn't supposed to." She chuckled and squeezed Amy around the waist. "And stubborn, that child coulda given lessons to a mule." She shook her head. "Had to swat this girl's behind more'n once, I tell you."

Scott clumped around the office, opening drawers and tossing out sheets of paper. Finally he sat down behind his desk. "Sedonia, could you and Amy take the children and wait in the hall? I have some questions I have to ask Mrs. Gardner." He cleared his throat. "Soon as the other deputy gets here, I'll take all of you to—"

Sedonia silenced him with a wave of her hand. "Never you mind about us, boy. I got my Buick outside, so we'll just be on our way."

She met Elsa's frightened gaze. "Rest easy, girl. Doc Prescott and I been looking after Lomitas Island's kids for a lotta years."

She squatted down to eye level with Marne and Kyle. "Your mommy is tired. While she's taking a rest, she wants you to stay with me and Amy and Amy's daddy." She lowered her voice. "We'll help the Christmas elves make your mommy a present."

Marne's blue eyes widened. "You know the Christmas elves?"

"Sure do." Sedonia's face crinkled into a smile. "Me and the Christmas elves are just like that," she said, crossing one finger over the other.

* * *

Marne cried all the way, wailing, "Daddy hurted. Mama hurted."

When they got inside her father's house, Amy hoped Sedonia would be able to work some of her usual magic on the children. Her hopes were in vain. Kyle drank half a glass of milk for dinner and that was all. Marne ate some chicken and promptly threw it up.

Sedonia bathed her and put her to bed. Kyle, who still hadn't uttered a word since she'd first set eyes on him, let Amy take off his shoes and socks, but refused to permit either her or Sedonia to remove his clothing.

Sedonia called her into the hall. "That child's hurtin' real bad, Amy. Won't matter a smidgen if he's clean or dirty, dressed or undressed, till the poor little thing has his cry."

Amy remembered something from her intern days. "I used to be a volunteer 'rocker' at Children's Orthopedic Hospital. Maybe that would help soothe Kyle."

Sedonia patted her arm. "Bless you, child. It sure can't hurt."

Amy carried him into the room they'd chosen for the children, wrapped him in a child-sized quilt, sat down in the rocking chair, and began to rock. After half an hour, Kyle's taut body began to soften. However, another half-hour of humming and rocking elapsed before he fell asleep.

She tucked him into the big fourposter beside Marne, turned on a night light, and left the door open. The children's room was situated between her bedroom and Sedonia's. One or the other of them would know if the children awakened in the night.

Notebook in hand, Amy went in search of her father. He shouldn't be far, she'd heard him come in while she and Sedonia were busy with the children.

She found him seated at Grandmother Prescott's trestle table in the country-sized kitchen eating leftover chicken casserole. "They're tucked in. Hope they sleep through." She sank onto a chair. "Sedonia's getting ready for bed."

"Good. She'll need her rest tomorrow." B.J. rose, poured

two cups of coffee, and set Amy's in front of her. "I put the evidence bags in the lab."

"Gardner's clothes, too?"

"Yep." He sat down. "The autopsy turned up something peculiar." He took a bite of chicken, chewed thoughtfully, and swallowed. "Damned peculiar."

Amy set down her cup. "Come on, Dad, stop being mysterious."

"Gardner had three bullet wounds spaced one centimeter apart in his thorax."

Amy drummed her fingers on the walnut table top. "Yes. Did you take x-rays?"

B.J.'s head snapped up. "Don't I always?"

She raised her hand in a calming gesture. "I was only asking."

"Anyway, I don't think he died of the gunshot wounds."

Amy stared at him. "Then what killed him?"

"Let me back up a little." B.J. laid down his fork and dabbed his mouth with a napkin. "The wounds were elliptical and funnel-shaped."

"So the bullets entered at an oblique angle—the same as the holes in the mattress."

"Right. One penetrated the atrium and lodged in the thoracic spine." He buttered a biscuit and continued his story. "The other two pierced the heart's left ventricle and, as you know, exited the back below the left scapula."

"Yes, go on."

B.J. leaned toward her. "When I opened the chest, I found a wound that pierced the aorta and extended down into the *right* ventricle."

Amy digested the import of his words. "Good Lord, if that wound preceded the ones made by the bullets, his chest cavity would have been engorged with blood."

"That's right. When the bullets hit, they must have let loose a goddamned geyser."

Amy nodded. "Had to, unless considerable time elapsed between the two events. Find anything else?"

"I remembered what you said about using barium sulfate to determine the shape of a knife blade." Smile wrinkles fanned out from his eyes. "Took a while to drip the barium into the narrow wound, but it worked." He gave her a sideways look. "Can't say you didn't teach this old dog some new tricks."

"And you are trying your daughter's patience. What showed up on the x-ray film?"

"The killer used an implement one centimeter in diameter and twelve centimeters in length. It has a broken tip."

"Something about the size of a knitting needle," Amy mused and jotted in her notebook. "Could you tell if it had a handle?"

"Found a round, one and a half centimeter contusion at the entry point."

"Good going, that puts a whole new light on the murder." She closed her notebook, stood up, and kissed him on the cheek. "I think I'll go examine some of the evidence."

"You need my keys."

"I have my own. Good night."

She traveled along a corridor leading off the kitchen. When she reached the end, she turned off the lab alarm. After negotiating an intricate locking system, she arrived in the basement where her father had assembled his own forensic lab.

She flipped a switch that triggered banks of fluorescent ceiling lights, and located the bags she wanted. With thumb forceps, iris scissors, and other equipment close at hand, she dumped the baby blue sweater onto a worktable. Fitting the temples of stereoscopic eyeglass magnifiers over her ears, she donned a clean white coat and sterile surgical gloves.

First she examined every inch of the garment under strong light, depositing hair, fibers, and other matter she found in tiny evidence packets. A thorough going-over in the purple glow of the ultra violet light followed. Then she exchanged her glasses for tinted goggles and turned on the laser.

After processing both Lukas and Elsa's clothing, Amy spent the next three hours doing lab tests, switching from stereomicroscope to comparison microscope to polarized-light microscope. When she finished, she picked up the phone and dialed the number Scott had given her.

"What do you want?" he asked in a sleepy voice.

She glanced at her watch—one A.M. Nothing like waking a man in the middle of the night to create a great working relationship.

"This is Amy. I'm sorry, I didn't realize the time."

"Hey, don't give it a thought. I'd only been asleep a few minutes. Do you need me? I mean . . . can I help. . . . Damn, I'm not used to talking to ladies late at night."

"Could I examine the Gardner house again tomorrow?"

"If I go with you. What's up?"

"A bunch of contradictory evidence and a gut feeling we overlooked something we shouldn't have."

Amy had just laid her head on the pillow when Marne started to scream, "Mommy, Mommy."

Amy dashed into the next room and scooped the little girl into her arms. "What's wrong, Marne?"

Marne dug her fists into her eyes. "Big bang."

"Honey, I didn't hear anything. Did you have a bad dream?"

Marne sniffed, nodded her head, and put her hands over her ears. "Bang, bang." A shiver went through her. "I want my mommy."

Amy gulped. Although she'd been expecting the question, she didn't have a ready answer. "Your mommy had to . . . go away for a few days."

"You gonna get her back?"

Amy hugged her. "I'll do my best." She sat down in a chair and began to rock. A lump in Marne's pajama pocket pressed against Amy's side. She plucked out the offending object and stared at the inch-high ivory figurine of a squat little man. "Where did you get this, Marne?"

"Found it on Mommy's bed," Marne said and yawned.

"Can I borrow it for a few days?"

"I guess so." She closed her eyes and fell asleep. Minutes later, she jerked awake and began to cry, "Mommy hurted."

Amy's eyes burned, her muscles ached, so she chose the easy way out. "How'd you like it if I got into bed with you?"

Marne looked up at Amy, tear-laden lashes framing china blue eyes. "Story, too?"

Story! Amy's mind went blank. It had been years since anyone had read her a bedtime story. "I'll try." She helped Marne into bed and crawled in between her and Kyle. He had his eyes closed, but she sensed his tenseness and knew he was awake.

Amy began a rambling story about a baby unicorn's search for his lost horn. Although she often had to stop and think, the children didn't seem to mind. Soon Marne dozed off. Kyle took much longer and when he did he made whimpering sounds.

The next morning, Amy crept out of bed, feeling as if she'd been through a wrestling match. She managed to shower and get dressed before Marne came looking for her.

Amy washed faces, brushed Marne's long ash blonde hair, and brought a little order to Kyle's mop of golden curls. With both of them in tow, she followed a tempting smell into the kitchen.

"Sit yourselves down," Sedonia said. "I got hot muffins and scrambled eggs." She laughed—a joyous sound that made Amy smile. "I'm cooking some of that turkey bacon you bought. If we don't tell Doc, he won't know the difference."

"Thanks, Doanie." Amy seated the children. "I doubt he thinks about sodium and cholesterol when he's cooking for himself." She poured milk and dished up the children's food.

Kyle drank his milk and nibbled at a muffin. Marne ate hungrily. "Mommy coming today?" she asked.

Sedonia set down a covered dish and took a chair. "Never you mind, little one. Your mama is missing you and Kyle."

Marne's spoon clattered into her plate. "But when's she coming—"

B.J. came in whistling a cheery tune. Sun, streaming through the bay window, glistened on the silver in his beard and moustache. His clean, freshly dried hair frothed around his bald pate in feathery gray ducktails. "Well, well," he said, in a hearty tone. "So these are our young houseguests."

Kyle glanced up, let out a squeal, tumbled off of his chair and bolted out. Amy ran after him.

In the living room the boy came to a dead stop before the cavernous opening of the stone fireplace, then screamed and lunged for her. Fingers grasping her clothes, shoes digging into her flesh, he climbed up her and wrapped his arms around her neck.

She held his quaking body and wondered what to do next. "Shall we sit here and talk about what scared you?" He shook his head violently. "What if we go back into the kitchen?" His hold tightened around her neck and he again shook his head.

Finally she resorted to her solution of the night before. She carried him to his room. As she wrapped him in the quilt, she pressed against his back. He flinched and whimpered. She smoothed the quilt over his rear and again he cried out.

A picture of Elsa's bruises sprang into her mind. Had the boy's father hit him, too? Was that why Elsa shot Lukas?

Handling him gently, she returned to the kitchen and seated herself in the glide rocker in front of the bay window. Kyle pulled his head down into the quilt until all she could see was his gray eyes.

"Kyle, the man with the beard is Dr. Prescott, and at one time he took care of all the mommies, daddies, and children on this island. He's also my daddy, and I think he's one of the nicest daddies in the whole world."

"And I never spanked her once, Kyle," B.J. added.

Lights danced in Sedonia's brown eyes. "Not that she didn't need it a few times."

Amy continued to rock. Sedonia and B.J. talked and laughed about island events while the radio played Christmas carols in the background.

When Kyle finally relaxed, Amy glanced over at Sedonia. "Do you kids know who makes the best gingerbread men on Lomitas Island?"

"Doanie!" Marne shouted.

"That's right, and from what I see over there on the counter, I'll bet she's going to whip up the most delicious, the most mouth-watering batch of cookies either of you has ever tasted."

Marne slid off her chair and twitched Sedonia's blue challis skirt. "Me too, Doanie?"

Sedonia patted her head. "Yes, siree, princess. Soon as I finish my coffee."

Amy raised Kyle's chin. "I have to go to work, Kyle."

B.J. scraped back his chair. "You going to meet Scott?"

"Yes, at eleven."

"Bring back some answers." He folded his napkin and got to his feet. "I'd better finish the job I started last night. See you all this evening." He waved and left the room.

Amy stroked Kyle's hair. "I'll find some toys for you and Marne. You can play right here. If you get scared, climb into my chair, pull the quilt around you, and rock. Can you do that?"

He pulled his face into a fierce scowl. Amy continued to smooth his curls. "This evening we'll find out if the little unicorn finds his horn. Won't that be exciting?"

At his solemn nod, she lifted him off of her lap and set him back in the chair. "Maybe you'd like to help Doanie and Marne with the cookies." She kissed him on the forehead. "Cookies are hard work."

"I'll say they are." Sedonia grinned as she and Amy cleared away the dishes. "I hope I can find someone with strong arms to roll out all that dough."

Amy's brown eyes met Sedonia's in a shared look of hope. "You just might, Doanie." She smiled, crossed her fingers, and went to find the toys she'd promised.

* * *

After three trips from her car on Westridge Avenue to the Gardner's front porch, Amy sat amidst her jumble of equipment. Since they'd left the day before, Scott had surrounded the yard with yellow crime-scene tape and put a padlock on the door.

At the entrance to the lane, Scott's car skidded to a stop. He got out and strode toward her. He wore no hat and the wind ruffled his sandy hair. Memories from the past flooded in on her.

He and his parents had moved to Lomitas at the beginning of her senior year in high school. From the minute she saw him, she'd thought of little else.

So did most of the other girls. They'd crowded around him wherever he went and he had his pick of the lot. When their English teacher told them to do a composition about someone they knew, she decided this was her chance to make him notice her.

The night before the assignment was due, she stayed up until two A.M. rewriting a story of how her father had tracked down an arsonist. She shuddered as she recalled the minuscule details she'd crammed into the piece.

The next day she'd suffered through half the period, hopeful one minute, dreading the next. At last she stood before the class with her sheaf of notes in her sweaty hand. The story's opening paragraphs dragged and her crisp reportorial style didn't come off as she'd planned. To make matters worse, she stumbled over the names of the arson accelerants and flubbed the quote she'd thought so clever.

Scott, who sat right in front of her, exchanged glances with his current date, a girl with long silky red hair and breasts the size of grapefruit. He smirked, yawned in an exaggerated fashion, and said, "Bor-r-ing" nice and loud. The whole class roared.

Amy grimaced, peeled back foil on a roll of antacids, and popped one into her mouth. Silly of her to dredge up the past—she had enough stress without adding more.

. "Good morning," Scott said as he climbed the steps. He beamed down at her. "Your call came as a nice surprise."

"I should have looked at my watch first."

"Who cares how late it was?" He laughed, threw wide his arms, and shouted, "Amy Prescott called me." He gave her a sidelong glance. "I can't believe it. *The* Amy Prescott called *me.*"

She searched his face for signs of mockery and to her surprise found none. She stood up. "Don't get carried away. I'm still a pompous, opinionated pain in the ass.

"I know, I know," he said with a grin. "But on a beautiful day like this, I can overlook anything." His gaze intensified. "I like you without glasses. Brown eyes as pretty as yours shouldn't be kept hidden." He took out a key and turned to open the padlock. "Hey look, somebody's tried to pry off the hasp."

Amy examined deep gouges in the doorjamb. "Why would anyone want to get inside? I saw nothing of any value in there."

"Damn," Scott muttered. "There goes my open-and-shut case."

Sunlight filtered through the open doorway behind them, but did little to disperse the gloom. Amy turned to Scott with a half smile. "You boarded up the windows."

"I've also got Gardner's truck in the impound yard. Found it parked near Enrique's Marina at Lomitas Harbor."

"You had a busy night."

Scott rubbed his chin and avoided her gaze. "After what you said about Tom, I didn't want you to think that I—" He flung out his hand. "I don't want to come out of this with egg on my face."

She broke into a wide open smile. "That makes two of us."

He blushed. "You don't make mistakes."

"Oh, yes, I do. Lots of them." She touched his arm. "Thanks for keeping an open mind."

His color deepened. "It's not every day a person gets to work with a forensic expert."

"I'm no expert, Scott. Far from it. The more I learn, the more I realize how little I know." She switched on a light. "Let's imagine several ways this murder might have taken place."

"But Doc found gunpowder residue on Mrs. Gardner's hands."

"I'd still like to try this exercise." She opened her notebook. "Elsa's on her way home with the children. What's Lukas doing in the meantime?"

Scott pulled at his lip. "He's waiting for his wife and he's mad. She comes in and he hits her with something."

"Dr. Ryan found wood splinters in Elsa's scalp wound."

Scott strode to the box beside the heating stove and picked up a piece of stove-length alder wood. "What about this?"

"Could be. Close at hand. Easy to grab."

"So she pulls the gun from her purse, backs him up to the bed, and shoots him."

"Hold on, Scott, we don't know the pistol is hers or that she had it in her purse."

"Oh, yes, I do. I spoke to the Anacortes gun dealer who sold it to her."

"I didn't want to hear that." She glanced at her notepad. "Here's something that mystified me. Lukas had the bloody imprint of a man-sized boot on the seat of his pants."

"Jesus! Maybe a male friend brought her home."

"That's one possibility." Amy and Scott started packing in her equipment. "Lukas also had semen stains on his briefs, the inside of his fly, and the front of his trousers."

Scott ran a hand over his face. "Anything else?"

"Two four-inch hairs on his sweater. Red ones with gray at the shaft's base. Dad discovered two more entangled in his chest hair and a chip of red nail polish."

"I'll bet she walked in on Gardner and the other woman."

146

Bile rose in Amy's throat as she remembered the day she found Mitch in bed with her best friend. Betrayed! Rage burned in her chest as it had two years ago. Resolutely she shoved the incident to the back of her mind. Neither Mitch or her ex-friend were worth tearing up her insides over.

Amy set up her light stand in the Gardner's bedroom, adjusted a binocular magnifier over her eyes, and focused on a pillowcase. Makeup smears slid into her range of vision. Nearby she found three strands of red hair and several curly black ones.

Amy gave the specimen containers to Scott and started on the quilt. "Last night I found some white modacrylic threads caught in Lukas's watchband."

"From what?"

"I don't know. If you get any ideas, let me know." She peered up at Scott. "Will you plug in that black plastic contraption in my satchel?" She darkened the room.

Scott triggered a switch. "Hey, we used to have these at the island dances." His teeth glowed a dazzling white in the rays of the ultraviolet lamp. He pointed to fluorescent dots on the blue quilt. "Is that what I think it is?"

"Probably." She drew a mark around the dots. "If it is seminal fluid, we'll get a DNA." She sank down on the edge of the bed. "But we'll need more than that—a lot more."

"If there was another woman, perhaps there was also a jealous husband or lover." Scott shoved the quilt into a bag and began packaging the rest of the bedclothing.

"Could be, I suppose." She raked her fingers through her hair. "Lukas had bruising across his throat and small hemorrhagic spots called petechiae on his face. That indicates someone applied pressure to his throat."

"Like this?" Scott's right arm encircled her neck. He squeezed for a moment and released her. "Would that do it?"

She touched her throat. "Might have. Describe the attack and how it came about."

Scott hitched his thigh on the table edge and focused on something above Amy's head. "Lukas and his redhead are, uh, going at it in the bedroom. He hears the front door slam and voices. At the same moment, Lukas reaches a—" the corners of Scot's mouth twitched—"a damned crucial stage in his lovemaking. Spooked, he leaps up and dumps his . . . his . . ." Scott's cheeks turned red. "Help me out, damnit. I'm not very good at this kinda talk in front of a lady."

"Try ejaculant."

"Yeah, that . . . all over himself. He rushes out to give his wife hell, and this guy grabs him."

"The assailant has a weapon."

Scott slid off the table. "How do you know that?"

"Dad says a sharp object about the size of a knitting needle entered Lukas's heart on a different angle from that of the bullets."

Scott scowled. "I didn't get to talk to Doc this morning. If you've got any more surprises, I want to hear them." His eyes glittered. "All of them—right now."

"Sorry, Scott, I only wanted a fresh perspective."

"Okay, okay, just tell me."

"The instrument entered from above, the bullets from a more oblique angle. And Dad thinks the object from above came first."

"That's crazy. If Lukas was stabbed, why did Mrs. Gardner use the gun on him?"

"Maybe to make sure he was dead." Amy went over to the children's bed. "The victim is lying here. His chest cavity is gorged with blood. We know the bullets struck him while he lay here. His body must have been covered, otherwise the walls and floor would be splattered with blood." She glanced at Scott. "Why would Elsa go to the bother? And where were the children?"

Scott stared back at her. "Jesus, don't ask me. I'm barely past square one."

Amy and Scott stood on Bridger Cove's salt-water-bleached dock. For the last hour they'd been going over the area surrounding the shack.

They'd come upon foot impressions of two men and also those of a woman who wore high heels. In the woods they'd run across an overgrown roadway that gave access to the cove. On it they found two sets of tire tracks—both recent.

Amy stared at snow-capped Mt. Baker off to the east and let her mind reprocess what they'd learned. "Where'd he dispose of the bedcovers?"

"Not in the straits. I know these currents, they bring everything back into shore. Besides, if this guy isn't an islander, he probably thinks our sheriff's department is from Hicksville and that he's perfectly safe. So he'll wait until he gets to the mainland to stash the blankets."

"Good logic." Her stomach growled. "Let's eat, I'm—" She broke off as a faint tapping sound came from beneath the dock. "What's that?"

Scott lay down on his stomach and peered underneath. "Hey, we're in luck." He found a dry branch in the woods, came back, and squatted on the rocky shore. "Get an evidence pouch ready." He made scooping motions with the branch until a piece of firewood floated into view.

Amy snatched it up. "I'll bet ten dollars this is what Elsa got hit in the head with." She peered beyond him. "Scott, can you get that object over there by that piling."

He maneuvered until he could pluck it from the water. He held the ice pick out to her handle first. "This the murder weapon you're looking for?"

She inspected it. "Got to be, the tip's missing."

Amy tossed the last bite of her ham sandwich to a waiting sea gull. Overhead three more wheeled in the cloudless sky and shrilled their protest. She pushed the picnic lunch Sedonia had packed closer to Scott. "Have you got room for the rest?"

A massive semicircle of granite protected them from the

wind, and with the warmth of the sun, the grotto felt almost summery. She took off her jacket, scooted backward on the half-log seat, rested her head against a slab of stone, and closed her eyes. "If I fall asleep, wake me. I'm pooped."

"You're entitled." Scott angled his body toward her and sipped his coffee. "You cast every foot and tire impression we came to. No wonder you stay so nice and slim."

Silence fell until Scott said, "I've seen you in town a number of times over the years."

Amy opened her eyes. "Why didn't you say hello?"

Scott licked his lips. "Scared, I guess."

"Scared? Why?"

His gaze met hers. "You know why."

A fine trembling started inside her. She glanced at her watch. "It's getting late."

When she started to rise, Scott caught her arm. "Please, Amy, don't run away from me again. I've waited twelve years. These things have to be said."

"All that was a long time ago." Her voice rasped and she stopped to wet her throat. "It's no longer of any importance."

"Oh, yes, it is."

She cast a suspicious glance his way. He hadn't cared then. Why should he now?

"You don't believe me, do you?" He took her wrists and turned her to face him. "At fourteen, I went fishing with my dad. A sea lion spoiled our catch. Dad shoved a rifle in my hands and said, 'Kill him.'" Scott swallowed hard and went on. "Just before I pulled the trigger, the sea lion looked at me. His big dark eyes were sad and liquid as if he was about to cry."

Scott massaged the back of her hand with his thumb. "That day, when I made everybody laugh at you, you looked at me and your brown eyes were just like that sea lion's. I knew right then, I'd killed something inside of you. After you ran out, I threw up just as I did after I shot the sea lion."

Amy spoke despite the lump in her throat. "I got over it."

His mouth twisted. "Like hell you did. I lay awake all

150

night trying to figure a way to undo what I'd done. In my family, men don't apologize for any reason. But I decided the easiest way to ease my conscience would be to say I was sorry and that'd be the end of it."

Scott bit down on his lip. "The next day I tried to give the speech I'd rehearsed. You looked right through me."

Waves tossed salt spray in her face and she scarcely felt it. "I was pretty mixed up in those days. Had been ever since my mother ran off." She started to get up but he held her fast.

"I tried to do the first noble thing in my whole damned life and you treated me as if I was nothing. From then on, I couldn't get you out of my mind."

She stiffened. "Don't be ridiculous. You weren't aware I even lived on the island."

"Didn't I? Every morning I ran ten blocks so I'd be across the street when Doc let you off at the courthouse."

Amy chewed the inside of her lip and watched a golden crowned sparrow teeter on a salmonberry bush to trill his three-note song. "You only came to torment me."

He regarded her with brooding sadness. "No, I was hurting for you. You held yourself taut as a wire. Your face looked like marble."

"How about you? The girls said you'd turned into a drag. Dropped out of athletics. Made the honor roll."

"I had to keep my vigil, Amy. If anyone else tried to bruise your spirit, I intended to be there to protect you. When you went to the library, I went to the library. I even studied a little, when I wasn't watching you."

A sandpiper skittering amongst the seaweed reminded her of herself. Then, as now, she'd thought if she ran fast enough she could escape the pain pursuing her. "I felt your presence, but I couldn't look up. I was afraid of what I'd see in your eyes."

He sighed and shook his head. "Months went by and I never saw you smile, not once. I thought if you'd just cry or yell at me, maybe you'd come back to life. So one day I knocked you down. Your hands and your knee bled. I knelt beside you, tried to hold you."

"And I slapped you so hard my hand stung for a week. Scott, what's the point of all this?"

"I need to be forgiven."

She sighed. "That kid stuff shouldn't matter anymore."

"It matters—it matters a lot."

"Okay, you're forgiven. Can I go now?"

He pulled her to her feet. "Put your arms around me."

"I will not."

He wrapped her in an embrace. "You're so chock-full of hurt and pride and anger you're as stiff as that little Gardner boy."

His words jarred her and she shrank away from him.

He drew her back. "Goddamnit, Amy, put your arms around me. You're going to get held whether you like it or not."

He rubbed her back. "You've had so much hurt. First, your self-centered mother. Then the kids teasing you about your father cutting up dead people."

She lifted her squashed nose from his shirt. "Who told you?"

"Doc. He and I have talked about you a lot." He smoothed her hair and pressed his lips to her forehead. "You understood his work solved puzzles. The kids who teased you didn't give a damn." He rubbed his cheek against hers. "But they were no worse than me. I never gave other people's feelings a second thought either—until I saw the harm I'd done to you."

His arms tightened around her. "Why did you marry Mitch?"

A spasm clutched her chest and she began to tremble. "I thought he . . . he loved me."

"That smooth-talking bastard didn't know the meaning of the word." A muscle bunched in his throat. "Three months after you got married, I caught him in one of the hidden coves. He had a girl cornered. He was hitting her and ripping off her clothes like a beast in rut. I rammed my knee into his groin so hard I hoped he'd never recover, and threw him in the ocean. The poor girl shook all the way home."

Scott continued stroking her back. "You're a good person, Amy. A beautiful, wonderful person. And you deserve to be happy."

"I don't know if I'm capable of happiness."

"You will be if you let yourself trust again."

His gentle voice found the spot deep within her where she hid her pain. She clutched his shirt and sobs wrenched her body.

At dinner Kyle kept his face turned from B.J., but he did eat some soup and a few crackers. When he finished, he climbed into the rocker and pulled the quilt around him.

Amy crouched down beside him. "While Sedonia and Marne are making fudge, why don't you and I do a project of our own?" She spied a drawing tablet she'd given him that morning. On it he'd drawn the figure of a man and scribbled over the picture with a black crayon. The hard stabbing lines made her stomach tighten.

She looked up, met his watchful gaze, and helped him down from the chair. "We need garlands to decorate the house." She led him down the hall. As they went by the living room, he pressed tight to her side and edged past.

At the end of a side corridor, she flipped a light switch, entered a narrow door, and took his hand. "The decorations are in the attic. I'll need help bringing them down."

At the top of the stairs, she noticed the shadowy corners and feared he might bolt. "When I used to come up here and play, I'd pretend I was a pirate with a shiny sword."

She took a crook-necked cane from an umbrella stand. "If you see something that frightens you, you can slash it and smash it like this." She swished the cane this way and that and handed it to Kyle. With a fierce expression, he grasped the shaft with both hands, holding it as if the crook was the end of his club. "Ready?" His features set, he thrust out his jaw and nodded.

She wound her way between barrels of chinaware, past a table that held a child-sized Santa with elves to match, and detoured a cherry wood armoire. Behind her, she heard a crash.

She glanced over her shoulder. "Kyle . . . ?" No answer. She squirmed around the armoire. "Kyle, are you all—" Kyle had the papier-mâché Santa Claus on the floor. Growling deep in his throat, he beat the figure with his cane. He cracked the face, split the body, and still he kept on. When the figure lay in brown pulp pieces, he flung down the stick and burst into tears.

Amy wrapped her arms around his sweat-soaked body, but made no attempt to stem his weeping. He needed release as badly as she had. She carried him down to his bedroom and rocked him.

"He—he—" Kyle began between shuddering sobs.

Tears stung her eyes. He'd won his battle.

"He said he'd n-never bring us a-a-nother present."

His father? The other man? "Who, Kyle?"

He peered toward the open door. "S-Santa."

His reaction to her father flashed into her mind, and she tightened her arms about him. "You mean a man with a white beard who looked like Santa Claus?"

"No . . . no," he wailed. "He had a red coat, long white hair, and . . . and a white beard." He swabbed his eyes with his fingers. "He hurt my mommy."

Amy's heart bumped against her chest. Had he seen what happened? She drew a quick breath. "How did he hurt her?"

"He hit her with a stick." A sob shook him. "She fell down and wouldn't get up."

Amy stroked Kyle's hair. "Did he hit you, too?"

"He kicked me." He clutched her arm. "He said if we didn't shut up and get in the bedroom we—" he began to tremble—"we'd never see our mommy again. And . . . and now," his voice rose, "she . . . she's gone . . ."

Her mind raced. She wanted to find her father and talk to Scott, but first she needed a few more answers.

She hugged him. "Your mom will be home soon, Kyle." She tilted his chin. "You've got my word on it."

"You promise?"

"Cross my heart." She drew a big X on her chest and smiled at him. "Now how about a nice bath?"

She set him on his feet and led him into the bathroom. While he undressed, she turned on the tap, poured in her own special bubble bath, and worked up a froth of bubbles.

When she helped him into the tub, she gasped as she caught sight of his back. The bruise on his behind he'd gotten from the man who hit Elsa. The purple belt marks crisscrossing his back had probably been put there by his father.

She squeezed a spongeful of water over his bony shoulders. "Where was your daddy when you came home?"

"On our bed."

"Sleeping?"

"I guess so. I bumped his foot when I passed him. He didn't yell at me like he usually does."

"After Santa sent you and Marne into the bedroom, what did you do?"

"I pushed the door open a little so I could see Mommy."

Amy sent up a prayer. "Did she get up off the floor?"

Kyle shook his head and tears overflowed his eyes. "Daddy says boys don't cry, but I thought she was dead."

Amy cradled his head in her arms. "In this house, you can cry all you want." She stroked his cheek. "What did Santa do?"

"He grabbed the toy gun that fell out of Mommy's purse." Kyle's face puckered up. "I t-think she b-bought it for me for Christmas." He let out a howl. "And he went and took it."

Thoughts crowded into Amy's brain. Lukas, dead or wounded, lay on the children's bed. Elsa came in, the man knocked her out. Her purse spilled its contents. The man saw the gun and decided to make it look as if she killed Lukas.

"Did you see anything else?"

"He dragged Mommy across the room, then he kicked the bedroom door shut."

She washed his face, sudsed and rinsed his hair. "Did you dress up in a costume at Halloween?" She wrapped him in a towel.

"Uh-huh. I was Batman."

"That man at your house wasn't a real Santa. He was only wearing a Santa suit. A real Santa would never have hurt you or your mommy."

He peered up at her. "Are you sure, Amy?"

She nodded. "When you were in the bedroom, did you hear anything?"

"The gun." Kyle struggled into his pajamas.

"Have you heard gunshots before?"

"Sure. On the farm Daddy practiced all the time."

Amy gave him a hug. "I have to go see your mom."

He regarded her with a sad expression that twisted her heart. "I hope she gets rested real soon."

Amy felt tears sting the back of her lids. "So do I, Kyle, so do I."

Scott met Amy and B.J. at his office. "Santa Claus committed murder two days before Christmas!" He raked his fingers through his hair. "For God's sake, don't tell anyone else or we'll be run off the island."

Amy, still sheepish about him seeing her cry, gazed at the floor. "Kyle's story matches the evidence."

B.J. shifted in his chair. "Didn't Amy tell you about the long modacrylic fibers attached to Lukas's watchband?"

"I think so, but—"

"That's what wigs and beards are made of, Scott."

"Okay, okay." Scott picked up his key ring. "Let's go talk to Mrs. Gardner. The public defender has been in so she knows her rights." He led the way down a corridor. Two iron-barred cells flanked one side. Elsa lay on a cot with two pillows propped under her abdomen.

She jumped up and clutched the bars. "How are the children?"

"Kyle's finally talking." Amy touched her hand. "Tell us what happened when you got home yesterday."

Elsa licked her lips. "Marne had to go to the bathroom. So I left the groceries in the wagon and hurried the kids up the steps." She twisted a lock of hair around her finger. "The door wasn't locked. It should have been. I used my key when I left." She shrugged. "The lock doesn't work half the time."

Scott, who'd been standing back, moved up alongside Amy. "Did the kids go inside first?"

She nodded. "I wanted to bring in the groceries."

Scott flipped open his notepad. "But you didn't."

"Marne screamed, and I rushed back to see what—"

"Go slowly," Amy broke in. "Remember each thing you did."

Elsa narrowed her eyes. "I'm not supposed to say anything about—" she blinked back tears, "about Lukas getting shot."

Amy glanced at Scott. "Can she tell us what she saw when she opened the door?"

Scott scratched his head. "I don't believe that'd hurt."

"But . . ." Elsa laced and unlaced her fingers. "I—I can't . . ." She sank down on the cot and put her head in her hands. "I just can't remember." She turned to them with pleading eyes. "I was on the floor by the kid's bed. I—I thought Lukas had hit me. I heard the kids crying in the bedroom and I didn't know how they'd gotten there. Then I saw Lukas and . . . and the b-blood running out from under the Christmas tree, and I just knew I—" She clapped her hand over her mouth.

B.J. took hold of the bars. "Who did Lukas work for, Mrs. Gardner?"

"Some friend of his."

"Did he make good money?"

"Look at this dress." Elsa spread her arms. "You saw the dump we lived in. Do you think we have any money?"

"Your husband was wearing expensive clothes and jewelry."

Elsa stared at him. "How could he? When he went to work yesterday morning, he had on his blue coveralls just like always. Besides, the only good clothes he had was a pair of white jeans."

"No gold chains, no Seiko watch?"

She eyed him suspiciously. "You trying to pull something? Lukas never owned anything like that in his life."

"Did he have any enemies?" Scott asked.

"I don't know."

Amy consulted her notebook. "Do you mind me asking how you happened to come to Lomitas Island?"

"Up north close to the Canadian border, we stayed at a farm that belonged to a friend of Lukas's. Lukas got a letter from him and told me we were moving here."

"Did you know his friend?"

"No. Lukas wouldn't even tell me his name." She got up and began to pace. "I saw one of his letters once. A bunch of dates. Didn't make any sense. He didn't even sign his name."

"Did Lukas work the farm?"

Elsa swung around. "Are you kidding? He wouldn't even fix the well. Brought back water when he went out at night to make deliveries."

"What kind of deliveries?"

"Lukas didn't say." She glared through the bars. "And I knew better than to ask him."

"Did you ever see this friend of his?" Scott clicked his pen and looked at her with a hopeful expression.

"Once I saw him from a distance."

"Is there anything you can tell us about him?"

"Nothing I can think of. . . . Oh, he drove a real fancy car."

"Did you recognize the make?"

She shook her head. "It was silver-colored. I'd never seen one like it before. Lukas said he'd have one just like it some-day." She laughed—a harsh bitter sound. "He always talked like that—and us unable to buy shoes for the kids half the time."

Amy moved closer to the bars. "Forgive me, Elsa, but I have to ask this."

Elsa grimaced. "Go ahead. I don't have much left to hide."

"Did Lukas know a middle-aged woman with red hair."

"Woman!" Elsa spat the word. "He had blondes, brunettes, redheads. Was always taking off with one of them." Her features hardened. "He came back, but only because his friend made him." She slumped onto the cot. "Go away and leave me alone."

Scott poured Styrofoam cups of coffee and handed them around. "Looks like we're going to be busy."

B.J. sat forward. "Sedonia says three men played Santa yesterday. Don Hatch at the school gym, Earl Jenkins at the church, and a member at the Seafarer's Yacht Club. Earl was at the church from one until three. So that lets him out."

"Might be more than three Santa suits on the island." Scott's lips tightened. "And who the hell would notice an extra Santa or two this time of year."

"Which means we're dealing with premeditation." Amy sipped her coffee. "Our killer thinks on his feet."

"Yeah, those bullet wounds sure muddied the picture." B.J. got to his feet. "I think I'll go talk to Don Hatch."

Amy chewed the edge of her lip. "I wished I'd brought my own car. I'd like to run out to the yacht club."

Scott smiled at her. "Great idea. Let's you and I drive out there, have a drink, and kind of mosey around."

"That wasn't what I—" She glanced at her father for help and got a shrug in exchange. She gave an exasperated sigh. In another age, her father would've made a fortune as a matchmaker. "Okay, let's get going, Scott. Maybe we can get Elsa out of jail before she delivers."

Candles flickered in cut-glass globes, reflecting off the mirror in front of them and making wavey streaks on dark water outside the window.

Amy fidgeted on the tufted blue velvet seat, twiddled her straw in her Brandy Alexander, and sucked in a gulp. The trip out to the club with the stereo playing soft music had been nice—too nice. If she had any sense, she wouldn't be sitting here with his shoulder brushing hers, their thighs almost touching. His nearness turned her into a trembling nincompoop. The bartender finished filling an order and Amy came alert.

Scott clinked the ice in his empty glass. "How about another one, Phil?"

"Sure thing, old buddy."

"I hear the club had quite a party for the kids."

"Best one yet." He set Scott's drink in front of him. "Barringer did a great St. Nick. Surprised the hell outa me."

"Oh, how come?"

"He's a tightwad. Expects extra service but never leaves a tip. And he's mean as a constipated bear when he gets drunk."

"Barringer?" Scott sipped his scotch. "Don't believe I know him. What's his first name?"

"Max. He's been around for a couple of months. Owns one of those forty-two footers over at the marina."

"Big time, huh? I'll have to check it out one of these days. Your Santa stay through the whole bash?"

"Yep. One to four. My kids had a blast."

Scott downed his drink and turned to Amy. "Ready to go?"

She slid off the stool. "Merry Christmas, Phil."

"You too, Amy. Nice seeing you again."

Scott steered her outside and along the boardwalk until

they reached a sheltered nook overlooking the moonlit water. "Do you think people change at Christmastime?"

"In books and movies. Never saw it happen in real life."

"Must have missed something." He smacked his forehead. "Can't get my brains to work when I'm around you."

"You had one drink too many. That's all."

"No, just enough to give me courage." He brushed her cheek. "Amy, I've wanted to kiss you forever."

Sorrow engulfed her. He'd liked her all along. Still, if she hadn't ignored him, he might not have given her a second thought. In either case, it was too late—much too late.

"Scott." She attempted to move away from him but he wouldn't let her. "I never mix my work and my private life."

"Oh, no?" He tilted her chin. "I'm going to kiss you and keep on kissing you until you unbend." He brought his warm, sweet-tasting lips down on hers and the world stopped revolving.

She wanted to respond, needed to respond, yet her mouth wouldn't go soft and she didn't lean into him as she should have. She hoped, with the liquor he'd had, he wouldn't notice.

He drew her closer, pressed her body to his. "Honey, I want you. I've wanted you for so long, my whole being aches with it."

Amy backed away. "I think it's time you took me home."

He let out a noisy breath. "Amy, Amy, don't you ever let anyone into that closed world of yours?"

"Once was enough."

Amy let her mind wander as she sauntered along a floating walk between two lines of boats at Enrique's Marina. This morning she and her father had gone through all the evidence.

Debris from the shack floor had yielded intriguing flakes of black paint. And she'd gotten an excellent boot impression from the Christmas-tree angel's satin skirt.

Now to find a Santa to match the boot. Don Hatch had been eliminated as a suspect. That left them with Max

Barringer—unless their murderer hadn't attended any of the parties. She shivered, drew the hood of her coat around her ears, and continued walking until she caught sight of *Orca,* Barringer's boat.

If he was the one, would he have come in by sea? She remembered the two sets of car tracks and decided he'd use something quieter to sneak up on his wife and her lover.

She made a mental note to learn something about Mrs. Barringer—if there was one—and moved a little closer. A portly man in a blue-plaid mackinaw was at work near *Orca*'s dock.

"Hi there, miss." Bright blue eyes under bushy gray eyebrows sparkled at her. "Ain't seen you around before."

"I'm Amy Prescott." She put out her hand.

He shook it vigorously. "Name's Jim Colby." He laughed and his red-apple cheeks glowed. "Call me Sunny, everybody does."

She smiled. "With your face and physique, I'll bet you're in big demand this time of year."

"That's right." He jabbed an ice pick into a block of ice, split it in half, and divided it between two ice chests. "Got a pack of grandkids, so I bought my own outfit."

A flake of snow settled on his nose and he grinned. "Hey, looks like we're gonna have a white Christmas."

A tall, heavyset man strode out on the boat's deck. "Get that goddamned ice in here, Colby. I don't have all day."

Sunny jammed the pick into the tie-up post and closed the chests. "Guess I'd better hitch up my reindeer." He winked. "Max hates all this holiday folderol." He smiled and waved as he boarded. "Merry Christmas."

"Same to you." As she turned to go, her gaze lit on the bright yellow handle of the ice pick. The price sticker wasn't even smudged.

She dashed back the way she'd come, jumped in her car, and sped up the road to the yacht club. Crossing her fingers, she raced into the lounge.

Phil gazed at her with sleepy eyes. "Mornin', Amy."

"I'd hoped you'd be here."

"Day man's sick. What're you doing out and about so early?"

"Gathering a little information for Scott." She settled herself on a stool. "Phil, how tall a man is Barringer?"

He pursed his lips. "A good six foot, I'd say."

"And the Santa at your party, how tall was he?"

Phil scratched his crew cut. "Come to think of it, he was about my size." He squared his shoulders. "I'm five-ten if I stretch a little." He leaned across the polished mahogany bar. "You mean Max sent a substitute? Why would he do that?"

Amy slid off the stool. "That's what we'd like to know."

Scott, Amy, and B.J. sat in a red vinyl upholstered booth in Rena's Cafe. Scott's attention alternated between his cheeseburger and a yellow legal pad. "Okay. I've got down the stuff Amy learned at the marina." He regarded her for a moment. "Pretty blouse. That gold color puts lights in your eyes."

"Thank you." She gazed out the window, pretending to be interested in cars laboring through gathering snow. After last night. she intended to see he kept his distance.

Scott turned to B.J. "You got anything to report?"

B.J. grinned and spread his hands on the hatch-cover table. "Spent the morning having a manicure. How do you like it."

Scott glanced from B.J. to Amy. "Is he ribbing me?"

She inspected her father's cuticles. "Nope. Did you get your money's worth?"

"I'd say so. Mrs. Barringer has her nails done every week. She was supposed to be in today but didn't show."

"Does their brand of lacquer match the chip you found?"

"To a T. My manicurist says Cheryl Barringer is fortyish and has red hair: a dye job. And she's partial to younger men. Always has one in tow when her husband's out of town."

Scott nibbled a French fry. "If you had a sample of her hair, could you match it to the ones you found?"

B.J. selected a piece of cantaloupe from his fruit plate. "Not so a court would accept it."

"Mrs. Gardner remembered three letters of that silver car's license plate." Scott spooned sugar into his coffee and took a swallow. "EMG, that's her initials. I checked with Virgil's Auto Shop. The plate on Barringer's silver Rolls matches."

"So . . ." Amy speared a piece of cucumber from her salad. "That proves Lukas and Barringer knew each other."

"Right, Amy." The long gentle look he gave her brought the blood surging into her cheeks. "However, I need more than we've got to prove Mrs. Barringer was with Lukas the day he died."

Suddenly Amy remembered the little ivory man she'd borrowed from Marne. She reached into her purse and set the figurine on the table. "This might have belonged to her. It doesn't look like something Elsa would wear."

"A Japanese netsuke." B.J. examined the squat little man. "The manicurist said Mrs. Barringer had a bracelet with a bunch of these on it. Said she wore the bracelet constantly." He pushed the netsuke across to Scott. "Where'd you get the thing, kitten?"

"Marne found it on her parent's bed the day of the murder."

"That's why someone tried to get into the shack." Scott scooted out of the booth. "I'm going to get a search warrant. If I get lucky at the Barringers', Elsa Gardner could be spending Christmas Eve with her kids." He smiled down at Amy. "I'll check in with you later, pretty lady."

Kyle and Marne met Amy at the front door. "Where's Mommy?" Marne asked.

Amy set several bulging sacks on the hall table, shook snow off her coat, and hung it on the hall tree. She knelt to eye level. "She might be here later."

Kyle glared from beneath puckered brows. "You promised."

Amy embraced both of them. "All kinds of wonderful surprises happen at Christmas, don't they?" The children nodded. "So let's close our eyes and wish for your mom."

Marne pushed Amy's shoulder and she opened her eyes. "Yes?"

"Can I wish for a doll, too?"

Amy ruffled her hair. "Of course you can." She caught Kyle's hopeful glance. "Remember, Kyle, the Santa you saw was only a bad man pretending to be Santa Claus."

Kyle's lip protruded. "But how'll the real one find us?"

His question stumped her. "I . . . uh . . . stopped at the electronic store and faxed him a letter." Her newly acquired inventiveness amazed her. "He knows where you are."

"You sure?"

"Absolutely."

He smiled and took her hand. "Come see what we did."

In the jewel-toned living room of burgundy, French blue, and mauve, Sedonia stood in front of a Noble fir. The tip soared upward as if striving to reach the huge open beams of the cathedral ceiling. Sedonia braced her hands on her hips. "Did you ever see the likes of this, girl?"

Amy viewed the glittering decorations. "Never. It's magnificent, Doanie. How'd you do it all by yourself?"

"Magic." Sedonia included the children in her secretive glance. "The elves came. Didn't they, kids?"

Marne snickered behind her hand. "Big, big elves."

Amy grinned at the children. "Is she spoofing me?"

"Doanie told the boys that brought the tree, they could have some cookies if they put on the star and the lights." Kyle laughed out loud. "Elves sure do eat a lot."

Amy exchanged a happy glance with Sedonia. "I have some presents to wrap. Then I'll come help you."

The telephone rang and she snatched it up. "Scott?"

"I found the boots you want, Amy. Old tight-fisted Barringer painted a pair of khaki-colored rubber boots so he'd look like the other Santas."

"How about the bedcovers?"

"Yep, and the Santa suit, too." He chuckled. "That man doesn't throw away a thing."

"Any bloodstains on the suit?"

"Yep, and Doc says it's the same type as Gardner's."

"Did Mrs. Barringer see her husband kill Lukas?"

"She claims she ran out of the shack so fast she doesn't know what he did. She's sporting a black eye and a big bruise on her cheek, so I'm inclined to believe her."

"What about Barringer?"

"His boat was headed for Canada with several boozed-up couples aboard when the Coast Guard stopped him. Barringer said they were having a Christmas party. However, the Coast Guard found several bales of marijuana hidden in the bilge."

"Did they arrest Jim Colby, too?"

"Nah, he's only been with Barringer a couple of weeks. And you were right, he did fill in for Barringer at the yacht club Christmas party."

"So, drug smuggling paid for Lukas's expensive tastes."

"Mrs. Barringer says she gave him the clothes and jewelry. Kept them at her house so Elsa wouldn't know."

"But he must have had *some* money of his own."

"Sure did. He hid a wad under the floorboards of the shack. She says they were planning to run off together."

"The dirty, rotten bastard."

"Ah, at last, something we can agree on." He laughed. "See you soon."

Blowing snow almost hid Scott's car from their view as he pulled into the driveway. Hatless and coatless, Kyle and Marne raced outside. Amy hurried after them.

Scott, carrying plastic bags in one hand and holding onto Elsa's arm with the other, met them halfway. "Take it easy, kids. Your mom's not feeling so good."

"But Mommy," Marne tugged on Elsa's skirt, "you gotta. Santa's coming."

"Oh, my Lord." Elsa stopped short. "I haven't been able to . . . What'll I do?"

Amy took her free arm. "That problem's all taken care of."

"Thanks, Dr. Prescott. You and your father have been so good. Letting us stay here and all. Deputy Margeson says we can't go back to—" She shuddered and hunched her shoulders.

"We have plenty of room, Elsa. And call me Amy."

Scott urged them inside and gave Mrs. Gardner one of the sacks he held. "Doc will be along in a while." He winked at Amy. "Some special stuff coming in on the ferry."

"Sounds like he and I had the same idea." She smiled at Scott. "You've made this an extra nice Christmas for all of us."

She took Elsa's coat and hung it on the hall tree. "Did Dad examine you?"

She shook her head. "He said to call Dr. Ryan. But if I can take a shower and lie down for a while, I'll be fine."

"Come along then and I'll show you your room." She glanced at Scott. "Go on into the living room."

"Don't worry about me." He grinned and rattled the sack he clutched. "There's something I have to do."

When she rejoined him half an hour later, she caught him taping something to the archway into the living room. Over the doorways to the dining room and the kitchen, she glimpsed the same tiny red bows. "What are you up to, Scott Margeson?"

"I'm hanging merry Christmas insurance." He took a slim velvet box from the pocket of his brown tweed blazer. "This is for you."

Amy stared at the box in surprise. "But I—"

"No buts." He fastened the gold necklace's clasp, stood her under the mistletoe, and brushed her lips with his. "Special day, special woman, special things." He rubbed his cheek against hers. "You are special, Amy. Very special."

She had difficulty getting her breath. This is what she'd hoped and prayed for once. But now—

"Amy, Amy." Kyle pelted down the hall. "Mommy's making funny noises."

Amy exchanged startled looks with Scott. "Oh, no—"

She ran to Elsa's room. "Are you all right?"

Elsa wiped her damp forehead. "My labor's started." Tears overflowed her eyes. "I'm sorry to be such a bother."

Amy sat on the edge of the bed. "Elsa, you and the children have brightened our lives." Elsa groaned and Amy jumped to her feet. "I'd better call Dr. Ryan."

Scott met her in the hall. "Is she . . . ?"

Amy nodded. "I'm going to alert the doctor." She hurried into the living room and dialed his number. When his exchange said he'd taken a patient to the mainland, her stomach swooped. "He's gone, Scott. What're we going to do?"

Scott put his arm around her shoulders. "You're a doctor, aren't you?"

"But I haven't delivered a baby since I did my OB rotation, and that seems like eons ago."

He chuckled. "Maybe it's like riding a bicycle—you never forget."

"It's not funny, Scott. I'm scared."

Scott cupped her face in his hands. "The Amy I know can do anything she puts her mind to."

Amy clasped his hands. "I hope you're right."

She ran to the kitchen. "Doanie, Elsa's in labor and Dr. Joe isn't available."

Sedonia gave her voluminous apron a jerk. "Then it's up to us, girl." She took a basin from the pantry and turned on the tap. "I'll get Elsa ready. You take care of the rest."

Amy hugged her. "You're a treasure, Doanie."

"Go along with you, girl. We got work to do."

Amy and Scott raided B.J.'s stockroom and piled supplies on a table at the foot of Elsa's bed. "How's she doing, Doanie?"

"Won't be long. I sent the kids to the kitchen to play."

Amy grabbed Scott's hand. "I need your help." She dashed across the hall to her room and stepped out of her high heels.

"Quick, unbutton those damned buttons on the back of my dress."

He worked red glass buttons through their ribbon loops. "Lady, this is *not* the way I fantasized undressing you."

Amy laughed and wriggled the red wool dress over her hips, revealing a red lace teddy. "That's the breaks, pal."

"Sure is." He turned her and pressed a kiss to the curve of her breast. "That's for now."

For now. His words sent an unsettling warmth through her as she jerked on freshly laundered jeans, pushed her feet into loafers, and snatched a white coat from the closet. "I'm as ready as I'll ever be."

"What can I do?"

"Keep the children busy.

"I don't know anything about kids."

"Amy," Sedonia called, "you better get in here. This child ain't waitin' around for no—body."

Amy gave Scott a shove. "Showtime."

Amy set the Rosewood cradle Scott had brought down from the attic by Elsa's bed and went to help Sedonia with the baby. When she opened the door to the kitchen, everyone was talking at once.

Scott drew her into the group circling the small table where the baby lay. "Look at all her dark hair, Amy. And her tiny little hands. Did you ever see such small fingernails in your whole life?"

B.J., his cheeks still cold from being outside, put his arm around her. "Great job, kitten."

"Elsa did the work. About all I did was catch the baby."

Kyle grasped her hand. "What'll we call her?"

"Your mom says Carol fits a Christmas baby."

"Yeah, it's pretty." He looked up at Amy with a solemn expression. "Your daddy says she's our Christmas present. Will Santa still stop here?"

"Will he, Amy?" Marne danced around her. "Will he?"

Amy glimpsed B.J.'s sparkling eyes, the smile that wreathed his face. "I'm sure of it." She hugged them. "And soon as I change my clothes, we'll have a Christmas Eve party."

Scott followed her into the hall. "I'm very good at buttons."

"More than just buttons, Scott." She fastened her arms around his neck and kissed him—kissed him with fervor, her lips soft, her body pliant and pressed fully against him.

When she finally released him, she felt as if her whole being had come alive. "You're a nice man, Scott. A wonderful man." She rested her palm against his cheek and met his steady gaze so he wouldn't think she mocked his words of a few days ago. "You're sweet and you're kind and you deserve to be happy."

He encircled her with his arms and a wicked glint flared in his sultry eyes. "I have a few ideas along those lines I'd like to pursue."

About the Author

Louise Hendricksen lives with her family in Renton, Washington. Her first Dr. Amy Prescott mystery, WITH DEADLY INTENT, will be published by Zebra Books in December 1993. Her second Dr. Amy Prescott mystery will be published by Zebra Books in September 1994. You may write to Louise c/o Zebra Books.

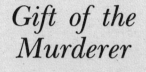

Gift of the
Murderer

by

Toni L. P. Kelner

I was glad I had saved Liz's present for last. Maybe it would help make up for Mrs. Hamilton's earlier abuse. "I believe this is for you," I said, handing her the glittery gift bag.

"For me?" she said, looking pleased. "Who did this come from?"

"A good elf never tells," I said solemnly. "Union rules."

She smiled and opened the bag. I could see my cousin Clifford watching from where he was playing Christmas carols on his guitar. The present was from him, but he was too shy to want Liz to know that. Liz reached into the bag and pulled out a long knife, the blade smeared with something dark.

"What on earth?" she asked.

"I don't know," I said. I looked over toward Clifford, but he looked as confused as I was. "I think there's been some kind of a mistake," I said, but was interrupted by a shriek from a few feet away.

Mrs. Hamilton had keeled over in her wheelchair, and one of the other residents pointed at her and shrieked again.

Liz dropped the knife back into the bag and thrust it toward me so she could run to Mrs. Hamilton. I was only a few steps behind her, though I didn't know that there was anything I would be able to do.

Liz put her hand on Mrs. Hamilton's back as if to straighten her up and then jerked her hand away. I was the only one close enough to see that her hand was covered in blood. A hole through the canvas back of the wheelchair matched the old woman's bloody wound.

I think Liz and I realized at the same instant that the smears on that knife had to be blood, which meant that I was carrying the weapon that had been used on Mrs. Hamilton.

I'll admit that I didn't have much Christmas spirit when my husband Richard and I came home to Byerly. My grandfather had been gone less than a year, and I wasn't sure that I wanted to celebrate without him. Still, I was trying to get into a holiday mood and had even agreed to help my cousin Vasti throw a party at the old folk's home a few days before Christmas. The last thing I expected was to end up investigating a stabbing.

Of course, if I had had one lick of sense, I would have called Vasti and canceled when the storm started that afternoon. But no, I let Richard talk me into going out in the middle of the worst ice storm to hit the mountains of North Carolina in years. It took us twenty minutes to chip out the car, and the roads were coated with ice.

I held just as tight as I could to the armrest the entire time we were driving and tried my darnedest not to back-seat drive. Finally I couldn't help but say, "There's a stop sign just around that curve. You might want to start slowing down.' "

"Yes, dear," Richard said.

"Sorry. It's just that driving in this mess makes me nervous."

"Hey, I live in Massachusetts. No puny North Carolina winter can scare me."

After several years up North, I should have been used to winter weather, too, but I wasn't. "Of course in Boston they have snowplows to keep the roads clear," I reasoned. "And driving in ice isn't anything like driving in snow."

"Yes, dear."

"Sorry," I said again. I managed to stay quiet for another couple of minutes, but then said, "Take your time. We've got half an hour before we're due at the old folks' home."

"Isn't it supposed to be 'nursing home'? Or maybe these days it's a senior citizens' center."

"You're probably right." I felt the car slide and gritted my teeth. Normally nothing in Byerly was more than ten minutes away from anything else, but we had already been on the road for twenty minutes and we weren't there yet.

"You're just afraid we're going to get into an accident and you'll have to go to the hospital dressed like that," Richard said with a grin.

I pulled down the sun visor on my side, looked into the mirror on the back, and made a face at myself. "Do I look as foolish as I feel?"

" 'The little foolery that wise men have makes a great show.' *As You Like It*, Act I, Scene 1," he replied.

"Thanks loads. That makes me feel much better." Thanks to Vasti, I was dressed in green tights and a red garment that Richard said was a jerkin. My coat covered most of the outfit, but not the shoes and hat. The bells on the curled toes of my red slippers jingled every time I moved, and the plume on the Robin Hood hat constantly fluttered in and out of the corner of my sight.

"I think you look adorable," Richard added. "Just what I'd like to find in my Christmas stocking. Except that an elf shouldn't be frowning. Maybe we should have a little elf practice so you can learn to go 'hee hee' and 'ho ho' and important stuff like that."

I looked at him accusingly. "You're enjoying this, aren't you?"

He grinned.

"Keep it up," I said. "I'll tell the other members of your department that Boston College's Shakespeare specialist has been quoting from *Rudolph the Red-Nosed Reindeer.*"

"Such cruelty," he said, shaking his head. "And so close to Christmas, too. You're liable to get coal in your stocking instead of that new software you've been hinting about. Just think of how happy those senior citizens are going to be when you and the others show up."

"They're going to laugh their fool heads off at us," I grumbled.

"You don't want to spoil the party, now do you? Remember what the Bard said. 'A woeful hostess brooks not merry guests.' *The Rape of Lucrece*."

"Vasti's the hostess, not me. I'm just an elf."

"Well, if you didn't want to be an elf, you shouldn't have volunteered."

"I *didn't* volunteer," I protested. "Vasti volunteered me." Vasti had originally arranged for four cousins to be elves at the Christmas party she was throwing at the Byerly Nursing Home, but when our pretty cousin Ilene got a better offer and backed out, Vasti was left one elf short.

To be fair to Vasti, I hadn't fought her too hard when she suggested I take Ilene's place. I was hoping that the party would inspire at least a little of the Christmas spirit I was missing this year.

I shoved the feather on that darned hat back into place and looked at Richard in his blue jeans and Shakespeare sweatshirt more than a little resentfully. "Vasti could probably come up with a costume for you."

"No, thanks," he said. "I don't look as good in tights as you do."

Finally I saw the sign for the nursing home. "There it is. Turn just past that post," I said, and was glad when we managed to turned past the post and not into it. Not surprisingly, there weren't many cars in the parking lot. Most folks had enough sense to stay home on a night like this.

Still the place looked like it was ready for a Christmas party. Colored lights outlined the entrance, and there was a wreath in every window. I recognized Vasti's style. As far as she's concerned, if it's worth doing, then it's worth overdoing.

With Richard and me helping each other across the parking lot, we just barely kept from falling on our behinds. Vasti was pacing across the lobby just inside the front door. I guessed that as the hostess of this shindig, she rated a higher rank than I did. Instead of an elf suit, she was dressed in a red velvet dress with white fur around the sleeves and collar, and had a perky Santa hat on top of her brown curls. I would have thought boots would fit the costume better than red patent-leather pumps, but Vasti always did have a weakness for high heels.

"It's about time!" she said when she saw us. "I didn't think y'all would *ever* get here."

"You said seven o'clock," I said, checking my watch. "It's only a quarter till now." I thought that was pretty good, considering the ice storm.

"Seven? Laurie Anne, I know I said six-thirty. The triplets are late, too."

I thought about arguing with her, but decided it wasn't worth the effort. "Well, we're here now."

"You can leave your coats in the closet behind the reception desk," she said, "and then come on down to the recreation room." She tapped her foot while we hung up our coats, and then led the way.

About halfway down the hallway, she stopped to let Richard and me pass her.

"What's the matter?" I asked, stopping too.

"Oh nothing," she said, and started up again. "I guess I should have gotten you a bigger elf suit."

I followed her as best I could while trying to catch my reflection in every shiny surface we passed. "It doesn't look too tight to me," I said.

"Now don't you worry about it," Vasti said. "Most of these old geezers can't see far enough to notice figure flaws."

What figure flaws? Maybe I wasn't Hollywood material, but I didn't think I looked *that* bad.

By now we had reached the recreation room. I had to admit that whoever Vasti had talked into doing the work had done a wonderful job of turning the institutional room into a place where you didn't mind having a party. Tinsel garlands and electric candles were scattered all around the room, and each of the tables circling the room had a silk poinsettia centerpiece.

179

There was an enormous Christmas tree in the center of the room, decorated with lots of blinking lights and shiny balls. A long table filled with platters of party food lined one wall, with punch bowls on either end. There was a small platform in one corner with music stands.

"Did I tell you that Clifford is coming to play Christmas carols?" Vasti asked.

"That's a great idea."

"I was just going to play tapes, but he said he wanted to come." She lowered her voice to what she thought was a conspiratorial whisper and said, "Don't tell him I told you, but I hear he's sweet on Liz Sanderson, one of the nurses here. I think she's Hoyle Sanderson's little sister. You remember Hoyle, don't you? Now, he's blond but she's a redhead, so I can't decide if it's natural or not."

"Is Clifford serious about her?"

"Oh he's serious enough, but he's too doggone shy to tell her that. I don't know what on earth he's afraid of."

I did. I had been painfully shy in high school and through a good part of college. Clifford was afraid he'd be laughed at, just like I had been.

Vasti went on, "I've got half a mind to tell Liz that he's got a crush on her just to get it over with. Then maybe he'll quit mooning over her."

"Vasti, don't you dare."

"Why not? The worst that could happen is that she'd tell me that she's not interested and ask me to break it to him gently."

The problem was, Vasti had never broken anything to anyone gently in her whole life. "Vasti," I started, but then reconsidered. If I left it alone, she'd likely forget about it anyway. Instead I said, "What do you want us to do? Everything looks pretty well set up already."

She picked a clipboard up off of a table and made a big show of looking at it. "Laurie Anne, you can arrange those Secret Santa gifts under the tree so they look pretty." She pointed to several boxes filled with wrapped packages. "You and the other elves will be handing them out later."

"Isn't that Santa Claus's job?" I said.

"No, because Arthur and I are going to be mingling and making sure that everybody is having a good time."

"Where is Arthur anyway?" Richard asked.

"He had a City Council meeting. Civic leadership takes up *so* much of his time." She sighed theatrically, which would have been more effective if I didn't know how much she loved being the wife of a city councilman. "I just hope he can make it through the storm."

She looked at her clipboard again. "Richard, those boxes on the table have cookies in them. You can set them out on those platters. All right?"

" 'I will be correspondent to command,' " he said. *"The Tempest,* Act I, Scene 2."

She paused a minute before deciding that he had said yes, and then said, "Now y'all two get busy, and I'm going to find a phone to see if the triplets are coming or not."

As I reached for a package, she added, "Laurie Anne, you might better be careful about bending over. I don't know how much strain those tights can take." With that burst of Christmas cheer, she disappeared into the kitchen.

Being an adult, I didn't let her comments bother me. Well, I stuck my tongue out at her retreating back, but I did put the presents around the tree like she had asked. Then I went to see how Richard was doing.

"Aren't you done yet?" I asked in what I thought was a fair imitation of Vasti's soprano. "What on earth are you waiting for?"

"I'm trying, but Vasti baked enough cookies for an army," he said.

"Heaven forbid!" I said. "Vasti doesn't bake. She must have got someone else to bake them for her." I looked inside one of the boxes. "See? I know those are Aunt Nora's double-butter cookies. She always decorates them so pretty, I'd recognize them anywhere." I reached for a particularly fetching reindeer and then paused.

"Richard," I said, "tell me the truth. Do I look heavy in this outfit?"

He stepped back and studied me from a couple of angles. "To quote the Bard," he said, and then gave a piercing wolf whistle.

"Richard! This is a hospital. Sort of, anyway." I looked around to make sure no nurses had run in to see what was the matter. "Thank you, love, but that's not the kind of answer I was expecting."

He shrugged. "I calls them like I sees them."

"And what play did that come from?"

"Who said anything about a play? That's what Shakespeare used to say to Mrs. Shakespeare."

"Oh yeah? Then why did he only leave her his second best bed in his will?"

Vasti's return interrupted our literary discussion. "The triplets didn't answer their phone, so I guess that they're on their way. Richard, are you planning to finish that today?"

Richard saluted. "Yes, Mrs. Claus. Sure thing, Mrs. Claus. Right away, Mrs. Claus." Even Vasti had to grin as Richard made a show of rushing around like a chicken with its head cut off.

Richard and I had just finished arranging refreshments to Vasti's satisfaction when Idelle, Odelle, and Carlelle arrived, with Clifford in tow. The triplets were dressed in elf costumes like mine, but Clifford had escaped Vasti's penchant for costume and was just wearing a nice red and white sweater with his blue jeans. All four of them were carrying more wrapped presents.

"It's about time," Vasti said. "The party starts in five minutes."

Actually we still had twenty minutes left, but Idelle knew how useless it was to argue with Vasti as well as I did. "Sorry, Vasti. We had to finish wrapping the last batch of presents after work, and the roads are just terrible."

182

Then the sisters noticed me and Richard, and, as if one, said, "Laurie Anne! Richard! We didn't know you were coming! Just let us hug your necks!"

Richard and I were immediately surrounded by hugging and kissing cousins, followed by less effusive but equally sincere greetings from Clifford.

"Doesn't Laurie Anne make a cute elf?" Idelle asked her sisters.

"I don't know how Richard is keeping his hands off her," Odelle agreed.

Carlelle said, "He just needs a little encouragement. Vasti, where'd you hang the mistletoe?"

"I didn't think mistletoe would be appropriate at a party for senior citizens," Vasti said stiffly.

"That's all right," Idelle said. "We brought some." She dug into her pocketbook, produced a sprig tied with red ribbon, and held it up high over my head. "Richard, Laurie Anne needs a kiss."

" 'The kiss you take is better than you give,' " said Richard, and he kissed me soundly, much to the delight of the triplets. *"Troilus and Cressida,* Act III, Scene 5."

"That's enough of that," Vasti said. "We've got work to do." She handed out assignments, and we went to work.

Richard and I were hanging the mistletoe when he whispered, "How am I supposed to tell the triplets apart when they're dressed alike?"

"Check their necklaces," I said. "Each one is wearing her initial." Actually I was used to the triplets dressing identically most of the time, so this was no worse than usual. I did notice that while my outfit was nearly the same as what the sisters were wearing, their jerkins were a good three inches shorter than mine.

Vasti must have realized the same thing, because I heard her say, "I didn't realize your outfits were so short when I bought them."

All three of the sisters raised their eyebrows in innocent surprise, even though we all knew that Carlelle was an expert seamstress and that hemming those jerkins wouldn't have taken her any time at all.

"Short skirts won't do you much good around here," Vasti said with a sniff. "Even you three aren't desperate enough to chase after men old enough to be your grandfather."

"But there's always the doctors," Idelle said cheerfully.

"And the orderlies," Carlelle added.

"And maybe even male nurses," Odelle said.

"I see y'all have given this some thought," Vasti said. *"Some* of us are here out of the goodness of our hearts to spread some Christmas cheer."

Idelle made a rude noise. "Who do you think you're fooling, Vasti? Everybody knows that the only reason you put this party together is publicity for Arthur. Showing off how civic-minded he is."

"Well, helping out a husband is better than trying to catch one," Vasti snapped.

I decided it was time for some peace on Earth. "As long as the old folks have a good time, it doesn't really matter why we're here, does it?"

"I suppose not," Idelle admitted.

"And speaking of old folks," Vasti had to add, "we better get a move on. Our guests will be here any time now."

I was arranging the packages the triplets had brought under the Christmas tree when Clifford came up behind me and touched my shoulder. He was carrying a silver gift bag with a cascade of curling green and red ribbons tied around the handle.

"Laurie Anne, you're going to be handing out the gifts, aren't you?"

"The triplets and I are," I said.

He held out the bag. "Could you add this one to the stack?"

"Sure." I didn't see a tag. "Who's it for?"

"It's for Liz Sanderson. She's a nurse here."

Knowing how shy he could be, I didn't say a word, just put the bag under the tree. He was still standing there when I turned back around.

"I thought it'd be nice if she got a Secret Santa gift, too. All the residents are getting them," he said.

"That's very thoughtful of you, Clifford."

"I just didn't want her to feel left out. She works real hard."

"I'm sure she does."

He nodded a few times rapidly, and then said, "I better go tune my guitar. Bye now." He walked away quickly.

Richard approached while Clifford was escaping and asked, "What's the matter with him?"

"I think he doth protest too much," I misquoted, and explained what Clifford was up to.

"Ah, young love," Richard said. "Reminds me of my first Christmas gift to a girl."

"What was that?"

"A paperback copy of *Romeo and Juliet* with photos from the Zeffirelli film. I hoped it would inspire the lovely Jennifer to imagine me as Leonard Whiting and herself as Olivia Hussey."

"Did it work?"

"Yes and no. She fell in love with Leonard Whiting."

"Her loss," I said, and gave him a consoling kiss before finishing up with the packages. "There," I said when done. "As pretty as a Christmas card."

"I'll say," said Richard with a grin.

"I meant the tree."

"Of course," he said innocently.

We wandered over to the refreshment table, but the triplets had everything under control. Vasti rushed by a time or two with clipboard in hand, but I couldn't figure out why since we had finished all the work.

"It's time," she finally wailed, "and Arthur isn't here yet. The secretary at City Hall said he left ages ago."

"He probably got held up by the storm," Odelle said.

"It was terrible driving over here," Carlelle added.

"Like driving on a sheet of glass," Idelle said.

"But we can't have a Christmas party without Santa Claus,"

Vasti protested. Then she looked at Richard. "Richard, do you suppose—?"

"No," Richard said. "For one, I'm not Santa Claus material." That was true enough. You didn't often see a lanky, brown-haired, beardless Santa. "And for another, you haven't got a spare red suit."

Vasti nodded, acknowledging defeat. "Oh, well. The photographer from the *Byerly Gazette* probably won't make it either."

"Thank the Lord for small favors," I whispered to Richard. "I am not about to have my picture taken while wearing an elf suit." Especially not for publication in the local paper.

Vasti looked at her clipboard one last time and nodded decisively. "We may as well get this show on the road. Clifford, play "Jingle Bells." Richard, you can serve punch. Elves, y'all go stand around the tree. And smile everybody! It's Christmas."

We all obeyed, right down to the smiles. Like she said, it was Christmas. The double doors on the end of the room opened, and the nursing home residents slowly started coming in. When I saw the happy expressions on their faces, I decided it had all been worth it. Driving in the storm, doing what Vasti said, even wearing the elf suit.

The last folks to come in were in wheelchairs, mostly pushed by nurses, and I looked to see if I could spot the young lady who had caught Clifford's eye. I knew her as soon as I saw her. She was by far the youngest nurse there, and no matter what Vasti said, her red hair looked natural to me. There was just a sprinkling of freckles over her nose, and she had a curvy little figure that would have looked a lot nicer in an elf suit than in that starched nurse's uniform.

"Cute, isn't she?" Odelle whispered.

"Not bad, if you like them young and pretty," Idelle said.

"Look at Clifford," Carlelle said with a giggle. "He looks like he's been struck by lightening."

Well, not quite, but pretty close. If Liz had looked in his direction, there was no way she could have mistaken his expression for anything other than unabashed adoration. Then he caught himself and concentrated on his guitar playing.

"Isn't love wonderful?" Carlelle sighed.

"You should know," Idelle said. "You've been in love three times this week yourself."

Odelle said, "When she gets a look at that doctor, she might try for four."

The three of them moved to converge on an admittedly attractive doctor. Meanwhile, the residents were converging on the refreshment table, and I went to help Vasti dispense cookies and other goodies. Richard was doing a booming business filling glasses, and I could tell he was dispensing Shakespearean quotes along with the punch.

Once the first flurry was over, I managed to edge over to where the lovely Liz was making sure a particularly frail-looking patient had everything she needed. Just to help out, of course, not because I was nosy.

"Are y'all having a good time?" I asked them both.

The older lady looked confused. "She wants to know if you're having a good time," Liz said in a much louder voice. The lady bobbed her head and nibbled on a cookie.

"Mrs. Good is a little hard of hearing," Liz explained to me, "but she really is enjoying herself. They all are. We really appreciate y'all coming over here."

"It's our pleasure," I said, and was glad to realize that I was telling the truth. "I'm Laura Fleming, by the way."

She looked a little confused, so I sighed to myself and added, "Some people call me Laurie Anne." As a matter of fact, almost everyone in Byerly did, no matter how hard I tried to change their ways.

"That's right. You're the one who lives in Boston, aren't you?"

I nodded. "There aren't many secrets in Byerly."

She smiled. "No, there aren't. Besides, I know some of your cousins. Ilene and Vasti, of course. And Clifford."

Had I noticed a certain emphasis on that last name? "I think he mentioned you to me," I said nonchalantly.

"Did he?" she said, and she didn't sound a bit nonchalant. She looked over to where he was playing and singing "Christmas in Dixie." "He's got such a nice voice. Reminds me of Garth Brooks."

Yes, there was definitely attraction on both sides. Now, how would I get them under the mistletoe? Stop that, I told myself firmly. I was getting to be as bad as Vasti.

Speaking of Vasti, she was getting ready to speak. She waved for Clifford to stop singing, and stood next to him. "Is everybody having a nice time?" she asked in a voice loud enough that even Mrs. Good would have no trouble hearing her. She waited for an affirmative murmur, and then said, "Well, we're all real glad. I do have some bad news for you, though. Santa Claus got stuck in the ice out there, and he's not going to be able to make it. But don't you worry! He sent some of his very favorite elves with a whole bunch of presents for you folks. Y'all just stay where you're at, and the elves will be coming around in a minute."

That sounded like a cue for us elves, so we met by the Christmas tree. Vasti and her clipboard joined us.

She said, "Now all of the packages are labeled, so you shouldn't have any problem handing them out."

I said, "How do we know who's who?"

"I sent around pins for everybody with their names on them a couple of days ago. They're *supposed* to be wearing them."

Now that she mentioned it, I saw that all of the residents where wearing red and green badges. Whatever faults Vasti might have, she did know how to arrange a party.

Vasti consulted her clipboard and asked the triplets, "Did y'all put together a list of what you got for people? I want to cross-reference it with my Secret Santa list."

"We didn't quite finish typing it up," Carlelle said in a tone that meant that they hadn't even started yet. "You don't need it right now, do you?"

"I suppose not," Vasti said. "Laurie Anne, you would not believe what some of these people wanted for Christmas."

She rolled her eyes. "All kinds of candy when they know it's not good for them and frilly lingerie they don't need any more than the man in the moon. One old coot wanted dirty magazines. Now what good are dirty magazines going to do an old man?"

"Maybe looking is better than nothing," I said.

"And what if he gave himself a heart attack?" she asked indignantly. "How would I explain that? I told the triplets to just ignore any silly gift ideas like that."

The triplets nodded dutifully.

Vasti said, "Now you four get busy, and I'll go see how the refreshments are holding out." She clattered away.

"Did you three get stuck buying and wrapping *all* of the presents?" I asked. There were thirty or forty residents, and it looked like there was a gift for each of them under the tree.

"Well, most of them," Carlelle said. "Every patient is somebody else's Secret Santa, and those that are able did their own shopping. We just shopped for those who couldn't."

Idelle said, "You didn't think Vasti did any of it, did you?"

"I think she likes to organize things so she doesn't have to do any of the work herself," Odelle said.

"That's not fair," Carlelle protested. "She works hard telling everybody else what to do." The other triplets and I snickered, and she realized how that had sounded. "You know what I mean. Besides, we love shopping, now don't we?"

The other two sisters nodded.

"Laurie Anne, I'd love to come see you in Boston," Idelle said. "Christmas shopping must be so much fun with all those stores you have up there."

"To tell you the truth, Richard did most of our shopping this year. I just couldn't get into the mood," I said.

"Really?" Carlelle said. "I just love Christmas shopping. All the sales and the people and the Christmas music and all."

Actually most years I had felt the same. It's just that every time I went into a store this year, I kept seeing gifts that would have been perfect for Paw. And Paw wouldn't be here this Christmas.

"Anyway," I said, not wanting to pursue the subject, "we better get going before Vasti Claus sics the reindeer on us."

While we handed out gifts, Clifford led the residents in Christmas carols. If Liz noticed that he was watching her while he sang, she didn't show it directly. Still, she tended more to the residents who were close to the singing than to those who weren't.

Apparently the Secret Santas had done a good job choosing gifts. I heard right many ooh's and aah's. I had always heard that Christmas was for children, but you wouldn't have known it from watching these people. They were having themselves a good old time.

I was on my way back to the tree to pick up another gift when I saw one man having troubles getting his package open. "Can I give you a hand with that, Mr. Biggers?" I said, after checking his nametag.

"That would be real nice," he said.

I pulled the paper off for him, broke the tape holding the box shut with my thumbnail, and then put it back on his lap so he could open it himself.

"Thank you kindly." He pulled the box top off, looked inside, and grinned like the cat who ate the canary. "My, my, my," was all he said.

I looked in to see what had him so pleased. The box was filled with copies of *Playboy* and *Penthouse*. Mr. Biggers lifted a few pages, peered inside, and grinned even wider. "My, my, my."

I saw Vasti approaching, and I guess Mr. Biggers did, too, because he slid the lid back on top of the box.

"Did you get a nice present?" Vasti asked brightly.

"I sure did," he said. "Just what I wanted."

"Aren't you going to show it to me?" she said.

"Oh, this isn't anything you'd be interested in," he said, with a sideways look at me. "Just a bunch of sports magazines. I dearly love reading about a good game."

190

"Well, I hope you enjoy them." She clattered away.

Mr. Biggers winked at me and said, "Merry Christmas, young lady."

I wondered if the gift had been purchased by one of the triplets or all three in collusion. Even as children, there had been nothing they enjoyed half as much as putting one over on Vasti. No wonder they hadn't made her a list.

Encouraged by my success in spreading Christmas cheer, I looked around to see if there was anyone else I could speak to. I saw a wheelchair-bound woman off in a corner by herself. "Hello there Miz . . ." She wasn't wearing a name tag, and only looked at me balefully when I paused for her to insert her name. She probably never had been a very pretty woman, but with that expression, she was downright intimidating. My Aunt Maggie would have wanted to know how much she'd charge to haunt a house. "Hello, there," I finally said. "Did you get a nice present?"

She mumbled something, and I realized that only the left side of her face was actually moving. The right side just sagged.

"I beg your pardon?" I said.

She grimaced and mumbled louder, but I still couldn't understand. Fortunately another patient walked up with two cups of punch. His nametag said "Frank Morgan."

"I'm afraid Mrs. Hamilton is a little hard to understand right now," he said. "Just give her another week in physical therapy, and she'll be quoting Shakespeare like that young fellow who was pouring the punch."

Mrs. Hamilton said something, and this time I caught enough of it to tell that it wasn't very nice.

Mr. Morgan winced, but just said, "Here's your punch, Sadie," and tried to hand it to her. Instead of taking the cup, she shoved it aside, knocking it out of Mr. Morgan's hand and splashing punch onto the floor.

"I'll go get something to wipe that up," I said, but Liz must have been seen what had happened because she appeared with a paper towel.

"Accidents will happen," she said smoothly, and wiped it up. "Mrs. Hamilton, did you want another cup of punch?"

I swear I could see the blood rushing to Mrs. Hamilton's face. She struggled for a long moment with what she wanted to say before finally spitting out, "BITCH!"

There was a moment of silence, and I knew the whole room must have heard her. Liz went white, and I realized just how young she was. She was probably still in her early twenties, too young to be able to take that without it hurting her feelings.

Mr. Morgan said, "Maybe I should take Sadie to visit with the others." He started to push the wheelchair but had only gone a few steps when Mrs. Hamilton used her good arm to switch on the electric wheelchair and move away from his grasp. I saw rather than heard him sigh, and he followed along after her.

Everyone else in the room went back to what they had been doing, leaving me and Liz still standing there.

"Are you all right?" I asked.

"I shouldn't let her upset me like that," she said, more to herself than to me. "She's old and she's real sick."

"I'm sure she didn't mean it."

"Actually she probably did," Liz said with a half smile. "Sadie Hamilton has been after me ever since I started working here, probably because she knows how young I am. The other nurses keep telling me that if I can put up with her, I can put up with anything."

"Is she that bad?"

"Any of the residents can get grumpy sometimes, but Mrs. Hamilton is just plain mean. She's been even worse the past few weeks. She had a stroke the week after Thanksgiving, and she pretty much lost the use of the right half of her body. She could probably get some of it back in physical therapy if she'd just try, but she won't. She just mumbles the most awful things at us when we try to show her. How can you help someone like that?"

"You can't," I said.

Liz nodded. "I know, but I have to keep trying." She spotted the punch glass on the floor and picked it up. "I better get back to work."

"Me, too," I said, and returned to my station at the Christmas tree to finish handing out presents. We were just about done when I saw the bag for Liz still sitting there. That's when I got the idea of giving it to her to cheer her up and instead handed her the knife that had been used to stab Mrs. Hamilton.

Liz had been trained well. Even after seeing the wound, she hesitated only a second before checking for a pulse.

"Is she . . . ?" I asked.

"She's alive," Liz said, and then called out, "Get Dr. Buchanan!" Another nurse ran to comply.

"You better call the police, too," I told Liz in a quieter voice. Liz nodded, and I saw the doctor coming in at a run. I stood back out of the way while he and Liz exchanged a few words and then wheeled Mrs. Hamilton out of the room, still slumped over in the wheelchair.

I looked around for Richard. The other residents didn't seem as upset as I felt they should have been. After a slight pause, they kept on eating cake and drinking punch as if nothing had happened. Even the woman who had been shrieking had quieted down and was nodding in time with the carol Clifford was playing.

Of course, I told myself, they didn't know Mrs. Hamilton had been stabbed. As far as they knew, she had succumbed to another stroke or maybe a heart attack, and probably neither of those were unusual around here. Should I tell them? I couldn't think of a good reason why I should, at least until we knew more.

I finally spotted Richard coming out of the kitchen with a tray of cookies. I met him at the refreshment table and pulled him into a corner.

"What's the matter?" he asked as soon as he got a good look at me.

"Didn't you hear the scream?" When he shook his head, I told him what had happened.

As soon as I finished, he said, "Are you sure that's the knife that was used on her?"

"Of course I'm not sure," I snapped, "but I would hope that there aren't any other bloodstained knives floating around the place."

"Is there anything else in the bag?"

"I don't know." I pulled the bag open, but all I saw was the knife and some red tissue paper. "I don't want to touch anything." I looked around the room. "The awful thing is that whoever did it is probably still in here. I mean, we'd have noticed an outsider."

"I assume the police are on the way."

"I hope so. I told Liz to call, and I'm sure the doctor would want them here, too." We stayed there watching the party uneasily and listening for the siren which would mean that the police had arrived. Instead Liz came over to me.

"Laurie Anne? Chief Norton wants to talk to you." Richard nodded, and I followed her.

"Is she here?" I asked as we walked.

"No, she's on the phone." She led me to a paneled office marked "Dr. Buchanan." "Chief Norton is on line three." She closed the door behind her as she left.

I picked up the phone and punched the blinking button. At first, all I heard was sirens and yells. "Junior?"

"Is that you, Laurie Anne?" she said, speaking loudly enough to be heard over the cacophony.

"It's me."

"Hold on just a minute, will you? I've got myself one hell of a mess to deal with out here. Three carloads of fools drinking beer ran into one another, and now they want to fight about whose fault it was."

That explained the noises I was hearing. I could just picture Junior in her blue jean jacket and cowboy boots wading into the middle of it. Even though she was only five foot three, she'd have them in order pretty quickly.

I had known Junior since we were five years old, and even then she wanted to follow in her father's footsteps as chief of the Byerly police department. Her name was the result of Andy Norton's wish for a son to name after himself. When his fifth daughter was born, he named her Junior. Naturally his sixth child was a boy. He became Andy Norton III, Trey for short, and Junior's deputy.

Junior finally came back to the phone. "Are you still there?"

"I'm here."

"Tell me, Laurie Anne. Why is it that every time you come to town, something like this happens? No, don't answer that. I don't have time. Tell me what's going on up there."

I quickly told her what little I knew.

Junior said, "The doctor says that Mrs. Hamilton is going to make it, but it was damned close. Another inch or so, and she'd be gone. I hear you gave Liz Sanderson a gift bag with the knife that did the job."

"I think so."

"Where is it now?"

"I've got it." I hadn't known what else to do with it.

"Good. Don't let it out of your sight. Liz said there was no tag. Do you know who it was from?"

"Yes," I admitted reluctantly. "My cousin Clifford asked me to give it to her."

"Is that so?" she asked, and I just knew she had raised one eyebrow.

"Not the knife," I added hurriedly. "I was watching him when Liz pulled it out of the bag, and he was as surprised as she was. The bag wasn't sealed or anything, and it's been under the Christmas tree all evening. Anyone could have seen it and put the knife in."

"We'll see. What else was in the bag?"

"I haven't looked."

"I imagine you've got fingerprints all over the outside by

195

now, so we won't worry about that, but don't put your hand inside. Just hold the bag by the bottom and spill out whatever's in there."

I cleared some papers off of the desk blotter, and then did as she instructed. The knife fell out first and was followed by two other items. "It's a Garth Brooks cassette tape, still sealed, and a little gold cardboard box. Like a gift box."

"See if you can use a pencil or something to open that box without touching it."

"I'll try." Fortunately Clifford hadn't taped it shut, and I used two paper clips to get it open. "It's a pair of gold earrings. Hoops." I leaned closer. "They aren't real gold, but they are pretty."

"Anything else in the box?"

I poked around with a pen. "Just cotton padding."

"How about in the bag?"

"Tissue paper."

I heard someone on Junior's end call her name, and Junior told me, "Hold on." A few minutes later she said, "Now what kind of knife is it? And remember not to touch it."

To tell the truth, I wouldn't have touched it even if she had asked me. "It looks like a regular kitchen knife. Wooden handle, used but not real old. It looks shinier along the point, like it's been sharpened."

"It would have to be right sharp to go through the wheelchair and into Mrs. Hamilton's back."

"I suppose so."

I heard someone yelling for her again, and Junior must have dropped the phone she was talking on, because I heard it bounce off something. Or someone.

This time she was gone longer, and I could hear her cursing long before she came back to the phone. "Laurie Anne, I've got a problem."

"Are you all right?"

"I am, but one of these fools just hit Trey upside the head and knocked him cold." Before I could ask, she added, "I'm sure he's going to be fine, but now I'm going to have to deliver this baby all by my lonesome."

"What baby?"

"I don't have time to talk about it right now, Laurie Anne. Is there a Bible anywhere around there?"

I didn't even ask, I just looked around the shelves. "I don't see one."

"Well, get a book, any book, and open it up."

I grabbed a *Physician's Desk Reference*.

"Put your left hand on the book and raise your right hand."

I did so, wondering what she was up to.

"Shoot, now how does it go?" Junior said. "Do you, Laurie Anne Fleming swear to uphold the laws of Byerly, North Carolina, and the United States, not necessarily in that order. Say, 'I do.' "

I said, "I do."

"Then by the power invested in me as Chief of Police in Byerly, I hereby make you a deputy of the Byerly Police Department, with all the rights and responsibilities I decide to let you have. You can put your hand down now."

"Junior—"

"Laurie Anne, I wouldn't ask you if I didn't have to, but I don't have any idea of how long it's going to be before I can get there. I'd ask for someone from the county or the state to take over, but they're all tied up with the ice storm same as I am. Besides, you and I both know that you're going to be asking questions anyway, don't we?"

"Probably," I admitted. I was getting a reputation around Byerly for curiosity.

"That's what I figured. This way you're obliged to tell me everything you find out, not just the stuff that doesn't affect your family."

That smarted, but she was right. I had avoided giving Junior information in the past when I thought it might cause more harm than good. "I've always told you everything eventually, haven't I?"

"Yes, you have, and that's why I'm trusting you now. At

the very least, I need you to make sure that whoever it was that tried to kill Mrs. Hamilton doesn't try again. If you find out anything else in the meantime, that's fine, too. All right?"

I could think of a good dozen reasons why I should tell her no, but of course what I said was, "All right, Junior." If she could deliver a baby in the middle of an ice storm, I could do this.

"Good. I'll be there when I can. Bye." She didn't wait for me to say goodbye back.

I hung up the phone and maneuvered the knife and Clifford's presents back into the gift bag while I tried to decide what I should do next. Like Junior had said, the first priority was to protect Mrs. Hamilton. Obviously someone had to be with her at all times. The question was, who? What if I used the very person who wanted to kill her as a guard? Who could I trust?

Myself, of course, and Richard. And Vasti and the triplets and Clifford. Then I stopped. Junior was trusting me to be at least somewhat objective, and if they hadn't been my cousins, I wouldn't have crossed them off the list so quickly. I had to be fair about it. I was going to assume that Richard was innocent no matter what, but that was as far as I could go without more proof. I could post Richard in Mrs. Hamilton's room, but I didn't think he'd be thrilled about my trying to find a murderer on my own. And actually, I wasn't too thrilled about the idea myself.

A knife in the back sounded like a solitary act to me, so maybe I could conclude that only one person was involved. If so, that meant that the solution was to use two guards at a time. That would have to do.

Liz was waiting for me outside the office, pacing nervously.

"Is Chief Norton on the way?" she asked.

"I'm afraid not. She's tied up because of the storm."

She looked even more nervous. "Then what are we going to do?"

"Don't worry," I said, trying to sound a lot more confident than I felt. "She's deputized me temporarily."

198

She didn't look impressed, and I can't say that I blamed her. I don't know that I would have trusted a deputy in green tights myself.

"Where's Dr. Buchanan?" I asked. "I need to ask him some questions."

"He's in the infirmary."

"Can you show me the way?" She nodded, and I followed her.

I had never liked nursing homes. They smell too much like hospitals, and they're too quiet. Now that I knew that there was an attempted murderer on the loose, this place was downright creepy. I stuck close to Liz and watched all around as we walked.

The infirmary consisted of a treatment room and a small ward of half a dozen beds. One bed had been curtained off, and Dr. Buchanan had just closed the curtain behind him when we came in.

"Dr. Buchanan? My name is Laura Fleming. Chief Norton has deputized me to take charge here." I thought that the phrase "take charge" was properly official without promising too much. "I'd like to ask you some questions about Mrs. Hamilton's injury."

"Fine," he said, looking at his watch, "if you can ask them in a hurry."

"Are you going somewhere?" I asked, following him as he kept on moving. Liz trailed along behind me.

"I just got a call from the hospital in Hickory. I see patients there as well as looking after the residents here, and they need me tonight. There have been a number of weather-related incidents."

"What about Mrs. Hamilton?"

"She should be fine. The wound was deep but no vital organs were hit, and there was relatively little loss of blood. We got to her before she could go into shock. The nurses will monitor her for complications, of course, but I don't foresee any difficulties."

"I see," I said, a little breathless from trying to keep up with him. "Could you slow down a bit?"

"Sorry."

"Does what you said mean that this wasn't an attempted murder after all?"

"Oh, I wouldn't say that. Another inch and the knife would have hit her heart. I'd guess that the heart was the intended target, but the difficulty of stabbing through the wheelchair back deflected the aim."

"Does that imply that the person knew what he or she was doing?"

"Combat knowledge, you mean?"

"Or medical," I said. Liz didn't look happy at that suggestion.

Dr. Buchanan stopped a second to consider it. "In most groups of people that would be a reasonable assumption, but not here. You see, most of our residents spend a fair amount of time reading up on their bodily processes. Comes with growing old, I suspect. Most of the residents' library is made up of medical books of one kind or another. Anyone here could easily have researched the issue."

By now we were at the front door and Dr. Buchanan was pulling on an overcoat. He asked, "Was there anything else? I really need to get to the hospital."

At the moment I didn't have any other questions. I wasn't sure what Junior would say about my letting a possible suspect leave the scene of the crime, but I didn't think I had any right to stop him, under the circumstances. Besides, I was almost certain he had not been in the party for very long after the triplets made their play for him. The three of them together did tend to scare men off.

I said, "I guess not. Chief Norton will probably want to talk with you later on."

"Fine. I expect to be at the hospital for some time to come." He turned to Liz. "Let me know if there are any problems with Mrs. Hamilton or any of the others."

"Yes, doctor. Be careful out there."

I must admit I would have preferred for him to stay. A doctor made a comforting authority figure, and I wasn't too happy with assuming the role myself. "Who's officially in charge of the home now?" I asked Liz after he left.

"I'm not sure. Usually Mrs. Higgenbotham would be. She's the head nurse for the night shift. Only she couldn't make it in tonight because of the ice storm. And Mrs. Donahue, the administrator, left early for the same reason. As a matter of fact, we're on a skeleton shift because so many people stayed home. There's only six nurses, counting me, two orderlies, and the cook."

That kind of decided it for me. If I didn't take charge, no one would. I said, "The first thing we have to do is to make sure that Mrs. Hamilton is protected. Someone needs to be with her at all times."

"One of the nurses is in there now. I'll make sure she stays there."

"Good. I'll be sending one of my cousins to join her."

"What for?"

"Until we know who tried to kill Mrs. Hamilton, we can't trust anyone to be in there with her alone."

"Surely you don't think that one of us—"

I cut her off by holding up my hand the way Aunt Maggie always does. "I don't think anything yet. The point is that we have to protect Mrs. Hamilton the best we can. Is she conscious?"

"No, she's under sedation."

"Fine. If she should come to and say anything, I need to know at once. Come with me so you can show my cousin back to the infirmary." I walked briskly away, imitating Dr. Buchanan's walk and hoping that she would follow. Fortunately she did.

The party was still going on, but clearly the news about Mrs. Hamilton had begun to spread. Instead of mingling, people had gathered into tight little knots around the room. I noticed that no one was going near the spot where Mrs. Hamilton had been stabbed.

Richard was standing with Vasti and my other cousins. What I really wanted was a few minutes alone with him, but I could tell from the expression on Vasti's face that I wasn't going to get it. As soon as she saw me, she put her hands firmly on her hips. "Where have you been? What is going on around here? Where's Junior? How am I supposed to throw a decent party when I don't know what's going on?"

If Dr. Buchanan leaving hadn't convinced me, that would have. I couldn't afford to hesitate in taking charge, because if I did, Vasti was bound to leap into the vacuum. I might be unsure about my own skills, but I knew all too much about Vasti's.

As soon as she stopped to take a breath, I jumped in with, "Y'all must know what happened. Junior can't get through the ice storm, so she's put me in charge. Carlelle, Liz is going to take you to the infirmary to keep an eye on Mrs. Hamilton. There's a nurse there if she needs anything medical, but I want you to stay there and make sure no one bothers her. Don't leave her alone, not even to go to the bathroom, unless you get word from me."

The triplets looked at each other for a second, but after the silent conference, Carlelle nodded. "All right." She followed Liz away.

By now Vasti had her breath back. "Laurie Anne, just what in the Sam Hill is going on?"

I ignored her. "Idelle, I want you to go outside and check the parking lot. There were only a few cars there when we got here, and they should all be covered in ice. See if there are any without ice, and if there are, get the license number. And see if you can tell if any cars have left."

"How is she going to do that?" Vasti wanted to know.

Idelle said, "I'll check to see if any of the parking spots aren't iced over yet, of course." She also left without questioning me.

"Laurie Anne," Vasti said, "are you saying that whoever it was might still be lurking around?"

Obviously I was, so I went on. "Richard, can I have your

handkerchief?" He handed it to me, and I gingerly pulled the knife out of the gift bag I was still carrying. "Odelle, check the kitchen and see if there are any other knives like this around. I want to know if the knife came from here." She took a good look at the knife, nodded, and headed for the kitchen.

"Laurie Anne—" Vasti started, and I knew I was going to have to come up with something for her to do.

"Vasti, I want you to keep the party going. Don't let anybody leave the room, but don't scare them either. Get the nurses to help you if you need them." I touched her shoulder. "I'm counting on you to keep these folks calm."

Though she looked a little suspicious, she nodded and said, "Well, all right then. Why didn't you say so in the first place?" She started corralling nurses and residents.

"What about me?" Clifford said.

"I want you to come with me and Richard for a minute," I answered, and we went into a quiet corner where I could still see what was going on.

"Clifford," I said as gently as I could, "did you know that the knife was in the gift bag?"

"Of course not! The first time I saw it was when Liz fished it out of the bag."

"I found a Garth Brooks tape and a pair of earrings in the bag, too. Is that what you meant for Liz to have?"

He nodded. "She's real fond of Garth Brooks."

"And that's all that was in that bag when you gave it to me?"

"That's all. Does she know it was from me? Liz, I mean?"

"Not yet," I said. He was so concerned about his crush being found out that he hadn't even realized that he was a suspect. "You heard what Mrs. Hamilton said to Liz, didn't you?"

"Everybody in this room heard it," he said indignantly.

"You must have been pretty angry at her. Feeling about Liz the way you do."

"You bet I was! I know she's old and all, but she's got no

call to be talking to people like that. Especially not to Liz."
He finally caught the implication. "Laurie Anne, you don't
think I stabbed her, do you?"

"No, I don't," I said truthfully, "but I had to ask. That
knife showing up in your gift right after Mrs. Hamilton was
so mean to Liz does look funny."

"I guess it does," he admitted. "If it had been a healthy
man who said those things, I probably would have started
something, but I never would have with a sick old woman.
And you know I would never have stabbed anybody in the
back like that. Anyone could have stuck that knife in the gift
bag. All kinds of people were all around the Christmas tree
tonight."

"Did you see anyone in particular over there?" I asked
hopefully.

He shook his head. "I wasn't really paying attention because Vasti had me playing carols."

"Did you see anyone over near Mrs. Hamilton? Before she
collapsed, I mean?"

Again he shook his head. "I don't think so. People were
coming and going so much, I don't know where anyone was."
Then he added with a shy grin, "Except for maybe Liz."

"How long have you known Liz?"

This time he knew where I was leading. "Long enough to
know that she'd never do anything like that. Ever since she
was a little girl, she's been just as nice. She told me herself
that the residents say ugly things to her all the time, but she
knows that they don't really mean it."

"All right," I said. Asking him about Liz had been foolish
anyway. He wouldn't have a crush on her if he thought she
was that kind of a person. "Richard and I are going to see if
we can find out who did this. In the meantime I want you to
help Vasti keep people calmed down. Play them some Christmas music. Maybe that will help."

"All right," he said. He picked up his guitar but then hesitated. "You believe me, don't you, Laurie Anne?"

"Of course I do, Clifford," I said, and I guess he could tell

I meant it. All right, I wasn't being objective, but I had changed Clifford's diapers. There wasn't a mean bone in that boy's body.

As soon as Clifford went, I hugged Richard. "I'm afraid we've been drafted. Or at least I have. Are you game?"

" 'I will be correspondent to command,' " he said. *"The Tempest,* Act I, Scene 2."

"You used that one already today."

"Did I? 'Heaven lay not my transgression to my charge.' *King John,* Act I, Scene 1. So where do we start?"

"With Mrs. Hamilton, I think. She's from Byerly, but I don't know a whole lot about her."

"Are you implying that you know about everyone else in Byerly?"

"Not everybody, of course, but most everybody. By their family if not any other way." I pointed to a bearded man in a red and green sweatshirt. "That's Mr. Honeywell. I went to school with his grandchildren, and he used to play Santa Claus at our Christmas party." Then I nodded at a skinny woman with hair dyed jet black. "Mrs. Peabody has been dying her hair that color for as long as I can remember, but she always does it at home because she doesn't want anyone to know that it's not natural."

"I was completely fooled," Richard said dryly.

"Since I don't know Mrs. Hamilton, I guess our first step is to find out about her." Liz picked that moment to return.

"I left your cousin with Mrs. Hamilton," she said, "but I still don't think it's necessary."

"Maybe not," I conceded, "but better safe than sorry. Now if you don't mind, I want to ask you some questions about Mrs. Hamilton." From out of the corner of my eye, I saw Clifford looking at us worriedly. "Maybe we could use Dr. Buchanan's office." I wasn't about to question Liz with Clifford watching me like that.

As soon as we got there, I waved Liz to one of the visitor chairs and took the desk chair myself. I thought I might as well try to look official. Richard picked up a pad of paper

205

and a pen from the desk and then pushed his chair back behind mine. Obviously he was going to let me run the show.

I took a deep breath. "I guess my first question is, do you know of any reason why anyone would want to kill Mrs. Hamilton?"

"No!" she said, and I guess she must have realized she answered a little bit too quickly. "I know you're thinking about what she said to me tonight, but believe you me, she's said the same and worse before. To all the nurses, not just to me."

"Does she just fuss at you nurses, or does she bother the other residents, too?"

"Oh, she's like that with everybody: nurses, doctors, other residents, the kitchen staff, even other people's visitors."

"Does she not get visitors of her own?"

Liz shook her head. "Not since I've been here. She's got a couple of daughters who live in the state, but they never come to see her. They'll send a card once in a while, but that's about it."

No wonder she was angry all the time. Under those circumstances, I would be, too.

"What about her will? Is she leaving them any money or anything else valuable?"

Liz shook her head again. "It's the daughters who pay her bills here. I don't think she has any money of her own, other than her Social Security check every month."

So much for that idea. "Does she have any particular enemy here at the home? Somebody she's really offended, rather than just pestered."

Liz took a minute to think about it. "I'm not sure," she said slowly. "Mrs. Good said she took her box of candy last week."

"Not really a killing offense, is it?" Richard said.

Liz shrugged. "Probably not, but you'd be surprised at how seriously our folks take that kind of thing. Mrs. Good's family sends her a box of candy every year, and she hoards it for a couple of months before she'll finish that last piece. It may not sound like a big deal to you, but you have to remember that Mrs. Good can't just drive to the mall to get another box. She's got arthritis so bad that she can hardly stand up. That candy means a lot to her, and she was *so* got away with when it disappeared. She insisted that we search Mrs. Hamilton's room."

"Did you?"

"Yes, we did, just to reassure her. We got Mrs. Hamilton's permission first, of course, and wasn't she furious! I think she said yes just to make Mrs. Good look bad. We searched everywhere but couldn't find hide nor hair of it. And after all that, Mrs. Good still wouldn't believe it. She claimed that Mrs. Hamilton must have hid it somewhere else."

Mrs. Good's unreasonable anger sounded promising, but I couldn't honestly suspect her. "I can't see how an arthritic woman could have stabbed Mrs. Hamilton," I pointed out.

"I guess not," Liz said, and then she shook her head. "I don't know of anything else. Of course, the residents don't tell us everything that's going on."

"Why is that?" Richard asked

"Maybe they think that coming to a nurse would be like tattling," I guessed.

"That's part of it," Liz said. "And then I think they just like it this way because it gives them something to do. They'd rather fuss and fume among themselves." I must have frowned, because she added, "I'm not putting them down, really I'm not. Boredom is the biggest problem these people have. After a while, one day is an awful lot like another. If their feuds keep them entertained, who am I to interfere? Anyway, what I was leading up to is that maybe you should talk to one of the other residents."

"Is there anyone who was a particular friend of Mrs. Hamilton's?"

"Mr. Morgan would like to be, for some reason. The other nurses say he's been sweet on her ever since she got here, and no one can figure it out. She certainly doesn't encourage him. She's just as mean to him as she is to everybody else."

207

"Could you find him and bring him here?" I asked.

"Sure."

She was gone long enough for me to ask Richard, "How am I doing?" and for him to reply, " 'Exceeding wise, fair-spoken, and persuading.' *King Henry VIII,* Act IV, Scene 2."

Then Liz brought in Mr. Morgan, performed introductions, and left. Mr. Morgan was thin but seemed heartier than most of the men in the home, and was dressed in a bright red pullover and gray slacks.

"Is Sadie all right?" he asked. "Liz wouldn't tell me a thing."

I weighed the idea of not telling him what was going on against the reality of my having no reason to ask him questions if *something* hadn't happened. Reality won. "Someone tried to kill Mrs. Hamilton," I said, watching his face for a reaction. All I saw was concern.

"Is she all right?"

"The doctor says she's going to be fine, but it was close."

He took a deep breath, and said, "Poor Sadie. First the stroke, and now this. Do they know who stabbed her?"

"I didn't say anything about stabbing," I said quickly. Was solving the crime going to be this easy? Of course not.

Mr. Morgan smiled. "Honey, this is an awful small place. Mrs. Robertson thought she saw blood when Mrs. Hamilton passed out, and Morris Nichols was watching when Liz pulled that knife out of the gift bag. We put two and two together a while ago, especially when no one would tell us anything different. We're not children."

"You're right," I said, acknowledging the reproof. "I'm sorry, but we didn't want to scare anybody until we had a better idea of what was going on. As soon as we're done here, I'll make some kind of an announcement."

"I think that would be a good idea. Now what did you want to talk to me about?"

"Did Liz tell you that Junior Norton deputized me?"

He nodded.

"What I'm trying to do is to take care of some of the

208

groundwork for her, maybe find out who might have wanted to hurt Mrs. Hamilton. Liz tells me that you're pretty close to her."

Mr. Morgan leaned back in his chair. "Well, I don't know if you'd call us close. Sadie doesn't let anybody get too close."

"I understand that she can be difficult sometimes."

He grinned widely. "Difficult, my right eye. Sadie Hamilton is the most ornery woman I have ever met. Never has a nice word for anyone, and no one but her ever does anything right. She curses like a sailor, and I've never known her to pass up a chance to tell anybody just what she thinks about them."

"I expect she's nicer once you get to know her," I ventured.

"Not so you'd know it. She tells me off two, three times a day."

"Then why . . . ?" I wasn't sure how to phrase the question.

"Then why do I put up with her? I like her, plain and simple. She keeps my blood moving. Sadie says I'm too damned nice, and I think she's right. My mama and daddy raised me to be polite, no matter what, and that's how I've always been. Not Sadie! She always says what's on her mind, lets it all hang out, like the young folks say now."

Actually I hadn't known young folks to say that in quite some time, but I nodded anyway. "She sounds kind of like my Aunt Maggie. She's never been one to mince words either."

Mr. Morgan said, "Most of us old folks are too shy to speak our minds. We know we're in the way, so we act just as nice as we can to make sure people still want to be around us once in a while. Sadie just doesn't give a darn about what other people think." He looked at Richard. "You must know *The Taming of the Shrew.*"

" 'Her only fault, and that is faults enough, is that she is intolerable curst and shrewd and froward,' " Richard quoted. "Act I, Scene 2."

"That's Sadie to a T. I never did like the end of that play when the shrew is all tamed. I'd just as soon she stayed a shrew, like Sadie has."

"Until she had the stroke, that is," I said.

He nodded sadly. "Oh, she's still got the feelings inside her, you saw that at the party. She just can't get the words out. It makes her all the madder and frustrates her something terrible. I pure hate to see her like that."

I realized that we had gotten off the track and thought I better bring it back around to the attack on Mrs. Hamilton. "With her being so ill-tempered, do you think that there's someone she had particularly angered?"

He considered it for a minute and then slowly shook his head. "I can't honestly say that I know of a soul that really wants her dead, if that's what you mean. Sure she makes people mad, but not like that."

"Liz said something about Mrs. Good and a box of candy," I said, feeling silly.

Mr. Morgan waved away the suggestion. "Young lady, surely you don't think anybody stabbed Sadie over a box of candy."

"No, not really."

"And another thing," he continued, "Margaret Good had no business claiming it was Sadie who took that candy. She made such a big to-do over it when it came in the mail, showing everybody what a big box it was and talking about how generous her daughter was to send it. All along knowing that Sadie's brats don't so much as call her on the telephone, not even when they heard about the stroke. Margaret even left the box in the TV room to rub it in. If you ask me, it served her right when somebody made off with it."

"Was Mrs. Hamilton feuding with anybody else?" I asked.

"Before her stroke, she was on the outs with pretty much everybody," he said, grinning again. "Sadie told everyone in sight that Mrs. Houghton's husband used to run around on her, and Mrs. Houghton was right put out about that. Especially since it was true. Then Sadie threw out a vase of Charlie's flowers because she said she was allergic to them. And she got to the TV room first one morning a while back and insisted on watching game shows all day long when she knew a bunch of the other ladies wanted to watch their stories.''

"Soap operas," I translated for Richard. He was rushing to write all of this down, but I didn't really think he needed to bother. I could see why Mrs. Hamilton hadn't been very popular, but none of this was exactly motive for murder. Oh well, maybe Junior could use the information somehow.

"Anything else?" I asked.

"I think those are the most recent problems. If you want me to go back a few months or so—"

"No, I think this will be enough to start on. I appreciate your time, Mr. Morgan."

"That's all right, young lady. Do you think it would be all right if I went to see Sadie now?"

"I think she's still unconscious, but I guess it would be all right." Even if he was the one who tried to kill Mrs. Hamilton, he wasn't likely to overpower the nurse and Carlelle in order to try again.

Idelle and Odelle came in as Mr. Morgan left.

"Are you ready for us?" Odelle asked.

I nodded. "What did you find out?"

"It's hard to tell," Idelle said, "but I don't think anyone's been out of the parking lot since we came in. Other than Dr. Buchanan, that is. I suppose someone could have come in or out on foot, but it's awful slippery out there. I fell down twice myself."

"Are you all right?" I asked.

She grinned and rubbed her tail end. "Only hurt my dignity."

"What about the knife?" I said to Odelle.

"I talked to Mrs. Cummings the cook and she said they have a set of cooking knives just like the one you have. And there's one missing. It's been gone since last week, so she already bought herself a new one that has a different kind of handle."

Last week? That implied premeditation to me. "Did she have any idea of who could have taken it?"

211

Odelle shook her head. "She said they don't really lock up the kitchen because there's never been any reason to. Residents come in for snacks all the time, and last week a bunch made gingerbread houses."

"So unless someone came in last week to steal the knife and then managed to sneak back in tonight in the middle of an ice storm, it must have been one of the residents or a staff member," I said. That left Clifford and the rest of my family out, I added to myself, but I had never really considered them suspects anyway.

Unfortunately I was still stuck with every one of the residents and staff members who had been at the party. Plenty of suspects but no motives.

"What do you want us to do now?" Odelle asked.

"Has Vasti got things under control back at the party?"

"You know she has," Idelle said with a snicker.

"Then maybe you two can go check with Carlelle in case she needs something to drink or to go to the bathroom."

They nodded and left.

"Well?" I said to Richard. "Any ideas?"

"We could bring in those soap opera fans. I know some people are ardently devoted to them."

"Thanks a whole lot. Next time you can be the deputy."

He shook his head emphatically. "No, thank you. I'm quite content to play the role of faithful dogsbody."

I put my head on my hands. "What have we got here anyway? In a roomful of people, someone stabs a little old lady through a wheelchair. Why stab her? I mean, she's a patient. Wouldn't it have been easier to slip something into her medication?"

"Not necessarily," Richard said. "Drugs are monitored pretty closely."

I nodded. "Okay. Then why at the party? Why not late at night?"

"The purloined letter approach? Whoever it was must have known that he or she wouldn't be noticed."

"Then why now? She just had a stroke, for heaven's sake.

What harm could she do to anyone? I don't think she could even monopolize a television set the way she is now."

"Maybe she was an easier target. From what people have been telling us, how easy would it have been to have snuck up on her before?"

I sighed. "Maybe Junior should have deputized Vasti instead of me because I haven't got a clue as to what's going on."

Richard put his arm around me. "You're doing fine. All Junior wanted you to do was to protect Mrs. Hamilton, and you're doing that. The rest is up to Junior, remember?"

"I guess," I said unwillingly. "It's just that it would be awfully nice to be able to hand the solution over to Junior when she gets here." I stood up. "Anyway, I promised Mr. Morgan I'd make that announcement. Coming, faithful dogsbody?"

"'I will follow you to the last gasp with truth and loyalty.' *As You Like It,* Act II, Scene 3."

Word must have spread that I was playing detective because the people in the recreation room quieted down when Richard and I walked in. Vasti was doing her best to hand out more cookies, but I don't think anybody was taking her up on it. Clifford was playing a song over by the podium, and I waited until he finished before starting.

"Can I have everybody's attention?" I said unnecessarily, since they were all watching me already. "I'd like to make an announcement." The people moved closer. "Y'all probably all know about Mrs. Hamilton by now. She was stabbed, but she survived the attack. The doctor said she's going to be fine." I waited for that to sink in before going on. "Chief Norton can't get through the storm to take charge herself, so she deputized me."

There was talking among them at that, and I thought I heard my grandfather's name mentioned. Like I had said earlier, there were no secrets in Byerly, so these people almost certainly knew I had taken an interest in such things before. Maybe that meant they'd trust me.

213

I continued, "I've been trying to see what I can find out about what happened, and that's where you folks come in. Did any of y'all see anyone around Mrs. Hamilton acting funny, someone who might have stabbed her?" There was a lot more talking, but no one seemed to have anything definite to say. "All right, then how about this? The knife used to stab Mrs. Hamilton was stuck in this bag afterwards." I held up the gift bag. "Did any of you see someone messing with this bag or putting anything into it?" Again the response was negative. I was disappointed but not surprised. If anyone had seen anything, word would already have reached me.

I went on, "Now you folks know as much as I do, but I'll answer any questions you might have."

A fearful-looking woman raised her hand, and I nodded at her. "How do we know that the murderer isn't going to come after someone else?"

I did feel right foolish when she asked that. Until then I had just assumed Mrs. Hamilton was the only target, and I didn't have any real reason for thinking that. Foolish or not, I didn't suppose it would be very comforting for me to admit my mistake to these people now. "That's why we've been keeping all of you in here," I improvised. "Safety in numbers."

A man muttered, "Safety in numbers didn't help Sadie Hamilton."

I pointed out, "That's because she wasn't expecting anything. Now all of you are on your guard."

"Does that mean that the murderer is still here?" the first woman asked. "Here in this room?"

There was no way around that one. "I'm afraid that's just what I mean. As far as we can tell, no one has left the home since Mrs. Hamilton was stabbed."

Now there was a wave of muttering and sidelong glances. I wanted to reassure them, but I resisted. These people deserved the truth. I didn't expect whoever it was to go after another target, but I couldn't be sure.

I looked at a clock on the wall. It was close to midnight,

and these folks were going to have to go to bed soon. How could I protect so many of them?

"It's getting late," I said, "and I know you're getting tired." Goodness knows I was. "My cousins, my husband, and I are going to stay here for the night." I probably should have checked with them first, but between the ice on the roads and a thwarted murderer in the building, I didn't think they'd argue. "I think we should all spend the night in here." There was some comments made, both from nurses and residents, but I talked over them. Hospital beds had wheels, didn't they? "We'll just roll in beds, and stick together. Nobody else is going to get hurt."

There was a lot of conversation, but I didn't hear any loud objections, so I decided I was going to get away with it.

"Liz, Vasti, and Clifford are going to be in charge of getting everybody everything they have to have for tonight, so if there's something special you need, just tell them."

Clifford looked blank, but Vasti called out, "People, I'd appreciate it if you'd go sit down until we get things set up." There was some movement but clearly not enough to suit Vasti. "Come on now!" she said, clapping her hands sharply. "We haven't got all night."

This sounded like as good a time as any for me to leave, and I pulled Richard along with me.

He asked, "Where to now, fearless leader?"

"I'm not that fearless," I answered. "I want to get out of here before Vasti comes up with something for me to do."

This time the door to the infirmary was flanked by two of the triplets. I know they were trying hard to look menacing, but it just didn't work with those elf costumes.

"How's she doing?" I asked them.

"She was stirring just a little bit a while ago," Carlelle said.

"I think she might be awake by now," said Odelle. "Are you going to interrogate her?"

I nodded and opened the door as quietly as I could. They had opened the curtain around Mrs. Hamilton's bed to give them more room. A nurse I didn't know and Idelle looked up as I came in, and I saw that Mr. Morgan was sitting by the bed holding Mrs. Hamilton's hand.

Richard tapped my shoulder and mouthed that he was going to stay outside, and I closed the door behind me. "How is she doing?" I whispered.

"I think she's waking up," Mr. Morgan said. "Are you going to question her?"

"I'm going to try," I said. "Do you think you could stay and interpret for me? She was pretty hard to understand earlier."

"Certainly."

Idelle and the nurse moved out of the way, and I pulled a chair up to the bed. Mrs. Hamilton did seem to be moving restlessly, and I hadn't been there but a few minutes when she opened her eyes.

She glared accusingly at me, then gave Mr. Morgan a somewhat friendlier look and mumbled something.

"She wants to know what she's doing here," Mr. Morgan said. "What should I tell her?"

"You know her better than I do. Do you think she can handle the truth?"

He nodded. "A lot better than she could our *not* telling her." Then to Mrs. Hamilton he said, "Sadie, this is kind of hard to believe."

She mumbled something else, and even without understanding the words, I could tell she was impatient.

Mr. Morgan said, "Sadie, somebody stabbed you. Somebody tried to kill you."

She didn't say anything for a while, and I was trying to decide if she had understood him or not when she blurted out, "Who?"

"We don't know who," I said. "We were hoping you could tell us. Somebody came up behind you at the party. Did you see anybody?"

She shook her head and said, "Die?"

I smiled in what I thought was a reassuring manner. "No, ma'am, the doctor says you're going to be just fine." Her glare told me that she was not reassured, but I thought I knew why. "Don't worry. We're going to make sure that no one hurts you again." I was wrong.

In the clearest words I had heard from her, she said, "Should have let him kill me."

I looked at Mr. Morgan in shock, and he started wringing Mrs. Hamilton's hand. "Sadie, don't say things like that!"

Her only response was to pull her hand away from his and determinedly shut her eyes.

The nurse and Idelle were both shaking their heads sadly, and Mr. Morgan kept whispering, "Sadie? Sadie?" I didn't have anything else to say, so I just left.

"You be sure and stay with her," I said to Carlelle and Odelle. They grinned and saluted, but I knew they'd stay.

"Well?" Richard asked once we were out of earshot. "Any accusations?"

"She said she didn't see anything, but I don't think she would have told me if she had. Richard, she *wants* to die!" I was on the verge of tears, and I guess Richard realized it.

"Come on," he said. "Let's find someplace quiet." He led me into what looked like a nurses' lounge, sat me down on a couch, and put his arms around me.

I took half a dozen deep breaths to fight back the tears. "It was so awful," I said. "She actually said that we should have let whoever it was finish the job. We're doing all we can to protect her, and she doesn't even want to be protected. How can she give up like that?"

"She's old," Richard reminded me. "According to Mr. Morgan, she's been miserable ever since her stroke. It's not unusual for people to get depressed at a time like that."

"I know, but it's Christmas."

"More people get depressed during the holidays than at any other time of the year."

"I know," I said again. "But . . ." Then I stopped. Was what Mrs. Hamilton was feeling all that different from what I had been feeling? And she had a whole lot more reason to be depressed than I did. My grandfather was dead, it was

217

true, but he would have been the last person on earth to want me moping around. Suddenly I felt very ashamed, both for blaming Sadie Hamilton for her depression and for wallowing in my own. "I really have been a Scrooge this year, haven't I?"

Richard pulled back and looked at me. "Where did that come from?"

"Just thinking about Mrs. Hamilton." He was still looking at me. "It's hard to explain, and right now we've got work to do."

"Are you sure you're all right?"

I nodded. *"I'm* not giving up. Maybe if Mrs. Hamilton sees how hard we're working, she'll realize she's got something to live for."

"Maybe," Richard said, "but don't count on it. This is Byerly, not 34th Street."

I nodded, but I don't suppose I really believed him. I wanted a Christmas miracle for Mrs. Hamilton and maybe a little one for myself while I was at it.

Vasti spotted us as soon as we came back into the recreation room and gestured for us to join her.

"You go ahead," Richard said. "Surely someone must need me to lift a bed or something."

"Coward!" I said to his back.

" 'The better part of valour is discretion.' *King Henry IV, Part I,* Act V, Scene 4."

Vasti really had got the job done. The party food and tables were gone, and the room was filled with rows of beds. A line of curtained panels ran down the center, and two signs pointedly labeled the halves LADIES and GENTLEMEN. A few folks were already pulling off their shoes and socks and climbing into bed.

After all her hard work, I couldn't very well ignore her demand for my attention. "Vasti, you have done a wonderful job."

"Oh, this," she said, waving her hand airily. "Nothing to it. What I wanted to tell you is that I think I solved the case!"

"Really?" I said, hoping I didn't sound too sarcastic. If I had, she didn't notice it. "Look what I found!" She held out a Whitman's Sampler box of candy.

I guess I looked blank.

"This box of candy was stolen from Mrs. Good. A nurse saw it and told me all about it. You see—"

"I've heard the story. Are you sure that's the same box?" I said, not sure why I should care.

"Mrs. Good identified it herself, and I had the devil of a time convincing her that she couldn't have it back."

"Why couldn't she?"

"It's evidence," she said as if it were the most obvious thing in the world. "I found it in Mrs. Hamilton's room."

Now that was interesting, although puzzling. Hadn't Liz told me that they had searched the room when the candy went missing?

"Her room is one of the closest, so I thought we could wheel her bed in here. She's not going to be using it tonight, after all. Anyway, this was in the drawer of her nightstand."

I didn't even bother asking Vasti what she had been doing in the nightstand. "So you think the candy has something to do with the attack?" I said.

"It must have. And there's more." She lifted the lid of the box, and I saw that there was only one piece of candy missing. "Look at that piece there," Vasti said, pointing to a nougat.

I did so, careful not to touch. "What?"

"Just look."

I got closer and saw what I thought was a fingerprint. "It looks like someone picked it up." Knowing Vasti, I was pretty sure I knew who it had been.

"It's been tampered with," Vasti said triumphantly. "It looked funny to me, and when I looked on the bottom, I found a needle mark. Don't you see? It's been poisoned."

"Did you get one of the nurses to take a look?"

"Of course not. One of them might be the murderer."

She had a point, of course.

"Pick it up and see for yourself," Vasti said indignantly.

"No, I trust you, and I don't want to disturb any evidence. If it was tampered with, what do you suppose it means?"

"Isn't it obvious? It means that Mrs. Hamilton was intending to poison Mrs. Good, and Mrs. Good retaliated."

"Vasti," I said slowly, "do you really think Mrs. Good could have stabbed someone?"

"Well, maybe not. But it has to be connected somehow."

"Maybe," I conceded. "If it has been poisoned, I'd think that a more likely idea would be that someone had tried to kill Mrs. Hamilton before and hadn't succeeded."

"That could be it, I suppose," Vasti said grudgingly.

"I'll tell you what. You hang on to the candy, and we'll have Junior send it to a lab for testing. They'll be able to tell us for sure."

"All right," Vasti said, somewhat mollified, and went to tell an orderly what he was doing wrong.

By then the residents were pretty much settled down for the night. The nurses and orderlies were stationed in chairs throughout the room, making sure everyone was taken care of. I saw that Clifford had pulled up a chair right next to Liz's, and while they weren't speaking, the way they were looking at each other said a lot.

"How's it going?" I asked them.

"Pretty well, I guess," Liz said. "Maybe they'll get some sleep, anyway. Clifford was a big help." She smiled at him, and he smiled back. "They'd be a lot happier if Chief Norton was here. No offense, Laurie Anne."

"No offense taken. I'd rather that Junior was here, too."

I saw Vasti supervising Richard, who was shoving in a chair I recognized as coming from Dr. Buchanan's office. "I don't know about you people," she said, "but I'm worn out." She plopped down onto the chair, and leaned back. "I'm going to try to get some sleep."

I thought longingly of one of the other chairs from that office but said, "The triplets worked all day, and I know they're beat, too. I better take over so they can get some rest."

"I don't think so," Richard said. "I think you should get

220

yourself a chair and grab forty or fifty winks. I'll stay with Mrs. Hamilton."

"Are you sure?"

"Absolutely." He pulled a worn paperback of *The Winter's Tale* out of his back pocket. "The Bard and I will keep watch together."

I gave him a hug and a kiss. "You are wonderful, you know."

" 'The naked truth,' " he said with a grin. *"Love's Labour's Lost,* Act V, Scene 2." He bowed with a flourish before he left.

By the time the triplets arrived, I had found chairs for all of us, and they quickly settled down, wrapped themselves in blankets Liz produced, and fell asleep. I must admit thinking that it was ridiculous that anyone could sleep in a situation like this, but I only had time to think about it for a minute before dozing off myself.

I awoke to a loud whisper. "Nurse! Come here!"

Liz muttered, "Now what?" and tiptoed her way toward a bed next to the window. A minute later she was back. "Mr. Biggers said he saw someone walk by the window."

"Is he sure?" I asked.

"Positive. I had to promise him that we'd go check or he'd be on his way out there himself."

I looked toward the window unenthusiastically, not thrilled by the idea of going out in the cold and ice, when darned if I didn't see a shadow myself. "I think there is someone there!"

Liz shrank back toward Clifford. "Maybe it's the murderer. What are we going to do?"

"I guess I'm going to go see who it is," Clifford said in a much deeper voice than he generally used. "Have y'all got any kind of a gun around here?"

Liz shook her head. "There's a softball bat in with the sports equipment."

"That'll do. You two better stay here and keep an eye out."

221

"Clifford," Liz said, her hand on his arm. "You aren't going out there alone, are you?"

"No, he's not," I said firmly. I was older than he was, and if anything happened to him, his mother would kill me. "I'm going, too. Liz, I wouldn't wake the others until we know for sure what's going on."

"That's right," Clifford said. "We don't want to make too much noise. That might warn him."

Common sense told me that making noise was exactly what we should do, so our prowler would pick up and go, but I was still hoping to solve the puzzle for Junior. Besides, I rationalized, who was I to spoil Clifford's big moment?

Liz watched him adoringly as we armed ourselves with aluminum softball bats and put on our coats. "Be careful," she whispered after us. Well, after Clifford anyway.

"You stay behind me," Clifford said as we stepped out onto the icy sidewalk, and I saw no reason to argue with him. Just staying upright was taking all of my attention, and I cursed myself for not finding something to put on my feet instead of those darned elf shoes. I did reach down and pull the bells off.

We walked around the building slowly and as quietly as we could. I wasn't sure, but from the broken ice, it did look like someone had walked down the sidewalk ahead of us. We were just about even with Mr. Biggers's window when I saw a large figure walking slowly, peering into windows.

I tugged at Clifford's sleeve, but he had seen him, too. He gestured me forward, and together we crept closer. Only I guess we weren't creeping quietly enough, because suddenly the prowler turned right toward us.

Clifford raised his bat threateningly and called out, "You over there! What are you doing here?"

The man said, "Hey now, put that down," and stepped into the light.

I started laughing. Our prowler was wearing a red hat with white trim and had a long white beard. That's right—it was Santa Claus.

It wasn't really Santa Claus, of course. After a minute more I recognized Vasti's husband. "Arthur? What on earth are you doing out here?"

"I know I'm late," he said, coming toward us. "I got stuck in the ice. I'd have gone on home, but I saw Vasti's car in the parking lot and thought the party must still be going on. I was hoping I could get her attention from out here."

"Why didn't you just come on inside?" Clifford wanted to know.

"Vasti told me not to let anyone see me before I made my big entrance. I wasn't sure if she'd still want me to give out presents or not."

We started back for the front door. "I'm afraid you're way too late to give out presents," I said, and then stopped.

"What's the matter?" Clifford asked.

"Presents," I said softly. "Where was her present?"

Arthur said, "Whose present?"

"Mrs. Hamilton's!" I said. "Come on!"

We went as fast as we could, and I threw off my coat and dropped it on the floor in my hurry to get back to where Vasti was sleeping.

Liz looked up as soon as I came in, but I went right on past her. Let Clifford explain, I thought as I went to shake my cousin. "Vasti! Wake up!"

"What? What's going on?"

"I need your Secret Santa list."

"What for?"

I saw her clipboard under her chair and grabbed it. "Is this it?" Without waiting for an answer, I started flipping through the pages. I found the list of residents, the gifts they wanted, and their Secret Santas. "Thank goodness you're organized," I said to Vasti, and looked for Mrs. Hamilton's entry. There it was, in black and white. I can't honestly say that it was the name I expected, but it did make sense once I found it. Especially when I thought about the candy.

By now Arthur and Clifford had caught up with me and were greeting and being greeted by their significant others.

223

"Clifford," Liz said, "are you all right? I was so worried." She looked up at him, and he took her in his arms. No mistletoe was required for the kiss that followed.

"Arthur? Where in the Sam Hill have you been?" Vasti said. "And straighten that beard. You look right silly."

I left them to their explanations and went to the infirmary. I took my time because I wanted to think about just what I was going to say when I got there. I tapped lightly on the door, and Richard let me in.

"What's up?" he asked.

"I think I've got it," I said quietly.

The nurse had that dazed look of someone staying awake by sheer force of will. "You can go grab a cup of coffee if you want," I said. She didn't ask for explanations, just nodded and went out.

Mr. Morgan was still perched by Mrs. Hamilton's bed, watching her sleep. "How is she?" I asked.

" 'O sleep, O gentle sleep, nature's soft nurse!' " Richard said. *"King Henry VI, Part II,* Act III, Scene 1."

"I think we better wake her up," I said.

"Wake her up?" Mr. Morgan said. "What for?"

"I think she needs to know who it was that tried to kill her," I said.

"I'm awake," a churlish voice said from the bed.

Sure enough, Mrs. Hamilton was glaring at us all. "Good," I said, and took the nurse's chair.

"Mrs. Hamilton," I said, "I think I know who tried to kill you, but I need to ask you something first." Her only response was a grunt, but she didn't take her eyes off of me. "My cousin found Mrs. Good's box of candy in your room. Did you take it?"

I could tell from the way her face turned red what she was going to say before she said it. *"No!"*

I nodded. "That's what I thought. I'm guessing that someone left that box in your room a week or so ago. Is that right?"

She looked suspicious, but she nodded.

"There was one piece missing from the box. Did you eat it?"

She made a face. "Half. Tasted bad."

"I imagine it did. It had been tampered with."

"Poison?" she wanted to know.

"I think so."

She blinked several times. "Who?"

I didn't answer her directly. Instead I looked up at Frank Morgan, who had been listening attentively. "Maybe Mr. Morgan will tell us."

He got very still. "How would I know?"

"Or maybe you'd rather tell us what you got Mrs. Hamilton for Christmas."

He didn't say anything, so I went on.

"I checked Vasti's list, and you were Mrs. Hamilton's Secret Santa. Only there wasn't any gift for her under the tree. And you weren't on the triplets' shopping list because you told Vasti you'd get her something yourself. What did you get her?"

"Nothing," he said. "She didn't want anything."

"Didn't she? Is that what she said?"

He looked down at his hands for a long moment, then shook his head and looked at Mrs. Hamilton while he answered me. "You don't know what's it like, you *can't* know. Sadie's an old woman, but she's always been strong and independent. She didn't like being here, but she could stand it as long as she could keep doing for herself. Then she had the stroke, and she couldn't even go to the bathroom by herself anymore. Most of her body is just dead." He looked up at me. "Do you know how you'd feel if you were in that shape?"

I shook my head.

"I'll tell you how you'd feel. You'd want to die, just like Sadie did. She wanted to die worse than anything. She wouldn't fill out a gift list, said she didn't care. I went to her and asked her if there wasn't something I could get for her. She looked me straight in the eye and said as clear as could be, 'I want to die.' "

He took a deep breath. "Don't think it was easy for me to do, because it wasn't. It was the hardest thing I've ever done in my life, but I couldn't just leave her like that. I took Mrs. Good's candy and put a sedative in it because I thought Sadie would go easy, that they'd think she went in her sleep. I didn't realize it would taste bad. I just thought it hadn't worked, and that's when I decided to steal that knife and use it. I thought that way she'd die quickly, but I guess I didn't hit the right spot."

He looked back at Mrs. Hamilton, who was watching us carefully with her one good eye. "I sharpened it up as good as I could and made sure to hit you on the side with no feeling so it wouldn't hurt. I didn't want it to hurt." His voice broke. "I'm sorry, Sadie, I wanted to help you and I've only made it worse."

Mrs. Hamilton struggled for a moment and finally said, "Jail?"

"I guess that's right. I'll be going to jail."

"For me?"

He looked confused. "I'm not sure I follow you."

"Jail? For me?"

He looked at me, and I said, "I think she's asking if you were willing to go to jail for her?"

Mrs. Hamilton nodded as hard as she could in confirmation.

Mr. Morgan said, "I guess you could say that. To be honest, I was hoping it wouldn't come to that." To me he added, "I would have confessed if it looked like anyone else was going to get into trouble."

I nodded, believing him.

"For me?" Mrs. Hamilton said, and she sounded almost in awe. Her next sentence was garbled, but I think she said, "No one does things for me."

"That's not true, Sadie," Mr. Morgan protested. "Lots of people do things for you."

She shook her head. "You. You tried. For me. Why?"

Mr. Morgan cocked his head. "Because I thought that's

what you wanted. I care for you, Sadie, you must know that. And it's Christmas. I wanted to you to have what you wanted."

"Did want it," Mrs. Hamilton said. "Not now. Don't want it. Live."

Mr. Morgan took her hand in his. "Really, Sadie? I'm so glad."

I halfway expected her to jerk her hand away from him, but she didn't. Instead she fixed her eye on me and said, "Jail?"

I nodded. "He'll be going to jail all right."

"No!" she said vehemently.

"You don't want him to go to jail?" I asked, wanting to be sure she meant what I thought she meant.

She shook her head vigorously. "No jail."

Mr. Morgan looked astonished. "Sadie, are you sure?"

"No jail." Then to me, she said, "You fix."

"Mrs. Hamilton, I don't know what I can do. I'm not really a deputy."

"No jail. Fix it!" Then she closed her eyes. Even in that condition, she had dismissed me as plain as day.

Mr. Morgan looked at me. "Can you do that?"

I thought about it a minute. "Well, since Mrs. Hamilton is still alive, I don't know that Junior can do anything without her pressing charges. I expect she'll want to have a good long talk with you, though." I hesitated. "Assuming that this is the first time you've ever tried anything like this, that is."

"Of course it is!" he said. "What kind of person do you think I am?" He glared at me for a minute and then relented. "I suppose you had to ask that. I swear, I never tried to kill anyone before."

"All right," I said. Of course, I was going to warn Junior to check over the nursing home's records just to be sure that there hadn't been any suspicious deaths, but I didn't see any reason to mention that.

I called the nurse back in and decided that she would be enough protection for Mrs. Hamilton now. Richard and I de-

227

served the rest. Which, unfortunately, we were not going to get for a while yet.

We had barely got back to the recreation room and found empty chairs when we saw blue lights flashing from the parking lot. Junior had finally arrived. She had thoughtfully not used the siren, so the others kept on sleeping, but I knew that she was going to want me awake to fill her in.

It didn't really take all that long to tell, once Junior quit laughing over the elf suit I had nearly forgotten I was still wearing. "I think that's about it," I said. "If I remember anything else, I'll let you know."

Junior just kept shaking her head. "I knew you'd try, but I didn't have any idea that you'd put it together so quick."

Quick? It felt like I had been at the nursing home for days. "What are you going to do about Mr. Morgan?"

"Well, I'm going to have to talk to Mrs. Hamilton myself, but if she really doesn't want to press charges, I expect I'll be able to find some loophole or another."

"Good. And now I would like to formally resign my position of acting deputy."

"Resignation accepted, but don't expect any kind of severance pay."

"No? Did I not do a good job?"

"You did fine," she said, "but you're out of uniform."

She started snickering again.

"Ha ha," I said, with very little good humor. Then to change the subject, I asked, "Did you get that baby delivered all right?"

"The mama did all the hard work. About all I did was catch the daddy when he passed out. A healthy girl, by the way. They were all set to name it after me until they found out what my name is."

"Junior Junior wasn't quite what they had in mind?"

"Not hardly."

I yawned so wide it almost hurt. "How are the roads?"

"Getting better," she said. "You shouldn't have any trouble

driving now if you take it slow, and the ice will probably all be gone by afternoon."

"Good," I said.

"I expect you want to get some sleep," she said. "I know I do."

"That's part of it," I said, and indeed the first part of my plan was to take off the elf suit and climb into bed. But after I got some rest, I was going Christmas shopping.

About the Author

Toni L.P. Kelner lives with her husband in Malden, Massachusetts. Her first Laura Fleming mystery, DOWN HOME MURDER, was published by Zebra Books in June 1993 and is available at bookstores everywhere. Her newest Laura Fleming mystery, DEAD RINGER, will be published by Zebra Books in February 1994. You may write to Toni c/o Zebra Books

A Christmas Question

by

J. Dayne Lamb

Chuck Berry let go with, "Out of all the reindeers, you know you're the mastermind . . ."

"Honestly, Teal!" Diana Quinn started to laugh.

"Well, what did you expect? I think Chuck's a pretty good antidote to your history of one suburban Christmas with Madison after another. Remember, that's why you asked me out here tonight."

"Um," Diana said, but she shifted around on the couch like her mind was on something else.

"I'll bet you two actually watched *White Christmas* every Christmas Eve," Teal continued, undaunted.

"Every other—"

"With a Handel's *Messiah* sing-along on off years at the Wellesley town hall." Teal Stewart nodded. "Right?"

"Just about." Diana grinned a sparkle into her green eyes. "The *Messiah* was in a church."

"Run Rudolph Run" petered out. The Marquees began to blast out "Santa Done Got Hip." Diana lifted the *Cool Yule* box from the coffee table.

"Hunt?" she asked. Pale crescent brows arched over her eyes.

"Umm. One urban Christmas after another. He prides himself on an extensive collection of alternative holiday music. That CD showed up in my stocking last year."

"Ah yes, to remind you of the way things used to be, I bet," Diana said.

233

Teal's blue-gray eyes clouded as she considered the suggestion. How many years had she lived with Hunt? How many years since they parted? Time's passage left an uneven balance. "Used to be" was long ago.

"I doubt it." Teal pushed back the stray chestnut hairs tickling her face.

"That's what Madison would have meant. 'Just see what you gave up. Weren't you a little fool to let go of me.' He's repulsive." Diana pantomimed gagging as she arced bright red painted nails to her mouth and as quickly settled back, hands clenched in her lap. "At least you can still like Hunt. That's lucky. I think about my soon-to-be-ex-husband and I want to kill somebody. Him, preferably. I actually married the creep."

"When you were a baby," Teal said. "Just graduated from college and twenty-one. Don't be so hard on yourself."

"I have to be hard on somebody."

"Madison's a better target," Teal suggested.

"I guess," Diana snorted.

The women stared into the fire. A hint of wood smoke spiced the air. Outside was bright with cold.

"What's Hunt doing tonight?" Diana asked.

Teal shrugged. "Where's Madison?"

"Somewhere with a stake of holly in his heart and a sprig of mistletoe jammed down his throat, I hope. Anyway, I assure you, nowhere near me or the town of Wellesley this Christmas Eve. Part of the preliminary agreement." Diana laughed. "Isn't this always the way? He insisted we move here and now I'm the one who's stuck!"

"But only until the divorce is final," Teal offered. "Then you can live wherever you like, right?"

"Teal, for someone as smart as you are and a certified public accountant to boot, you can be so gullible. Madison doesn't want this divorce. He'd rather make my life as miserable as he possibly can and drag it out for years. Even when it's over, it won't be. Not really."

"Because of Scott?"

"Um-hum. Madison is his father so—"

"You're tied to the jerk even after the final decree," Teal finished.

Diana flipped her palms up. "One way or another I'm chained to Madison for life."

"Scum," Teal said.

"Pond scum." Diana sighed.

"Listen to us on Christmas Eve," Teal said. "Too much wassail."

"No, not enough." Diana took a long drink of the mulled wine. "I can understand him acting awful to me. I wounded his male vanity."

"Chopped it into little pieces, actually," Teal suggested.

"Okay, I wasn't discreet, but how can he be such a rotten father to his own child? He never calls Scott between visits—and those are spent taking the kid to the movies. He's never spent two hours alone with his son for all his whining that I ruined the perfect family. I don't know, Teal. I wasted thirteen years married to a man I can't even stand to think about right now."

Teal watched Diana pace from window to window as she toyed with the electric candles centered on each sill.

"What are you looking for?" Teal asked. "Madison lurking around the house?"

"That's not funny," Diana snapped.

She settled back beside Teal on the couch. The friends made a nice contrast. Teal, tall and rather more elegant than pretty, and Diana, all fiery red hair and temper compressed in a small flashy package.

"I thought Scott was Madison's big reason to fight you on the divorce. Isn't his argument to the court that he deserves the right to be an active, daily father to his boy?"

"And I deserve to be an astronaut despite my lack of inclination or effort. Sure, that's what he said because the courts love it, but I tell you, the man hardly knows his son. How could he? Madison was away from home for hours and hours each week. But now he can manipulate Scott to get at me.

He even pumps his son for information. 'What is Mommy up to? Who is she seeing?' This goes on every other weekend!"

"Who are you seeing? Hank?"

Diana nodded. The tension around her mouth softened. "Um."

"That must be driving Madison crazy." Teal pushed off the couch. "Time to start on the tree? I brought stuff from the Chinese year."

Diana chuckled. "You and your themes. Did you ever decorate an ordinary tree? You know, multi colored lights and lots of shiny, mismatched balls?"

Teal didn't look amused. "I'm following the Stewart family tradition—" The giggles leaked out. "Which I learned at my mother's knee. In all things, express your individuality."

"Right." Diana snorted. "Wasn't the Chinese year the year you served that weird pastry? I remember Hunt gave me a piece called something lovely like 'Lotus moon over sea.' One bite and I slipped the rest to Argyle."

"You and about everyone else at the party. Our poor deerhound really was sick as a dog the next day. Hunt's deerhound now, actually." Her laughter and words trailed to a stop.

Teal missed Argyle's jumping at the sound of her key in the door. She missed the big gray dog, his head in her lap for a scratch, his familiar animal smell. More than she missed Hunt maybe. She unwrapped a tiny brass and silk lantern and hung it on a branch. The first ornament on the bare tree danced.

"There. It's a start," Teal said.

"I miss those theme Christmas parties. I tried the make-our-own-ornaments approach with Scott last year. He might have been a little too young." Diana pulled a blue ball out of the box and put it back. "Do you remember the year what's-her-name made a sock mouse with the beady jet button eyes? I think Madison came up with a paper chain. I should have walked then on the grounds of mental cruelty expressed by a total failure of creativity."

"I didn't think they had grounds like that anymore," Teal said.

"Probably not," Diana agreed.

Teal looked across at her friend. Diana wasn't selfish exactly, just someone who thought first of herself. What she wanted. It never seemed to occur to Diana there might be consequences. Most of her life, there hadn't been, not negative ones. Diana was smart and funny and spoiled. Someone Teal could hardly have imagined as a friend. But Diana was, and a close one. Teal shook her head.

"You're right." Diana shook her head back, misunderstanding Teal's look. "It is weird how, in a no-fault state, Madison can get his pound of flesh through the courts. You and Hunt were lucky. You didn't have to go through a legal divorce. If I never see the turkey again after all this, it will be too soon."

"Our separation wasn't that easy. Don't expect so much of yourself so soon." Teal snapped open a paper fan and searched for a bare spot in the tree.

"Benefited by the years of hindsight, what do you think went wrong?" Diana asked. "I used to envy you two."

Teal stopped to stare. "You, married to the perfect husband with the perfect house, envied me?"

"Just goes to show what we don't know about someone else's life. What did go wrong?"

"Probably what I told you when it happened. I got busy. He got busy. We never saw each other or when we did—"

"I would have given anything to have had that relationship with Madison. Not see him," Diana said.

"Oh stop! You liked it well enough to put up with him for twelve of the thirteen years. You even loved the social stuff out here, Diana, admit it. Scott in private school, you the doyenne of that charity, Madison climbing his way up—"

"The corporate ladder? God, Teal! I made more money working than he did until Scott came along and you know what Clayborne Whittier paid us in the early years. Sometimes I worry about Scott's genes with Madison being his father. Can someone be born to mediocrity?" Diana said.

237

"Madison's not that bad. I mean, he's bad, but he's not that bad. And he's certainly not stupid. What about Hank? Is he so smart?" Teal concentrated on the tangled joints of the silver fish she held to avoid Diana's eye.

"Smart enough to show me what I've been missing. Thirteen years, Teal. I can't imagine how we ever produced a son. Forget trying for a daughter. When I see Madison, my skin crawls."

"And when you see Hank? Don't answer." Teal flipped up a hand. "There are some things even best friends shouldn't know. Are you planning on helping with your tree or what?"

"I'm finishing my wine."

"Of which we've both probably had enough." Teal flopped down beside Diana and raised her glass. "To a merry Christmas Eve!"

The glowing embers cast long shadows across the wall. Teal made out the distorted curves of a bunch of mistletoe. The berries dangled from the center of the bow Diana had tossed across the mantel. *Cool Yule* ended. Flames hissed in the sudden silence and the antique farmhouse creaked. The warm light picked out the strands of gold in Teal's chestnut hair and burnished Diana's copper to a vivid red.

"More music?" Teal didn't ask with much energy. Wine and warmth conspired to make her sleepy.

"Uh-uh." Diana pushed herself upright. "I'd better set up Scott's bike. I like your idea of stringing the ribbon from the tree to the garage. I hope he's surprised."

"He will be," Teal said. "And the old winding ribbon trick will increase the suspense—"

Diana laughed. "You certainly aren't a mother. Boys of seven are very impatient. Chances are after all my work, he'll look at that damned two hundred dollar bicycle and wonder why he didn't get another Nintendo which is what he thinks he wants."

"Are all moms so cynical? He may be overjoyed," Teal said. "If he isn't, I'd be happy to trade him for the bike."

Diana grunted and rose. "He's probably asleep by now,

but do you mind standing guard on the steps in case? I'm not doing all this just to have him catch me."

"Sure." Teal stood.

Diana wasn't exactly short, but at five feet seven Teal was the taller.

"The front steps, please. They aren't as squeaky and they're closer to his bedroom," Diana directed. She was back at the side window, staring out.

"See anything interesting?" Teal asked.

Diana spun around. "No."

"Just one question—"

Diana stiffened. "Yes?"

"What do I do if he does wake up?"

"No big deal," Diana said. "Just make a commotion to warn me. I shouldn't be long."

"When you're done with the bike, there is still the tree." Teal pointed to the near-bare boughs of the fir.

"No problem. You can't imagine how nice it feels to be putting it up on Christmas Eve like in my family. Civilized! Madison insisted we buy our tree before Thanksgiving and decorate it the minute we finished the turkey! By Christmas the poor thing was naked of needles and as dry as a bone. Honestly."

"Well, consider yourself finally free to do as you please."

"Almost free," Diana muttered. "Almost."

Teal settled on the big landing, halfway up. The old farmhouse reminded her that Diana and Madison Quinn had presented an image of the couple most people could only hope to be. Well-to-do, attractive, blessed with a son and this beautiful house. What a contrast between appearance and reality.

Few women became accountants when Teal and Diana first met. Fewer still became certified. Back then—Teal laughed aloud at the thought. Back then—what a sad comment on the world of commerce and industry for someone only in her thirties. Times had changed. Some.

Anyway, back then she had noticed Diana immediately in the group of new hires starting with Clayborne Whittier, the international accounting and auditing firm. Gender, as much as the red hair, made Diana stand out. Teal had the advantage of one month's seniority. Diana quit the firm after two years, but their friendship, begun as colleagues, grew.

Teal and Diana continued to meet for quick visits after work or for longer talks on the weekend. Diana liked the excuse to escape her husband and Wellesley. Boston reminded her of a time before she considered Earth's Best applesauce to be gourmet food. Once in a while, Teal and Diana took a lunch of roasted chicken sandwiches and white bean salad at Artu on Prince Street in the North End. Afterward they'd sip espresso at the Café Vittoria and pretend to be in Italy.

Diana had been one of the first people Teal talked to about Hunt when everything started to go south. Huntington Erin Huston, architect, to be exact. First lover, then lover and companion, then—well, who knew? Sometimes friend, seldom lover. Not what it was.

Diana became more than an amicable acquaintance in that period of emotional transition. Teal made the decision to separate from Hunt, but being the one to initiate the breakup didn't mean it didn't hurt. Diana had understood.

Which was more than Teal could say of herself about the sudden changes in Diana's life these days. Getting fed up with Madison? Sure. Actually Teal wondered why it had taken Diana so long. Teal never had cottoned to Madison Everett Quinn. But Diana's scorched-earth approach gave Teal pause.

Diana never had acknowledged her unhappiness. Year in and year out, life was going along fine. Madison moving up the career ladder, Scott a budding Einstein in first grade, Diana busy with the fulfillment of motherhood and Wellesley. Teal wasn't fooled, but she didn't mind. Their friendship had developed its unique intimacy based simply on an enjoyment of the other. Their respective daily lives had little meaning.

The day Diana first mentioned Hank, Teal understood her friend would not simply engage in a quiet affair, not Diana of the hot temper and burning hair. And Diana proved Teal right. She flaunted her new passion and as good as told Madison her feelings for him and for Hank within about a day. Small wonder Madison sought to redeem his pride by making her life hell over the divorce.

Diana's behavior generated a good deal of talk in her upper-middle-class town where affairs were, by unspoken protocol, conducted with discretion. Diana offended more than Madison. She didn't endear herself to the good burghers of Wellesley, and she had been counted among that crowd. Now Diana had to live with the unhappy discovery that her change in marital status left her on the outside in town.

The pungent smell of balsam wafted up the stairs. Teal heard voices as she came out of her reverie. Voices raised in a Christmas carol and growing louder. She hoped the group would come up to the house. At home on Beacon Hill in Boston, she loved the tradition of sharing her wassail bowl. But no, not tonight—the sound of voices began to fade. Teal crossed her fingers to bring them back later, perhaps after they did the other side of the road.

A muffled thud came from the direction of Scott's room. Rustling. A child's night cough. Teal tensed as she imagined small feet hitting the floor. She stood and peered up. Nothing. She sat back down.

"Mommy! Mommy!" Scott screamed as he tore around the corner.

Teal bolted upright and spread her arms. Scott set his jaw and skidded to a stop. He so resembled a determined Madison that Teal started to laugh. Her mistake. His U-turn for the kitchen stairs caught her by surprise. She wasn't going to get to him, not soon enough to spare his mother.

"Diana! Diana! Scott alert," Teal shouted as she sped down to the first floor.

She made it in time to see Scott hurl himself into his mother's arms as Diana stepped in from the garage. Teal prepared her face to exchange one of those looks over the little boy's head. The kind of look E. Teal Stewart and Diana S. Quinn often had enjoyed at the expense of unsuspecting Clayborne Whittier partners, but Diana didn't raise an eye. She kept her attention riveted on her son.

"Mommy! Mommy has Santa come?" Scott asked. He bounced up and down on bare feet. "I want to look. *P l e a s e.*"

He tugged at his mother's hand and in that moment froze. Two pairs of eyes followed his. The thin line of blood gathered speed to roll across Diana's palm and splatter crimson to the floor. Diana's chin shot up.

"Nothing," she mouthed to Teal. "Honestly. Assembly required—wouldn't you know." She wrinkled her nose and turned to her son with a reassuring hug. "I'm okay, honey. It's nothing, a scratch."

"It's yuck!" the seven-year-old said. He scuffed the wet blob with a toe. Red mottled the rug under his foot.

"Help Mommy wash and then I'll take you back up to bed," Diana said.

"No," he cajoled. "I want to see what Santa left under the tree."

"Maybe we should see if Santa drank his milk and ate his cookies instead," Diana suggested. "He'll be awfully upset if you peek before his visit. If the milk is still here, it's straight up to your room. All right? No looking. No tree—"

Diana's voice faded around the corner as she piloted Scott into the kitchen. Teal returned to the living room. The fire had died to a dark-ember glow, and the heat released more scent of balsam from the tree. The empty room embraced her, warm and cozy. Outside, the distant voices continued to raise in Christmas song, but now the words grew clear as the group came closer.

"Pa-rum, pa-rum, pa-rum-pa-pum-pum," drifted across the still night. Teal stepped to the window to monitor the carolers' second approach. The feeble light of a street lamp and a brilliant moon illuminated their way. Teal heard snow crunch under foot as the singers turned in at the path to the Quinn house. She could not see them yet because of the garage. The march hesitated and, in a moment, the footsteps sounded a retreat as the group retraced the route to the street.

Why, Teal wondered? She felt unaccountably disappointed. Why did they leave before coming to the front door?

The scandal—of course! Diana said she as good as had a scarlet letter carved into her forehead. Her brazen conduct had set the neighborhood and town to censor her. Teal registered anger against her disappointment. Who were these strangers to judge? And on Christmas Eve?

C r a s h !

The jolt cut off the next thought as the tree dipped and tottered. Teal reached for the trunk. The balsam righted in its stand, but the ribbon Diana had tied to the bottom and unwound to the garage was pulled taut.

Teal knelt to loosen the knot. The idea of a present at the end of a line wasn't really hers but her mother's, another family tradition. The feel of the satin, smooth against her hand, brought memories of a different Christmas Eve. The one when a twelve-year-old Teal snuck down to the tree after everyone else was asleep.

She found a bright pink ribbon girdling the trunk. At the end, she discovered more than her first three-speed bike—she discovered the truth of her mother's warning. It was no fun to outwit a surprise. Still, Teal recalled years of happy riding on her first big-girl bike.

Bike! Scott's bike. It must have fallen. It must have been the crash. Teal prayed she wouldn't find a mess of scratches and dents. Diana must not have heard from all the way upstairs. Teal tracked the satin guide line from the living room, past the kitchen, and into the darkness of the garage.

She flipped on the light switch and squinted against the sudden glare to complete the trail with her eyes. The ribbon slid across the concrete floor before it rose to end in a bunch of mistletoe showing green and pure white where it nestled into the heart of the bow.

Teal froze. The ribbon rising to the bow. The mistletoe. The end of the line and the surprise. But this ribbon wasn't tied to any old bike. This ribbon was jammed between Madison Everett Quinn's grinning lips.

"No!" Teal cried and slapped her hand to her mouth.

The clear yellow plastic of an ordinary screwdriver handle angled up from four inches below and to the left of Madison's tilted chin, from out of his chest. Teal stumbled over a wheel and pressed her fingers to the side of his throat. She counted a slow three. Nothing beat. No pulse. No hope.

Madison Everett Quinn slumped on the cold floor very, very dead.

She didn't waste time with thinking. The bicycle hauled upright in a second. She settled the kickstand. No scratches. No dents. She jerked the tool-closet door open and grabbed Madison under the arms. He didn't make it easy. He resisted, slipping from her hold, awkward and leaden.

What did she expect of a corpse six feet long? She stuck a foot in the door and managed to two hand him until he wedged in. She freed the bow and pressed the door closed on his sagging grin.

The ribbon dangled, fancy end down. Blotches of Madison's saliva mottled the back of the bow, but she wasn't going to concentrate on them. Or on him. A few globes of the waxy berry rolled around on the floor. Teal narrowed her somber eyes on the bike. A quick shake of the decoration would have to suffice. She looped the handle bars with ribbon and topped the seat with the festive bow.

She checked the curl of the red line as she returned inside. Not too slack, not too taut, and at the far end, she secured the end to the tree as if it had never been otherwise. Different sensations came back into focus. Her heart pounding. The stifling heat of the fire. The deadly quiet. Teal dropped to the couch.

"Teal? You there?" Diana called as she came down the stairs. She rounded from the front hall into the living room. "Did I hear something? Did I hear you go out?"

Teal didn't blink as she nodded.

The effect was as good as a match to a fuse. Diana shot across the room for the garage. Teal followed at a stroll.

"The bike . . ." Diana's voice dribbled off. She stared from the sleek, red two-wheeler and back to Teal. She fingered the bow like it was a bomb.

"Surprise? Surprise?" Teal couldn't hide the edge in her voice.

"You shouldn't have . . ." Diana pressed a length of ribbon between her palms. Over and over.

"What are friends for?" Teal asked. "The assembly— surely that was the hard part."

"Yes," Diana murmured. Her eyes darted around the room. "Is . . . is everything all done? Put to rights?"

"You tell me," Teal said. She gestured to the bike. "Looks pretty good."

"I guess." Diana hesitated.

Maybe, in a moment, Diana would talk. Maybe. Teal crossed her fingers and hoped. Diana began to open her mouth and Teal leaned forward.

Ding-dong.

The bell echoed from the front door. A small tinny sound this far into the house. Diana's mouth closed.

Ding-dong.

"Hank," the women said in unison. They remained fixed where they stood.

Diana's focus bounced from the red and chrome, across Teal, past the one car parked in the two-car garage. It circled back again. Her feet rocked toe to heel to toe. The bell rang again.

"I think Hank wants us to come," Teal said. "Would you like me to let him in before he decides to take on the door?"

Diana sucked in her lower lip. "No. I'll go. It's just . . . are you sure you finished? You didn't have to, you . . ."

A moment of Diana's voice trailing to silence preceded the next ring. Then pounding sounded from the front of the house.

"He might wake Scott," Teal suggested.

"Oh no!" Diana moved.

Teal watched Diana's hair swing around the corner. It was beautiful hair, bright and alive. Then all trace of Diana disappeared. Teal turned to inspect the garage.

The rafters were hung with the debris of an active, athletic family. Skis and poles, a battered Sunfish mast, an inflatable rubber boat. Beneath, Diana's Volvo rested, its engine cold. The bicycle occupied the space for a second car beside the first. Beneath the bike wheels, normal wear marked the floor. Oil stains. A smattering of needles shed from the tree. Shriveled, brown oak leaves blown in from outdoors.

Dirt. And something darker.

Teal squatted. The something darker turned into something damp and a blackening red on closer inspection. Something like blood.

"Teal? Are you going to join us?" Diana stood in the door.

Teal lurched upright as her friend descended the two steps into the garage. Her elbow caught the ribbon and the bike tottered. It did not fall.

"What's that? What were you looking at?" Diana stared down. She smacked her foot over one dark blob.

"Blood," Teal said.

Diana jerked back. "I never realized my stupid scratch could make such a mess. Scott can't discover his present set up on a floor covered with this. I'd better clean up."

She finished talking already busy at the utility sink at the back wall. Water thundered into a pail. The other evidence, Teal realized, numb. Diana unhooked a mop from the pegboard wall.

"Do you always leave this side door unlocked?" Teal asked. She pointed.

Diana raised her head from her self-appointed task. "What are you talking about? Oh, that door. No. Never."

Teal rotated the outside handle. The action demonstrated the door was not locked. A cold wind swirled into the garage.

"Well?" she asked. "Well, almost never unless I forget," Diana amended.

246

"What do you use it for?" Teal asked.

"Firewood deliveries and stuff like that." Diana returned to pouring Lestoil in the pail.

"You don't have the truck pull into the empty space right there?" Teal pointed to the area Diana scrubbed beside the bike.

"Not when Madison lived here. Then we had two cars, remember. It's habit now, I guess." Diana straightened. "Teal, what are you really asking about?"

"It could be unsafe. A woman and child alone in the country—"

"This from the individual who refuses to live anywhere else but the middle of a city? And don't tell me Beacon Hill is safer than Wellesley." Diana clattered the mop and pail in the sink before she faced Teal. "Are you ready to come in and talk with Hank or do you plan to spend your Christmas Eve inspecting my garage?"

Diana acted like she had before the bicycle crashed to the floor. The old Diana, back in control. The room had been put in order, the bloodstains washed and gone. She had nothing to fear.

They started up the steps. Teal reached out to kill the light.

"No." Diana placed her hand on Teal's arm. "Wait. I opened the toolshed and left it unbolted before Scott came downstairs. If he gets up early, he could get into it and hurt himself. Let me—"

Teal was faster. She rocketed from the stairs. "I've got it, see?"

Her back leaned against the door and she shoved. She tried not to show the strain of Madison's dense and resistant two hundred and ten pounds flopped against the other side. The latch clicked, and Teal shot the sliding bolt at the top of the door.

"Let's go!" Teal grinned.

The fire had been fed and new flames leapt and roared. Hank greeted Teal with a twirl under the sprig of mistletoe

247

he held above her head. His lips brushed her cheek, the gesture of a friend.

"Joyeaux Noël, Teal!"

Henry Clement instructed French at Scott Quinn's exclusive private school and coached the town's public youth soccer league. Part of Hank's charm was that he did pretty much what he wanted. Money and status weren't his thing. He made enough to live in reasonable comfort, but not in a style to which Diana had grown accustomed.

Diana had confessed her ambivalence to Teal. "He's not exactly poor, but . . ." she had said.

No, not exactly poor. He lived in Wellesley and drove a very old, very beat-up Porsche. Poor by the standards of people like Diana maybe, Teal had agreed.

"That's just it—I shouldn't mind," Diana had said.

"But you do?"

"Well, yes. A little. Maybe. I don't want to be unfair to Scott just because I love Hank, and actually I'm not so sure for myself. I like money. What it can buy. The freedom, I guess."

Teal almost laughed. "Like all the freedom you had with Madison to be the person you wanted to be? Come on, Diana. Hank and you could do fine, but it won't be like with Madison, no. And you won't be paying the same price. I hope."

It had been the only advice Teal could give.

"Et qu'est-ce que vous avez fait ce soir?" Hank pointed to the tree and laughed. *"Rien, je crois."*

Diana's expression grew a shade testy.

"We haven't done nothing, exactly," Teal answered. "Just close to nothing on the tree."

"Shall we get to it?" Diana asked. "And in English."

"Mais oui," Hank said and danced Diana around the room. He ended their waltz beside the balsam. "Where do we start, *ma cherie?"*

"With these," Diana said as she laughed. She held out last year's tinsel, carefully saved in a box.

"Surely you aren't too cheap to buy the stuff new," Hank said.

Teal giggled. This was beginning to feel familiar. A few friends, a fire, wrangling over how to decorate the tree.

Reality cut short her serenity. How many Christmases had she discovered an estranged husband, ready for the morgue, on a friend's garage floor? Before how many trimming parties had she hurried to hide a body? There was another way to describe what she had done tonight. Tampering with evidence fit just fine.

And what about Diana? The friend who confessed to her love of freedom and money had sloshed water and soap across a floor spotted with Madison's spilled blood. Teal had watched without saying a word. Detective Malley wouldn't approve. He'd have another term for what Teal had done. Accessory after the fact. It wasn't a pretty notion.

"Teal? Teal, are you listening? I said I almost didn't make it here on time tonight." Hank was smiling.

Teal knew she was supposed to ask why. "Why?"

"I took it into my head to drive to Freeport—"

"Aye-ah?" Diana teased. "To Maine's famous twenty-four-hour L. L. Bean? Oh Hank, you didn't need to do that." She had dropped the accent. "And I think you made it a little early." Teal squirmed as Diana beamed.

"Scott wanted fishing gear, right?" Hank asked, holding Diana with his big brown eyes.

Okay, okay, Teal wanted to say. You hope to woo the mother through the kid. Hank sometimes had that effect on her. An adult with attitude—Peter Pan's. The charm of men like Hank, aside from his considerable good looks, was the refusal to do it the grown-up way.

"Anyway, what a zoo," he continued. "I thought I was smart, waiting until Christmas Eve. Everyone else must have been thinking like me. The store was up to here with people."

"It doesn't ever close, does it?" Teal said.

Hank shook his curly hair and grinned. "Nope."

"Yes, they do, don't they? On Christmas Day?" Diana said.

"I bet it's open," Hank countered.

"Oh, come on, they must close—"

"Can we change the subject? You sound married," Teal said.

"Horrors!" Hank jumped back to hug Diana. He winked at Teal. "Sure. And speaking of married—where is the old man spending the holiday?"

Hank liked to tease with a jibe. Teal remembered that from their first meeting.

"Oh, a Bostonian," he had said. "Do you paak the caa in Haavad yaad?"

Very clever—yeah, right.

"No," she'd replied, her teeth on edge. "And there isn't a Brahmin in town who would be caught dead talking like that."

Teal actually didn't much like teasing. She certainly didn't like being teased. At least Hank had dropped it there and didn't go on to rib her about her profession. Why did so many people act stupid when an accountant was both female and good-looking?

Teal noticed that Diana wasn't reacting all that well to the teasing herself right now.

"Stop it, Hank! You don't care one whit about Madison, and I'd just as soon not talk about him tonight."

Diana riveted her attention on the carpet. The rug was a fabulous Persian, but she must have seen it a million times since she owned it. What made the geometric pattern fascinating tonight?

"I only wondered if he was making the same effort I did on the fishing gear to see his precious son, is all," Hank said. He shrugged.

Teal remembered the day Diana told her about Hank. Diana's choice of restaurant had been the first hint something was up—she did not like to meet on Boston's swankiest shopping street, but for this morning, she chose Mirabelle on Newbury Street despite the terrible parking.

Then there was Diana's hair gleaming like a new copper sun, the sprinkle of gray banished. Everything about her had

250

glowed burnished and beautiful and on fire. She dispensed with the small talk quickly. Yes, good croissants and good coffee, she agreed and then got on to her subject.

"I've never felt as alive," she had said. "Teal, this man has touched something dormant in me. Hank is so witty and brilliant. And fun. The sex is—well, I love the lanky, crazy guy, honestly. I think you will, too. Let me show you his picture. See!"

Diana slipped the Polaroid from her wallet and handed it over like a teenager in love. Hank stood tall and slender, his hair and eyes dark. Madison measured tall enough, but thick and blond. Beside Madison, Diana had appeared frail and petite. Beside Hank she looked about right as he rested his chin on her head and held her wrapped in his arms. They were laughing.

"What do you think?" she'd asked Teal. "Isn't he something."

"Umm. Something that could torch your relationship with your husband, that's easy to see," Teal replied as she passed the image back.

Diana regarded the photograph. "He could ruin everything, couldn't he? My marriage, the reputation in town I've worked to achieve, and my role as a mother, if Madison turns into a prick. But Teal, I'm not sure I want to live without him. I'm not sure I can. Without what he does to me. Am I crazy?"

Teal had sat, mute, picking at croissant crumbs. Who was she to say?

"I asked in part because—" Hank paused and Teal tuned back into the present.

"Because if Madison found me here, he could go nuts on you. Diana, the court order—"

"Forbids you from being in my house or seeing my son. You don't have to remind me, but he agreed not to interfere with Christmas. He's probably on his way home to his mother." Diana twisted a colored ball between her fingers.

Her toe traced the outline of a figure woven into the rug.

Teal saw a smear of dried blood at the tip. Diana had cleaned up the floor but not her shoe.

"I still don't understand how a court can let him get away with running your life in this day and age," Hank threw out.

Teal thought he must like to toss gasoline at lit matches.

"Because he was—" The shiny gold ball burst and showered jagged stars across the rug.

"Because?" Hank prompted.

"Because he is willing to stop at nothing to get back at me, and my lawyer said I should give him that for now, all right? It will never stick in the final divorce. Can we drop the subject of Madison? Do you see him anywhere near here? No. And he won't be, so forget him!" Diana looked at the empty hook dangling from her fingers and burst into tears.

Hank murmured words like *honey* and *sorry*. Teal squirmed. Third wheel—there was a great expression. It wasn't much fun being third of three.

Intimate words and more intimate actions animated the couch. Teal considered her position. Two is company. Three's a crowd. Besides, there was something else she had to do. Had had to do for a while.

"I'll get us a plate of cookies," Teal said. Neither Hank or Diana took any notice.

Spice scented the warm kitchen. Teal fingered a scrap of sugar-cookie dough stuck to the counter and surveyed Diana's interpretation of a farmhouse. A huge Viking stove, cabinets of hand-hewn wood, and a painted tile floor contrasted with Teal's Euro-chic kitchen at home.

She had installed a special rubber floor herself, the kind used in fancy gyms, at Hunt's suggestion that the material would save her legs. Tile might be pretty, but it made the cook's life too hard. Actually nothing in the farmhouse reminded Teal of her town house. *Chaque à son gout,* as Hank might say. Each to his own. That's what made life interesting. Teal laughed and reached for the cookies. And saw the telephone.

The instrument's cheerful yellow coordinated with the rustic decor. It hung about nose level in front of her face. She had no reasonable excuse to avoid doing what she should have done half an hour ago. Maybe tonight was Christmas Eve and maybe she didn't want to interrupt a family celebration with a professional call. But if she didn't call him, the obvious alternative was worse.

Her finger trembled as it pressed out each one of the seven numbers. Her ears pounded with her blood's roar, the sound of an ocean of regret. This was no way to treat a best friend on Christmas Eve. Surely Diana deserved some slack. Teal slammed the receiver to its hook. She could leave the question unanswered for tonight. What else were friends for?

Teal panted like she'd been running for miles. Or dragging and heaving a body across a floor. Madison's body. It had resisted her pull like a dead weight. Because he was dead. She had to make the call. Not even Diana could ask more of Teal than this. She punched out the digits, fast.

The line rang. And rang.

"Hello?" A reluctant, querulous tremble colored the greeting.

"Detective Malley, please." Teal winced.

"Why?" the woman whined. "This is Christmas Eve! My son is not on duty!"

"Dan. I'd like Dan, please. I am sorry to be disturbing him on Christ—"

The older women dropped her end. Teal jumped away from the receiver at the bang. Static and then a second voice came on the line.

"Hello?"

"Your mom, Dan? I am sorry. This is Teal Stewart—"

"I recognize you, T-t-teal," Dan said.

She could imagine his slow, considerate nod.

"Yes, of course." Teal didn't want to think about the reason they had exchanged too many telephone calls and become too familiar with the other's voice. Yet here she was with another body. "I need your help."

"Of course. What's it all about?" Dan asked.

Teal did not intend to answer, not directly. What she needed was help with the plan. The plan to trap—the thought broke off. She wasn't going to think about that.

"I know this sounds weird, but I need you to ask the Wellesley police to find the caroling group out here. Then, if a few of the police could join the group and serenade the Quinns' house—" Teal held her breath.

"Y-y-you're joking." Dan's flat voice did not ask a question.

Teal wished she could laugh like a fool and say she was and mean it. Apologize. Hang up the telephone. Open the garage closet tomorrow morning and find it empty.

"No, actually. I wouldn't ask, except that it is important. Very important, Dan. I thought maybe a Boston homicide detective would have more pull out here than a visiting CPA. It may sound silly, but I wouldn't put you out for nothing, honestly."

Madison Everett Quinn had been a lot of things. Egotistical. Stubborn. According to his wife, a rotten lover. Fulfilling the Peter Principle at work and a bore at home. He had been a father. A husband. A son.

However described, whether loved or unloved, loving or cold, he had not been nothing.

"Wellesley? You want me to call the Wellesley station and give them orders. Why d-d-don't you make it easy? How about I'll call and boss around the Moscow police."

"It really is important, Dan—"

"Then tell me more," he said.

"The thing is, I can't."

Teal stared down at the plate of cookies on the counter beside the phone. Her free hand automatically rearranged the gingerbread figures one-two-three in a row. Boy-girl-boy stared up with six blank, raisin eyes.

"What do you mean, you can't? You mean you w-w-won't."

"It's hard to explain from this distance . . . on the phone."

Very hard to explain. What could she say to her friend the

254

cop? I have a small confession to make, I hid the body? I stood by and watched the prime suspect scrub the blood away with a mop? Oh, who are these folks? Just some people I know, the types who get a messy divorce? The wife has a lover and is the beneficiary of a great big insurance policy on her husband? Teal sighed.

Boy-boy-girl gazed from the plate.

No. She didn't like that.

Girl-boy-boy.

Not quite. The next progression left the tan figures where they started. Boy-girl-boy.

Two's company. Three's a crowd.

Teal shifted the plate away from her with a jerk. The first boy slid to the edge and farther. He dropped and cracked in two. A leg broke off.

Teal heard Dan breathing.

"I need help. Please," she whispered.

His sigh carried across the miles. "Dad had friends in Wellesley. They'd be retired now, but who knows. Maybe one of them has a kid in uniform like me. That's the best I can do. Just tell me again this is important, not some two-bit theft of your friend's yard decorations. And tell me it doesn't involve you directly. Please."

She could imagine Dan's earnest young face. The smartest, youngest, and most sincere Boston homicide cop, that's what she thought. Homicide Detective Daniel Malley was about to go out on a limb on nothing but her word. She could name more personal friends who would have come up with much less. He deserved the truth.

"Important and ugly and involving someone close to me. The best gift I could get this Christmas is to find—"

"—Out you're wrong, I see. S-s-so. Give me the details. What caroling group? And where are you? . . ."

She didn't tell him that wasn't quite it, that what she needed was to convince herself by establishing the final proof of guilt. Then justice must take its course. A tear beaded at the corner of her eye. Teal shook her head. She could not afford to cry.

She answered Dan's routine questions while she stooped to pick up the pieces of the gingerbread boy. She lobbed them into the trash. That cleanup was easy. Not like the other one-two-three would be.

"Will you be all right until these guys arrive?" Dan asked.

"Sure," Teal said before she put down the telephone. Sure, she'd be fine.

She added figures to the plate. Boys and girls. Angels and santas. No more trinities. She couldn't let herself think it would turn out that horrible and that easy.

"What took so long?" Diana asked from where she knelt fishing an ornament's hook over a low branch.

"Discretion, yes?" Hank smiled and handed Diana another orb. "You're the perfect friend, Teal."

She wasn't sure about that.

"The tree—what do you think?" Diana asked. She emerged from the greenery, hands on her hips.

Her face was all red, Teal noticed. Like she'd been holding her breath.

"Close to perfection." Teal circled. "I love that one."

She pointed to a fragile silver moon. The thin, blown-glass crescent beamed a smiling face across to the branch of a companion gold sun.

"I do, too," Hank agreed. "I had to make her hang it since Madison gave her the moon, wouldn't you know—"

"It's not that simple." Diana gritted her teeth and shook her head.

"My advice is to forget him and enjoy the goods." Hank grinned.

"Like everything is that easy," Diana snapped.

"Cookie, anyone?" Teal offered.

The sugared angels and stars restored a show of good humor. The three sat on the couch to eat and evaluate their progress on the tree. One or two ornaments were repositioned. Teal added a last pagoda and a tiny tasseled scroll of a Chinese love scene. Hank strung up his offering of a jolly *Père Noël*.

Teal tried to catch Diana's eye behind his back, but Diana resolutely stared ahead. For a minute the Christmas Eve scene felt like a poorly staged play. Teal wanted to reach out and pat comfort to Diana, but she could not. She could not go that far to pretend everything would be okay.

"Let's switch on the lights," Hank suggested.

Diana raised her head with a jolt. "The lights—oh, no."

She stared Teal straight in the face and her voice cracked. "No—I totally for—"

"—got!" Teal yelped.

"Why are you two about to roll around the floor in laughter?" Hank asked.

"Madison," they chorused.

Diana wiped at the tears of mirth streaking her face. She wrestled for control of her voice. "Madison always strung the lights on the tree—"

"Even at my Christmas parties," Teal added, as if that should illuminate the matter.

"His male thing, I guess. Anyway, without him here, we never thought . . ."

Hank stretched and stood. "Better late than never. I'll manage to string them up without breaking a thing. Where have you got them hidden?"

"It doesn't matter. I like the tree the way it is, and no matter how careful you are, something will be smashed to pieces." Diana patted the seat and gestured Hank closer.

"No. I can do it if you both help and we are very careful. What's a tree without lights?" He arched his brows.

Teal squinted at the tree. Three pairs of hands at work had left it hung with baubles and tinsel and things vaguely Chinese. But Hank had a point. No lights didn't look quite right. The moment a darkened living room twinkled and glowed meant it was Christmas Eve.

"Won't Scott be disappointed?" Teal asked. "I mean, I think Hank's right that we can do it. Where are the lights?"

She walked to the decorations box and began to rummage.

"They're not in there," Diana said, her voice low.

"Then where?" Now Hank stood.

Diana pointed to the garage. "It's okay. I'll go." She pushed by Hank.

"No, really. Let me," he said.

Diana shook her head. "They're buried somewhere in the tool closet. It won't take me long, while you—"

Teal sprinted past them both. Damn. The stupid lights would be stored in that closet.

"You two stay. I'll be right back," she called over her shoulder.

"No. I'll go with you," Diana said. She hurried to the door.

"Wait! Are we acting like kids or what?" Hank said. "Diana is right—we'll probably ruin half of what's up. I have a few old candle clips at home with candles from Germany. It won't take me five minutes to drive there and back. The effect of their dancing flame is lovely—"

"Unless the whole tree goes up like a torch," Teal said.

"She's right. It's too dangerous. This isn't a live balsam and even then I'm not too sure. Scott will live without lights." Diana shrugged.

"What's that about?" Hank pointed to the red ribbon snaking through the living-room door and down the hall by the kitchen.

"It leads to Scott's present from me. A bicycle. He'll follow it from the tree tomorrow and find his bike at the end. Would the trick have excited you as a boy?" Diana asked.

"Indeed. What a clever idea," Hank said. "When did you have the time? Or is the final setup in the morning?"

"No. No. Earlier this evening. Everything is assembled and ready.

Teal handed a cup of wassail to Diana and raised the ladle. "And for you?" she asked Hank.

"Nothing, thanks. You both enjoy a glass while I check out this bike if you don't mind." He waved.

"What do you think, Teal? Isn't he great?" Diana said after Hank left.

Teal watched Diana tear a fringe around her paper napkin. The garish holiday pattern overlapped a stake of holly with a sprig of mistletoe. Teal flipped her napkin over.

"I'm not sure he's exactly to die for," she said.

"Honestly," Diana exploded. "You know what I mean!"

"And what do you mean to do now with Hank?" Teal whispered.

"What did you say?" Diana snapped her head up. "Listen to me. I sound as moody as a teenager—"

"—in love," Teal finished.

"Dion and the Belmonts, top ten 1959." Diana giggled. "Why does my mind love holding trivia?"

A log hissed.

"Shh," Diana said. "Do you hear sleigh bells?"

The room was silent as they listened.

How many years had she known Diana? Teal wriggled her fingers and counted. Better than five, less than ten. Friends. So, what should she say? Should she say, Diana, what were you doing in the garage?

But Teal knew what Diana had been doing in the garage. She had been fighting with Madison. Teal sighed.

"What's wrong?" Diana asked.

Teal shrugged. "Holiday blues."

Diana nodded. "Me, too. A little."

They fell quiet. Teal expected Diana to hammer her with questions and chatter about Hank. But Diana remained mum.

Teal never remembered feeling this much tension with her friend. She read the hands of the mantel clock. If Malley had any luck, the singers should arrive soon. Diana ladled out a third cup of mulled wine. No footsteps sounded Hank's return. Teal took a deep breath. Now or never, this was it.

"Diana?" Teal heard her voice dip and rise. "When the bike fell over while you were upstairs with Scott and I went out into the garage?"

"Yes?" Diana darted a glance at Teal over the rim of her

259

punch glass. Then she smacked her drink to the table and glared. "Do you have any idea of how miserable he says he'll make me if I go through with the divorce? God, I despise his wounded male pride or whatever the hell it is! Don't ever get married, that's my advice."

"It's not much of a worry so far. The right person hasn't asked me." Teal sighed.

"Right person, wrong person—what did I know back then? Pinned all through college, can you believe? Madison was the only man I ever slept with until Hank freed me. No wonder I never understood the tale of Sleeping Beauty. But this maiden has awakened. And she'll never go back. I'm not proud of myself. I'm not proud of how I did what I did, but life with Madison was life in a prison. Can you see and forgive me?"

Teal tried to hold her expression to a neutral smile. She loved Diana. Self-centered, smart, funny—even on a bad day, Teal loved Diana. Friends owed each other compassion and support and honesty. And she wasn't being honest with her friend right now, but Teal couldn't face telling Diana how this Christmas Eve had to end. She wasn't going to seize the moment.

"Hank's been gone for a while," she said instead.

Diana shot her a look. Yes, Teal wanted to say, I am avoiding your question. It doesn't matter if I see. It matters what happened. Teal smiled a fake holiday smile.

"What do you think he's doing out there?" Diana asked, her voice testy. "I'll go see."

She banged out of the room. Teal leaned on her elbows and stared into the fire. A log cracked a shower of sparks across the hearth. She picked an artificial Sequoia cone from the basket and threw it on the burning logs. The heat exploded the chemical coating into tongues of blue and purple and green.

Like the cool nights in California, Teal thought, when she and her friends scavenged real Sequoia cones from the beach. Soaked in the minerals of the Pacific, they added color to graduate student bonfires. California, where life had seemed safe. A state before ugly realities like Madison Quinn lying cold as a corpse on the garage floor.

Teal wished wisdom came with age, but she couldn't claim that it did. She wished the carolers would hurry. She couldn't stand another minute of wondering if she'd done the right thing.

There had been days during the breakup with Hunt that she'd hated him. Been enraged at everything he said, everything he did. Had wanted to throw his architectural models and books and tools out of the apartment's front door. Had wanted to chop at him with a knife maybe. But she hadn't. She moved herself out instead, and sometimes now they even got along more than amicably. Friendship hadn't seemed possible back then.

It would never, ever be possible for the Quinns.

Laughter breezed in with the banging of doors. Teal strained to hear. Diana's giggles and the sounds of a kiss. More distant voices sang. "God rest you merry gentlemen . . ." drifted to the house from the street. God rest the gentleman, indeed.

Teal spun around as Diana and Hank walked in with a rustle of cold air.

"What do you think?" she croaked.

"Some machine!" Hank said. "Nothing like my first two-wheeler, that's for sure."

Diana's happiness made her face pink and radiant. "He's worried I'll spoil my son, but what do you believe?"

Her hand motioned to the gaily wrapped fishing pole under Hank's other arm. The one he didn't have around her.

"Where was that?" Teal asked.

Hank grinned. "I brought it in from my car—"

"Which is what took him so long," Diana said. "Now I feel like a potential piker only going for the two hundred dollar bike. There was one at three."

"And the worry about spoiling your son?" Teal chided. "Hmm?"

261

Diana's face clouded. "Maybe I am trying a little too hard right now. But it's difficult for a boy to lose a father, much as I'd just as soon Madison be—"

"Listen!" Teal jumped in. Don't say it, Diana, she thought. Don't say *dead.* "Listen! I hear voices."

Feet stamped along the snowy walk. Voices chattered then outside Diana's house, paused, and lifted.

"God rest you merry gentlemen, Let nothing you dismay. Remember—"

Hank was up and heading for the foyer.

"Wait!" Diana said.

Hank swung around. "What's wrong, honey?"

"They'll wake Scott."

"That's all? Scott can come down to hear them if he wants, and we have plenty of wassail." Hank turned to throw open the door.

"O, tidings of comfort and joy!"

Teal didn't think Diana felt that way. The redhead stiffened her jaw into a smile as she joined Hank to extend a hand in welcome. Teal wondered if her lover had any idea of what inviting in the group would do to this night. She glanced from his face to Diana's and back. Diana's lips vibrated with anxiety and her eyes darted over every individual in the singing crowd. Hank looked handsome and relaxed.

"Please everyone, come in for some Christmas cheer," he said. He waved to the living room and directed the removal of hats and coats.

Teal mingled with the group forming in front of the tree. She turned as a last person joined them. Dan Malley! Teal swallowed a gasp. Wasn't he able to find a member of the local police? No, she amended, it looked like he had. The burly guy beside him. Hank passed around wassail and offered the plate of cookies. Except for Diana, everyone exchanged Christmas greetings.

Diana hung back in the hall, her face in shadow. All at once, the carolers reassembled into a chorale unit as if on cue. Cups down, cookies eaten. A woman stepped forward.

"Now, what can we sing to thank you?" she asked. She moved her eyes from Teal to Hank until she found Diana. "I am so glad you changed your mind. It's all for charity, you know."

"What is?" Teal asked to cut the attention from Diana.

"Our singing. That's what I was trying to explain to the lady of the house before—"

"But I was too busy!" Diana as good as screamed.

Dan Malley had sidled from the back of the chorus to the side nearest the entry.

The woman took a quick step back. "Of course. I understand. We're so happy that your friend here called to ask us back."

The woman pointed at Hank. His smile lowered at the corners of his mouth. Teal tensed. The woman's singling out Hank could ruin the charade. Malley must have been the one to fool the group into returning, but the woman naturally connected Hank to the male voice.

" 'Silent Night,' don't you think?" Teal hastened to suggest. "Please."

"Silent night, holy night, All is calm . . ." soared into the room.

Hank's smile returned. He pulled Diana forward and stood behind her, her head to his chest. Teal considered this picture of an adoring couple. Was this why Madison had been murdered? For love? Teal felt sick.

Or had pure rage raised the hand that struck the blow? Or both?

Teal wasn't sure she wanted to know. She would prefer to leave Diana's private life private. But there was the fact of Madison's death.

Malley caught Teal's eye with a question. The burly guy began to act restless. Teal looked back at Hank and Diana. Did Hank suspect the real reason behind this musical visit? What had Diana said to him in the garage? Nothing, Teal bet, because if he knew, he never would have welcomed in the singers. She was sure of that.

The song ended with all calm in the room, all bright in the blaze of the fire. Now or never.

Teal swung around and raised her head. She had to avoid Diana's vulnerable face. Hank returned Teal's gaze.

"Diana said she was too busy to invite the carolers to sing. What was your excuse, Hank? You did something to rid this house of the group when they returned. Did you speak to them beside the garage?"

Hank jerked backward, pulling Diana with him.

Malley closed off access to the hall, fast. A petite woman skirted the room to block the passage to the kitchen. Forget the stereotyped burly guy, Teal realized. He did not move.

The leader of the group swiveled her head from Hank to Teal in confusion.

"He waved us off when he was busy trying to rub the red paint off his shoe. We'd seen the lady of the house working on a red bike earlier." She smiled at Hank. "Were you assigned some last-minute painting? I've found that projects never go well on Christmas Eve."

"No, they don't," Teal agreed. She could not shift her eyes away. She could not blink.

The rest of the group laughed, except for Malley and the policewoman and Hank.

Diana squirmed from his arms to face him. "What is everyone talking about? What paint?"

"Blood. Not paint, blood." Teal intoned no question to her statement.

Diana swung to glare at Teal. "You aren't making sense. That was my blood I cleaned up. You saw the cut. The damned screwdriver." Diana waved the bandaged back of her hand. "Hank didn't arrive until—"

"No, Diana. Madison's blood, not yours," Teal said.

Diana shook her head. "That's crazy. Hank wasn't anywhere near here when Madison came to see me."

Diana gasped and clamped a hand to her mouth.

"When Madison came to see you?" Teal said.

Diana sighed. "I didn't want to tell you. It's such an old,

stupid story. He came. We fought. What else is new? I didn't want to ruin tonight for Scott or Hank or you."

"Madison was with you when I called out the warning about Scott, wasn't he?" Teal said.

Diana rocked her head. "Yes."

"You must have been confused when you found me in the garage without Madison when you returned from putting Scott back to bed," Teal spoke gently.

"Yes. Madison threatened to stay all night if he had to. He wanted to spend Christmas with his son. He wants sole custody, you see. Or says he does. He wouldn't know what to do with Scott—"

"He must have infuriated you," Teal said.

Diana snorted. "I was so mad, I socked him with the bow and mistletoe still in my hand. Phew! Lot of good that did. He just laughed and clowned around pretending to eat the bow. Then you warned me about Scott. When I found you in the garage, I was sure Madison had tried to lobby you. He must have because he hadn't been successful with me. He's not the type to give up voluntarily."

"He didn't leave," Teal said. "Ask Hank."

Diana furrowed her forehead as she lifted her face to meet the eyes of her lover. "What is she talking about?"

Hank tried to shrug. "I haven't the faintest idea."

The room resembled a still life of a party filled with holiday good cheer. Ornaments reflected distorted firelight from the tree, lazy smoke curled up the chimney, and stockings hung from the mantel. The carolers balanced cups of wassail and strained to understand the first hint of tomorrow's town gossip. Not one moved.

"Tu est un peu malade?" Hank asked Teal. "No one seems to understand what you're talking about."

"No, I'm not sick," she snapped. "And you know exactly what I'm saying."

Hank's voice dropped. "No, I don't, and you are embarrassing yourself and me in front of these good people."

"Then let me show you." Teal gritted her teeth.

She tore past the policewoman. Malley fell in behind Hank and the rest of the party pressed to follow. Teal sprinted down the few steps to the garage and ripped open the closet.

"Light," she yelled. Diana flipped up the switch.

"See!" Teal gestured in a sweep.

Slumped just inside the open door lay a big tan bag of road salt. A snow blower leaned against the back wall and tools hung from a pegboard. That was it. No Madison or any other body. No trace betrayed the former occupancy of a corpse.

Teal's rage drained to confusion.

"Very funny on Christmas Eve. Is the joke over?" Diana chopped out each word with her teeth. "Do we have Ms. Sleuth's permission to go back inside?"

The group leader directed her charges to the front hall.

"It is time for us to leave. You were lovely to invite us in," she said to Diana. She accepted the cash Hank offered. "Thank you so much and God bless you and yours this Christmas."

Coats and hats were gathered and put on. Malley sidled over to pair himself with Teal in the commotion.

"What the hell is going on?" he hissed. "W-w-what did I miss in this charade?"

"Dan, I tell you, I dragged Madison Quinn's body from the center of that garage to hide him in the closet. I watched my friend mop up her husband's blood all the while she believed it to be hers. I am not crazy. This all happened this evening. Dead bodies don't get up and walk—he just cannot be gone!"

"You did what? You discovered a murder and didn't call the police?" Dan jerked his gloves on.

Teal sighed. "Okay, you're right. But I called you—"

"And the body has disappeared, Teal. If it was ever there to b-b-begin with."

"Hey Dan, this is me, remember? Not a flake. Not a crazy."

Someone opened the front door. The air hit Teal in the face with the smell of a frigid night. It reminded her of the group's arrival, the outside clinging to their coats, caught in their

266

gloves. Hank's smell when he returned, one arm around Diana and the other balancing Scott's fishing rod.

"Stop!" Teal shouted. She began to push through the crowd. "His car!"

Hank bolted. A quick turn on his heel and he was through the house before the policewoman knew what to do. Malley skidded on a throw rug and tripped Teal. None of them paid heed to Diana as she slipped out the front door. Car tires squealed from the drive. The policewoman, Malley, and Teal arrived in the garage to see tail lights turn from the drive into the street.

"Where's the telephone?" Malley asked. "I guess you aren't crazy—"

"But I should have figured it out the minute he invited you all inside like he had nothing to hide. I was so busy being pleased with my scheme to trap him, I didn't pay attention." Teal raised her head from her hands. "I feel like a dope."

"No time for that." Malley sprinted into the kitchen for the phone.

The policewoman herded everyone else back to the living room. The burly guy no longer seemed to mind; he foraged the plate for a cookie. Any other day and Teal would have been amused that she took him and not the competent her for Dan's recruited Wellesley cop. Today, nothing seemed funny.

"Where's Diana?" Teal asked.

Diana wasn't meant to run away. The entire effort had been to protect Diana from wrongheaded blame. From the damage of circumstantial evidence and the likely zeal of misguided cops. She could not be gone, not after all this.

The bike's crash had set Teal off. The fall began the process which ended with most of the incongruities settled in place. Like the carolers starting up the path and then doubling back. Not once, but twice. Or Diana's confusion when she saw all the blood. The drops were too much to have come from her hand, but she couldn't explain them to herself any other way. Hank's tale about almost arriving late when he had come early. And from beginning to end, Teal's faith. Diana had not, could not, would not kill her husband.

But where was she? Teal opened her mouth to cry out. "Diana?"

"Here."

Teal whirled around.

"Right here," Diana said. "And he is with me."

Hank stepped into the light.

"But how?" Teal asked.

"I stood in the middle of the street. It was run me down or come back. I hated my husband, Teal, and I can't hate his killer, but I couldn't watch him escape. Not even for you, Hank."

Tears coursed down Diana's face and dripped on her blouse. Hank dropped to his knees and encircled Diana's legs with his arms.

"I only meant to scare him away. That's all. Just make him leave. I knew I was early and when I passed his car parked down the road, I told myself to drive by. Come back later. Then I saw you in the garage with the lights on and Madison screaming, his face contorted in rage. You hit him and he laughed at you. When you turned and ran—"

"Because of me," Teal murmured. "My shout about Scott."

Hank kept talking, his face buried against Diana's body. "Anger made me crazy. I pulled up with my car to block him in the garage and I got out. I told him to leave you alone. He came at me waving that screwdriver and grinning with a mouth full of mistletoe. I yanked the tool out of his hand and he went for my throat. One blow. One blow. It was him or me."

Diana stroked his head.

"You saw me, didn't you?" Teal said. "When I came out and moved the body. That crash, it was Madison clipping the bike as he hit the floor. You saw me from the street as I hid the body. You must have been going crazy wondering what I knew, waiting for a chance to move him—"

"I don't think anyone should say anything more." Dan un-

268

wound Diana's hand from the back of Hank's neck. "I'm sorry. The Wellesley police are on their way to join their colleague here and take him in."

The fire had died hours ago and the embers lay on the grate, gray and cold. Bells rang out from every church steeple in the town.

"Christmas morning," Teal said.

"Christmas morning," Diana agreed.

She rubbed a length of red ribbon between her palms, then let go to watch it flutter down on the floor by the tree.

"Look!" she said in a flat voice as she pointed. "Isn't that another ornament?"

She knelt to remove the wrap of tissue. A miniature crèche of mother and child dangled from her fist. Her composed face turned to the tree, and she slipped the hook over a bow. The crèche hung free.

"I remember the year Scott was born, the year you brought this that Christmas Eve." Diana smiled at Teal and came to life.

"And I promised to sit for you when the baby came. Scott was a real education for me." Teal smiled back.

"The act of a real friend." Diana sighed. "Teal. I saw the question mark in your eyes all evening. I was so guilty thinking you knew about my fight with Madison, and you were doing everything you could to protect me despite your doubts. What you must have thought when you found his body! I wish I could be as sure of my innocence myself. Thank you for your gift of—"

"Faith?" Teal said. "Isn't that what Christmas is all about?"

About the Author

J. Dayne Lamb lives with her husband in Boston, Massachusetts. Her first Teal Stewart mystery, QUESTIONABLE BEHAVIOR, is on sale now. Her next Teal Stewart mystery, A QUESTION OF PREFERENCE, will be published by Zebra Books in July 1994. You may write to Dayne c/o Zebra Books.

The House on the Hill

by

Pat Warren

Dead. Santa Claus was dead.

Her eyes wide with shock, Kate Kennedy took several staggering steps back from the body she'd literally stumbled across as she let out a choked sound, half scream, half gasp. She nearly fell over a large decaying log as she regained her footing. Her eyes frantically scanned the area, but she could see no one. Panting, she tried to let her rational mind take over.

It wasn't like her to panic. A registered nurse, she'd seen dozens of dead bodies. Besides, it wasn't the dark of night but only late afternoon, even if rain clouds had shadowed the usually sunny Arizona sky. And she was familiar with this wooded area, having grown up a mere twenty miles away. She'd never run across anything sinister here, except in her overactive imagination.

Until today.

The bearded man in the red suit lay on the hard ground next to a cottonwood tree, a gnarled root touching his white hair. He wasn't moving, not even a little. Clutching the Nikon hanging from its strap around her neck, she wondered what he was doing here in these suburban woods. Why wasn't he sitting in some gaily decorated mall promising children he'd bring them shiny sleds and Cabbage Patch Dolls?

Dark blood stained his red jacket around what appeared to be a bullet hole. Perhaps he wasn't dead, just badly hurt, Kate thought. Although her first instinct had been to turn and run, her conscience wouldn't let her. She was trained to save lives. She couldn't leave, despite her apprehension, if there was a possibility that the man was still alive.

She bent over and pressed two shaky fingers to his neck, searching for a pulse. His skin was still warm, but she could detect no heartbeat. Hurriedly she straightened and glanced uneasily over her shoulder.

If he were still warm, that meant he hadn't been shot all that long ago. When she'd pulled off onto the side of the dirt road bordering the woods, she hadn't seen a sign of any other vehicle. She remembered that there were a couple of isolated houses back in among the trees, but only crude paths led to them. On this chilly December afternoon with the threat of rain, it would be unlikely that Santa and whoever shot him would have been wandering around on foot. A nervous shiver raced up her spine as she narrowed her eyes and looked around again. She could see nothing but a few skittery birds.

Usually she took Highway 19 when she drove from her Phoenix apartment to her parents' home in Palo Verde south of Tucson, rarely traveling the back roads. But today she'd purposely detoured to take pictures of the deer she knew often wandered down from Coronado National Forest. On this trip home for the Christmas holidays, she'd planned to show her two young nephews the snapshots, passing them off as Santa's reindeer.

Except this Santa was in no shape to drive his sleigh tonight.

Since she was here, it was too good an opportunity for an amateur photographer to let pass, Kate decided as she lifted her Nikon and adjusted the aperture. She took two shots, then one more from a second angle. Replacing the lens cap, she started back toward her car. She'd stop in town at the sheriff's office and report what she'd found. Even though it was Christmas Eve, surely someone would be there.

Kate felt the first raindrops as she cleared the trees. Her Mustang was parked where she'd left it. No other cars around. Hunching her shoulders, she pulled the folds of her leather jacket closer around her camera to keep it dry. Thunder reverberated overhead as she tugged her car keys from her jeans pocket. Squinting up at the leaden sky, she realized they were in for a downpour as she opened the driver's door.

Suddenly she heard the sound of a powerful engine and turned to see a blue four-wheel drive approaching from behind. The storm had darkened the area, but the vehicle's lights weren't on. Frowning, Kate realized that the driver was careening all over the road and probably didn't see her.

"Hey!" she shouted and jumped in front of the Mustang just as he zoomed past her, too close for comfort. Her heart in her throat, she sucked in several deep breaths as she watched the Blazer race down the road. "Damn fool," she muttered as she got behind the wheel and locked her door. Maneuvering her car back onto the road, she stepped on the gas, anxious to get away from dead bodies and crazy drivers.

But she'd only gone a short distance when she spotted the lights of another vehicle in her rearview mirror. It was a dark car advancing very quickly. Kate's hands gripped the wheel as she wondered what in the wide world was going on.

She sped up and so did the other car. In the mirror she could see two shadowy figures inside. They were close enough that she felt their front bumper tap her back one. Growing more anxious by the moment, Kate eased the car to the right, hoping they'd pass. She could see a wide ditch running parallel to the road. Straining to keep the Mustang from slipping, she felt nervous perspiration trail down her spine.

Carefully she made it around a sharp curve in the road only to glance out and see that the car had shifted alongside and was nudging the Mustang none too gently. Too furious to be thoroughly frightened, Kate inched more to the right. She loved her car and this fool was scratching it in some crazy game.

But a sudden new thought had her sobering. Could the men in the car have had something to do with Santa's death?

Kate stepped down hard on the accelerator. The dark car

sped up even more, then banged sharply against the Mustang. It was the final blow. Kate lost control, and the powerful little sports car lurched into the ditch, swayed precariously as it slowed, then stopped abruptly as the front wheels encountered a pile of rocks.

Slammed forward by the momentum, only Kate's fierce grip on the steering wheel kept her head from hitting the windshield. Belatedly she realized she'd forgotten to fasten her seat belt in her haste to get moving. Opening her eyes, she saw the tormenting vehicle race out of sight.

Kate sat for a moment catching her breath, thanking her lucky stars that at least she wasn't hurt. But she was still a long way from her destination. She knew her family would worry if she didn't show up soon without calling. An attempt to start the car had her hitting the wheel in frustration as the motor refused to catch. The car was probably wedged in too tightly to go backward anyway, she decided with a sigh. The rainfall was growing heavier, and occasional flashes of lightning slashed across a murky sky. Just what she needed, Kate thought, an electrical storm.

She couldn't just sit here. The dark car might return. Gingerly she opened the door and managed to climb out. No streetlights along this stretch of road. It wasn't pitch dark yet at five, but it soon would be. Kate zipped her jacket closed over her dangling camera, grabbed her purse, and locked the door.

A pathway led into the woods just a few feet away, looking just wide enough to accommodate a car. Hopefully it would lead to one of the houses nestled in among the trees. Ducking her head, Kate set out.

Even trying to stay under the protection of trees, she was getting thoroughly soaked. After a while she stopped and peered ahead, trying to spot the outline of a house or perhaps lights in either direction. It was difficult to hear anything above the rain and rumbling thunder, so she had to rely on her vision. Surely even the killer hadn't lingered in the woods in this weather. With that thought, Kate trudged on, trying to follow the path.

She'd gone only a few more steps when a jagged bolt of lightning split the sky. Frozen to the spot, Kate stared as a tall palo verde fell across the trail she'd been following, landing no more than ten yards from where she stood. Trembling, she darted out of the trees, remembering the warnings about electrical storms. How had she wandered into this nightmare? she wondered as she brushed wet hair from her face.

Squinting, she could make out lights in the distance. Skirting the fallen tree, she gazed upward and saw a house on the hill with lamplight shining from its windows. It loomed eerily ahead, looking somewhat like a location in a Stephen King film. Still, any port in a storm, Kate thought as she settled the strap of her bag more comfortably on her shoulder.

But a sharp crackling sound off to her right had her swiveling, then crouching behind the bulky tree branches. Had the sound been another tree plummeting or perhaps a deer seeking shelter? Or a human tracking her? As she studied the wooded area, she thought she saw a shadow separate itself from a tree and move toward another tree. Her heart began to thud wildly.

Should she wait or run for it? Then suddenly she saw the shadow move again, more distinctly this time. And it was coming nearer. Perhaps she could startle whoever it was with the only weapon she had. Unzipping her jacket, Kate eased out her camera, removed the lens cap, and flipped on the flash attachment. Setting the focus, she waited.

There it was again. Rising, she got off two quick shots, then turned and began to run. She wasn't about to stick around to see if he would follow. Tucking her camera into her jacket as she ran, she prayed the people who lived in the house on the hill would be receptive to hearing a rather bizarre tale.

Kate had nearly reached the lawn when she heard a discharge, then felt a whizzing sound rush past her head. *Dear God! He was shooting at her.* With the help of a spurt of adrenaline, she made it across the grass to the porch in record time. Racing up the wooden steps, she all but collapsed at the door. With her last ounce of strength, she raised her fist and began to pound.

Mike Tanner carefully set down the bottle of scotch and a glass filled with ice cubes on his coffee table and frowned. Had that been someone on his porch he'd heard or just a noise of the storm? In this remote location, he seldom had uninvited guests and rarely invited anyone. Which is the way he liked things.

As Palo Verde's sheriff, he had to deal with people every day. Always short-handed, he didn't take much time off. It would be just his luck that on the first day he'd checked out early in months, someone would come looking for him.

The evening had started off badly. His carefully laid plans had been interrupted when his Irish setter had run off like a wild animal. Mike had had to jump into his Blazer and go looking for him. He hadn't found Shamus and had returned home spitting mad. Every time the silly dog disappeared for hours, he either got into a fight and wound up dragging his tail, or he ate some garbage somewhere and was sick for days. Well, to hell with him, Mike had decided. If Shamus was going to do something stupid, he'd have to suffer the consequences.

So he'd returned and put on some chili to cook, then hauled out his usual companion for recent Christmas Eves past: a fresh bottle of scotch. Mike wasn't ordinarily much of a drinker. But Christmas Eves were different. He hated the holiday, the sentimentality, the memories that haunted him. The only thing that kept the wolves at bay this time of year was to get blitzed. Which he'd been about to do, carefully and methodically.

Until he'd heard the pounding at his door, which was sounding too desperate to ignore. Mike went to see who it was.

She all but fell inside, a slender woman with short brown

hair that clung wetly around her pale face and dark eyes wild with fear. Mike grabbed her arm to keep her from pitching forward, but she brushed him aside and slammed shut the door.

Leaning against it, she struggled to speak. "Please, you've got to help me. He's got a gun." Her voice hinted at hysteria bubbling just below the surface.

"Take it easy." Mike led her into his living room, guiding her toward the hearth where a fire he'd lit minutes ago crackled in the grate. "Sit down and catch your breath."

Mike thought of Palo Verde as a sleepy little community, one where the last recorded fatal shooting had taken place thirty years ago. Which was one of the major reasons he'd moved here just over two years ago. As an undercover cop in Los Angeles, he'd seen too much, buried too many people he cared about.

After the last devastating investigation had ended, he'd taken the recommendation of a friend and applied for the job of local sheriff. Dealing with speeders and an occasional whisky-inspired domestic quarrel may have sounded terribly boring to some, but Mike liked it just fine. He hadn't seen a civilian toting a gun since he'd arrived.

Yet this woman claimed to have seen someone with a gun near his home, someone who knew how to use it.

Mike went to get a towel from his half bath, handed it to her, and watched as she rubbed her hair dry. Seating himself on his leather footstool, he leaned forward, bracing his elbows on his knees. "You want to tell me what happened?"

Still shaky, Kate glanced across the living room at the three bay windows, her eyes widening. There were no blinds and only abbreviated tie-back drapes, exposing the room to any-one outside. "You can't close the drapes," she muttered, more to herself than to him.

"No." Privacy wasn't a problem in this remote area. He sat facing her, waiting.

Kate swallowed hard, then shrugged out of her jacket. Carefully she took off her camera and placed it on the hearth alongside her. She felt somewhat calmer, yet far from safe. Still, she had to trust him. There was no one else.

"Someone out there shot at me," she began, staring into the fire. "Barely missed my head."

"Who is he?" Mike asked.

"I don't know."

"Why is he after you?" He hadn't seen a car when he'd let her in. "How did you get here?"

"It's a long story." At last Kate turned to look at him. He was a big man, tall and lean. He had a rugged, outdoor face that needed a shave. His hair curled into his collar and his eyes were a cool gray. Assessing eyes filled with doubt. She prayed she hadn't stumbled from the frying pan into the fire. "Is your wife home?"

"I don't have a wife." Mike watched renewed fear leap into her eyes. "Don't be afraid. I'm the sheriff. Mike Tanner." He reached into his pocket and flipped open his ID for her to see.

Checking it, Kate released an audible sigh of relief. "You must have a gun. Go out there and get him."

Mike kept his features even and hung on to his patience. He'd questioned many distraught people and knew it usually took them a long time to get out the details of their story, mostly in erratic spurts. "Maybe you'd better answer a few questions first. For starters, what's your name?"

"Kate Kennedy. I'm from Phoenix. I'm a registered nurse at Good Samaritan Hospital and I . . ." The wind tossed a heavy splash of water against the front windows, the sound startling her. "Look, we're wasting time."

She sounded normal enough. "Why is this man shooting at you, Kate?" He hadn't heard a shot, but the storm might have muffled the sound.

"Probably because he's the man who shot Santa Claus."

This time Mike couldn't prevent his face from registering incredulous disbelief. Of all nights for a wacko to appear on his doorstep.

Watching him, Kate shook her head, realizing how she

must sound. "You probably think I'm crazy. He's not *really* Santa Claus. A bearded man dressed in a red suit is dead not far from here, next to a cottonwood tree. I stumbled over his body. I didn't think he was still around, but I guess the killer must have seen me. He's out there with a gun."

Mike just sat staring, wondering what in hell to do with her.

Growing annoyed at his silence, Kate stood. "I can see you don't believe me. Fine. If you'll tell me where your phone is, I'll call someone to come get me."

"Phone's probably out," he said, rising. "Happens every time there's an electrical storm in these parts." Mike walked to the end table and picked up the receiver. "Sure is."

Damn. Kate felt like crying, like hitting something. Preferably this jerk who was making her feel like she'd slipped a cog. "I can prove it, you know." She pointed to her camera. "I took pictures."

"Of a dead Santa Claus?"

"Yes," she all but hissed at him. "He's in the woods, not half a mile from here." Her gaze swung to the windows. "And the person who shot at me is out there, too."

Slowly Mike rose. All right, he'd humor her. Walking to his chair, he picked up his gun from the end table. "I'll go have a look." Pulling on his jacket, he stepped outside.

Kate wanted to peek out the front window, but remembering the bullet whirling past her ear, she decided to wait by the fire. She dug her comb out of her purse and ran it through her hair, hung her jacket to dry on the chair back and slipped out of her wet shoes.

The local sheriff. That part was lucky. A sheriff who didn't believe her. Not so good. But if he found the man . . .

It was a full ten minutes before Mike returned, shaking water from his hair. Tossing his jacket onto the hall coat tree, he walked over to where she stood by the fire looking up at him expectantly.

"I couldn't see anyone." He placed the gun on the table, then sat down wearily. He sent a longing glance toward the bottle of scotch, the ice melting in the glass. "All right, tell me everything right from the start."

Just then they heard a crackling noise. Then all the lamps went out, and they were left with only the light from the fireplace.

It was turning out to be a rotten night in more ways than just the storm, Lloyd Gilmore thought as he huddled into the turned-up collar of his raincoat. Cold, wet, and worried wasn't exactly how he'd planned to spend Christmas Eve. And unless he came up with a way out of this jam, things would only get worse.

"What do you think they're doing there in the dark, Lloyd?" Freddie Temple asked as he took off his wire-rimmed glasses and blotted the rain with his crumpled white hand-kerchief.

The power failure wasn't going to help, Lloyd decided. At least with the lights on, they'd been able to track their move-ments through some of the windows. "They'll light candles, I hope. Maybe an oil lamp." He shivered as the gusting wind blew rain into the meager shelter provided by the carport attached to the free-standing garage.

"Ramsey's not going to like this," Freddie whined. "He's not going to like this at all."

Lloyd's temper, never far from the surface, flared. "And who the hell's fault is all this?" He'd been telling Ramsey for months to get rid of Freddie, that he was a liability to the organization. But Ramsey insisted no one could doctor books the way Freddie with his accounting background could. But after tonight, the boss might seriously look for a replacement.

It wasn't just the Santa thing, bad as that was, Lloyd thought as he brushed water from his dark hair with a thick hand. Now there was this girl who had a picture of the body. And maybe of them.

"I didn't mean to do it," Freddie insisted, replacing his glasses. "You were there. It was an accident."

"You think anyone's going to believe that? You think Ramsey's going to want to bring the cops in on this?" In all fairness to Freddie, how could they have known that Max would get demanding or that he'd have a gun hidden in that Santa suit?

"We'd have been okay if that woman with the camera hadn't come along." Freddie paced alongside a blue Blazer, literally wringing his hands.

"Yeah, well, she did come along. We've got to get that film somehow." Who would have believed she'd pick the sheriff's house to run to? Of all the lousy luck.

"You cut the phone lines so they can't call for backup," Freddie said, trying to be logical. "We've got Max's gun. We can overtake them, one guy and a small woman. How hard can it be? If we break in the front door, grab the camera, and . . ."

Lloyd whirled on Freddie. "And what? Did it occur to you that she knows we're out here, that she probably told him everything, and they're just waiting for us to make a move? Or that the sheriff certainly has a gun? Mike Tanner knows Ramsey and might recognize us as working for him. Or do you want to storm in and shoot them both, make it three killings? What do you think Ramsey'll say to that?"

Freddie's eyes behind his thick glasses blinked rapidly. "So what are we going to do?"

Good question, Lloyd thought. Damn good question. As always, even sometimes with Ramsey, he'd have to do the thinking. Ramsey'd hired him as muscle, an ex-jock who was strong as an ox. The sporting-goods stores Ramsey owned were legit, but the big money came from the betting syndicate they'd built up over the years into an organization that controlled all underground gambling in the state. It was a slick operation, and Lloyd was the watchdog. Anyone who wanted to see Ramsey had to go through Lloyd.

Suddenly a sneeze shook him. Swell. He'd probably catch cold to round out this beaut of a night.

"Lloyd, what are we going to do?" Freddie asked again.

He had several ideas. But first they had to take care of something. "I'll think of something. Come on."

"Where are we going?"

"Just shut up and follow me." Staying off the main path, he led the way back into the woods.

Mike sat watching the candlelight flicker across Kate's face. Her story sounded just ludicrous enough to be believable. But though she looked to be sane and sensible, and told her tale without hesitation, he was dubious.

Ten years on the force in Los Angeles had shown him just how inventive people could be. No book of fiction he'd ever read could possibly top some of the whoppers he'd heard. And every one of them spoke as if they were reciting the gospel truth. Would this face lie? they seemed to ask.

Everyone lied, Mike had come to believe. Some were better at it than others. That was the only difference.

"Let's think about this," he began, leaning forward, trying the reasonable approach. "Only a couple of reasons I can think of for a man to be wearing a Santa suit. He was a paid Santa working the season, probably in some mall. Or he'd wandered away from a costume party. Do you agree?"

Kate ran a hand through her hair, stopping to rub a spot over her left eye where a headache was beginning to grab her attention. She hated the doubt on Mike's face. "If you say so. Look, I didn't hover over the body and speculate who he was or why he was wearing the red suit. I checked to make sure he was really dead, took a couple pictures, and got the hell out of there. Call me strange, but I get nervous standing around in a gloomy woods in a rainstorm with a dead body at my feet. I don't linger contemplating motives."

Strange was exactly what he would label her. "But motives are exactly what we have to discover. Why was Santa out in the woods? Why would someone want to kill the jolly old fellow? Maybe because he didn't bring him everything on his list last year?"

Her eyes narrowed, but she tamped down her temper. And swallowed her apprehension about what she was about to suggest. "I can see I need to prove this to you." She stood, stepping into her shoes. "If you have a flashlight, I'll show you the body."

He should say no. Marching out in the pouring rain just to appease a nut case was beyond the call of duty. Still, he knew it would gnaw at him until he made sure.

Mike got up and went to find his flashlight.

On the grassy lawn, Kate glanced toward the carport and saw a blue Blazer. "Were you out earlier in that?"

"Yeah. I went looking for my dog. Why?"

"You nearly ran me over just as I'd come out of the woods. My Mustang was parked on the side of the road."

"I didn't see you or your car."

"Probably because you didn't have your lights on and you were driving like a maniac all over the road."

Mike clenched his teeth. "Are we going, or aren't we?"

Kate started walking.

It was dark as pitch in the woods, only the eerie beam Mike held lighting their way. In his other hand, he had his gun. He may not believe Kate, but he didn't believe in being careless either.

The rain had lessened but hadn't let up. Kate couldn't help looking every which way, half-expecting the man who'd shot at her to leap out from behind a tree. Some protection this laid-back sheriff would be. He carried his gun, but she'd wager he hadn't fired it this decade.

She was having trouble judging the distance. She'd driven at least half a mile before the dark car had forced her off the road that paralleled these woods. But one cluster of trees looked like another. She had little choice but to trudge on and hope she wasn't leading them in circles. Her credibility with Sheriff Tanner was already in short supply.

It seemed as if they'd been walking forever before she recognized a landmark. The thick section of mesquite had to be the place. Then, in the flashlight's glow, she saw the decaying log she'd nearly tripped over. "He's got to be there, just past that log," she told Mike.

He let her lead, holding the light for her.

Kate circled the tall cottonwood around to the far side. Looking down, her mouth dropped open.

Santa was gone.

"He was here, right here," she insisted, her voice sounding shrill even to her own ears.

"You're sure this is the tree?"

She glanced around half-heartedly even though she was certain. "Yes, this is it. I remember that section of root sticking up over there. He was on his back, his head nearly touching that root."

Mike bent down, taking the flashlight beam lower. No sign of blood, no indentations in the piney earth. He'd almost been rooting for her to be right. If he'd have found one clue, one shred of evidence to back up her story, he'd have agreed to investigate.

Straightening, he looked at her. She seemed so sure. In the spray of light, he studied her eyes. "When your car landed in the ditch, did you hit your head?"

Letting her fury surface, Kate balled her hands into fists. "Damn you, there was a body here, I tell you."

She was stubborn and spirited. He'd give her that. And not half bad-looking, even soaked with rain and mad as a wet hen. Too bad she was looney tunes. "We'd better get back to the house before we both catch a cold."

Kate's anger had her marching with strides that kept her alongside him easily. No matter what he thought, she knew she was right. What had happened to the man in the red suit? "Those two men in the car that forced me off the road were probably involved. They undoubtedly came back and hauled him away."

"Carrying a body makes a man pretty heavy. I didn't see any deep footprints. Did you?"

She didn't bother to answer that. "Let's go into town and get my film developed. That will prove my story."

"It's eight o'clock on Christmas Eve. Nothing's open."

Kate's shoulders sagged. In all her twenty-nine years, she'd never experienced a more frustrating Christmas.

Mike kept walking. Hopefully the power would come on soon and the phone service would be restored. From somewhere he'd find a tow truck to haul Kate's car out of the ditch so she could be on her way. For both their sakes.

Maybe she was on some medication that had her hallucinating. Or perhaps she had an overactive imagination always seeing mysteries where there were none. For now, maybe she simply needed to rest.

As for him, she'd already ruined his plans, he thought, remembering his unopened scotch. Just what he'd needed to make his favorite holiday perfect, a crazy lady who sees dead Santas under cottonwood trees and men who aren't there shooting at her.

With an annoyed frown, Mike placed his hand on Kate's elbow and hurried her along.

They were walking in the clearing near the house when Kate heard a noise coming from the direction of the woods. With a gasp she grabbed Mike's arm just as he swiveled toward the sound.

Shoving Kate behind him, he cocked his gun and directed the beam of light toward the noise. In a moment a large ball of red fur came hurling at them out of the darkness, and he let out a relieved laugh. "Shamus!" he yelled, crouching to thump the dog on his back. "Don't worry. It's my dog," he explained.

Kate's heart was pounding so loudly she thought she'd drop right there on the wet grass. It was all getting a bit much for her. Wearily she dragged her feet toward the porch, leaving Mike to follow with his Irish setter.

"Where you been, boy?" Mike asked as he and Shamus stepped onto the porch. "Out scavenging, I imagine." Shamus shook himself mightily, spraying them both. "Cut that out," he said, reaching around Kate and unlocking the door.

Kate hurried inside out of the cold and the dog bounded

after her. Mike raised his foot to step over the threshold just as a shot sounded from somewhere behind him.

Instinct had him ducking as he heard the bullet slam into the wooden door frame. Diving inside, he slammed the door shut.

Holy shit! There *was* someone out there shooting at them.

"Gimme that gun!" Lloyd grabbed the weapon from Freddie and stuck it into the waistband of his pants. A rush of anger had him shoving the slight bookkeeper into the dark carport. "What the hell are you doing, shooting at the sheriff?"

"I was trying to put him out of commission so we could get the woman's camera," Freddie sniveled. "I wasn't aiming to kill."

Lloyd wished he had the patience to count to ten. "Now he knows we're still out here. We've lost the element of surprise. Jesus, but you're stupid."

Offended, Freddie rubbed the shoulder Lloyd had slammed against the wooden post. "Oh, yeah, well, you got any better ideas, hotshot?" He'd never liked Lloyd and couldn't understand why Ramsey listened to him. The man was nasty-tempered and no better than a common thug. When they got out of this mess, he'd try again to persuade the boss to let him go.

"Just shut up, okay?" Frustrated, Lloyd glowered at the windows of the house, wondering what the sheriff would do. Tanner had no way to call for help. If he did come out looking for them, he'd be an open target. Lloyd doubted he'd risk that.

If only Freddie hadn't let the sheriff know they were still around. They'd gone into the woods to haul Max's body into the trunk of their car just in time. They'd seen them returning from the direction of the woods. The woman apparently told Tanner about the body she'd found. She'd probably led him to where she'd remembered Max was. Lloyd almost laughed, imagining Tanner's face at the scene. The case of the missing Santa Claus. He'd probably thought she was a nut case. And would have continued to think so until that fool Freddie messed up again.

Lloyd shoved his wet hands into his damp trouser pockets. He'd hoped the sheriff, not believing her story, would have tucked her into his spare room and gone to sleep himself, thinking he'd get rid of her at first daylight. He and Freddie might have had a chance to sneak in and grab the camera. Now Tanner might not believe everything she'd told him, but he surely knew someone was outside his house with a gun.

And now there was that dog to complicate things. He'd have to come up with a new plan.

"It's cold out here," Freddie complained, shivering. "What are we going to do, Lloyd?"

"Keep still and let me think." Lloyd moved to the back of the carport as much to get away from Freddie as to keep an eye on the rear of the house in case the sheriff decided to sneak out and catch them unawares.

A flash of lightning lit up the dark sky momentarily, followed by a loud thunderclap. Damn, if only this rain would stop, Lloyd thought as he hunched up his shoulders.

"Do you believe me now?" Kate asked as she rubbed her hair dry by the fire for the second time this evening.

At the front windows, peering around the limited protection of the narrow drapes, Mike searched what he could see of the yard for signs of movement. He saw nothing, though he knew there were many hiding places—the woods, the carport, the area below the slope of the hill. The person with the gun could be anywhere.

He turned back and walked to the fireplace. Finding a towel, he began to dry off a trembling Shamus. "Describe the man in the dark car who forced you off the road."

"There were two men, but I could only see vague outlines of heads in the rearview mirror."

Terrific. Mike bent to add more logs to the fire. "All right, tell me what the man in the Santa suit looked like." Poking at the blaze, he listened to her description, a scowl forming on his face. "Great. Sounds just like Edmund Gwenn in that sentimental Christmas story they show on television every holiday. Maybe the beard was fake."

"It wasn't. I had my fingers on his throat. White hair, white moustache, and beard. All real."

He straightened, then sat down on the hearth. "He's not from around here. I know most everyone in Palo Verde."

"Then you must know my folks, Tom and Ann Kennedy. And my brothers, Sean and Jack."

Mike looked at her again, more carefully this time. There was a family resemblance. The Kennedy brothers ran the local hardware. They were good people. Okay, so maybe she was telling the truth. "Yeah, I do. Nice folks."

"Hallelujah. Perhaps you'll decide I'm not crazy after all." Kate knew her story must have sounded bizarre, but he sure was a hard sell. She stood up, slipping off her wet jacket. "Or do I have to get shot for you to believe me?"

Grabbing her hand, he pulled her down beside him. "I don't think we ought to stand up. They can probably see us in the light from the fireplace. We make too good a target through those front windows."

She shuddered at the thought. "Do you think they'd come right up onto the porch and . . ." She couldn't complete the thought.

"Let's not take the chance." Grabbing two large pillows from the couch, he set them on the carpeted floor. "This way we're out of range." He settled on one and leaned back against the hearth. Shamus lay down at his feet, tired from his earlier wanderings.

"So what are we going to do, wait them out?"

"Since there're probably two of them and we don't know how many guns they have, it'd be pretty foolish to rush outside, don't you think?"

"I guess so."

Reaching to the end table, he picked up the phone. Still out. They were relatively safe in the house. Over forty years old, it was well-built. He doubted that even two men would come storming in with guns blazing. Everyone for miles around knew it was the sheriff's place. As soon as daylight began creeping over the hill, they'd have to take off or become targets themselves. Of course, it wasn't even midnight yet.

"I'm going to have a look around," Mike said, taking both the gun and flashlight. Upstairs and down, he cautiously checked all the windows and both doors. They were as secure as he could make them, he thought as he returned.

Just then, his beeper went off, startling both of them. Mike removed it from his pocket and turned it off.

"Aren't you going to call them to . . . oh. I forgot you can't call them." Kate's hopes fell, then rose again. "Maybe it's your office and when you don't answer, they'll come check on you."

Mike sat down alongside her. "Unlikely. They'll figure the storm knocked out the phone line. It's Christmas Eve. Everyone's home with their families."

And Kate heartily wished she were. "Who do you suppose was beeping you?"

"Probably Hank, my deputy, wanting to tell me he was locking up the office for the night. He's on call, so he'll be available from his home." A thought occurred to him. "What about your folks? You said they were expecting you. Do you think they'll come looking for you?"

Kate shrugged. "It's possible. Or they might think I got held up at the hospital, which often happens." She heard a rumble of thunder. "Of course, with this storm, they might get worried."

"Even if one of your brothers found your car, I doubt if he'd march into the woods in a rainstorm."

She had to agree. Stretching out her legs, Kate leaned back and sighed, trying to relax as she looked around the room. It was sparsely furnished, almost barren, with no frills. And not a sign of Christmas anywhere. "You don't celebrate Christmas?"

"No."

Well, that was clear enough. What fun. She'd get to spend Christmas with Scrooge himself. Oh, well, she'd tough it out, get through somehow and . . . And the lights suddenly came back on. "That's better," Kate said, finding a smile. "Do you think we could put on a pot of coffee?"

Mike thought he could use a cup himself. "I'll make some." Keeping low to the floor until he was past the windows, he moved toward the kitchen. Shamus followed, cocking his head at his master on all fours.

Kate wished she dared peek out the front windows to see if she could spot the two men. But she hadn't imagined either of those two shots, and the memory kept her seated. Brushing her hair back, she lamented over the silly urge she'd had to go looking for deer. If she'd have passed on by, she'd now be in her parents' cozy home, probably just finishing a big dinner and moving to sit around the decorated tree. She'd have her nephews, Jeff and Joey, snuggled up to her. Her brother Jack would be tuning his guitar, and they'd soon be singing carols just a little off key. She closed her eyes, picturing the scene.

"Here we go," Mike said some minutes later, holding out a mug of steaming coffee.

"Mmm, it smells wonderful." She sipped cautiously, feeling the heat slide down and warm her. Shamus came over, sniffed at her, then lay down at her feet. Kate stroked his thick fur as she glanced at Mike seated on her left. She found herself wondering about her reluctant host. "How long have you lived here?"

"Two and a half years."

"But you're not from around here?"

"Born in Tucson."

Not terribly chatty. Still, they faced a long night together. They couldn't spend it in silence. At least she couldn't. "Were you in police work in Tucson, too?"

"No, in L.A." Mike was curious, too, but not necessarily about her background. Curious about the two characters who were after her. "When was the last time you were in Palo Verde?"

"Last July for my mother's birthday. Why?" She drank more coffee, beginning to feel a little better.

"I'm wondering why two guys you don't recognize are taking potshots at you. Can you think of a reason?"

"Not really."

Something didn't add up. "Okay, so you took a couple of pictures of the body. But you couldn't make out their faces in the rearview mirror, which they probably guessed. Even if you took the film to the police, what makes them think you can tie them to the dead man?"

"Well, I'm not sure they'll come out, but I also snapped two pictures of them chasing after me just before I reached your house."

Mike sat up straighter. "Why didn't you tell me this before?"

"Because you didn't believe anything else I told you."

Frowning, he turned to stare at the bottle of scotch, debating whether he should pour a generous dollop into his coffee. Probably not a good idea, considering two alleged Santa Claus slayers were slinking around his house. "That has to be it. They think you've got them on film, along with a picture of the body."

"I'd better take the film out and put it in a safe place." Kate set down her mug and rose to get her camera from the end table. Across the room, she bent to pick it up just as a muffled sound from outside had her turning toward the window.

The next thing Kate knew, she was being thrown to the floor, her knees buckling under the heavy onslaught of Mike's tackle. As he took her down, a gunshot could be heard, then breaking glass, followed by the dull ping of a bullet hitting the brick fireplace. In the aftermath, they heard the wet thud of receding-footsteps, then Shamus barking furiously.

For several frightening moments, Kate lay beneath him, trying to catch her breath, allowing her heartbeat to normalize.

Finally Mike lifted his head and looked at her. "I told you not to stand up."

He was heavy on her, his masculine scent suddenly making

her very conscious of his body pressing on hers. "You're right. I shouldn't have."

Her eyes held remnants of fear and a sudden new awareness. Inches from her, he could feel the warmth of her breath on his face. Then a log shifted in the grate, and Mike shook his head. What the hell was he doing thinking about this woman when some crazy man was shooting into his living room?

Drawing back, he eased from her. "I'm going to turn off all the lamps. Stay low." He moved about the room until the only light was from the fireplace. She'd crawled over to sit on the floor alongside the couch against the far wall, away from the windows.

Keeping down, he grabbed her camera, removed the film, and dropped the roll in his pocket. "There, now they'll have to come after me."

"I'm sorry I involved you in all this."

Mike set aside the camera and leaned back as he shrugged. "It's my job." He turned to Shamus who was pacing along the windows barking his head off. "It's okay, boy." But the dog kept up his noisy protest.

Kate found her hands weren't quite steady. "Have you been shot at a lot?"

"Yeah, a lot. It doesn't get any easier."

"So now what?"

"Now we wait." He picked up his gun from the nearby table. "I've got lots of ammo. We're not visible over here. They've got two choices: come flying through the window or take off and hope the pictures don't turn out."

"Which do you think they'll do?"

By way of an answer, Mike cocked his gun.

"You missed! I know you missed." Freddie was fairly crowing he was so pleased.

"I *meant* to miss, you fool." Lloyd was exasperated and wet to the bone, a bad combination.

"You yelled at me for shooting at 'em, but it's all right if you do it." Wrapping his arms around his thin body, Freddie shook his head. "I don't understand you."

"Your shot let the sheriff know we're out here. My shot hopefully made him curious enough to come looking for us." He'd turned on the Blazer's lights and opened the driver's door, thinking that if Tanner looked out, he'd want to investigate. The plan wasn't ideal, but it seemed their best chance.

It wouldn't be that hard to overtake him, Lloyd felt certain. The gun the sheriff wore was pretty much for show. Around this sleepy burg, he probably hadn't fired his weapon in years. Crouched on the far side of the Blazer, Lloyd tested the weight of the thick board he'd found earlier. All he had to do was get close enough to whack Tanner with it and knock him out. With the sheriff unconscious, getting the film from the girl wouldn't be much of a problem.

If only he could keep Freddie from stumbling over his own two flat feet.

Freddie raised up and squinted through the misty rain toward the house. "He's not coming out, Lloyd."

Lloyd ground his teeth. "I can see that." He'd already walked around the perimeter of the house. There was no back door, just the front and side. He could see both from where he stood.

Lloyd sneezed twice. This had to work before pneumonia set in. Damn the sheriff. What the hell was he doing in there? Furious, he threw down the piece of wood and yanked the gun from his belt. "Stay here. I'm going to take a closer look." Cautiously he crept out and made his way around the front porch toward the windows, staying low.

"Shamus, will you stop that?" Mike watched the dog howling at the front door. The Irish setter was fairly quivering in his anxiety to get outside.

"Come here, boy," Kate coaxed. But the stubborn animal only barked with more vigor.

"All right, I give up." Bent low, Mike moved to the door. "Go on. See if you can scare those two into high-tailing it out of here." He watched Shamus scamper out onto the porch. But instead of racing down the steps, he detoured to the left and renewed his barking at the railing.

Surprised, Mike kept his eyes on the dog through the slight crack in the door, holding his gun at his side. Shamus dipped his head, his nose sniffing at the bottom of the railing, then rose to race toward the stairs. He was almost there when another shot rang out, grazing the dog's back and causing him to drop to the porch floor, yowling in pain.

"Sonofa. . . ." Mike opened the door and shot back, aiming in the direction of the gunfire. He heard running footsteps as he crouched low, hurried out to gather Shamus in his arms, and moved back inside to slam the door shut. The wiggling dog was bleeding and mad to boot as he carried him into the kitchen.

"Oh, no," Kate said as she followed them. The poor dog.

"Grab that big towel and spread it on the table, will you?" Mike struggled with the dog's squirming weight. "It's all right, Shamus. You'll be just fine." He set him down and examined the wound. "It's not bad. There's peroxide in that cupboard above the stove and some other first-aid stuff."

Kate took him the things he asked for, then moved to soothe Shamus, whose dark eyes looked at her sadly. "I know it hurts," she singsonged to him, petting his head.

"I should have known better than to let him out there," Mike muttered, his mouth set in a grim line. "I can't seem to keep even my dog from getting hurt."

"What kind of man shoots at a dog?" Kate asked, thinking aloud. She flinched as the dog shuddered when Mike poured the cool liquid on his wound.

"Most criminals are more like animals than this dog is," Mike commented bitterly.

"I'm sure if you worked in L.A. you've seen more than your share." She handed him the antibiotic ointment she'd found and a sterile gauze pad. "You must have had to keep your feelings distanced from all that or it would seep into your personal life."

He sighed, a ragged sound. "Sometimes that's not possible. Sometimes it is personal, and you want to strike back, to give them a dose of their own medicine." He wound gauze stripping around the dog's body to keep the bandage in place, at least for a while. "Only you've sworn to uphold the law, not break it."

He sounded more than just weary. There was a bone-tired ring to his words that seemed to come from deep within. "A cop really doesn't have much recourse, does he?"

"Not much." Mike reached for the tape and cut off a piece. "He can run away, but he takes his memories with him. So sometimes, when it all gets too much, he drinks to forget, only even that doesn't work very well." Finished, he stroked the dog gently. "There you go, Shamus." Carefully he set him on the floor.

Kate remembered the bottle of liquor on the coffee table in the other room. Had he been planning to lose himself in that before she'd come banging on his door? Suddenly she wanted very much to know. "Did someone you care about get hurt by some criminal you were involved with back in L.A.?"

At the sink, Mike washed his hands. "Not hurt, killed. Not just someone I cared about. My wife."

"Oh, Mike." She went to him, touched his arm. "I'm so sorry."

"Yeah, me too."

"What happened, or would you rather not tell me?"

He reached for a towel and began wiping his hands. "We'd been in this Italian restaurant, the one where we'd met, celebrating our six-month anniversary. Natalie was so happy. I was busy watching her as we walked out, and I got careless. A dark car drove by and two shots were fired. Both hit her. I was investigating this drug syndicate. Those bullets were meant for me. Natalie died in my arms."

Kate didn't know what to say, couldn't think of anything

297

that could possibly make up for that kind of pain. Again she touched his arm, tightening her fingers, feeling inadequate.

Mike sucked in a deep breath as if to shake off the bad memories. "Three years ago today, Christmas Eve."

That explained his lack of interest in the holiday. Mike Tanner was a virtual stranger, yet her heart ached for him. Her mother always said that nursing was the right profession for Kate because she bled for everyone. Acting on instinct, she opened her arms and eased him into her embrace.

He stiffened at first, then a breath shuddered from him, and he lowered his cheek to rest on her hair as his arms went around her. Offering compassion, Kate held on, letting him absorb her comfort.

Lloyd felt ready to chew nails. Everything they'd done had backfired. They hadn't lured the sheriff out, except long enough for him to pick up his dog. He hadn't meant to shoot at the dog. But the snarling animal had been about to lunge off the porch to sink his teeth into him. He was certain he wasn't badly hurt.

And still Tanner stayed inside. Damn!

He watched Freddie crawl into the back seat of the Blazer to warm up. They were getting nowhere fast, and it was already past midnight. Max's body was probably beginning to stink up his trunk. Ramsey was likely wondering where they were, maybe sending someone to look for them. But whoever he sent probably wouldn't think to search these woods. They were in a hell of a fix and it was up to him to get them out of it. But how?

Lloyd stared at the old house, willing his mind to come up with a plan. Then suddenly he had it.

Walking around to the other side, he nudged Freddie in the Blazer. "Come on. We have to go back to the car. I've got an idea that's definitely going to work."

* * *

298

They were dozing in the warmth of the fire that Mike had stoked again. Kate lay on the couch and Mike on the rug beside it, his head cradled on a pillow. They were far enough away from the windows to be out of firing range, yet they had a view of the yard and porch. Mike's gun was near his outstretched hand.

He'd felt a little awkward after the intimate moment in the kitchen where she'd held him as if it were the most natural thing in the world, Mike acknowledged. Then she'd moved away somewhat shyly and made a bed of fresh towels for the wounded dog by the hearth. She was the most generous and open person he'd met, especially on such short acquaintance. Yet he had no doubt she was sincere.

Such caring puzzled him. Almost as much as it puzzled him why the whole story of his wife's death had tumbled out of him so easily. That had never happened to him, not with his friends much less with someone he'd met hours ago. Perhaps because it was the third anniversary of Natalie's death and the whole dreadful scene had been on his mind. Or maybe this woman who'd appeared out of the night was just a damn good listener. In either case, she hadn't made him feel embarrassed for having told her, and he was grateful.

If he believed in such things, he'd almost believe she'd been sent to save him from wallowing in his own self-pity. Or at the very least from a serious hangover.

Mike rolled over, punching the pillow into a more comfortable position, then settled down. But the sound of glass breaking coming from the back bedroom had him sitting up in a hurry. Grabbing his gun, he got to his feet as Kate jumped up.

Then they heard the explosion.

Racing back with a barking Shamus on his heels, Mike shoved open the bedroom door cautiously. The room was in flames.

"What is it?" Kate asked from behind him.

"Someone tossed a Molotov cocktail through the window," he explained as he picked up a small area rug and began to beat at the fiery drapes. Mike cursed himself for not getting around to buying a fire extinguisher.

Kate saw the Coke bottle with the flaming liquid in the center of the double bed, the blankets all ablaze. "What can I do to help?"

Mike was coughing from the smoke already filling the room. The air coming in through the broken window was fanning the fire, which was spreading from the bed and drapes to the carpeting. And he couldn't even call the fire department. Turning, he grabbed Kate's hand and pulled her from the room.

"We've got to get out of here before this spreads everywhere. Get your coat and shoes on." Tucking his gun in his waistband, Mike went to the kitchen, then shoved a couple of boxes of shells into his jacket pocket before putting it on. At the front he peered outside.

"How are we going to get out of here with those two probably lying in wait?" Kate asked.

Mike walked to the door. "I'm going to go out shooting long enough to make sure the area around my Blazer's clear. Can you shoot a gun?"

She sent him a hesitant look. "If I have to. I'd rather not."

"Can you handle a four-wheel drive?"

"I think so."

"Good, because you'll have to drive while I ride shotgun. Wait here until I signal you to come out."

"What about Shamus?"

"I'll carry him when I come back for you." Mike checked the gun's chamber, then quietly opened the door. Crouching low, he moved to the railing facing the carport. Why were the Blazer's lights on and the door open? He hoped the battery hadn't run down or that they hadn't disabled it. Eyes searching the area, he thought he saw two shadows but couldn't be sure. Shooting hand steady on the bannister, he shot toward the shadows. Four blasts then he paused. He heard swearing and saw a tall shadow race toward the trees. Patiently he shot twice again and saw a shorter figure follow the first. That should do it.

"Let's go," he whispered, scooping Shamus into his arms. "Stay close to me."

She did as they rushed toward the relative safety of the Blazer. Settling the dog in the back with him, he handed Kate the keys as she jumped in behind the wheel. Fortunately it started on her first try. Mike reached for his radio, then noticed the cut wires dangling below the dash. Of course, they'd ripped them out.

"Back out, then swing toward the road." Quickly Mike reloaded, then braced his gun on the side windowsill as she followed his instructions. "Go around the palo verde on the right side where the ground isn't so soft."

Kate maneuvered the Blazer handily. But as they rounded the front of the fallen tree, they heard a shot fired from not too far away, coming from the left. Mike answered in kind as the dog on the seat barked his support. "Step on it and get us the hell out of here, but keep your head down," he shouted.

Feeling like a gangster's moll driving the getaway car in a B-movie, Kate pressed down on the gas. Another shot grazed the roof, and Mike twisted about to shoot backward. He saw smoke billowing from the bedroom window and the flames spreading. Damn, he really liked that house. His landlord wasn't going to be any too happy either. The Blazer lurched over a rough spot on the path, then raced toward the highway.

Heart pounding, Kate promised the fates that if they'd get her out of here in one piece, she'd never stray from the beaten path again. Even as she completed the thought, a bullet came screaming in through the open side window and slammed into the windshield, shattering it into a zillion pieces.

Kate gripped the wheel and screamed.

Kate rolled the Blazer to a stop in front of the one-story stucco sheriff's office just as the sky in the east was showing signs of lightening. Mercifully the rain had slowed to a drizzle. Not another moving car could be seen on the road in either direction on this early Christmas morning.

Christmas. Kate turned off the engine, folded her arms across the steering wheel, and lowered her head. A dead body, a Molotov cocktail, men she didn't even know shooting at her as she drove wildly out of the woods. Shattered glass sprinkled all over the front seat and floor. The trembling that had begun back at the house seemed worse. Her hands were cold and clammy and her stomach jumpy with nerves. She struggled to keep from crying.

Mike stepped out, gathering Shamus in his arms. "I've got to call the fire department. Can you make it inside?"

Silently Kate trailed after him, glancing over her shoulder in both directions. She wondered when this feeling of danger following her would end. Inside she sank onto a leather couch as Mike picked up the phone. Shamus lay down at her feet, put his head on his crossed paws, and let out a shuddering breath. "I know just how you feel," she told the dog.

Mike hung up the phone. "They're on their way."

"I hope they can get the fire under control before you lose everything." He was the sheriff and it was his job to help, yet she felt terrible about ruining his evening, his house.

"Yeah, me too." He glanced at his watch. Not yet six. He fingered the roll of film in his pocket. His friend, Johnny Brice, owned a camera shop not far away and lived in an apartment above it. He could wake him and ask him to develop the film, check out the faces. It wasn't much, but it was the only lead he had.

However, first things first. Turning, Mike studied the slender woman huddled in the corner of the couch, her arms wrapped around herself protectively. She'd been through a lot and looked ready to fold.

"I should probably call my folks," Kate said halfheartedly. "They'll come get me and—"

"Not just yet. Your parents would be no match for those two guys with guns." Mike was well-aware that he wasn't the target. The men wanted the film, but they probably also thought that Kate could identify them. The fact that they'd been bold enough to shoot several times into the sheriff's house indicated they were serious and not about to give up.

At first he'd thought he'd take her with him to the camera shop. But he could see she was dead on her feet and perhaps even suffering from shock. "I want to make other arrangements, to make sure you're safe while I get this film developed." The less he dragged her around in full view, the better. The sheriff's office with its cinder-block walls and two rear jail cells was about as solid a refuge as he could think of. "Will you trust me for a little while longer?"

Kate didn't have the strength to object. She wanted to go to her parents' house, to feel familiar arms around her, to put this nightmare behind her. But she didn't want to put her family in jeopardy either. Those bullets had been frighteningly real. She'd go along with Mike and hope for the best. "All right." She closed her eyes and leaned her head back.

Mike picked up the phone and dialed his deputy's number. Six rings and no answer. His other deputy, Carlos Mendoza, had taken several vacation days off to go visit his family in Mexico for the holidays. Hank Longren had worked late last night. Unmarried and childless, Hank usually spent his time off sleeping or hanging around Jimmy's Grille. Mike decided to beep him. Hank called back in three minutes from his Jeep's radio. "Where are you?" Mike asked.

"On my way to Oak Ridge," Hank answered, naming a trailer court south of town. "Possible domestic violence."

What rotten timing, Mike thought. "As soon as you're finished there, I need you back here at the office." Quickly he explained the situation that had developed last night, that he was leaving Kate Kennedy in the building, and that two men were after her. "They may not show, but just in case, I want you here pronto."

"Gotcha," Hank said. "This shouldn't take long. Ned Pearson's wife called, said he's been drinking all night and started cuffing her around. I may have to bring him in to sleep it off."

Mike hung up and walked around the desk to the couch. "Hank'll be here soon." He held out the .38 he'd taken from his drawer. "You said you know how to use one of these."

Kate stared at the gun without enthusiasm. "Yes, but I'm not nuts about the idea."

"Me either, but I think it's important to get this film developed before those two guys disappear. I doubt that we were followed, but you never know." He nodded toward a dozing Shamus. "He'll warn you if anyone's coming. The camera shop's not far, and I won't be gone long." He met Kate's worried eyes. "With any luck, I'll have you back with your family by noon. Deal?"

She nodded. "I just want this over with."

She looked small and scared. Mike didn't blame her. She'd offered him comfort back at the house. He could do no less. "Come here," he said and drew her up into his arms.

Kate's anxiety had her clinging to him in a way she never would have a mere twenty-four hours ago. She felt herself trembling and wished she were made of sterner stuff. Raising her head, she made a stab at looking confident and unafraid.

Her vulnerability got to him. But when he lowered his head to her, comfort wasn't what was on Mike's mind. Her mouth was soft and giving, her arms tightening around him. A quick flash of desire slammed into him, something he hadn't felt in three years. Pulling back, he stared into eyes as surprised as his own.

Then, because he wanted to know if the first had been a fluke, he kissed her again. This time he let her go and found his hands were none too steady. "Kate," he began, and cleared his throat, "when this is over . . ."

Stepping back, she nodded. "We'll talk."

"Lock the door behind me." With that, he left.

Kate locked the door, then slowly turned to Shamus. "I hope you're better at this waiting game than I am," she said shakily.

* * *

Mike parked in the back lot behind the strip mall. Walking around front, he noticed a tan Cadillac parked in front of the office next to the camera shop. There was a small boy asleep in the passenger seat. As he leaned down for a closer look, the office door opened and Ed Ramsey stepped outside carrying a bulging leather briefcase. Straightening, Mike nodded.

" 'Morning. I see you have E. J.," Mike commented, aware that Ed had been involved in a nasty custody suit over his son during his recent divorce. As he recalled, Ed had lost.

"Yeah, for the holidays," Ed said as he placed the briefcase in the open trunk alongside several boxes and two large suitcases.

Mike knew Ed Ramsey more by reputation than as a friend. He owned several sporting-goods stores around the state, but it had been rumored even before Mike returned to Arizona that Ramsey was involved in an illegal betting operation. Yet no one had been able to pin anything on him so far. Mike had kept an unobtrusive eye on the big man who favored expensively tailored Western clothes and often wore a large white Stetson.

Seemingly in a hurry, Ramsey closed his trunk and wiped his brow with a white linen handkerchief.

"Going on a trip?" Mike asked, wondering why Ed was sweating in the chilly morning air.

"Yes, just me and my boy." Ramsey opened the car door.

It seemed a little odd, leaving so early on Christmas morning. But perhaps the boy's mother had only turned him over to Ramsey last night. "Well, have a good trip."

"Thanks." Behind the wheel, Ramsey started the car, then pulled away from the curb and hurried down the street.

Mike watched the Cadillac disappear from sight, then climbed the stairs to wake Johnny.

It took nearly an hour before the sleepy Johnny handed Mike the finished prints. He hadn't been too thrilled to be awakened, but though he'd grumbled, he'd trudged downstairs and gone to work after instructing Mike to make a pot of strong coffee. After three cups, Mike was more than a little anxious as he examined the pictures.

There were several shots of deer taken from quite a distance, just as Kate had told him. Mike came to the snapshots of the dead man wearing a Santa suit and studied them closely. He didn't recognize the portly man with the white beard. Next there were two prints that were obviously taken at dusk with a flash. In one he could see a man alongside a tree holding an object in his hand. In the other there were two men, but he couldn't make out their faces.

"Can you enlarge these two for me, Johnny?" Mike asked.

Johnny groaned. But he set down his cup and picked up the negatives.

Fifteen minutes later, Mike was staring at a somewhat grainy face he definitely recognized. Lloyd Gilmore was Ed Ramsey's right-hand man, a stocky streetwise thug who was more bodyguard than business associate. The item he was holding was clearly a gun. The tall thin man Mike didn't know.

Could Ramsey's hasty departure earlier have anything to do with his sidekick being in the woods near Mike's place last night? And who was the dead man?

"Do you recognize either of these men?" Mike asked Johnny. The shopkeeper had been a resident of Palo Verde for over ten years.

Johnny straightened his glasses. "The guy with the gun is Lloyd Gilmore and the taller one wearing glasses is Freddie something. They both work for Ed Ramsey. I've never seen the guy with the hole in his chest." He looked up at the sheriff. "Somebody killed Santa? Better not let the word get around, especially on Christmas Day."

"Yeah, right," Mike said, putting the snapshots in his pocket. "Don't say anything to anyone about this for now, will you, Johnny?"

Johnny struggled through a yawn. "Okay by me." Overhead, the sound of excited footsteps could be heard. "Terrific. My kids are up."

"Sorry I had to wake you. I owe you one, buddy." Outside, Mike looked around. Still no morning traffic. He headed for his Blazer around back.

A dead man in a Santa suit. Two men who work for Ramsey stalking Kate in his woods, one holding a gun. Ramsey, nervous and sweating, leaving town with his son. How did it all tie in? Was there even a connection?

Maybe Kate could supply some of the missing pieces. Mike swung the Blazer onto the road and headed for his office. Ten minutes later, he pulled up and was relieved to see Hank's Jeep parked in front. Hopefully Kate hadn't been alone too long.

He opened the door and was met by the silence of an empty room.

His heart leaped to his throat. "Hank?" he called out, walking inside. Before he cleared the desk, he heard a moan from the back followed by an angry bark.

He found Hank on the bunk in one of the cells, trying to sit up as he rubbed the back of his head. It took Mike a few precious minutes to unlock the cell and get Hank settled on the couch in the front office, then to release Shamus from the bathroom where he'd been confined. "What happened?" he asked Hank as he returned with a cold cloth for his head.

Hank's tongue was thick, but he finally managed to get out his story. He'd finished at the trailer court, leaving the drunken husband finally passed out in his own bed. He'd arrived at the office to find a tan Cadillac parked around back. Gun drawn, he'd cautiously entered the back way but hadn't gotten far. A brawny guy had ambushed him in the hallway, disarmed him, and thrown him in the cell.

"What about the woman, Kate Kennedy?" Mike asked, his nerves jumping.

Hank ran a shaky hand over his eyes, trying to focus.

"You'll never guess who had her in a strong-arm grip. Ed Ramsey, the guy from the sporting-goods store, you know?"

Yeah, he knew. "How'd they get past Shamus?"

"Damned if I know. He was locked in the bath when I got here, barking like crazy." Hank tried to stand, but the dizziness overcame him and he sat back down heavily. "I'm sorry I let you down, Mike."

At the phone, Mike dialed 911. "It's okay." He gave the operator the details about Hank and told them to send someone to take him to the hospital. From what he could see, it looked as if Hank had a concussion at the very least. Mike moved to the door. "I hate to leave you, but I've got to go find them."

"Yeah, yeah, go. But watch out for that short guy. Ramsey called him Lloyd or Floyd. Mean as shit. It wasn't enough to lock me up. He came back in and whacked me with the butt of his gun."

And that same Lloyd had Kate. Mike balled his hands into fists.

"Try the north road out of town," Hank went on. "I heard Ramsey say they had to hurry before they closed the bridge on account of the rain. The only bridge I know of is the old wooden one heading north." Hank touched the knot on his neck and groaned.

Hearing that, Mike dialed the sheriff of Green Valley, the nearest community to the north of Palo Verde, hastily explained the situation, and asked for backup in the vicinity of the old bridge. The sheriff said he'd get right on it.

At the door, Mike turned. "Thanks, Hank. EMS will be here right away." Outside Mike climbed into his Blazer and checked his weapon. He didn't know what had driven Ed to this point, but it would seem he was a desperate man. Where was the tall fellow, Freddie, and Ramsey's son who'd been asleep in the car?

Tires squealing, he turned around and raced toward the highway leading north.

Another woman entrusted to his care was in danger. Dear God, Mike prayed, don't let history repeat itself.

Gripping the wheel in both hands, Mike drove as fast as he dared on the slick pavement. The rain had stopped but the heavy downfall had left the entire area drenched. He passed over sections of the highway that were flooded, and he could see that the drybed washes so common to Arizona were full to overflowing with the accumulation. His eyes scanning ahead and behind, he could see no tan Cadillac, and his frustration mounted.

He wondered how long it would take Green Valley to send him some backup assistance.

The street leading to Highway 19 and Tucson due north forked suddenly, and Mike swerved to the right just in time. The shoulder of the road was soft and muddy, but the four-wheel drive climbed effortlessly back onto the pavement. If Ramsey was headed for northern Arizona or planning to veer off west toward California, this would have to be the route he'd take. His mouth a thin line, Mike stepped on the accelerator.

He was nearly to the city limits when he saw the Cadillac. The swollen river filled with churning water had caused a collapse of a portion of the old bridge on the far side. He could see a large wooden section being dragged away by the rapid current. A lucky break for him, Mike thought as he pulled the Blazer as close as he dared.

The Cadillac apparently had started onto the bridge then stopped, probably when the far section had pulled loose. They were in a precarious situation, half on and half off the old wooden structure. Remembering Lloyd's gun, Mike climbed out cautiously and stayed behind the protection of the Blazer. The tinted windows of the Cadillac were steamed up, making it even more difficult to see inside. The driver revved the engine, then turned it off.

Mike raised his gun. "Get out of the car, everyone," he ordered. "Hands up and no funny stuff."

A long silence followed. Mike checked his pockets to be sure he still had his boxes of ammo. Carefully he took aim and fired a warning shot into the air. Again he repeated his instructions. "Come out, nice and easy, and no one will get hurt."

Finally the driver's door opened and Ramsey stepped out. He cocked his head at Mike, attempting a friendly smile. "Mike, let's talk this over."

"I said *everyone* out of the car," Mike repeated.

Ramsey opened the back door and said something to those inside. Mike watched Kate climb out slowly, holding in her arms the sleeping child. She looked tired and understandably tense but otherwise all right. Next, out stepped the burly Lloyd Gilmore holding a gun to the back of Kate's head. His smile wasn't friendly at all.

"We can make a deal, Mike," Ramsey said more loudly.

The boy stirred and awoke. Kate carefully set him on his feet but kept him near her as he sleepily rubbed his eyes. Ramsey placed a beefy hand on the boy's shoulder. "You don't want to hurt a child and a woman, do you, Mike?"

Where in hell was his backup? Mike straightened, keeping his gun aimed at Ramsey, yet watching the others. Kate's concern for the boy was evident as she kept a protective hand on him. Lloyd looked capable of shooting them all. "What the hell is going on here, Ed?" Mike asked, hoping to buy some time.

Ed Ramsey ran a hand over his thinning hair. "No one was supposed to get hurt. I want you to believe that, Mike." He'd talked with the woman. She'd told him that Tanner knew the whole story and that he had the film. He'd had ample time to have had it developed. Damn that overanxious Freddie. Ed tried to look like the reasonable businessman he pretended to be.

Mike wasn't buying his Mr. Nice Guy routine. "Someone did get hurt though. You want to tell me about it?"

Ramsey swiped at his damp brow. "Things got out of hand, I agree. It's just that my ex has been giving me so much grief over visiting E.J. that she finally pushed me over the edge. She wouldn't let me see my own kid at Christmas. Can you imagine?"

"Go on," Mike said.

"She was making me crazy, you know. So I got this idea. I hired a guy to dress up like Santa Claus at this party I knew E.J. was going to attend. Max is a two-bit actor, works in Little Theater, and he jumped at the chance. So he coaxed E.J. away from the party telling him I was waiting for him. And I was. So we drove away and met Freddie and Lloyd on this road not far from your place. I drove to my house with E.J., and the guys were supposed to pay Max off and take him home."

A chilly gust of wind blew rain from nearby trees across E.J.'s face, and he burrowed into Kate. She picked him up and cuddled him to her, ignoring Ramsey's hand moving to her arm. Mike felt certain she wouldn't allow the child to be harmed, not even by his father, not if she could prevent it.

"So why'd they shoot Max?" Mike asked.

"He got unreasonable," Lloyd piped up, impatient with all this time-consuming explanation. He was a man of action, not conversation. Ramsey felt they could talk their way past the sheriff, but Lloyd had his doubts. He'd play it Ramsey's way a little longer. "He wanted more money than we'd agreed on, and he tried to blackmail us. Freddie tried to get the gun from him and it went off. An accident, that's what it was."

Mike could see that Ramsey wasn't sure he believed Lloyd. Nor was Mike. Everybody tried to talk their way out of a murder charge. What better way than to say it was an accident?

"We were just about to take off when *she* came along," Lloyd said, glancing at Kate with disgust. "Stupid broad, taking pictures in the rain." His face was a mixture of anger and incredulity.

"So you tried to chase her off the road and followed her to my house?"

"Yeah. All we wanted to do was get the damn film."

"You shot my dog and you set my house on fire."

Ed swung around to look at Lloyd. "You didn't tell me that."

"I didn't have time," Lloyd said defensively. "Look, Ramsey, Freddie's dumped the body by now. We've got to get moving before someone comes along." He waved his hand toward Mike. "He's only one guy. Let me take care of him before—"

"Shut up." Ramsey was hanging on to his control by a thin thread. Everything was going wrong. He'd worked so hard to set up his operation, and because Freddie had fumbled, it could all fall apart. And now Lloyd was getting jittery. He heard his son whimper in the woman's arms. He couldn't order someone shot in front of the kid. E.J. was only four, but he'd remember. He'd make one more stab at convincing Tanner.

Ed shifted his feet restlessly. "Look, I don't want any trouble. I'll release the woman if you'll let me take my boy. We can turn around and be across the border into Mexico in an hour. Be reasonable, Tanner. All I want is my son." He should have listened to Lloyd and gone south to begin with, Ed realized belatedly. But he'd been so sure they'd be better off in California. He hadn't given a thought to this rickety old bridge. Another costly mistake.

Just then another section of the bridge on the far side slipped into the rushing water with a thunderous splash.

Lloyd glanced at the swaying bridge, then at Ramsey before swinging his gaze back to Tanner. "That's it. I've had it with this begging and pleading." Moving fast, he grabbed Kate around the chest and pulled her hard against himself, the gun in his other hand still aimed at her head. She struggled to hold on to the boy, but he only tightened his grip on her. "Throw your gun over here, Sheriff, or I shoot her and the kid *now*. I'm not kidding."

Gritting his teeth, Mike strained his ears, trying to hear a siren in the distance, wishing he did. Lloyd had him and he knew it. He tossed his gun along the ground toward them but

312

just out of Lloyd's reach. He had another one under the seat in the Blazer if only he could get to it.

Ramsey bent to pick up Tanner's gun and was about to pocket it when Lloyd stopped him.

"Uh-uh. Hand it here. I'm not throwing away years of work because you get all sentimental over your kid, Ramsey. Get over there with the sheriff."

The shock on Ramsey's face wasn't faked. Looking dazed, he handed the gun to Lloyd, then backed over to Mike's Blazer. "What in the hell do you think you're doing?"

"Saving my skin. We worked well together, Ramsey, but I'm not serving time because of a mistake Freddie made or because you decided to spend Christmas with your kid."

"Just a damn minute," Ramsey said, trying to regain control as he took several steps forward again. "I can work the kidnapping charge out with my ex. As for Max's killing, as you said, it was Freddie who pulled the trigger. Let's not be hasty. Let my son go and we'll——"

But Lloyd was wet, tired, and out of patience. He fired at the ground just inches from Ramsey's hand-tooled leather boots. His mouth twisted into a sneer at the way the tall man jumped back, almost into the sheriff's arms. He'd suspected Ramsey was a coward at heart. He'd always had Lloyd to do his dirty work for him. And most of his thinking. Well, no more.

Lloyd had watched Ramsey tuck his cashbox into the trunk. Who needed him? He'd go alone, be across the border in no time. He spoke Spanish like a native. They'd never catch him there.

But first he'd have to take care of his witnesses.

With a brutal shove, he thrust Kate toward the wobbly bridge railing. She barely managed to stay upright and not drop the boy, who was now crying loudly. He wasn't crazy about the idea of killing a woman or a kid, but he had no choice. "Say your prayers, lady." Lloyd raised the gun.

Kate didn't have time to consider her options. Swiveling about, her hold on E.J. tightening, she jumped off the bridge

313

through the opening in the broken railing. Closing her eyes, she prayed she could save them both.

Furious, Lloyd took aim.

"Don't shoot," Ramsey yelled. "You could hit E.J."

But Lloyd was past caring. He shot toward the bobbing heads once, then again. Without waiting to see if he'd hit his target, he turned back toward the two men.

Then suddenly he decided on an abrupt change. He hadn't killed anyone up to now. Just in case they ever caught him, maybe he should keep it that way. Pointing with the gun, he waved Tanner and Ramsey onto the bridge. "Over there, both of you." They did as he said.

Lloyd got behind the wheel of the Cadillac. He knew the radio in the Blazer was out, so the sheriff couldn't phone for help. Tanner was already peering over the railing, looking for the woman and kid. He was such a do-gooder he'd probably try to save them rather than follow him. In either case, he'd never catch him. Seeing Ramsey's expression as he realized that Lloyd was about to run off with his money pleased him enormously. Grinning, he turned the Cadillac around and drove off, the tires spattering mud in all directions.

Ramsey gripped the railing. "Tanner, do something," he pleaded. "I can't swim. My boy's going to drown."

Mike studied the churning water, praying that Kate was a good swimmer, that neither of them had been hit by Lloyd's shots. At last he saw her struggling with the boy in her arms, trying to keep both their heads above water. The swollen river rushed along like the Colorado rapids. It looked as if she could use some help, but what about Lloyd who was getting away and Ramsey who would be facing a kidnapping charge?

It took him only seconds to decide. There was only one decision he could live with. Once before, he hadn't been able to prevent someone he cared for from dying. He'd felt guilty and tormented ever since, jinxed.

He had to help the two in the water. Ramsey and Lloyd would be found sooner or later, even if they got away now.

Tuning out a sobbing Ramsey, Mike quickly stripped off

314

his jacket and shoes, then turned and jumped into the raging water.

It was rough swimming, the current swift and deadly. He could see Kate more than a hundred yards ahead of him, trying desperately to get to the shore. The boy's head bobbed up, then went down again as the swirling water sucked them under. Mike increased the length of his strokes, fighting harder.

He didn't know if Ramsey had taken off in his Blazer or if he was waiting to see what would happen to his son. Maybe by now his backup had arrived. But he couldn't think about any of that now. He had to concentrate on his goal of reaching Kate, of taking the burden of the child's weight from her. She had to be exhausted. Already his own arms felt like lead weights. He struggled on.

Almost to her, he encountered a rock that scraped his side, tearing his shirt. Swearing mentally, he pushed on. Finally he felt he was near enough so she could hear him. "Give him to me," he yelled.

Gratefully Kate passed the frightened child to Mike. They were maybe two hundred feet from the shoreline at this point. It seemed more like two hundred miles. Her shoulders ached fiercely as she forced herself to take longer strokes. She'd lost a shoe, and she had a bruise at the back of her head where the current had slammed her into a rock. Just a little farther, she prayed.

The boy was no longer struggling as Mike held him in a chin grip, and that worried him. The water was so deep that even near the bank it was over his head. Easing E.J. into his arms, he finally reached the edge and grabbed onto a rock, pulling himself closer. With no small effort, he lifted the child onto the soggy grass, then heaved himself up.

He turned back and stretched a hand out to Kate. "Grab hold," he shouted. But the current lifted her and tossed her back out. Mike glanced at the boy and frowned. He wasn't moving. He took the time to shift him onto his stomach and lift his arms. Then he turned back to assist Kate.

She made it on the second try with barely enough strength left to climb up onto the marshy grass. Still her first thought was for E.J. "I know CPR. Let me—"

"I know it, too," Mike told her, kneeling alongside the boy. "You rest." And he went to work.

It seemed like forever, but finally E.J. coughed, sputtered, and spit out some water. Then he began to cry, and Mike knew he'd be all right. He handed the boy over to Kate, who was sitting up.

"It's all right, honey," she told him as she held him to her. "You're fine now."

Mike stood and looked toward the bridge. Only his Blazer was there. Apparently Ramsey had fled the scene. He remembered that the keys were in his pocket.

"They got away," Kate said, her gaze following his.

Mike came back and stooped alongside her. "Not for long. We'll get 'em."

She was soaking wet, streaked with mud, her clothes torn, her hair plastered to her head. She was holding a child she'd risked her life to save. He'd never seen a woman who looked more beautiful. Wordlessly he raised a hand to brush a strand of wet hair from her cheek.

"You came after us," she said, her eyes bright. "I wouldn't have made it without your help. E.J. and I would have both drowned." Kate placed her hand over his. "Thank you."

Maybe he wasn't jinxed after all, Mike thought.

Mike had never seen anything quite like the Kennedy clan on Christmas Day. The big old ranch house owned by Kate's parents was stuffed to overflowing with relatives, friends, neighbors, kids, and dogs. There were even a couple of corrals around back housing a chestnut mare and a black stallion.

The dining-room table was laden with more covered dishes than Mike—an only child—had ever seen at one gathering, with the possible exception of a restaurant buffet. Though he hadn't walked in hungry, he'd found himself finishing two filled plates at Ann Kennedy's insistence. Perhaps that more than anything spoke of his level of comfort among Kate's family.

From across the room, Kate saw Mike fill his coffee cup at the sideboard. Slipping away from her sister-in-law, she moved to his side. "How are you doing?"

"Just fine." He took a sip of hot coffee, his gaze taking in the houseful of people. "Your family's awfully welcoming."

She smiled and dared to slide her arm around his waist. "I think so." Her eyes went to the decorated evergreen in the corner of the family room, its shimmering star reaching nearly as high as the cathedral ceiling. "Nice tree, eh?"

"Yeah."

Kate turned to face him. "Does it bother you being around all this Christmas stuff?" She'd hesitated in asking him to join them, not wanting him to be alone, yet concerned about his memories haunting him.

Mike thought about that a moment, remembering the Christmases of his youth. "No. This is how it should be. I've had a lot of good holidays. It's just that lately I could only remember the bad ones."

She sought to lighten the mood even more. "You have to admit this is probably one of the most unusual Christmases you've had."

"That it is."

"Isn't it ironic, Lloyd Gilmore going through all that only to get stopped near the border because the Cadillac had expired license plates?"

Mike grinned at the mental picture. The State Police had phoned him, and, after hearing his story, they'd thrown Lloyd in jail until the paperwork cleared to extradite him. Meanwhile they'd picked up Ramsey after he'd hitchhiked to his house and Freddie, who'd led them to Max's body, which he'd thrown into a dumpster at a shopping mall. "Poetic justice, I call it."

"Sherry Ramsey was sure glad to get E.J. back." They'd called her and she'd raced right over to pick up her son.

"He's going to have quite a story to tell his preschool class, isn't he? He's such a cute little boy."

"Yeah. I can see why Ramsey hated losing him." Mike finished his coffee.

"I can also see why Sherry wouldn't want Ed Ramsey to have the child since she probably knew he was involved in criminal activities. I suppose now his whole operation will be thoroughly investigated."

"I'm sure it will."

"That Lloyd is a piece of work."

"But he sure can track. I don't know how he managed to find you at my office."

She met his eyes, her own serious. "I hope you're not blaming yourself for that. No one can evade someone who's determined to find you. Besides, the important thing is, you saved us both. You have to feel good about that."

"I do." His eyes warmed. "You know I do."

Through the patio doors, Kate caught a glimpse of the sunset turning the sky crimson. "Let's go out a minute." She heard the mare whinny and, from the far corral, the stallion's answering snort.

"A mating call, do you think?" Mike asked around a grin.

Placing her hands on his shoulders, Kate smiled up at him. "Sounds like it to me." Rising on tiptoe, she kissed him. "Merry Christmas, Mike."

"Yeah, maybe it is at that," Mike answered.

About the Author

Pat Warren is a bestselling and critically acclaimed romance novelist who has recently turned her attentions to the mystery/suspense genre. Her titles include NOWHERE TO RUN, hailed as a "spine-tingling, reader-pleasing tale of action, romance and suspense," as well as her debut suspense novel, 'TIL DEATH DO US PART, which was praised by one critic as a "topnotch thriller." Pat lives in Scottsdale, Arizona, with her travel-agent husband and is the mother of four grown children.

THE MYSTERIES OF MARY ROBERTS RINEHART

THE AFTER HOUSE   (0-8217-4246-6, $3.99/$4.99)

THE CIRCULAR STAIRCASE (0-8217-3528-4, $3.95/$4.95)

THE DOOR   (0-8217-3526-8, $3.95/$4.95)

THE FRIGHTENED WIFE   (0-8217-3494-6, $3.95/$4.95)

A LIGHT IN THE WINDOW (0-8217-4021-0, $3.99/$4.99)

THE STATE VS.   (0-8217-2412-6, $3.50/$4.50)
ELINOR NORTON

THE SWIMMING POOL   (0-8217-3679-5, $3.95/$4.95)

THE WALL   (0-8217-4017-2, $3.99/$4.99)

THE WINDOW AT THE WHITE CAT
         (0-8217-4246-9, $3.99/$4.99)

THREE COMPLETE NOVELS: THE BAT, THE HAUNTED
LADY, THE YELLOW ROOM
         (0-8217-114-4, $13.00/$16.00)